HONEY

FROM
THE

ROCK

THE WYLDHAVEN SERIES
by Lynnette Bonner

OTHER HISTORICAL BOOKS
by Lynnette Bonner

THE SHEPHERD'S HEART SERIES

Rocky Mountain Oasis – BOOK ONE
High Desert Haven – BOOK TWO
Fair Valley Refuge – BOOK THREE
Spring Meadow Sanctuary – BOOK FOUR

SONNETS OF THE SPICE ISLE SERIES

On the Wings of a Whisper – BOOK ONE

Find all other books by Lynnette Bonner at:
www.lynnettebonner.com

HONEY FROM THE ROCK

Book Seven
WYLDHAVEN

Lynnette BONNER
USA Today Bestselling Author

Pacific Lights

Honey from the Rock
WYLDHAVEN, Book 7

Published by Pacific Lights Publishing
Copyright © 2022 by Lynnette Bonner. All rights reserved.

Cover design by Lynnette Bonner of Indie Cover Design, images ©
    Depositphotos_232384046 - Flare
    Depositphotos_21219423_DS – Texture
    AdobeStock_606424995 – Décor and Dividers

Other images generated by Lynnette Bonner using Midjourney and Adobe
Photoshop.
Book interior design by Jon Stewart of Stewart Design
Editing by Lesley Ann McDaniel of Lesley Ann McDaniel Editing
Proofreading by Sheri Mast of Faithful Editing

ISBN: 978-1-942982-22-7

To my friend Lesley:

We've come a long way on this writing journey together.
Thank you so much for all you do for me. My books wouldn't
be the same without your creative touch.

Our seasons may be changing; there may be a little more
distance between us; but I will always hold you close to my heart.

Love you, friend!

Psalm 81:13–16

If my people would only listen to me,
if Israel would only follow my ways,
how quickly I would subdue their enemies
and turn my hand against their foes!
Those who hate the Lord would cringe before him,
and their punishment would last forever.
But you would be fed with the finest of wheat;
with honey from the rock I would satisfy you.

Prologue

The fever burned pain in his bones with such intensity that he clutched for the ship's rail, nearly missing it in the darkness. His stomach revolted with each step, but he could not fail! He gritted his teeth against the clawing wind. A cough racked him, nearly taking him to his knees.

In the blackness above, the mizzenmast protested the battering gale with a loud caterwaul. Somewhere two pulleys in the rigging clanked against each other like an uncontrolled percussionist.

Arms folded tight, he leaned into the incline of the deck and put one foot in front of the other. He had to do this one last thing for his son. "Jus' a little further."

Ahead, he heard a *snick*, and light flared. Dismay froze him.

But it was only the watchman far down the deck lighting his cigarette.

Inhaling relief, he ducked behind a barrel and curled himself into a tight ball. Misery stabbed him. His lips juddered with agony.

The sailor strolled past, heading toward the other end of the deck. The acrid waft of the man's tobacco hung in the air briefly, before it was snatched away by the squall.

He lurched from his hiding place and curled his arms against the searing pain in his belly as he stumbled through the shadows toward the main cabin on the deck. Would that he were back in his bunk, but these night hours were the only time the captain wasn't in his cabin. This had to be accomplished now.

For Isaiah.

All of this was for Isaiah.

Finally! He'd reached his destination.

The hinges of the cabin door squeaked loudly. He winced, waiting to see if the watchman had heard, but the man was all the way on the other end of the ship now and the whistle of the wind and flapping sails had likely prevented the sound from reaching him.

Inside, all lay in darkness. To find the document, he would have to risk the light of a candle.

Still trembling with an ache like he'd never experienced before, he shrugged out of his coat and tucked it around the frame of the room's one window that overlooked the deck. The seaward porthole, he didn't need to worry about.

Sweat dripped into one eye. He dashed it away.

He took one of the matches from his pocket and struck it on the seat of his pants. A candle on the desktop waited for the flame, and the room soon glowed with golden light.

He lifted the silver candleholder and scanned the documents scattered on the desk.

Not here. But then, he hadn't expected it to be.

He began a methodical search and felt his despair rise when he rifled through the last drawer without attaining his goal. Setting the candle down, he sank into the chair and tented his fingers to ponder. Slowly, he scanned the room. Other than the desk, there was only the bolted-down chest beneath the porthole and a small table strapped to one wall.

He started with the chest, inside and out. But it also proved futile.

And the table held nothing, top or bottom.

Devastated, he squatted into a crouch. First, he'd lost Cassandra. And now he'd lost her home. The rent from it was his one hope to insure provision for Isaiah's future. Now it had been snatched away in one moment of thievery.

Anger surged and he slammed a fist against the floor.

He froze. Had the guard outside heard? The only sounds were the creaking of the ship as it fought against the waves. Relieved, he scooped his hands over his head and clasped them at the back of his neck. A floorboard caught his eye.

The end he had punched had sunk beneath the other boards by an inch. The other end had lifted by the same amount.

Lord of mercy, You do take pity on this poor fool, don't You?

He scrambled forward and pried up the board with trembling fingers.

There!

The prize he'd been searching for lay in the small hollow beneath the board, rolled and tied with a string. He slid the string off and flattened the parchment on the table to make sure it was indeed his, and when he was satisfied, he returned the board firmly to its place, snuffed the candle, and donned his coat. He stuffed the parchment into the inside pocket, and opened the door to the cabin a spare inch. Now he just had to make it back belowdecks without being seen.

Chapter One

Seattle, Washington – February 1898

"Wake up, mistuh."

The young voice intruded on Kin Davis's slumber. He moaned and clutched both sides of his head. A spike of pain felt like Jael's tent peg piercing his temple. The long wail of a ship's horn sliced through the morning.

He winced. Why so loud? And why was it so blasted cold today? He must have forgotten to close the window last night. He turned on his side and curled his arms against his chest. He'd get it in a minute. First . . . just a few more minutes of sleep.

"You gotta wake up. Now." The annoying voice trembled as a desperate hand shook Kin's shoulder. "They comin' this way. An' you gonna find yo'self deader'n Adam hisself and turned over fo' that corpse reward." The intruder jostled him more insistently.

Kin's fingers rubbed circles at his temples. His bed swayed. Swayed? Why was his bed moving?

Something pinched his shoulder.

"Ow." He swung his arm to push away the vexing interloper. "Leave me be, kid. I'm sleeping."

"That's it, mistuh. You done left me no choice."

There was a clang of metal, and then a sluice of ice-cold water jolted Kin upright with a gasp. He leapt to his feet, ready to take on his attacker, but a wave of dizziness nearly took him down again. With a grunt, he bent to prop his hands against his knees. Despite his dizziness, he was now wide awake and madder than a teased rattler. He shook his hair back from his face and swiped a hand over his eyes to clear them of water.

He was not in his tiny attic room—not even indoors. Instead, he found himself standing on the Seattle docks glowering at a boy who wasn't much taller than his lowest ribs. The boy held an empty bucket in one hand and he returned Kin's scrutiny with wary gray eyes.

"Give me that!" Kin snatched the galvanized pail and willed himself not to visibly shiver.

Water still dripped from his hair onto his shoulders. No matter his efforts, a shudder worked through him. He chucked the bucket into a pile of rope and crab pots. It clattered loud enough to give Jael's tent peg a couple of taps. Kin gritted his teeth against the stabbing torment.

The call of another ship's horn drew his gaze to the dawn-kissed Seattle harbor. The ship slid into the dock two slips over. Waves slapped at the pier Kin stood on, bobbing it in the Pacific. He broadened his stance to maintain his balance. The last thing he wanted was to end up taking a swim this morning. A bucket of water to the face was bad enough.

A frown crimped his brow. What was he doing sleeping on this pier? He fought for memory of the night before, but the last thing he seemed able to remember was stepping into the Merchant's Exchange Saloon after he'd left work yesterday.

He returned his focus to the kid. "Why'd you do that?" He gestured toward the bucket.

The kid, who wore a coat that was at least three sizes too big, thrust out an arm to indicate a dock down the way. "Savin' yo' life."

A silhouetted group of men moved together along the docks, poking and prodding every shadowy crevice and cranny.

"You find anything?" one of them called in a voice modulated to rise just above the sound of the surf.

"Not yet," another replied. "But we will. We always do."

In the burgeoning light of dawn, Kin noted the strip of fabric fluttering in the man's grip.

His heart rapped a tattoo against his ribs. His mouth went dry. He grabbed the kid's arm. "Thanks, kid. Let's get out of here." He rushed the boy off the pier and in the opposite direction of the approaching men.

The reavers were only one pier over now, but thankfully the murky dawn light gave enough cover to make escape possible.

Kin rested a hand on the kid's back and glanced behind as he urged him across the street. He'd been doing pretty good at staying away from drink lately. He'd purposely kept himself busy with his law studies on nights and weekends. In fact, he hadn't imbibed a drop all month . . . until last night.

He'd thought he had his demon beat. But yesterday Mr. Riggs had accused him of stealing, and told him if it happened again, he would lose his job. Kin knew exactly which employee was likely the real culprit. He'd been so angry when he left work that he hadn't been thinking straight when he'd entered the saloon. He'd obviously consumed too much and fallen asleep on the pier.

If the kid hadn't come along when he did . . .

Kin pushed the thought away.

Parson Clay, the man who'd raised him after his pa had died, would have told him the Lord had been watching out for him just now. He also would likely tack on some mention of how God had big plans for Kin's life.

He wanted to believe it. He really did. One thing was certain. Whether God had anything to do with it, or not, he had no doubt that the kid had indeed saved his life.

Not long past, with the Yukon Gold Rush in full swing, droves of hopeful miners had streamed into Seattle on their way north. Outfitting for the trek took time, and the temporary settlement camps were a breeding ground for disease. Seattle's streets had become so plagued with corpses that the city couldn't keep up. The council had voted to offer a reward of twenty-five dollars for every corpse any citizen brought to the morgue.

It hadn't taken long for a few unsavory types to realize they could make more money turning in dead bodies than they could in prospecting for gold, and homicides had swollen like the tide.

The council had to amend their offer. Money was now only paid for bodies that appeared to have died of natural causes.

So gangs roamed the streets with silk scarves. These, they could use to choke their victims without any visible markings.

Kin felt a tremor work through him as he tugged at the skin over his Adam's apple. He needed to get his mind off his near demise. He thumped the kid on the shoulder and motioned to one of the ladders that led down to the lower levels of the city. "You hungry? Least I could do is buy you some breakfast. What's your name?"

In the light shining from Mrs. Corbel's bakery window, he truly looked the boy over for the first time and felt his brow slump. The shivering kid was dressed in not much more than rags and the too-large coat that was inadequate for these parts this time of year. His thick black curls puckered in shaggy clumps, and mud caked his skin in places.

"I could eat, yessuh." The boy eyed the ladder dubiously, a cloth cap twisted tightly in his hands. "Name's Isaiah, jus' like that Bible prophet. Why these ladders be all over the place, leadin' underground?"

Kin led the way down the nearest ladder. "You must be new to these parts?" He stopped at the bottom and motioned for Isaiah, who still peered down, to join him.

After a moment's hesitation and a glance back along the street, the kid climbed carefully onto the top rung and descended one halting step at a time. Only when he was safely on the ground by Kin's side, did he answer his question. "Yessuh. My pa . . . Well, we was headed to the Yukon, but he took powerful sick on the ship here from San Francisco and . . . he passed on."

The kid's voice broke on the last words, and Kin felt the sharp pain of them like a knife to his heart. How well he knew what the boy must be feeling. How old was the kid? Eight? Nine?

"I'm sorry to hear. How long ago was that?"

Isaiah swallowed. "Las' week." He gestured up toward the street they'd just left. "First night, that gang almost got me. Only thing saved me was being small enough to fit through the slats of a fence and they couldn't follow. Only my clothes got torn."

Kin dropped a hand against the boy's shoulder. "I'd bet you haven't slept easy since you got off that boat. Where's your ma?"

Isaiah scuffed the ground with the toe of one boot. "She passed on when I was born."

Poor kid. Kin nudged Isaiah toward the bakery where he liked to get sausage pies. He needed to hurry, or he'd be late for work. Mr. Riggs wouldn't put up with that. Especially not after yesterday.

"Let me get you something to eat. And then I have to get. But I've got a room you can stay in for the day. Sleep. Even take a bath if you want."

Based on the condition Isaiah was in, Kin hoped the kid would decide to take a bath before climbing into his bed. "My name is Kin Davis, by the way."

As they made their way to the underground bakery, Kin motioned to a ladder. "You asked about the ladders. A few years ago, there was a big fire in town. Leveled the whole place." He kept their pace brisk. "Before that, the city had a lot of trouble with the sewers backing up at high tide. Since they needed to rebuild anyhow, they decided to build a level higher." The bakery door squawked loudly as he pushed it open.

Mrs. Owens looked at them from behind the counter. "What can I get for you this morning?"

Kin dug into his pocket with one hand, while holding up four fingers of the other and gesturing to the sausage pastries. He finished his story as he handed over the money. "We've been hauling dirt from the surrounding hills to raise the streets— that's been my job these past months." He nodded his thanks to Mrs. Owens for the pies and held two toward the kid. "Here. You eat one of those and save the other for later today."

Isaiah's eyes grew wide and he pushed the pastries back. "Mistuh, I can't pay fo' those."

Despite his words, the kid's gaze lingered on the pastries, longingly.

Kin took Isaiah's hand and settled two of the paper-wrapped pies there. He spoke around a mouthful he'd already taken. "Consider it small payment for you saving my life this morning. Now come on and I'll show you to my room. I can't be late for work."

Kin practically ran through the underground streets. In places, the above-ground walkways had already been built above their heads. Grids of glass skylights revealed the brightening sunlight and lit their way. At the corner of First and Yesler, he took a ladder to the top. One block over, he led Isaiah at a trot up the rickety stairs at the back of Mrs. Huston's building.

Kin's attic room was hot in the summer, and cold in the winter, but it kept him dry and was cheaper than anything else he'd been able to find in the city.

On the first landing, he dashed inside to the washroom, grabbed up a bucket, and put the pump handle to good use. He thrust the filled bucket at Isaiah, and set to filling another. With that done, he hurried toward his room once more.

"Come on, kid." They rushed up three more flights of stairs, and Kin bumped the door to his room open with his shoulder. He pointed toward the flimsy divider that sat in one corner and set his bucket near it. "There's a galvanized tub behind that, and a toilet. When you flush, you have to go down to the washroom for more water to fill the tank, but . . ." He skimmed the kid from head to toe once more, taking in his golden-pecan skin. "On second thought, I think it would be best for you to stay in my room out of sight for the rest of the day. You take my meaning, kid?"

Isaiah's lips twisted into an understanding grimace. "Yessuh. I understand."

"Good." Kin spoke as he shucked out of yesterday's shirt and tugged on his only other one. "Mrs. Huston, she's a kind lady. You've nothing to fear from her. But there are others who live in this building on the floors below, and I can't speak about them." With that, he gave a nod and headed toward the stairs. He called over his shoulder, "I work till six. Then I'll return and we'll get some dinner." He paused with his hand on the railing and looked back at Isaiah who peered at him, wide-eyed, from the bedroom doorway. "Take a bath before you crawl under my blanket, okay kid?"

Isaiah smiled. "Yessuh. Thank you, suh."

Kin gave him a wave of acknowledgment and hurried down the stairs.

The moment the man disappeared into the stairwell, Isaiah Coleman closed the bedroom door, sank onto the floor, held his head in his hands, and cried. "Lord, I done prayed fo' You to send me help and You answered. I don' know why You done took Pa. But You answered Ike, just like You did for some o' them Bible people."

Sobs shook him so forcefully that he collapsed onto his side. The floor pressed cool against his damp cheek. Relief and gratefulness gave way to a sorrow so deep it stole his breath and made it near impossible to inhale.

Pa gone. All alone in the world now. Nowhere to go.

He cried until the exhaustion of days on end without food or sleep dragged him under.

Hours later, he woke shivering from cold and hunger. He rose and jogged in place, swinging his arms to get his circulation moving. He wished for a fire. He wished for a lot of things. Pa had planned to outfit them for the Yukon once they arrived in Seattle. He'd been saving up for nigh on three years and when he'd heard about the gold up in the Yukon, he'd told Isaiah the Lord had good plans in store for them. They'd rented out their house and purchased their tickets.

But then Pa'd taken sick and died only hours before they arrived in port. And before Isaiah could get Pa's money from his billfold, the ship's captain had found and confiscated it. The captain claimed all of it was necessary to cover Pa's final expenses, but at the service in the pauper's cemetery, Isaiah had only seen him pay a single dollar for the digging of the grave and one more to the minister. When he'd asked for the rest of it, the captain had told him the remainder was owed to cover their passage.

Isaiah was fairly sure Pa had paid for their passage up front, but he was only a kid. Who would listen? Besides, without proof, he had no recourse.

So after the ceremony, he'd waited until the captain was busy talking with a couple other men, and then he'd darted away from the assembly of strangers who stood around Pa's grave. He hadn't gone back to the ship. He'd only had one other change of clothes in his knapsack anyhow. The only thing he'd cared about, he'd already been wearing and that was Pa's thin coat. It still carried his scent, plus the last thing Pa had admonished him before he'd slipped into unconsciousness was not to be parted from his jacket.

Days later, he'd been wandering the docks and praying for the good Lord to send him help when he'd literally tripped over Kin Davis's body.

At first, he'd thought him dead, and planned to steal his clothes, but when he'd realized he was simply dead-drunk, he'd started to walk away, yet something had made him stay. He couldn't quite say what it was since he was wary of the docks, but maybe his near-death brush from his first night in the seaport had raised a protective spirit in him. He hadn't wanted the helpless man to meet such a fate.

And now . . .

Isaiah lifted the one remaining sausage pie and sniffed it with appreciation. His stomach rumbled loudly as though belying the fact that he'd eaten a whole one only a few hours ago.

He forced himself to set the pie down and wait for later. Who knew how long it would be before he had food again? The man had said he'd return at six. But what if he forgot to come back for him?

Since he'd warmed slightly, he took one of the buckets and poured it into the galvanized tub behind the divider. Carefully, he shimmied out of his clothes and washed as good as he could with such a small amount of water in such a little tub. He used the water in the other bucket to rinse himself, gasping as the cold water sloshed across his skin.

He smirked. What he got, he supposed, for throwing that bucket of seawater in Mr. Davis's face this morning.

With a towel wrapped around himself, he started to dress, but grimaced at the sight and smell of his clothes and chose to use the leftover bath water to wash them, instead. Once they were rung out, he draped them over the divider, then crawled beneath the warmth of the covers.

He was asleep again, almost before he closed his eyes.

Chapter Two

Wyldhaven, Washington – February 1898

With her hands tucked behind herself, Cora Harrison leaned against the wall at the back of the sanctuary where the women of Wyldhaven had gathered. At the center of the room, Liora Rodante and Dixie Griffin sat amidst a circle of chairs, surrounded by a gaggle of womenfolk.

Cora smiled as both Liora and Dixie oohed and ahhed over the matching baby blankets that Charlotte Callahan had quilted for them.

"They're so beautiful!" Liora fingered the spring-green satin edging.

"Look at this stitching." Dixie clucked her tongue and traced a finger over the intricate vine Charlotte had sewn. "My, Charlotte, is there anything you can't do?" She raised her brows in awe.

Charlotte's lips pulled into a smile that offered thanks and a dismissal of the compliment all at once. Dixie and Liora set the blankets aside and each moved to open another gift, but something in Charlotte's expression snagged Cora's attention.

As soon as she was no longer the center of focus, the woman smoothed her skirts and dusted at a bit of invisible lint. Anyone looking at that moment couldn't have missed the sorrow dimming Charlotte's eyes.

But a quick search of the room revealed that Cora was the only one paying attention.

Before Charlotte could catch her watching, she returned her gaze to Dixie and Liora. They were each expecting a second child, and Charlotte had yet to conceive a first. Though Cora realized it was only a guess, she figured Charlotte's sadness stemmed from that.

At least Charlotte had a husband, Cora thought grimly, then immediately asked the Almighty for forgiveness. She ought to trust more in God's timing, but based on the distinct lack of eligible bachelors in Wyldhaven, she figured the Lord was going to have to do something supernatural to get her a husband. And in all honesty, she wasn't certain she was important enough to warrant such a miracle.

Oh sure, there was Taulby Ecklund. But Cora knew he only had eyes for Wyldhaven's beautiful redheaded schoolmarm, Zoe Kastain.

There was also the handsome bronc buster, Kane Carver. But he was so busy with his work and with supporting his younger brother and sister that Cora would lay down money on the fact that it would take one of the aforementioned supernatural events to get him to notice her, the mousy blonde woman who cleaned rooms at the boardinghouse.

Besides, she doubted Uncle Merle and Aunt Betsy would approve of a mere bronc buster as a suitor, no matter that they ought not get any say, seeing as Aunt Betsy had considered her nothing but a burden when she'd first come to town. Cora didn't live with or depend on them. A woman who paid her own way in the world should be able to make her own decisions about who she wanted to marry.

The problem was, she couldn't think of one man that held her fancy.

A pair of warm pecan eyes, nearly hidden by a shaggy swoop of dark, curly hair rose unbidden to taunt her with that lie. She gave herself a little shake and thrust the image away. No matter that Kin Davis had been a gentleman and rescued her two Christmases ago when she'd arrived in Wyldhaven—and no matter that he was the only man who'd ever ignited an ember in her belly—he wasn't the man for her. After the way Pa had left her and Ma to fend for themselves in the years before Ma passed on, she'd vowed that any man she took as husband would love the Lord God first and foremost. Besides, Kin had left town a little more than two years ago and hadn't come back even once. So it was plain that she'd had stronger feelings for him—sinful though they might have been—than he'd had for her.

The women in the room rose and began returning pews to their rightful places, and Cora gave herself a little shake, realizing she'd woolgathered the whole party away. She hurried forward to help Mrs. Holloway clear the table laden with food.

Priscilla Hines, wife of Wyldhaven's mercantile owner, collected her covered dish from the table and then paused to speak rather loudly to Charlotte. "Don't you worry, Charlotte, about the fact that you haven't conceived yet. The good Lord will send you a bundle of joy when He deems you fit and ready."

Cora winced. So maybe she wasn't the only one to have noticed Charlotte's discouragement, but did the woman have to be so demeaning in her attempt at support? When the Lord deemed Charlotte fit and ready? Wasn't that the same as saying she was currently unfit and unready?

From the way Charlotte's cheeks paled, Cora couldn't help but think she had certainly taken the words to mean as much. Cora stepped forward, though she had no idea what she might offer in way of comfort, but she was slower than Aurora Clay— the parson's wife—who hurried to Charlotte's side.

Aurora wrapped one arm around Charlotte's shoulders as she spoke. "I'm sure what Priscilla means to say is that all of us will be thrilled when we get to have a gathering like this on your behalf, Charlotte, and that she in no way intended to mean the Lord is withholding a child from you until He deems you worthy." On the last words, Aurora pegged Priscilla with a frown.

The woman's mouth gaped, snapped shut, then gaped again. "Of course, I in no way meant to imply—my apologies. It seems I'm forever putting my foot in my mouth." Face downcast, she fiddled with the lid on her cast iron Dutch oven.

Cora frowned. Her words seemed too syrupy to be sincere. But . . . Were those tears in her eyes?

Priscilla jerked her head up, chin angled. "Forgive me. I'd best get home to Jerry and David." She spun toward the door.

Not tears then. Maybe anger?

Charlotte squeezed Aurora's hand in thanks before hurrying to catch Priscilla near the back of the sanctuary. They were too far away now for Cora to hear their words, but after only a moment, Charlotte gave the woman a hug and then they left together.

Cora's eyes narrowed. Maybe she'd been too quick to judge the situation. Priscilla herself had never conceived. Perhaps she'd truly been trying to encourage Charlotte, but had spoken her words poorly? That didn't lessen the good intentions of her heart.

Whatever Priscilla's intent, Charlotte was very kind to have forgiven her so quickly like she did!

Aurora's shoulders sagged. She looked at Cora with soulful eyes. "Perhaps I spoke too quickly?"

"I was about to say something myself, so you weren't the only one to feel her words were rather thoughtless. But maybe she didn't intend them as they sounded?"

"Maybe." Aurora didn't seem at all sure.

Kane Carver stepped past the wall that separated the sanctuary from the doors. Hat in hand, he searched the room. His dark hair was a touch on the long side, and he used one hand to scoop it away from his face.

Cora took him in, from the dust of his hand-stitched boots to the soft brown of his eyes. Could she learn to care for the man? Would he even consider a woman like her? Her heart didn't thrill at the prospect, but he was a good man. She could learn to enjoy his company, couldn't she? Perhaps.

Cora's dear friend, Belle Kastain, and Kane's sister Maude hurried to meet him. Maude said something, and Belle reached to smooth a lock of Kane's hair that protruded at an odd angle, offering a chuckle that Cora could hear all the way across the room. Belle's gesture and the way Kane fiddled with the brim of his hat as he smiled down at her made Cora aware there was something more brewing between them than she'd realized. She would have to pry that bit of information out of Belle the next time they had dinner together.

She tucked her lower lip between her teeth. Looked like she wouldn't need to bother with trying to decide if she could learn to enjoy his company. Kane might be taken, after all. She forced her focus back to her companion.

Discouragement tugged at Aurora's lips, but from the faraway look in her eyes, she wasn't focused on the man near the door, even though she continued to stare in the direction Charlotte and Priscilla had disappeared. "I think you're right. I'll have to pay her a visit and apologize for my hasty judgment."

When Aurora reached for her nearly empty pie tin, Cora squeezed her hand. "Don't be too hard on yourself."

Aurora blew a frazzled breath. "It seems I've a very long way to go before becoming a proper parson's wife." She crossed her eyes.

Cora smiled. She wanted to ask Aurora if she and Parson Clay might be thinking of starting a family soon, but clenched her jaw before she blurted the inappropriate question.

Instead, she set herself to being useful wiping down the table and then helping Jacinda carry it to its place in the front corner of the church. During the week, the table was used as a desk for the town's teacher, Zoe Kastain, though that wouldn't be necessary for much longer. The town had already held several fundraisers to procure the funds to build a separate school building. And the final one was set for later this month.

Cora's heart did a little flip of excitement at just the thought. There would be music and dancing, plenty of good-natured competition, and various and sundry items for sale. Cora herself had crocheted several large rounds of lace to sell. And the proceeds from the gathering should be enough to get the schoolboard's approval to start building next month. The site for the schoolhouse was already platted across Wyldhaven Creek in the flat beneath the forest line.

Zoe twirled onto the platform just as Cora and Jacinda finished settling the table in its place. "I'm so excited!" Her words trilled and she gave another whirl that was strong enough to balloon her skirts. "These next couple of weeks are going to fly so fast. The students and I have so many final details to attend to! This time next year we'll be in our own building! Imagine!" She stretched her arms wide and grinned at the ceiling.

Cora exchanged a smile with Jacinda. "Someone is just a smitch over the moon."

"Am I ever!" Zoe clasped her hands to her chest and eyed the room. "I am going to miss this place though."

Jacinda's lips twisted. "You'll be in here every Sunday."

"I know. It just won't be the same."

Marshal Holloway poked his head around the back partition. "You ready, darlin'?"

Jacinda offered Cora and Zoe a parting wave as she hurried toward her husband. "Yes, dear. I just need to gather my coat."

As they trailed in Jacinda's wake and stepped into the church entry, Cora realized she and Zoe were the last two in the building. "How are you getting home?"

She only had to walk down the hill into town to get to the room where she stayed at the boardinghouse, but Zoe lived a couple miles outside of town.

Zoe gathered her coat from one of the hooks in the entry and peeked out the window beside the double doors. "Taulby is going to escort me."

Cora gave her friend a sly smile. "He's a mighty fine-looking gentleman." She only felt a little guilty for her attempt to ferret out whether Zoe was interested in the man.

Zoe's cheeks pinked. "He is."

Blushing must mean she was interested, right? Cora despaired. No matter how nice she found Mr. Ecklund to be, she would never attempt to coerce him away from his interest in Zoe. "And godly, too."

A nod was the only reply Cora got for that bit of teasing. She decided to let her teasing drop as she set to buttoning up her own coat. She knew that Zoe had harbored feelings for her childhood friend, Washington Nolan. But he'd been gone for a couple years now since he'd enlisted in the cavalry.

"Do you hear anything from Wash?"

A tiny frown crimped Zoe's delicate brow as she settled her powder-blue hat at a jaunty angle on her gorgeous red curls. "Not for a couple weeks."

Cora tugged on her gloves. "I'm sure he's just busy. Or the post has been slow."

"Yes. I hope so."

They stepped onto the church porch, and Zoe drew the door shut behind them.

Cora politely greeted Taulby, when he clambered from the bench of his wagon.

"Miss Cora." He tipped her a nod and offered his hand to assist Zoe aboard.

Cora bade them farewell and headed down the path toward town, but for some reason the interaction weighed heavy on her heart.

Was she the only woman in the world who didn't have a man interested in her?

Kin's teeth clamped together so tightly that his jaw ached as he stormed from Mr. Rigg's office. Two minutes. That was how late he'd been for work. And after two solid years of breaking his back for the man—and showing up early most of the time, he might add—he was dismissed. But only after he'd put in a full day's work—which the man declared he wouldn't pay for on account of Kin's tardiness this morning.

He barreled down the shaky wooden stairs two at a time, but when he got to the bottom, he hesitated. For the first time in two years, he didn't have any place he had to be.

His thoughts drifted to the saloon. He gave himself a shake. That bone-deep thirst would pass, but only if he mastered it. Yesterday he'd let it get the best of him, and now look where that had gotten him. Truth was, if that kid, Isaiah, hadn't come upon him sleeping on that dock, he'd be lying on a table down at the morgue about now. And if the cutthroats had somehow missed finding him in the dawn-shadowed docks, he likely would have arrived to work even later. Either way, it was his weakness for drink that had brought him to this place, and he had no desire to go back.

He started toward his tenement. Thankfully, he was paid up through the end of the month. That would keep him from having to dip into his savings at least for a couple weeks. He'd always been good at saving his money.

If there was one thing living with Pa had taught him, it was to save. There had been weeks, when he was a kid, when there had been no food in the house. Pa had practically lived at the saloon and had eaten the little bit of food he'd consumed there. Many a time, it was Wash Nolan's "extra" lunch sandwich that had been Kin's only meal of the day.

Now, looking back as an adult, he had a feeling he owed Wash and his pa more than a little for keeping him alive all those years ago.

Despite knowing how much he had in savings, he already fretted over the fact that he was out of work. What was he going to do?

The kid had mentioned the Yukon Gold Rush. He could do that. Take the kid with him. But prospecting involved many a long hard hour of work without one guarantee of reward. Give him a job that was steady and consistent any day over something as speculative as panning for gold. No. He didn't want to go to the Yukon.

He thought about the set of law books beneath his cot. He'd spent a good bit of coin on those books. And even more in time, studying them. Many a Saturday, and most evenings, he been studying law under Mr. John Townsend. The lawyer had been more than kind to help him understand what he needed to do to become a lawyer himself.

Kin wasn't quite sure when the idea had taken hold of him. He'd thought about law a few times when he lived back in Wyldhaven. But the impetus that had spurred him to begin his studies had happened just down the street.

When he first came to Seattle, he witnessed a crime. A woman had been knocked out and her reticule stolen. Kin had felt so helpless as he'd sat with her until her husband and a doctor had arrived.

Later, in court, even though he'd been able to identify the man who stole the purse, the criminal's lawyer had systematically torn Kin's reputation apart. He'd still been drinking heavily back then. That was one of the things that had driven him to give it up. But more than that, he'd wanted to fight back. Mr. Townsend had been the woman's lawyer, and he'd offered to help Kin learn the law for himself.

Mr. Townsend had been telling him for a couple months now that he was ready to take the exam, but he'd been too nervous to try. If he failed . . . Well, he didn't want to fail.

You good-for-nothin' idiot! You don't have the brains God gave a squirrel!

Kin shook away the memory of his father looming over him and the spilled coffee beans as he'd cowered into the corner of the cabin with his arms protecting his head. He sighed. Seemed all his life he'd been trying to escape the appraisal of his father—and always failing.

Parson Clay said things happened for a reason. It sure seemed unreasonable that he'd gotten fired for being two minutes late, so maybe the Almighty was trying to get his attention.

He paused at the street corner to wait for several wagons to pass, and angled a glance at the sky. *You couldn't have gotten my attention some other way?* He snorted. Great. Now he was talking to God? Would the all-perfect Creator even listen to a less-than-scratch two-bitter like him?

The traffic cleared and he continued toward home. He scuffed a boot against the dirt of the roadbed. Much of this soil had been hauled in and tamped down by his own hand. Labor, that was something he could do. But there weren't many jobs like this around town. Especially not this time of year. He kneaded the weary muscles at the back of his neck.

Each day had enough worries of its own—yet another saying from the Good Book which the parson had drilled into him as a boy. It was true enough, he supposed. Tonight, he'd take Isaiah to buy a new set of clothes and get them both some grub. Then tomorrow he'd figure out what to do about a new job.

He rounded the corner just this side of his building. Mrs. Huston stood on the walk speaking with two rough looking men. From the broad spraddle of their legs it seemed they were braced for the sidewalk to dip from beneath them at any moment. Sailors, then.

"You sure you ain't seen him?" one of the men prodded. He held a hand flat, indicating a height just above his waist. "About yay high and half—"

His partner cleared his throat loudly and tipped a nod to Mrs. Huston as though reminding him that a woman was present.

"Right. Sorry. Half black? Kind of mealy gray eyes that don't look right on a boy of his color."

Kin's heart rate kicked up a notch. For a split second it was due to anger at the man's demeaning and untrue words about Isaiah. But in the next second, when he fully realized that it was indeed Isaiah the man had described, Kin's gaze darted to Mrs. Huston. Had she seen the kid today? Would she tell these men if she had?

Of their own volition, his boots ground to a stop on the walk a few paces from the group. He needed to hear how this conversation played out.

"I told you, I've seen no such boy!" Mrs. Huston threw back her shoulders. "What do you want of him, anyhow?"

The sailors exchanged a glance. "He's one of our crew is all. We want to make sure he's safe. But we also need him back aboard."

Kin's eyes narrowed. His fists clenched so tight that his fingers ached.

"Well, I ain't seen him, so be off with you. I'll send word if I catch sight of him." Mrs. Huston flapped a hanky to shoo the men on their way.

Seemingly displeased not to have found the kid, the sailors turned to mosey Kin's direction. He recognized one. Farnham had worked several weeks for Mr. Riggs nigh on nine months ago now. Kin hadn't seen him since he'd been let go for punching another man over some misplaced tools.

Farnham nodded at him. "Davis."

Kin returned his greeting.

The other man lifted his chin. "What are you looking at?"

Kin shrugged and strode forward. He motioned toward the door to the tenement that they'd all been standing in front of. "Was just waiting for you to clear the doorway so I could go inside." He held his breath as he brushed past Mrs. Huston and started up the stairs.

Behind him, he heard the door close.

"Kin?" Mrs. Huston's voice was quiet but insistent.

He stopped with one foot on the landing and looked back at her.

She tucked her hanky into her sleeve and arched her brows. "You and I both know that boy isn't part of their crew. I don't know what they want with him, but it ain't good. However, I can't have trouble 'round here. Understand?"

Kin blinked slowly.

Mrs. Huston sighed and propped her hands on her hips. "Just keep him out of sight, you hear?"

"Keep who out of sight?" Kin's lips tilted with dry humor.

Mrs. Huston returned his smile with a nod. "Exactly." With that, she disappeared into her own apartment and shut the door with a firm push.

Chapter Three

The table at the back corner of the Seattle saloon lay in shadows. Just the way he liked it. He could keep his back to the wall and study the room, yet remain mostly hidden. He sank into a chair and hooked his bootheel against the crosspiece between the legs. When the barmaid came by, he ordered a plate of beans and a beer.

Only one, he promised himself. And it was only beer. He could handle that.

His men hadn't arrived yet, but he'd come early. He always liked to be early. It allowed him to get the lay of the land before anyone else.

He'd downed a quarter of the beer and almost the full plate of beans before they approached.

Even before they reached the table, he could tell they'd failed. Hats curled in their fists and slinking along like two cats just dragged from a water barrel.

He dropped his fork against his plate and pressed his spine to the slats of the chair.

He hated failure. His own most of all. Why hadn't he hidden that deed better? Yet these two's only task had been to find a paltry boy. How could they not succeed in something so simple?

"You didn't find him." He snapped the words as they gingerly eased into the seats across from him.

Farnham only swept a finger at a knot in the tabletop.

Carr spoke. "Not yet, Captain."

"Not yet. Not yet." He mimicked. "You two are as useless as a hole in a hull! Where have you looked?"

"Everywhere!" Farnham snapped.

"Everywhere, in a pig's eye! That kid isn't more than nine years old. He can't have gone far!"

Carr raised his hands. "We asked at every tenement and establishment in a ten-block radius. We'll work our way further out tomorrow."

"That's right, you will. Because what that kid has is mine. So you get back out there at first light. And if you don't find that kid, don't plan on picking up your pay, understand!?"

Farnham and Carr exchanged a look. It was nearly the end of the month. Maybe his edict wasn't fair. But he was too angry to care.

If he didn't get that deed back, he would have killed a man for no reason.

Besides, she would want him to have it. He didn't let his thoughts linger there.

He glowered at the two men still sitting across from him. "Go on. Get away from me. If you plan to get started at the crack of dawn, you'd better get some sleep."

"We were hoping to eat." Carr couldn't seem to meet his gaze this time.

In disgust, Captain Sherman thrust back from the table. "Same time and place tomorrow."

"Yes, sir."

He snatched up his stein and downed the contents. Blast but he wanted another. He stalked from the premises before his weakness could conquer him, leaving the two men to their repast.

His stomach was already sour and roiling. The stress of this situation just might be his undoing.

The next morning, Kin nudged the kid to awaken him. Isaiah grunted sleepily. He'd slept on the floor, using the extra blanket and pillow that had mysteriously showed up outside Kin's door the evening before.

Kin smiled at the memory as he sluiced down with cold water in the tub behind the divider. By the time he'd dried off, dressed, and emerged, Isaiah had his blanket folded and stacked somewhat haphazardly with the pillow at the end of Kin's bed.

He tucked away a grin. He'd give the kid credit for trying.

"There's a café about a block from here where we can get porridge and hot coffee. Sound good?" Then where should he start looking for work? The docks maybe. He thought again about the law exam but shook the inclination away. He wasn't ready. He needed to do a few more weeks of studying, at least.

Isaiah's lips twisted to one side and his gaze dropped to the floor. "I don't mean to be a burden to you. My pa, he had some money. But that captain, he took it."

Kin kicked himself, realizing the kid must have misinterpreted his introspection and thought he was worrying about having to spend money on him. Still, if the captain of his ship had stolen his money . . . "How much?"

Isaiah shrugged. "Maybe twenty dollars."

Kin contemplated. Twenty was a good sum, but not enough to go after. Besides, he didn't mind taking care of the kid. He ruffled a hand over Isaiah's head.

Isaiah raised tear-filled eyes to Kin's.

"Aw, kid. Come here." Kin stepped forward and rested a hand on the boy's shoulder. A flood of feelings from the days just after his own father had passed rushed through him. He sank onto the edge of the bed so he'd be more on Isaiah's eye level. "You had a good pa, did you?"

The kid nodded, as the tears spilled over to streak polished tracks down his cheeks. "Yessuh."

Kin hesitated, not wanting to rush ahead and offer empty platitudes as some had done with him. "I haven't said anything to you, but I lost my pa when I was just a little older than you are."

Isaiah searched his face. "You did?"

Kin swallowed. "I did. And I missed him something fierce." Even though his own father hadn't deserved the emotion. "I won't tell you that the days get easier, even though they do at some point. You'll always miss him. But you take life one day at a time and live it in such a way as to honor your pa. Pretty soon you'll be able to look back and see . . . well, you'll see that life is short and that the way we tackle it matters."

The truth of his own statement hit him like a punch in the gut. Had he ever uttered a truer phrase? For most of his sorry existence, he'd been living in a way that reflected his blamed excuse for a father, who'd been nothing but a mean drunk.

But there was another man. One who had disciplined him with a gentleness made all the more evident because it held no compromise. One who'd had no obligation to put up with an ornery cuss of a kid, but had done so anyway.

Kin straightened. From here on out he wanted to live in a way that would honor Parson Clay, the man who had sacrificed so much to take him in and raise him. He wanted to live in a way that mattered.

That thought shored up his backbone. He would go talk to Mr. Townsend today about taking that test. He could always try again if he didn't pass this time.

Kin returned his gaze to Isaiah. "It's okay to grieve over your pa, kid. I just want you to know that if you ever want to talk about it, I'll understand. And I don't mind helping you. Not one bit."

Isaiah nodded. "Thank you. I jus' want to pay my own way. That's all."

Kin stood. "Tell you what . . . As payment for breakfast, you can help me study all day for a big test I need to take. How does that sound?"

Isaiah sniffed. Lifted his focus. "I am a sight hungry."

Kin grinned. "That's what I'm talking about." He reached for their coats on the hook behind the door. "While we walk to the café, tell me about your pa. What was he like?"

Isaiah slipped his arms into the coat sleeves and lowered his nose to the collar, inhaling deep. Then he lifted a distant smile. "He told me stories. Always funny stories. Sometimes about a cow who thought she was the queen. Or a dog who wanted to sleep in the master's bed. I think Pa laughed more than I did." He hesitated, growing serious. "Pa had a good laugh."

As they trotted down the stairs, Kin settled a hand against the boy's shoulder. "I bet you have a laugh just like his, Isaiah."

"Ike."

Kin glanced down to meet a timid gaze.

"My pa called me Ike. You can too, if you like."

Kin dipped his chin. "All right. Ike it is."

They reached the bottom landing and Kin cracked the door that led outside to subtly check the walk in both directions and the area across the street. Seeing no one, he felt some of the tension leave his shoulders. "Let's get some breakfast. After that, it's just a couple blocks to the law offices where I need to set a date for my test."

Cora stood behind the front desk at the boardinghouse, attempting to balance last month's books. With a huff of frustration, she tugged the tabulations closer and reexamined them. Her calculations were off by eleven cents. But at least Mrs. Griffin's cash drawer had eleven cents *more* than Cora thought it should. If the books had to be off, that was the better predicament, she supposed.

The bell above the front door jangled and she looked up with a smile, relieved to give her mind a break from the tedious task of tracking down where she'd gone wrong in her figures.

A blond man strode toward her—likely fresh from the stagecoach she could now hear pulling away. She'd been so concentrated on her work that she apparently hadn't heard it arrive. If she had to guess, she'd say the man was only a little older than she was, and definitely from a city. He wore a brown suit and carried a matching rounded bowler in one hand and a shiny new leather valise in the other. He was clean-shaven and might have been accused of having a childlike face, except for the wisp of blond stubble gracing his soft jaw and upper lip.

His gaze sharpened with interest as it settled on her.

She wouldn't call him handsome—maybe something more like presentable. His shoulders were a bit sloped and his chin too receded.

But he definitely seemed intrigued by her. His blue eyes drilled into hers with an intensity that made her wonder what he might be thinking.

It was slightly disconcerting. Her hands fumbled to straighten the books. Heavens, it truly had been a long time since a man had scrutinized her in such a way. She glanced down, and then up again, wishing he would do something besides stare at her. "Good afternoon, sir. H-how may I help you?"

Mercy! She hoped he hadn't noticed the tremor in her question. He might take it wrong.

He'd stopped before the desk now, and a nervous smile tilted his lips. "I certainly hope you can help me, miss. I surely do. It is 'miss,' isn't it?"

There was an awkward tilt to his head and an assessing glint in his gaze, but he smiled with an easy camaraderie that left her at ease.

Still, the way he said the words made a curl of caution twist through Cora.

His charm, though flattering, seemed unpracticed and had probably not been put to use on all sorts of women. Despite that, there was something a bit unnerving about the way he continued to search her over.

She'd obviously been deprived of a man's company for much too long if the mere sight of a new man had piqued such curiosity.

From here she would withhold her judgment. After all, he was probably only in town for a night or two.

"It is miss, sir. And I'm pleased to say so." She waited a beat for her words to settle before adding, "Would you like a room?"

He plopped his bowler on the counter and swept her with an appraisal that slowly turned serious. "I apologize, ma'am, if I've made you uncomfortable. I forget myself sometimes. In the city, such questions are common between people of . . . our age. I didn't mean to cause you any discomfort. Please forgive me."

Perhaps her earlier thoughts had been incorrect. His statement seemed to prove that he'd often practiced such charm on other women. Yet his words were coated with gentility and concern.

She studied him. Was the man simply used to getting his way and perturbed that she hadn't responded to him? Or was his apology genuine?

"Yes. I'm here for a room." He offered her a coaxing smile. "Do forgive me?"

Cora gave in to the kindness in his eyes. She spun the ledger to face him and nudged the fountain pen closer. "There is nothing to forgive, sir."

"On the contrary, ma'am. I fear I've made you uncomfortable. 'Twas not my intention."

"All is forgiven, sir." Heavens, were her cheeks as rosy as they were hot? Best she get back to business. "I have two rooms left. Would you prefer a west facing one? Or east?" She forced a calm expression that she was far from feeling.

He lowered his gaze to the book, seemingly willing to let her change of topic slide. "Well now, I don't know." He signed his name with a scribble that Cora couldn't read, then lifted his focus to hers once more. "Which would you recommend?" There was still a hint of his charm in the twinkle of his blue eyes, but she could tell he was trying to withhold his personality to keep her at ease.

And somehow, it was working. Mercy. The man had her all in a muddle. She felt sweat break out on her forehead. One moment she'd felt distrusting of his charm, and then next she seemed to have been taken in by it. Was it only that a man was finally paying her some attention? Or was there something more here than she realized?

"I'll give you the western one." She lifted the key from the rack behind her and handed it to him. "It has a lovely view over the valley. Right up those stairs. Last room at the end of the hall on the right. Enjoy your stay."

He settled his round hat on his head and tugged the brim. "Miss." With that, he departed up the stairs.

Cora eased out a breath and sank onto the stool behind the desk. She felt her shoulders relax. She'd probably made more of that than it was, but she was thankful to have the man out of sight.

"Everything all right?"

Cora gasped and spun toward the voice. "Oh lands! You nearly sent me to glory before my time." She pressed one hand to her chest, nervous laughter bubbling up.

Dixie Griffin, the boardinghouse owner, stood in the dining room doorway wiping her hands on a towel. "Sorry. Was that a new guest?"

Cora nodded. "All the rooms are filled today except for number two."

"Wonderful." Dixie took in her face. "You sure you're all right?"

Cora flapped her hand. "It was nothing, I'm sure. That guest just . . . At first, I wasn't sure about him, but I've decided that he's quite charming." Now she was certain her face was as red as a hot poker.

Dixie searched her countenance and a slow grin spread. She glanced toward the stairs where the man had just disappeared. "What's his name?"

"Uh . . ." Cora bent to study the signature in the book. She slid it closer to Dixie. "Your guess is as good as mine."

Dixie looked at the scrawl and her brows winged upward. "Is he a doctor, do you suppose?" Her smile and the gentle swipe she was taking at her own husband's handwriting eased a little more of Cora's tension.

"How is Doc doing these days? It seems like an age since I've seen him around."

Dixie blew out a breath. "He's practically been run off his feet this week. But that's nothing new. And this time his busyness has relief in sight, because some of what's keeping him busy is that he's preparing the way for the new doctor who's coming to town."

"The new doctor? He's finally coming?"

"Yes!" Dixie's hands raised toward the ceiling. "Glory be! Flynn hasn't wanted to say anything until he was sure the man could come. He's supposed to be here by the end of the week. He's fresh out of medical studies in California. Flynn has been corresponding with him. Seems to think he's going to be a great boon for our town. I only hope that half the man's résumé is true."

"Well, I'm pleased that Flynn will have some more help. He and Aurora need the assistance."

"Do they ever." With one more glance toward the stairs, Dixie poked Cora's shoulder. "You let me know if our guest makes you blush again, will you?" Dixie winked.

Cora felt her embarrassment rise. "It really was nothing. He was very kind and apologetic when he noticed he'd made me uncomfortable."

Dixie's eyes narrowed. "How did he make you uncomfortable?"

Cora hesitated, but decided there was nothing for it other than to admit the truth. "It was the way he looked at me. A little too forward, perhaps. And his words were like . . . syrup." Blast! Was her face going to be crimson all day?

Dixie chuckled. "He really did make an impression. I can see that! Maybe the good Lord has finally brought 'round a man who can turn our dear Cora's head?"

Cora gave her friend the best glower she could muster through her smile and nudged her back in the direction from which she'd come. "Don't you have work to do?"

Dixie's laugh tinkled like bells. "I guess I had best return to the kitchen and finish the dishes."

"Yes'm." Cora gave a nod to urge her on her way.

Dixie was still chuckling as she disappeared, and Cora couldn't help but feel a wave of gratefulness to be working for such a caring and compassionate woman. The Lord truly had blessed her when Kin Davis had connected her with Dixie about this job.

Her vision blurred against one wall. Kin Davis . . . After all these years of his absence, why did that man still come into her thoughts? She wondered for the thousandth time where he was. Was he even still alive? She prayed for him often, but hadn't heard the parson speak of him for months now. Too bad that the man had been harder toward the Lord than a Cascade Mountain rock. She'd felt connected to him on so many levels, but that was an area where she refused to compromise. Her relationship with the Lord was too important for her to risk it by yoking herself to a man who didn't share that value. Even if she discounted the fact that he'd been a kind, thoughtful, and humorous man; her attraction to him would have pulled her toward him like a magnet, and to be pulled toward him would have distanced her from the Lord, no matter how diligently she might have tried to prevent it.

Besides, heedless of her attraction, he'd left town. And that told her plenty about the level of his interest in her. So all her thoughts didn't amount to much more than tea on a biscuit.

She released her thoughts of him with a sigh.

Her gaze fell to the accounting books and a grunt escaped. Now she just had to figure out where she'd made the mistake in her mathematics. Her nose crinkled. Blessed she might be, but it wasn't a very glamorous life.

After breakfast, Kin kept an eye on the surrounding people and buildings with a tension tightening his gut as Isaiah trailed him down the walk toward Mr. Townsend's office. He probably should have left the kid in his room, but Isaiah had perked up so much over breakfast that he hadn't wanted to return the kid to the solitude of the room and resurrect his morose thoughts and sadness over the death of his father.

So far, Kin hadn't seen anyone giving them undue attention. His worry was probably for nothing. What danger could a kid Ike's age be to a ship's crew, anyhow? Perhaps the men only wanted to make sure Ike was safe, as they'd claimed?

Kin blew a puff of dismissal. Not likely. At any rate, they'd arrived now. He nudged the kid off the street.

Mr. Townsend's office took up the first floor of a new brick and stone building on the corner of Pine and First. Gold lettering on the door's glass proclaimed "James J. Townsend, Esq."

A brass bell tinkled an announcement of Kin and Isaiah's entrance.

"Be right there!" Mr. Townsend called from behind the heavy gold drapes that curtained off an arched doorway. From past experience, Kin knew the man's cluttered desk lay on the other side—along with cabinet after cabinet of pigeonholed shelves, each one dedicated to the case of a particular client.

A burgundy brocade settee and two matching chairs clustered around an oval table to the left of the door. Kin motioned for Ike to have a seat, but couldn't seem to relax enough to be seated himself. Instead, he paced the short distance along the rear of the settee and back again.

The curtain rustled. "Kin!" Mr. Townsend hurried forward, hand outstretched in greeting. "I wasn't expecting you this time of morning! Everything all right?"

"Morning, sir. This here is my friend Isaiah Coleman. He's staying with me for a while."

Curiosity lit Mr. Townsend's eyes, but he was polite enough not to voice his questions. "Pleasure to meet you, young man!" He stretched a hand to Isaiah.

The boy stood. "Same to you." His handshake was firm and polite.

Kin smiled. The kid had been taught his manners, that was certain.

Mr. Townsend returned his gaze to Kin. He didn't prod this time, but Kin could read the concern in his gaze well enough.

"Riggs fired me. I was two minutes late to work yesterday."

"I'm sorry to hear it. It's his loss, if I know anything about you, and I do. He'll have a time finding anyone who works as hard as you."

Kin shuffled his feet, uncomfortable with the compliment. He never knew how to respond to something like that. "Thank you, sir."

"So what brings you here? Something to do with the boy?" His gaze skipped off of Ike.

"Uh, no sir. I thought . . . well . . . since I'm out of work, I thought I might take you up on your prodding to take the bar exam."

A grin bloomed on Mr. Townsend's face. "Well, I'll be!"

Kin rushed ahead. "I thought I'd study for a couple more days and then—"

"Nonsense! Nonsense!" Mr. Townsend waved him to silence. "I've had the test ready and waiting for weeks now. You don't need any more time to study. Follow me. There's no time like the present."

Kin hesitated. "But I've got—" He gestured to Ike.

Townsend waved away his concern. "The kid will be fine. He can pass the time with me. You like iced cream, son?"

Isaiah's eyes widened. "Yessuh."

Townsend smiled at Kin. "There. You see? We'll be fine. The boy and I will chip up an ice block and crank the handle while you take the test. I'll even bring you lunch and have dinner ready for you this evening."

Kin felt helpless to delay. Was he ready? He hadn't been prepared to take the test on the spot. "What happens if I don't pass?"

A flick of Mr. Townsend's wrist brushed the protest away. "I'm certain you'll do fine. No more protesting." The man practically pushed Kin toward the gold curtain. "Come on, Isaiah. Follow us."

In the back room, Mr. Townsend directed Kin to an empty table. From a chair, he removed a stack of crates filled with jumbled papers and plunked it behind the table. "Sit. Sit."

Slowly, reluctantly, Kin did. He rubbed the sweat from his palms onto the knees of his trousers. Swallowed. He should have known to do his studying first before coming to tell Townsend he wanted to take the test!

The lawyer rifled through a drawer. "When I was first studying law, we took this exam orally. But they are pushing us now to use a written test. So I've prepared a little something for you." With a flourish, he brandished a sheaf of papers from the depths of the drawer. Satisfaction gleamed in his eyes as he placed the stack in front of Kin and straightened them, just so. He plucked the fountain pen from his shirt pocket and laid it on top of the pages. "Right. You're all set. I'll be back in . . ." He tucked his hand into his vest pocket and extracted the watch connected to the gold fob that dangled from one of his buttonholes. The face of the watch popped open with a soft click. "Four hours, with some lunch. After that, you can take the second part of the test."

Second part of the test . . . Kin's stomach twisted tighter than one of Mrs. Griffin's kitchen rags at the end of a long day.

Behind Mr. Townsend, Isaiah's eyes widened. "That there is a long test!"

It wasn't the amount of time that bothered Kin, but whether he would adequately know the information required.

Mr. Townsend chuckled. He ruffled a hand over Ike's curls. "Gives us plenty of time to make and eat that iced cream."

With a sigh, Kin gave in and picked up the pen. "Go on then. I've got a test to take. But"—he pointed the end of the pen in Ike's direction—"you better save me some of that iced cream. And tell Mr. Townsend to put some chocolate in mine. If he's making me take this test right away, that's the least he can do."

Isaiah exchanged a smile with the lawyer, his teeth a slash of white between bunched cheeks. "Yessuh."

One glance at the first question immediately returned Kin's stomach to knots. He ought to have known that Mr. Townsend wouldn't make this test easy on him. He put pen to paper and scarcely even noticed when his two companions left the room.

Chapter Four

Cora was still at the front desk an hour later, attempting to find the mistake she'd made in tabulations. She'd gone back two weeks and hadn't found it. Now she was working through the third.

"Seems like some pretty serious work you've got going on there."

She jolted, taken by surprise, and only in that moment realized that his footsteps had been sounding on the floorboards for a few moments.

The blond man whose name she still didn't know smiled at her. "Sorry. Didn't mean to startle you."

He'd taken time to shave, she noted. His lack of facial hair emphasized his youth. Did the man's age even match her twenty?

"No. It's all right. I was just so concentrated on finding my mistake—" She gestured at the books. "—that I didn't hear you approach." She returned his smile. "How can I help you?"

He fiddled with the bowler hat in his hands. "I wondered if you might direct me to the clinic?"

Cora frowned. Was the man sick? Or was he in fact the doctor the Griffins were expecting? "Do you mean the doctor?"

"Well, yes, I suppose. Do you know where I could find a Doctor Griffin?"

Her excitement grew. He already knew Doctor Griffin's name. He had to be the new doctor, didn't he? "I suppose Doc is still out on his rounds. But if you'll wait one moment, I can fetch his wife. She can probably tell you better where he is."

"His wife is here?"

"Yes. She owns this establishment. One moment, please."

"Fine. Yes, fine. I'll wait right here."

Cora bustled through the boardinghouse dining room and found Dixie in the kitchen. "That new boarder? He's looking for Doc. Do you know where he might be?"

"He's not back yet." Dixie swiped a wrist across her forehead and gave the batch of jam she was cooking another quick stir. "He's still out at Camp Sixty-Five, but he should be home shortly, providing there were no emergencies out there today."

"That's what I thought. The man asked to be pointed toward the *clinic*."

Dixie chuckled. She lifted the pan and set to filling the waiting jars with an ease that came with long practice. "Poor unsuspecting city folk. Always expecting our little town to have the latest amenities." Her humor abated abruptly. "Is he sick?"

Cora shook her head and laced her fingers in a tight tangle. "I . . . I think he might be the new doctor." She suddenly felt sure her hunch was right.

"Oh lands! Here a few days early? Wouldn't that be a blessing! Belle?" Dixie called to Belle Kastain, who worked for her in the boardinghouse kitchen. "Would you be a dear and finish sealing this jam for me? The wax is already prepared and melting at the back of the stove. I think another five minutes should be enough." Dixie was already pulling off her apron.

"Of course." Belle smiled at Cora as she took Dixie's place. "Hi, Cora."

Cora returned her friend's greeting. "We still on for dinner in the dining room after you finish?"

Belle nodded.

"Perfect. See you in a bit."

Dixie rinsed her hands and quickly dried them, then Cora followed her out to the boardinghouse entry.

All energy and happiness, Dixie stretched a hand toward the man who paced the floorboards. "Are you Doctor Polson? Alexander Polson?"

A smile bloomed on his face, giving emphasis to his lack of a chin. "The very one." He accepted her handshake. "And you are Doctor Griffin's wife. He's mentioned you several times in his letters. It's a great pleasure to meet you, ma'am."

"I can assure you, Doctor Polson, that the pleasure is all mine. I can't tell you how relieved I am to have another doctor come to these parts to help lift some of the burden from my dear husband's shoulders."

"Yes, ma'am. I'm anxious to get started. I arrived a few days early in the hopes of acquainting myself with the clinic and its practices."

Cora rolled her lips in and pressed them into a thin line as Dixie cast her a wide-eyed look.

"I'm sorry to inform you—"

"—It's just that—"

The women both spoke together and then stopped with a chuckle.

Cora motioned for Dixie to continue.

"I fear, Doctor Polson—"

"Alex, please."

Dixie gave him a placating nod. "I fear, Alex, that our little town might not be as . . . civilized as you are expecting."

A frown settled between his blond brows. "I don't understand."

Cora felt sorry for the man. She hoped he would stay even after he learned that his duties would be more travel than standing in a clinic and waiting for the patients to come to him.

Dixie laced her fingers primly and gave the man a steady look. "There is no clinic. Even now my husband is out on his rounds at Logging Camp Sixty-Five."

"Logging Camp . . ." The doctor's words broke away, and his gaze searched out the window as though a view of the town might reveal the missing clinic to his travel-weary gaze.

Cora stepped behind the entry desk and straightened her books. But she couldn't keep her gaze from the distressed features of the poor doctor for long. Would he hightail it right back to the big city once Dixie finished her explanation? That would be a tragedy indeed. Doc and Aurora certainly needed his help.

"I don't understand?" The doctor's brow slumped into a veritable plowed field of perplexity.

She almost giggled as she thought how she would explain this conversation to Belle later when they had dinner. Forcing her mind back to the present, she realized she'd missed some of the conversation.

Dixie was still explaining. "And so, you see, surrounding Wyldhaven are a number of logging camps. A little like the tent cities one might find around a mining camp, only these are near the areas where trees need to be felled."

"Right. I see now." The man glanced down at his shiny shoes. He lifted one and tilted it in both directions. "I guess if I'm to do a lot of riding to logging camps, I ought to trade these in for a pair of sturdy boots." His self-deprecating smile was infectious.

Cora felt an ease in her spirit at his quick acceptance of Dixie's explanation. She smiled and nodded at him encouragingly. "Pop down to see Bill Giddens at the livery. He will fix you right up."

He slid his bowler through his fingers, gaze lingering. "I'll do that."

Beside him, Dixie quirked a brow at Cora.

She felt her face heat and returned her focus to the books. "Dixie, I'm afraid I'm off by eleven cents to your good, but I can't find it anywhere. I've been trying for a couple hours."

"Oh!" Dixie strode toward her. "I should have mentioned it sooner. A man left some extra money beside his plate during a rush, and I dropped it in the drawer without marking it down. That must be the extra. I apologize."

Behind Dixie's back, Dr. Polson gave a friendly roll of his eyes. "Sorry," he mouthed.

Cora didn't dare respond for fear of Dixie seeing it, so she merely lowered her gaze to the register again. "Right. Not to worry. I'm just happy to have found it. I'll mark it down now."

Dixie squeezed her shoulder and started toward the kitchen. "Thank you, Cora. I'm not sure what I would do without you."

When Cora lifted her gaze, Dr. Polson was at the door. He tugged at the brim of his hat, then stepped onto the street.

She blew a frazzled breath.

Why did she feel as though this new doctor's arrival in town would mean a new trajectory for her? It was an odd feeling. Was it the good Lord trying to make her aware of something?

Lord, whatever it is, direct my steps.

The next morning, Kin stood before Mr. Townsend in his office, staring down at his test score. "I passed?" He gaped at the score sheet in his hand as awe threatened to take his knees from under him.

Townsend's deep laughter filled the room. "You did, indeed, son. You did indeed. Been a long time since I've had any student score so well on an exam."

Kin lifted his gaze to the man. "So I can practice law now?" It was a stupid question. He knew the answer of course, but it didn't seem real.

The lawyer's meaty hand clapped one of Kin's shoulders. "You sure can. Anywhere in the state of Washington, as you know."

A longing for home washed over Kin. He suddenly knew what his decision would be. He'd left Ike in his room this morning. The boy had seemed in a better frame of mind, and Kin only planned to be here long enough to learn his score. He'd have to check with Isaiah. He hoped the kid would want to come with him, because he couldn't fathom leaving him here on his own. He'd cross that bridge when he came to it.

Ever since they'd left here the day before, he'd been keeping Isaiah hidden and trying to decide what to do. Isaiah hadn't seemed to know why the sailors might be looking for him, and on further questioning, he'd sworn up and down that his pa didn't owe those men anything. Kin believed him.

Kin stretched a hand to his mentor. "You've been very kind to me, Mr. Townsend. I want to thank you for all you've done."

"Nonsense, lad. Working with you has been my pleasure. I take it this is goodbye?"

Kin nodded, still feeling a bit of the wonder at finally having direction. "I think I'm heading back home, sir. Back to Wyldhaven."

"Well! That's good, son. Real good." He pumped Kin's hand like a handle on a fire wagon. "I wish you all the best. I truly do!"

"Thank you, sir. The way you've allowed me to read the law under you, well, it means a lot."

Townsend flapped a hand. "Go on with you now. And write me a letter once in a while, would you?"

"Yes, sir. I'll do that."

He felt a bit of nostalgia as he stepped out to the tinkle of the doorbell one last time, but a swell of joy—and yes, he'd have to admit it, pride—washed through him at the realization that he'd done it. He'd really done it.

Kin hustled through the streets of Seattle back to the boardinghouse. When he burst into his room, Isaiah jolted upright on the bed where he'd been reading Kin's copy of *Huckleberry Finn*.

Kin grinned at the boy. "If I leave Seattle, do you want to come with me?"

Isaiah's eyes shot wide. After a brief moment, his countenance fell and his shoulders drooped. "Don't suppose there's anythin' keepin' me here."

Relief swept through Kin. If he was honest, he hadn't known if the kid would want to come with him. And he knew he wouldn't have been able to leave the boy here on his own.

He tugged his small trunk from beneath the bed. "Pack up, kid. I'm taking you to the prettiest little town this side of the Mississippi." He gave a pointed look to Isaiah's reading.

Isaiah grinned. "I do like this story. Mr. Mark Twain sure do know how to make people laugh."

"That he does, kid. That he does. The train leaves in two hours. Nothing keeping us here. We might as well leave today as next week."

It only took them a few minutes to stuff all their belongings into the trunk. Kin stripped the bed and folded the sheets and blankets together. He instructed Isaiah to wait with the trunk, then carried the bedding down to Mrs. Huston's room.

When she opened her door, he gave her the bundle. "Ma'am, you've been a fair and kind landlady. I'm lighting out and won't be needing my room anymore."

She set the bundle to one side. "I'm sorry to hear that. Let me get you a refund for your remaining rent."

Kin held up a hand. "That won't be necessary. I know it might take a few days to find a renter. And I didn't give you any notice that I was leaving. I think it's only fair that you keep it. And . . . I appreciate you not saying anything about . . . well—" He chuckled. "—about the guest that I do not have in my room."

She returned his smile, but then gave a shake of her head. "Not sure what the world is coming to when there are thugs hunting down children in the streets. I pray you will be safe, Kin Davis. And that mite too."

"Thank you, ma'am." With a tip of his hat, he left her to hurry back and fetch Ike.

He just needed to send a wire ahead to Wyldhaven, then they'd buy their tickets and get a quick lunch in the diner near the station.

He'd be home by this evening. Anticipation quickened his steps.

Chapter Five

Bill Farnham slunk along the walk near the train station. He was supposed to be searching the tenements on the other end of Yesler, but the kid was gone. There was no point in looking for the little rat anyhow. Too bad they'd lost him though, because it was going to be a very slim month without his pay.

He gritted his teeth. It really wasn't fair of the captain to do that. After all the months he'd spent working for the man, too!

If he did somehow find the kid, it would be a miracle. And he wasn't holding out hope for that.

He'd much rather sleep on one of the benches in the cool air of the train station than spend the day walking in today's hot sun, looking for a kid he was never going to find.

Today's east-bound train was just about to leave and then the station would quiet right down and he could get a nice nap.

He sank onto the end of one bench near a mother and her baby in a basket. She cooed to the child and then tucked a blanket around him. The little tyke stuck his thumb into his mouth and promptly fell asleep.

The mother raised her eyes.

He shouldn't have stared. As a way of apology, he offered a smile. "Cute little guy."

"Thank you. He's right tuckered."

"All aboard!" the conductor called.

The woman rose with a parting waggle of her fingers, hefted the basket onto one arm and hurried toward the train.

Farnham shucked out of his jacket and swung his feet up. He'd planned to tuck his coat behind his head and close his eyes, but blinked instead at the sight of Kin Davis striding toward the train just two cars down. Kin Davis and the very kid Farnham had just been thinking it would be a miracle to find!

For one moment, he sat frozen, partially reclined on the bench. It was the thought of his paycheck that lurched him into action. He shrugged back into his jacket as he dodged around a cart loaded with trunks. "Kin Davis!"

Kin spun toward the sound of his voice, one hand resting on the kid's shoulder. His eyes widened for a moment, and then he bent to say something into the boy's ear. They both hurried forward. An attendant near the entrance took their tickets, and they clambered aboard the passenger car. Kin bent to study Farnham through the windows as they made their way down the aisle inside.

Farnham hesitated, hands plunked on his hips. He had no money for a ticket. But by the time he went to fetch the captain, the train would already be gone.

This was a dilemma. If he told the captain he'd seen the boy but didn't catch him, he was going to be in for a long lecture on the stupidity of his failure. But if he didn't tell the captain, then he would never see his pay.

Kin continued to watch him through the window.

What made him do it, he wasn't sure, but he formed his hand into the shape of a gun and pretended to pull the trigger in the kid's direction.

Kin's lips thinned. He remained watchful, scanning the area as though searching for Farnham's accomplices.

He was alone today. But next time, he would have company.

Giving Kin a jaunty wave, he turned and angled through the lines of people waiting to board. This train was headed east. First stop would be the station near Wyldhaven.

He paused at the ticket booth on his way out. Gave the portly woman behind the counter his most charming smile. "I was to meet my brother and his adopted son here, ma'am. But I fear I'm a little late. Can you tell me if you saw them buying tickets? I'm not sure if they made it on the train or not." He described Kin and the boy as best he could.

Her eyes lit up. "Yes. They just purchased tickets a while ago."

Farnham winced dramatically. "That brother of mine, he's a bit of a no good and I'm worried about my nephew. Can you tell me how far they bought tickets for? I'd like to check up on them once in a while."

The woman's lips pinched with a moment of hesitation, but then she must have overcome her doubts because she glanced at the register before her. Her fingers traced a line. "Looks like they are only going as far as Wyldhaven." She smiled. "Good news for you. That's not too far."

"Thank you kindly, ma'am." He tugged on an imaginary hat brim. "I appreciate the information."

"Would you like to buy a ticket?"

His heart gave a thump, but a lie came quickly to mind. "I have some responsibilities I have to deal with in town. I'll have to follow them on the next train. I'll get my ticket then."

With a wave, he turned and hurried out of the station before the woman could ply him with more questions.

The captain would likely be at his favorite saloon and might just give him his paycheck after all.

"Lost him!? What do you mean you lost him?" Rage seethed through Captain Sherman's chest. Why did he have such incompetents working for him?

Farnham shifted and ran trembling fingers down the buttons at the front of his shirt. His voice was barely audible when he spoke. "Well, sir. I caught a glimpse of the boy. Leaving town with a fella by the name of Davis."

"Why didn't you stop them?"

Farnham exchanged a look with Carr, who had come crawling into the saloon just before Farnham.

"You're talking to me, not him. Spit it out!"

Farnham wetted his lips. "I was at the train station. Asking around like you told us to. I was asking a woman if she'd seen the boy when I suddenly caught a glimpse of him climbing aboard with Davis."

"You're sure it was him? I don't want to go off on some wild goose chase."

"I'm sure. Through the window of one of the cars I saw Davis helping the boy to a seat. I ran, honest I did. But the woman at the counter said it was too late to buy tickets. The train pulled out of the station before I could get to them. But I found out where they were going. They only bought tickets as far as Wyldhaven."

"How did he get connected with this Davis fellow, I wonder? And how do you know him?"

Carr stepped forward. "Before he took work with you, Farnham used to work with Davis at Rigg's Dirtworks."

"He seemed a good sort of man. Hard worker." At the granite look the captain gave him, Farnham cleared his throat. "All I mean is that I think he'll take good care of the kid until we can catch up with them."

Captain Sherman tapped his fingers on the table. This was all a muddle. A very irritating muddle. He was tempted to let it go. Wash his hands of it. Yet every time he thought about that home—mansion more like it—right along the shore, a swirl of madness swept through him. Would he live there? Maybe someday. But until he was ready to roll up his sails, he could rent the place. It would bring a mint.

It should have been his.

His fist clenched.

Would have been his if it weren't for that conniving man who had wormed his way into Cassandra's heart while he was away to sea. A darkie, to boot! How could she have betrayed him in such a manner?

He lifted his hand and, when the barmaid stopped by, ordered a whiskey. "Make it a double."

Each time he remembered the pitying looks he'd gotten when he walked the streets of Santa Monica, a curl of bitterness swelled inside him. Women had given him sad smiles and then whispered to each other behind their hands.

"There goes the man thrown over by Cassandra McKnight for a former slave."

"She's Cassandra Coleman now, and married to a negro. Imagine!"

"Yes, I heard! How awful Captain Sherman must be for her to take a black man over him!"

Oh, they'd been careful that he never actually heard the words. But he was good at reading expressions, and sympathetic looks, and quiet giggles.

It had vexed him sorely. Still vexed him!

And then, planted with the vile man's cursed seed, his dear Cassandra had passed while giving birth to his abominable offspring! It was such a scandal! A former slave and his whelp living in the grandest house on Ocean Avenue.

Whatever had possessed the man to head for the Yukon, Captain Sherman might never know. All he'd known was that opportunity had come knocking when Coleman and his son had stepped onto the deck of his ship.

Had the man even known that he, the captain of the ship on which he'd purchased passage to the Yukon, had formerly courted his deceased wife?

He strongly doubted it.

He'd been gentle, at first. Asked sympathetic but probing questions. Grudgingly, he'd had to admit that Isaiah Coleman Senior was a quick wit. The man hadn't trusted him. He'd been able to see that right off. But the man's suspicions hadn't filled him with enough caution.

A few drops of poison in his food each night aboard ship, and his decline had begun slowly. A search of his cabin, while the man and his sniveling brat had been atop, had provided him with the deed he'd expected he would find.

But it had nearly brought him to a rampage when the rumors had proved true. Cassandra had indeed bequeathed her family estate to Coleman before she died. Unthinkable!

Even now, the memory caused his fist to clench on the table.

The barmaid set his drink before him and he dropped his coin onto her tray before he downed it in one gulp.

Cassandra must have been coerced. Perhaps Coleman had even killed her!

Sherman *thunk*ed his glass onto the table.

Cassandra would have wanted him to rescue her estate. She would have wanted it to go to him instead of the low man who had somehow ensnared her.

So he'd hidden the deed in the floorboards of his cabin.

He should have checked more often. But there was always a guard posted. No one should have had access to his stateroom. He hadn't even worried that the deed might be lost to him a second time.

It wasn't until they'd docked in Seattle and already had the man buried, that he'd discovered that Coleman must have snuck in at some point before he died and retrieved the document. Only the piece of string remained in the compartment beneath the board.

Had the man taken the deed with him to his grave?

Sherman's drink threatened to return to the tabletop. No. It couldn't be. The boy had to have it. He just had to. And that meant they must find him.

Cassandra would want it.

And so to honor her memory, he would hunt the boy down and make him sign over the property. could always have a fake one drawn up, but it would cause no end of trouble if the boy returned with the real document in a few years' time. No. It was better to fetch the legitimate papers.

He would have to cancel his next sail. But the income from the house would more than make up for the lost income of one trip to the Yukon.

He looked at the men across from him. "Buy three tickets on the next train. We're going after that boy."

Chapter Six

Kin had wired ahead asking Jackson Nolan to pick them up at the train station, but it was Lincoln Nolan who waited for them with his pa's buckboard. He couldn't deny that he was thankful to have arrived in town without any to-do. It was clear from Farnham's threatening pose back at the Seattle train station that he did indeed have some beef with Isaiah. What kind of grievance a grown man could have with a mere slip of a kid, he wasn't sure. But Farnham had been with the sailors searching for Isaiah that first day as well.

Whatever it was, it would behoove Kin to inform the sheriff that trouble might be brewing. Thankfully, Isaiah had been preoccupied with excitement over the train and Kin didn't think he'd even noticed Farnham or his threatening gesture. For the remainder of the trip, he'd been careful to keep his concern from Isaiah and he didn't plan to change that now. However, it wouldn't take too much questioning for the sailors to discover that he and Isaiah had purchased tickets only as far as Wyldhaven. Kin felt sure they hadn't seen the last of those men.

A problem for another day. For now . . .

He strode down the station steps and inserted levity into his tone. "Howdy, Linc." Kin pumped his hand. "Land almighty, I think you've grown a foot since I last was home."

Lincoln hung his head with a shy smile. "Yes, sir."

"Sir?" Kin laughed. "Aren't you the same kid that used to put frogs in my bait bin?"

Lincoln's smile grew to a grin. "Guess I'm guilty on that charge indeed. Jackson sends his apologies for not being here. He's been hired by the new mill in town and doesn't get off till later."

"Not to worry. This here is Isaiah."

Lincoln and Isaiah exchanged nods of greeting, and Kin was pleased to see Linc hold out a hand to Isaiah without pause.

Kin hefted his trunk and motioned with a nod for Isaiah to keep up as they followed Lincoln to his wagon in the lot. "What about Wash? You all hear from him?"

Lincoln's steps faltered for only the briefest of seconds, but it was enough for Kin's heart to plummet.

Lincoln lowered the tailgate of the wagon bed. "He was writing right regular, but his letters stopped a few weeks back. I'd be lying if I said Pa wasn't concerned."

The news nearly took Kin's breath. He dropped the trunk into the back of the wagon with a loud thunk that made the horses shift and bob their heads. He swept a hand to the back of his neck. "I'm sincerely sorry to hear that." The tailgate creaked like an old rocking chair as he latched it back in place.

Lincoln dipped his chin in appreciation and motioned for them to join him on the seat. "We're all hoping that his letters have simply been delayed for some reason. Pa keeps saying we can't borrow trouble from tomorrow, but . . ."

The way the sentence trailed off left a hollow feeling in Kin's gut. He tried not to think too much about Wash as they took the road away from the station.

The trip into town was uneventful and it wasn't until they drove onto the main street of Wyldhaven that he realized they'd taken the whole trip in silence.

He bumped Lincoln's shoulder with one fist. "Wash is the strongest, stubbornest person I know. I'm sure he's fine."

Lincoln swallowed. Sniffed a little. "Thank you."

To Kin's right, Isaiah squirmed and methodically studied each building along the street.

After a moment, he leaned close to Kin. "Where's the schoolhouse?"

Kin took a quick glance past the new building that had gone up since he'd last been home. It looked like it might be the mill Linc had mentioned. Beyond it lay the flat area on the other side of Wyldhaven Creek where for years it had been planned that a schoolhouse would be built.

Still no building.

He directed Isaiah's attention toward the church. "I guess classes are still being held in the church." He gave the kid a nudge with his elbow. "Don't worry any. I'll be sure to get you enrolled just as soon as I can." To Linc he asked, "Zoe still the teacher?"

Lincoln nodded with a little roll of his eyes. "She is."

Kin chuckled. "Let me guess . . . You wanted to be done with school, but she paid your pa a visit and talked him into sending you for 'one more year.'"

Lincoln sighed. "That about sums it up. I should be doing man's work. Instead, I'm squished into the back row scratching out ciphers that I'm never going to need to know."

Kin felt a swell of pride over his childhood friend now being the town's teacher. He thumped Linc's knee. "This will be over before you know it, Linc. Try to learn everything she sets in front of you. You'll never be sorry about that down the line."

Lincoln's lips were pressed into a tight line of disagreement, but he gave a lift of one shoulder. "All right."

Kin turned his focus to Isaiah. "Miss Kastain was one of my best friends, growing up. You'll love going to school with her as your teacher. And I'll make sure to talk to her and get you all the books you need."

Kin didn't miss the glimmer of gratitude in Isaiah's eyes as he said, "My pa would like that."

"Here we are." Lincoln Nolan pulled his wagon to a stop in front of the post office. He gave Kin a look. "You sure you don't want me to drive you on up the hill to the parsonage?"

Kin shook his head and motioned for Isaiah to hop down. "This'll be fine. The walk will do us some good after that long train ride."

Truth was, he was a little nervous about being back home and simply popping in on the parson unannounced. In a past letter, Parson Clay had told Kin about his marriage to Aurora. Kin couldn't be happier for them. He just wasn't sure if the extra bed in the room he'd shared with Tommy at the parsonage would now be occupied by a squalling bundle of joy.

They might not have room for him, much less Isaiah.

As Isaiah grabbed one handle of the trunk and Kin grabbed the other, he pointed in the direction of the path leading up the hill past the church. But a glimpse of Isaiah's wide eyes made Kin realize this was all probably a bit terrifying for the boy. He gestured to the little log cabin at the top of the hill. Smoke skewed from the chimney in a welcoming spiral. "That cabin up there is where I spent a lot of my growing up years. You already know the man who raised me is a parson. Of course, that building there, well, that's the church."

Isaiah nodded but his eyes were still as wide as a pair of horseshoes.

"Ike." Kin waited until he had the boy's attention. "I promise you these are good people. They are going to take care of you just like they took care of me."

Isaiah darted him a wary scrutiny.

Kin held up a hand. "I don't mean to say that I am going to leave you in their care. I'm not leaving you."

The boy's shoulders slumped in relief. "Yessuh."

"You hungry?"

A silent nod was Kin's only answer.

"Aurora—she's like my sister—she married the parson. Anyhow, if Aurora doesn't have dinner on, we'll come back down here to the diner and eat." He motioned across the street to Dixie's Boardinghouse. "Sound good?"

Isaiah gave another silent nod.

Kin kept quiet after that, figuring he'd done the best he could to ease the kid's mind about this whole situation. He would see soon enough that PC and Aurora would be welcoming.

When they reached the porch, they set the trunk that contained all their worldly possessions to one side of the door. Kin tugged off his hat, motioning for Isaiah to do the same. Then he took a deep breath and knocked.

From inside the house there came the sound of shuffling and Aurora's ladylike chuckle. Just the sound of it shot him through with a wave of nostalgic belonging.

He was home. Why had he waited so long to come back?

The door swung open to reveal Tommy, lanky and rough-shaven. For one brief moment, his jaw dropped. And then he surged forward, all gangly legs and arms. "K-Kin!"

Kin was almost knocked backward by Tommy's enthusiastic lunge of a hug. He braced himself with one foot as he clapped Tommy on his back. "Hey there, Tom Tom. It's been a long time. You're looking good. Real good."

"You l-look good. You f-feel good. And you s-smell good too." Tommy inhaled deeply.

Kin chuckled, feeling a bit awkward as Tommy practically buried his nose in his hair.

Isaiah grinned at him from beyond Tommy's shoulder.

Tommy still clung to Kin as though he never intended to let him go.

Kin nudged Tommy back. "All right. All right. You've got to release me now. I'm not going anywhere."

Reluctantly, Tommy released him, and allowed him a spare inch of space.

Kin pressed the tips of his fingers against Tommy's chest and urged him to retreat a little more. "It's real good to see you again, Tom Tom." He swung his hat to indicate Isaiah. "This here is Isaiah. You can call him Ike."

"H-hi." Tommy scanned Isaiah from head to toe and back again. "How c-come your sk-skin is so d-dark?"

Kin gasped a laugh. He opened his mouth to reprimand Tommy about the impoliteness of his question, but Isaiah beat him to it.

"Because my mama was white and my daddy was black. How come you're so pale?" Isaiah punctuated his question with a grin that showed he bore Tommy no animosity.

Tommy blinked a couple times. "I d-don't know."

Kin tapped Tommy's chest with his hat. "Next time you tell old Ike here that it's because both your mom and your pop were white."

Tommy nodded. His gaze swept Isaiah again. "H-he's like c-coffee with c-cream. I'm just c-cream." He thrust the back of his hand next to Isaiah's to compare. "He looks n-nice."

Isaiah smiled. He clasped Tommy's hand in both of his own and gazed up at him sincerely. There was a shimmer in the kid's gray gaze. "You look nice too, Tommy. Real nice."

"Th-thank you!" Tommy giggled and bounced up and down a couple times. To Kin, he said, "He th-thinks I look n-nice."

That was when Kin noticed PC and Aurora standing in the doorway behind Tommy.

Aurora grinned from ear to ear and burst past Tommy. "Oh, Kin! It is so good to see you!" She stood on her tiptoes and threw her arms around his neck. "Welcome home!"

Kin barely had time to get his arms around her before she had leapt back and motioned for them to follow her inside. "Come in. Come in. We were just sitting down to dinner. I'll throw a couple extra plates on the table."

"We don't want to be an imposition." Kin kept his gaze on Parson Clay's stern features that hadn't yet indicated whether he was welcome, or not.

Aurora didn't seem to notice. "Nonsense. Why would you be an imposition? This is just as much your home as it is ours."

Her voice trailed away as she disappeared toward the kitchen.

The parson stepped back and indicated they should come inside.

Kin nodded for Isaiah to follow in Tommy's footsteps. But he remained where he was, studying the parson's face.

PC had his lips pressed together in a tight pinch that made Kin think he probably wasn't as welcome as he'd hoped he would be. But he didn't want to disappoint Aurora, so he gave a nod and started to step past.

However, just as he came abreast of the man, one strong hand shot out to grip Kin's forearm.

Startled, he glanced up. And that was when he noticed the sheen of tears glazing the parson's eyes.

"Come here, Kin. It's so good to see you." PC pulled Kin into a warm clasp.

Being wrapped in the arms of the only man who'd ever truly been a father to him canceled all his doubts about coming home.

Parson Clay gave a self-deprecating chuckle as he pushed him back and swiped at his eyes. "Do come in. Come in." He reached past Kin to close the door. "I'll just grab the extra chair from the sitting room. Then I'm really looking forward to hearing all about how you've been."

Kin realized he maybe should have written more often than he had.

Dinner passed in comfortable conversation while Aurora and Preston plied him with question after question and filled Isaiah's plate so many times that the boy finally raised a hand and declared he was set to bust if he ate another bite.

After that, Isaiah and Tommy planted themselves in front of the checkerboard, and Aurora poured Kin and Preston each another cup of coffee, and then started washing the dishes.

Preston blew on his cup, studying Kin across the rim. "How has work been? What have you been doing?"

Kin filled him in on the job he'd worked hauling dirt to raise the streets of Seattle. And then before he could lose his nerve, he blurted, "And I've been studying law under a man named Townsend. Took the bar exam not long ago. I'm a lawyer now."

Preston's cup clanked against his saucer, and he grinned like a calf in alfalfa. "You don't say!"

Kin nodded. "Then, when Isaiah there needed to get out of the city, I thought we might as well come back and settle in Wyldhaven. See if I can set up a practice here. I know it's been a while since I've been in town. Any solicitors already set up here?"

"No. You would be the first." The parson still grinned from ear to ear. "Kin Davis. A lawyer." He stared into his coffee with a shake of his head. "If that don't beat all."

Kin opened his mouth. Closed it. Then pressed forward before he lost his nerve. "Made a decision not long ago."

"Oh yeah?"

"Decided that I'm tired of being the man my pa always claimed I would be. I want to be a man like you."

The parson's gaze drilled into his. "While I'm flattered, it's not me you want to be like, Kin. Not really."

Kin frowned. "Who else would it be?"

The parson pointed a finger toward the ceiling. "Jesus. That's who I try to be like. Any good you see in me is only because I'm trying to be like Him."

Kin sighed. Roughed a hand through his hair. "That seems like a mighty tall order. One I'm doomed to fail. I wouldn't even know where to start."

"You start one day at a time, each one surrendered to the Almighty."

Kin stared into his cup, feeling as though the task were too daunting. But he said, "Okay. I can try."

The parson smiled. "The good news is that the work of salvation is already complete, Kin. All you have to do is surrender."

There was that word again. Surrender? What did that even mean?

The parson leaned forward and gripped his shoulder. "Rescuing that lad, the way you did? That's something like what our Lord did for us. Isaiah didn't have to come here with you. But he surrendered to your leading. I'm praying for you son. And I'm right proud of the man you've become."

Kin allowed himself a moment to relish the wave of warmth that swept through him. Lord knew he'd had his share of disapproval from the man because of his shenanigans. It sure felt good to finally have done something that made him proud.

Now he just had to find space to set up a practice.

Nervousness rattled through him like a buckboard with no springs.

When the last of the dinner crowd had cleared out, Cora took a quick moment in her room to freshen up and then made her way through the empty dining room to the kitchen where Belle waited for her.

Belle still leaned over the sink, up to her elbows in suds as she tried to hurry through the last few dishes, but Cora talked her into pausing to eat with the promise that she would help her with cleanup once they finished their own meals.

Belle grinned. "You don't have to ask me twice!" She rinsed and dried her hands, then pulled two plates from the warming drawer.

As the savory scent of Dixie's rosemary pork chops, buttery mashed potatoes, and steamed cauliflower wafted toward her, Cora's stomach let out a loud rumble.

She covered it with one hand and a chuckle. "Pardon me! It's been too long since my noon repast, I suppose."

Belle tugged two forks from the drawer in the sideboard, pushed through the batwing doors into the dining room, and set the plates on their corner table. "I'm starving too! Sit. Sit."

Cora set bread, butter, and honey on the table and then sank into her seat. They said a quick prayer before they both dove into their meals like starving puppies around a bowl of mash. After they'd each taken several ravenous bites, they lifted their gazes to one another on a laugh.

Belle covered her mouth with one hand and spoke around a mouthful of potatoes. "I hadn't realized just how hungry I was."

Cora lifted her fork. "I, on the other hand, have been fighting off a fainting spell since the first wafts of this delicious meal drifted to me over two hours ago!"

Belle giggled and reached for the basket of rolls. She moved them to the middle of the table along with the crocks of butter and honey.

"Oh my. I do love honey!" Cora exclaimed as she snatched up some bread and swept a drizzle across half of a golden-brown top. "Is this from the Nolan farm?"

Belle nodded and took one of the rolls for herself. "It is. Now, no more keeping me in suspense. Tell me all about this new doctor."

Despite herself, Cora felt her face heat. She stuffed a bite of warm, yeasty bread and sweet, clover-y goodness into her mouth.

"You're blushing!" Belle grinned at her.

Cora tilted her friend a look and quickly swallowed her bite. "I just might be at that. I confess that I don't find him overly handsome, but he's quite personable, and that's much more important than his looks. There's also the fact that he's the first man to show an interest in me for a very long time."

A vision of teasing pecan eyes and swoops of brown curls taunted her with the memory of the last man to pay her any mind.

"Oh?"

Cora blinked away the apparition and stabbed a piece of cauliflower rather forcefully with her fork. She gave the steaming vegetable a little wave. "He stopped to talk to me several times today. And . . . I think he was making eyes at me."

"Of course he was. He'd be a fool not to." Belle grinned. "I'm happy for you. He's gone up in my estimation and I haven't even met him yet. And I know you have a good head on your shoulders."

Cora felt a wave of shyness. She flapped a hand at her friend. "Oh do go on with you. But I confess that it wasn't quite as . . . enchanting as I remembered to have a man show interest in me. However, it was somewhat relieving. I'd begun to think that I might be an old maid for the rest of my life."

Belle snorted. "Nonsense! You're beautiful!"

"Well . . . Thank you for saying so, but it doesn't seem that the men in this town feel the same."

"Oh, *pfft*. You can't pay them any never mind. Men like us to think they are bold and brazen, but really they're just as shy and scared of commitment as we are. If not more so." Belle gave a definitive nod, but her gaze lingered on Cora in a searching manner.

"What is it?"

"It's only . . . I wouldn't want you to rush into anything simply because you don't feel you have any other choices."

Cora felt a little taken aback. Was that how she perceived herself? Out of choices? She supposed that was true enough. She reached across the table to squeeze her friend's hand. "Never fear, dear Belle. I promise not to rush into anything. Speaking of men . . ." Cora eyed her friend across the table as she finished her last bite of potatoes. "Seems that you and Kane were rather . . . intimate when he fetched Maude from the women's gathering the other day."

Belle's cheeks turned a shade to match Dixie's new red-checkered curtains.

"I knew it!" Cora exclaimed triumphantly. "How long has that been brewing?"

"In all honesty, I wonder if the feeling is all one-sided." Belle blew at a strand of hair on her forehead. "I've had such feelings for him for months now, but he's said nary a word."

"Do tell."

Belle pondered for a moment before responding. "He came upon me when I was in rather a state one day when I was missing Pa something fierce. He was so kind and understanding. I think I fell for him on the spot. But I rather fear that he only sees me as a weak kitten in need of constant help."

Cora dropped her chin and gave Belle a stern look. "Anyone who truly knows you, knows that's not accurate at all."

"Well, you know what they say." Belle lifted one shoulder on a sigh. "First impressions are hard to erase."

For some reason, Belle's comments brought to mind Kin's quick wit, kind heart, and taunting grin.

Cora despaired of ever getting the man from her thoughts. "Yes, I know what you mean."

Chapter Seven

It was a glorious early March morning filled with golden sunlight and wisps of rising mist when Cora looked out her bedroom window the next day. She paused for a moment to tip her face into the sunrise, simply relishing the feel of the sun warming her skin. But all too soon, she realized she was going to be late for her shift if she dawdled much longer.

She rushed through her morning ablutions, and had only just reached the dining room, where it was her job to seat customers, when Dr. Polson stepped through the batwing doors.

She offered him a smile, determined to be kind yet also to keep Belle's advice from the evening before in mind. She would not rush into anything. "Good morning, Doctor. If you'll follow me, I'll get you a table near the window so you can enjoy this morning's glorious sun." She spun away from him without waiting for his reply.

His footsteps trailed behind her until she paused at a small table beneath one of the windows and pulled out a chair for him.

"Here you are." She straightened the set of silverware next to the empty cup. "What can I get you to drink this morning? Would you like coffee? Or perhaps a spot of tea?"

Dr. Polson settled his hat onto the finial of the chair but didn't take his seat.

She looked up to find him grinning down at her. "Did you say 'spot of tea'?"

He was teasing her, without a doubt. She lifted her chin and embraced her heritage, turning on the thickness of the accent she'd never quite been able to shed through the years. "Indeed, I did, gov. 'Owever, I'm right sorry to say we've narry a crumpet t'accompany it."

Dr. Polson threw back his head on a laugh and Cora felt satisfied to have ignited his humor.

After a moment, he slowly grew serious.

Oh, Lord, have mercy. The man's intent gaze all at once filled Cora with a recognition of her femininity and a horror to realize he was about to ask her a question she felt certain she would need to decline.

Just as she'd suspected, he clasped his hands behind his back and leaned toward her with a serious expression. "Miss Cora, I wondered if you might agree to—"

"Doctor Polson, good morning." Dixie stopped by them with the coffee pot in her hand.

Cora stepped back with a relieved shutter of her eyelids. God bless Dixie Griffin.

"I hope you slept well?" Dixie continued.

The doctor straightened. His gaze remained on Cora for a moment before he turned his focus completely to Dixie. "I did. Thank you."

Cora felt a jitter of nerves. What had the man planned to ask? She wasn't certain she was ready for anything like what she suspected he'd been about to request. She thought again of Belle's warning from the evening before and suddenly realized that Belle's advice was needless. She had absolutely no desire to rush into anything with any man. Even if he had made it clear he found her attractive. It was a freeing feeling.

Dixie seemed unaware that she'd interrupted. "Excellent. Flynn will be down in a moment. He is saying goodbye to our daughter, Ellery." Dixie's eyes crinkled at the corners. "She was having a hard time with the parting today. Please—" She tugged his chair further from the table. "Be seated. What can I fetch you this morning?"

"Ah . . ."

Cora tucked away a grin at the befuddled look on Dr. Polson's face as he sank into the seat.

"Whatever you recommend is fine, Mrs. Griffin."

"Fine, then. I'll bring you the same as Flynn. Pancakes and eggs and bacon. There are browned potatoes, too. And plenty of syrup and butter. It's a meal that will fill you up, and that's certain. Coffee?" Without waiting for his response, Dixie bent over his cup.

Cora noted by the wrinkles in the bow at Dixie's back that she was wearing her apron a little looser than normal today.

"Ah . . . yes. Thank you. With cream, if you have it?" The young doctor's gaze once more sought out Cora over Dixie's shoulder.

Dixie remained oblivious. "Of course. I'll fetch that right out. Oh, here's Flynn now."

As Doctor Griffin squeezed his wife's arm and then sank into the seat across the table, Cora realized the two loggers who had just entered the dining room were her excuse for escape. "If you'll excuse me, I really must see to the others." She tipped her head to the two men who waited near the doors.

He dipped his chin. "Good day to you, Miss Cora. Perhaps we can resume our . . . discussion a bit later?"

Her nerves flapped to life again. Her resolve strengthened. Surely it wasn't trepidation that she ought to feel at the prospect of a man asking her . . . asking her what? She still only had guesses as to what he wanted. She offered an obligatory, "Of course," then hurried away before the apprehension swirling through her could reveal too much to the assessing looks Flynn and Dixie leveled on her.

She tried to smile as she approached the men at the door to take them to a seat, but she feared she failed rather miserably.

Kin woke to find Isaiah's feet crammed into his armpit. While the parson and Aurora had not gotten rid of his bed, he'd rather forgotten how narrow it was. Still, the spring nights were too cold for either of them to sleep on the floor, so he and Isaiah had shared the bed—heads toward each end, and legs alongside each other. At least that was the way they'd started out. Somewhere in the middle of the night, he'd woken with Isaiah's knees in his back. And now, it seemed that the kid had gotten cold and invaded Kin's side of the bed.

Kin shoved the kid's feet to one side and scrubbed a hand over his face. "Isaiah, wake up. We have to get you to the school. I'd like us to be a little early so you can meet Miss Kastain before all the other kids arrive."

As though the words had launched him from the bed, Isaiah sprang to his feet. Before Kin could even roll to a seated position, Isaiah was splashing water from the washbasin against his face.

Across the room, Tommy gave a sleepy chuckle from beneath the quilt on his own bed. "H-he's b-bouncy in the m-mornings."

Kin suppressed a yawn. "Seems so."

"Not always." Isaiah flicked water from his hands and thumbed his suspenders over his shoulders. "But today I get to go to *school*! Ain't never been to a real school 'fore."

Kin frowned as he reached for the towel that hung on the bar at the side of the wash basin and handed it to Isaiah. "You've never been to school?"

Isaiah shook his head and patted his face dry. "In our neighborhood, we had two schools. One for white folk and another for black. The white school wouldn't have me 'cause I was too black. And the black school wouldn't have me 'cause I was too white." He hung the towel back on the bar. "Pa said he could pay to send me to one that was farther away, but it would have taken over an hour there and back and he didn't want me gone for that long each day."

"That must have been disappointing." Kin wondered about the kid's upbringing. If his father could have afforded to pay for schooling, they must have been fairly well-off?

Isaiah shrugged. "My daddy done taught me everything he knowed."

Kin didn't miss the tears that the kid did his best to blink away. He rose and roughed a hand over the boy's head. "Well, things are different here. You'll see. Tell me about your life in California."

Isaiah stared into the wash basin for a long moment, then lifted his head with a smile. "I miss the sound of the ocean." He motioned to the window. "Here there's wind, and branches clackin', and birds that chirp like they playin' a piccolo."

Kin didn't let on that he had no idea what a piccolo was.

"But back home, well, there ain't nothing quite like wakin' to the sound of waves poundin' the shore. And back there, the birds, they cry like they always missin' they mamas. They more like a squawky oboe than a high-pitched piccolo." Isaiah was smiling now. "And the sound of the wind in palm trees is some different than the sound of the wind here. Sharper there. More clatter to it, somehow."

"So your house was right on the shore?"

Isaiah nodded. "Yessuh. Right across Ocean Avenue from the prettiest golden beach you ever did see."

"What made your pa want to head for the Yukon?"

A lift of one shoulder, and Isaiah's face fell a little. "Pa said that after Ma died, the place didn't hold much appeal for him anymore."

"So he sold it?"

"Oh, no suh. He let it out, he said. He told me so when he was so sick there at the end on that ship. He made sure to tell me several times."

"I see. So you get some money from the house being let out?"

Isaiah wagged his head. "Don't know nothing about that. Weren't for you, I think I might have starved to death on the streets of Seattle."

Kin tucked the information away. He'd have to think about what he needed to do to get Isaiah his money. For now . . . He tousled Isaiah's hair. "Why don't you see if Mrs. Clay—" The sound of her name elicited a grin. Would he ever get used to calling Aurora that? "Why don't you see if Mrs. Clay needs any help with breakfast? I'll be out in just a minute."

"I h-help too!" Tommy exclaimed, following Isaiah out of the room.

Kin grunted and stretched aching muscles. He definitely didn't want to spend another night crammed onto the tiny bed with Isaiah's feet in his back. As soon as he dropped the kid off at school, he would mosey on down to the boardinghouse to see if Mrs. Griffin had any rooms available.

The thought of the boardinghouse brought to mind a pleasing face with hazel-gray eyes and golden-blond wisps of hair framing it. Did Cora Harrison still work for Dixie? He couldn't deny that he was more than a little curious to see. Likely, some lucky man had made her his wife by this time.

After gasping his way through a face wash from the just-this-side-of-ice water in the basin, he stepped out to the table.

Aurora was just settling a pot of steaming oatmeal onto a trivet. She beamed a smile. "Good morning, Kin. Sleep well?"

His back twinged with the question. "Slept fine, thank you," he lied.

"I did too!" Isaiah nodded happily from where he sat with his hands folded as he waited politely for breakfast. "After breakfast, Mr. Davis gonna take me down to meet the teacher so's I can go to school today."

Aurora poured Isaiah's glass full to the brim with creamy milk. "You will love Miss Kastain. She's a wonderful teacher who loves her students!"

"Sh-she gots p-perty r-red h-hair all piled on t-top of her h-head." Tommy's face was almost the same color as the mentioned coiffure.

Kin chuckled and couldn't resist teasing. "You got an affection for Miss Kastain, Tommy?"

PC cleared his throat and gave Kin a shake of his head as he approached and sank into his seat. His look said, "Don't encourage this."

He thought quickly. "I think she's beyond our reach, Tommy. Unfortunately, that Wash Nolan holds her affections."

Tommy nodded. "Y-yeah. I know."

Ike perked up. "Who's Wash Nolan?"

"He was one of my best pals, growing up. He's off in the cavalry now."

He didn't like the way PC and Aurora exchanged worried glances.

"M-maybe he w-won't c-come home." Tommy's tone was hopeful, though he looked guilty for it.

"We all hope that's not the case," PC said firmly.

Tommy hung his head. "Y-yeah. I'm s-sorry."

Kin returned his gaze to Tommy, who was still blushing and squirming in his seat with his head hanging. Of course, PC was right. Nothing could come of Tommy falling for any woman. It didn't seem fair. Not to Tommy. And certainly not to PC and Aurora, who would end up caring for him for the rest of their lives. And what if dear sweet Tommy outlived them? Then what would happen to him? The whole line of thinking shot Kin through with a hot surge of anger. It *wasn't* fair. Not in the least.

And yet God was the one who had created Tommy the way he was in the first place—or at least had allowed him to become so. None of them really knew if Tommy was born the way he was, or if something had happened to him. PC had taken him in after the town had rescued him from an outlaw gang. He had come into their lives full grown, but sweetly childlike.

What purpose could God have had in that? What need had He of such a loving simpleton? Just as quickly as his anger had risen, it faded away. There must be some reason because God never made mistakes. Kin sank into his seat, giving PC a nod of understanding.

It was in that moment that his musings registered with a bit of surprise. *God never made mistakes?* When had he come to believe that? He wasn't sure. What he *was* sure of was that here in this moment, he believed it with all of his heart.

They passed the rest of the meal in quiet conversation. PC was heading to Camp Sixty-Three today for a funeral and a baby dedication. Aurora was heading into town to help with final preparations for this month's last fundraiser for the schoolhouse. Tommy was instructed to paint until he got hungry, and then, after he ate the sandwich Aurora had left for him wrapped in paper in the icebox, to take Allegra on a walk.

"I thought I might ride out to see the Carvers at my place," Kin offered. "Would you like to ride with me Tommy? I don't think I'll have time today, but we can go tomorrow after you take Allegra on her walk."

Tommy's eyes widened in excitement. "Y-yes! Tommy l-like that!"

"All right, then. I'll rent us a couple of horses from the livery. But not until tomorrow, okay?"

Tommy nodded. "T-tomorrow."

PC took a sip of coffee. "Kastains are still boarding your mare?"

Kin nodded. "They are. I'll need to talk to Zoe about when might be a good time for me to come get her. But, until I have a place of my own, she might as well board there as here in town."

Aurora's words were soft when she said, "I know they've really appreciated the little bit of extra that boarding your horse gave them. But now that Susan has remarried, I think they are doing better financially."

Kin twisted his cup in a circle and eyed Isaiah across the table. It suddenly hit him full force that, just like PC and Aurora had taken on the care of Tommy, he'd taken on the care of Isaiah. Sure, he wouldn't have to care for Isaiah for his whole life, but . . .

Was he ready to be a father figure? He gulped apprehension at the thought. The last person he wanted Isaiah growing up to be like was someone like him! The kid certainly needed a better role model, and yet . . . If he could learn to be like Jesus as PC had instructed yesterday, maybe the kid would be all right. He certainly couldn't give him up without hurting his feelings. And he didn't want the boy to feel like he wasn't wanted.

"Thank you very kindly for breakfast, Missus Clay." Isaiah pushed back from the table. "You ready, Mr. Kin?"

Kin didn't miss the amused exchange between Aurora and PC over the way Isaiah had labeled him "Mr. Kin." He scooted back from the table. The kid was way more polite than most his age, Kin would wager. "I am at that. Get your coat."

Aurora spoke low as she watched Isaiah slip into his coat across the room. "That coat is awfully large on him, Kin. Doesn't he have one that fits him better?"

"It was his pa's. He won't be parted from it. I've already tried."

Tears misted Aurora's eyes, and Kin knew that she understood very well what it was to lose both parents at such a young age. "Well, then, he mustn't be parted from it, but perhaps this evening he'll allow me to alter it so that it fits him a little better. Kids can be very cruel over the smallest of details."

Kin felt the parson's gaze on him and met the man, scrutiny for scrutiny. Both of them transferred their gaze to Isaiah's in-between skin tone at the same time.

Kin sighed. Though he knew Zoe would be more than welcoming of Isaiah, and though Wyldhaven definitely wasn't California, he suddenly had a fist of apprehension clenching his stomach. If the only confrontation the kid faced at school was over his too large coat, it would be a miracle.

Chapter Eight

Charlotte Callahan felt restless. The house was spotless. All today's desserts for the diner were baked. She'd started at least three books and rejected all of them this morning. None had held her interest.

She checked the weekly to-do list she kept on the kitchen counter. She needed to bake the pies for the fundraising social, but she didn't want to start those for a couple of weeks yet.

She paced through the kitchen and paused in front of the window. It was a gloriously sunny day. Perhaps she ought to be outside enjoying it before summer swept in to steal the cool of the spring days filled with sunshine.

Her work coat hung on a peg by the back door. She slipped it on, following it with gloves.

Marching outside, she took the garden rake from the shed and then paused to study the empty fields around their cabin.

Their cabin sat on a hill that gave her a good view of the surrounding countryside. The path that led toward town swooped into a little valley and then climbed the other side, cutting a ribbon of brown through the new-growth gold of the fields. The leaves on the large oak near the top of the hill were a vibrant green and made a soft soothing sound as they waved in the breeze. Beyond that, the clear sky was such an azure blue that her heart ached with the beauty of it. An eagle soared, studying the field for some unlucky rabbit or mouse. A soft wind swept through the grasses, whispering to her to feel joy at being alive on a day such as this.

She lifted her face to the sun. Eyes closed, she inhaled the warmth of the loamy spring breeze. Her restlessness eased.

If she were honest with herself, her disquiet had started the moment Priscilla Hines had spoken those thoughtless words to her at the gathering the other day.

She hoped Priscilla hadn't meant to be unkind. After all, Priscilla herself had confided that she longed for a child of her own. However, no matter that Charlotte hoped the words had been spoken without malice, her heart seemed to have taken them in and chosen them as barbed pets.

When He deems you fit and ready . . .

"Oh Lord, You know how those words have tormented me so over the past few days. Is it because of me that you are withholding a child from us? Something I've done or haven't done? Your Word says children are a blessing, and I long for that blessing. Yet, You've withheld it from us. Please help me to be content. To trust, even when I don't understand. My heart hurts. I feel less loved by You, if You'll forgive me for saying so, because I know it isn't true."

She felt a coolness on her cheeks and realized tears had slipped free to track down her face.

Hoofbeats startled her, and she quickly spun to put her back to the cabin path and swipe at her cheeks.

"Charlie, darling? What's the matter?"

Charlotte's shoulders sagged in relief. Just the sound of Reagan's voice soothed a portion of her sadness. But how to explain to him what she was feeling without causing him pain as well? She remained where she stood, fist clenched around the handle of the rake to keep her grounded.

His saddle squeaked as he dismounted. Grass rustled beneath his boots. And then his hands were warm and firm against her shoulders. His thumbs kneaded at the knots of tension, shooting a welcome torture up her neck. He leaned into her and pressed his lips into the hair just above her ear. "What is it? I'm here. Talk to me." His thumbs kept working over her muscles.

After a long moment, she let the rake go. It clattered against the side of the cabin as she turned to collapse into him. Her cheek settled against the steady beat of his heart. Her hands smoothed over the taut fabric of his shirt until she could draw him closer with a firm hug.

Strong arms enveloped her. The stubble on his chin brushed her forehead as he dipped down to rest his head against hers.

And then she cried. Without a sound. Without movement. Without hope for change.

Because she suddenly knew that this was a dream she had to let go. There was no understanding it. No changing it. No reasoning with the inability to have children. It was simply a truth. A part of her that she couldn't wish away. And so, she must give in. Accept. Make peace with it.

Reagan held her in silence, the steady beat of his heart a sure comfort beneath her ear.

She remained in the comfort of his arms for as long as she dared. Finally, she eased back from Reagan and smoothed her palms over the damp patch on his shirt that had absorbed her tears. "What brings you home this time of day?"

He looked down at her, a worried pucker between his brows. "I was coming by to tell you I need to ride out to Sixty-Five to investigate a theft, so I won't be home for lunch." His gaze drilled into hers. "What is it, Charlie?"

She fiddled with the front pocket of his shirt and lifted one shoulder. "Just saying goodbye, I suppose."

"Goodbye?"

Her gaze blurred against the oak in the distance. "To the dream."

He touched her chin, drawing her focus back to his. "The dream of having children?"

She nodded, searching the blue of his eyes.

His thumb softly caressed her chin. "I love you. We're going to make it through this, you and me, together." His voice broke on the last word.

Her lips found the center of his palm and then she offered him a watery smile. "I know." She considered for a moment, and then whispered tentatively, "Am I enough, Reagan? Enough to make you happy? Satisfied?"

He cupped her face firmly and bent till she couldn't avoid eye contact. "Of course you are. Without a doubt. And what about me?" His lips quirked up at one side. "Can you settle for being stuck with only an old lawman like me for the rest of your life?"

A teary giggle spurted past her lips. "I can, indeed, Mr. Callahan."

"All right, then." He nodded emphatically. "I guess we are a pair meant for each other."

Charlotte stood on her tiptoes and gave him a soft kiss. "We are, at that." She blew out a breath. "But I have to find something to do, Reagan. More than baking desserts for the diner. I'm going stir-crazy here without much to occupy my time."

"All right." He nodded.

"Just like that?"

His brows rose in surprise. "You thought I'd try to stop you?"

She brushed the thought away. "I don't know what I thought. But I'm glad to know you'll support me."

"What will you do?"

Nothing came to mind. She gave a shake of her head. "I'm not sure yet, but the good Lord will bring something along."

"I'm sure He will. With a little aid from your ingenuity." Reagan smiled before he lowered his head to give her another lingering kiss.

After a moment, she gave him one last peck and a gentle push. "You can go to work. I'm fine now."

He pouted playfully and waggled his brows. "Maybe I don't want to go to work, anymore."

She laughed. "Do you want a sandwich to take with you?"

An exaggerated grumble was his only answer, and a pleading teasing glint beckoned her to cave to his desires.

Charlotte felt the thump of her heart against her ribs. My but the man was a temptation. However, he was expected out at the camp. Charlotte raised a firm finger. "All you are getting from me at this moment, Sheriff Reagan Callahan is a sandwich. Take it or leave it."

"Fine, I'll take your measly sandwich," he groused. "But"— he sidled a step closer and settled his hands at her waist as he lowered his voice—"I'll be back this evening with expectations."

A girlish giggle burst from her, and she felt her cheeks heat. "I promise to have something more than sandwiches prepared for dinner." She made a dash for the house then, leaving him lamenting and laughing behind her.

Isaiah nearly skipped along the path beside Kin, the tin lunch pail that Aurora had prepared for him swinging precariously by his side.

Kin realized he was walking a bit fast and slowed his steps. "Careful there, or you'll dump the whole passel into the dirt." He chuckled.

Ike tempered the arc of the bucket. "Wouldn't want that. She packed me late strawberries from her garden and the biggest piece of cake you ever did see. She told me she didn't want me goin' hungry for afternoon classes and that I could pop up to the house if what she give me wasn't enough."

"Gave."

"Suh?"

"If what she *gave* me wasn't enough. That's the correct way to say it."

The boy eyed him. "Yessuh. Gave."

Kin offered a shoulder-squeeze of encouragement. "You take her up on it too. Aurora always means what she says."

Ike chuckled. "Not sure my stomach'll be able to hold all the fixin's in this here pail, but I 'spect she knew that and give—uh, gave—me extra so's I could share with the fellas."

Kin plucked a shaft of grass and tucked the end into his mouth. "You might be right about that." He angled the kid a glance. "You nervous?"

Isaiah pondered for a long moment. Finally, he said, "I guess the truth never hurt no one. Yessuh. I got me a whole passel o' butterflies flutterin' around in my insides."

Kin grinned. He pondered his next words for a careful moment before finally speaking. "You'll be fine. Folks around here are a good bunch. And there are plenty of boys your age. You'll see." He eased out a slow breath, hoping beyond hope that he was right on that count. He'd decided against raising any caution that there might be concerns. Zoe wouldn't kick up any fuss or even bat an eye over the color of Isaiah's skin, but he wasn't so sure about some of the townsfolk.

Ahead of them, the bell started ringing and Kin realized that it had taken them longer to escape the house than he'd anticipated. They hadn't arrived early liked he'd hoped.

Kin glanced up to see Zoe's slight form topped by a mass of red curls, standing on the porch as she tugged the pull. He grinned. It did him good to see her again.

Children tromped up the steps and she paused to greet each one while still ringing the bell. But when Kin and Isaiah came to a stop at the bottom of the stairs, the rope fell limp in her hands.

"Kin Davis! I do declare!" Zoe hurtled down the stairs and threw her arms around Kin's neck.

From behind her back, Isaiah grinned and gave a sly pump of his dark brows.

Kin ignored the kid and relished the feel of his childhood friend's welcoming embrace. "Zoe. So good to see you."

She was thin. Concerningly so. He could feel her shoulder blades poking out as though she'd sprouted wings while he was away.

She pushed back from him. "I didn't know you were in town! When did you get home?"

"Just got in last evening." Kin motioned to Isaiah. "This here is Isaiah Coleman. Ike to his friends. Got an extra desk in that school of yours?" He took her in from head to toe. Her dress hung on her like it had been made for someone twice her size. His concern mounted. Yet, despite how much weight she'd lost, she looked as vibrant as ever.

"I certainly do!" Zoe faced the boy and stretched out a hand. "Isaiah, it's a pleasure to meet you. I'll let you tell me when you consider me enough of a friend to call you Ike." Her smile was so warm it could have thawed ice.

"Ma'am." Isaiah shook her hand like a perfect gentleman, even bowing over it at the end. "Happy to meet you. I'd be honored to consider you a friend."

Kin couldn't resist a chuckle. The kid was laying it on a bit thick.

But Zoe didn't seem to mind. She ruffled a hand over Isaiah's curls, drawing Kin's attention to the fact that the boy could use a haircut. "Well, don't you have polished manners. I'm so excited to have you join us in class!"

Isaiah beamed. "Thank you, ma'am."

Zoe met Kin's gaze for a moment.

Kin wanted to ask a whole slew of questions, but now was not the time. Instead, he said, "We should catch up—"

"—I'd love to get together for a chat."

They spoke over top each other, then laughed.

Zoe backed toward the stairs. "We must catch up. Would you be able to meet me for dinner this evening in the diner?" A sheen of moisture glossed her eyes, but she quickly blinked it away. "I'll pay my own way. I'd just love to hear how you've been these past few years."

Kin felt a tension grip his temples. Something was obviously worrying her, but she had her students to think of. He'd have to wait till this evening to find out what was on her mind. Did she know more than the Nolans about something that had happened to Wash?

His voice was a bit gritty when he replied, "I'd like that. Shall we say five o'clock?"

"Sounds perfect." She turned, placing a hand on Isaiah's back to urge him up the stairs, calling over her shoulder. "See you then."

Isaiah threw a wide-eyed glance over her arm.

Kin smiled as he lifted a hand of farewell to the kid. He'd wager those butterflies had started to flap their wings in earnest, but the kid would be fine.

He tossed the stem of grass he'd been chewing to the ground and turned to survey the town, hands propped on his hips. He might not be able to do anything about what troubled Zoe, but he did need to figure out what to do about starting a practice. He'd need to put up a building. He had plenty of money for that.

He swept his gaze along the street. What he needed was land. Where would the best place be?

Not to the south. That would be too close to the livery. From here on the hill by the church, he could see that street after street of rowhouses had been built on the west side of Second Street. He shook his head. He remembered when Wyldhaven had only been Main and Second.

The properties west of the rowhouses would likely be cheap, since they were so far from the heart of town, but he discarded that notion. He wanted to be closer to the business district. He turned his gaze toward the north side of Wyldhaven Creek. Just past the mill, across from the cleared lot where the new schoolhouse would be built, there was a piece of property. But that might be a bit noisy during the children's lunches and playtimes. His focus landed on the building Isaiah and Zoe had just entered. There was a parcel of land here just behind the church, up the hill from the mercantile. He strode past the building until he felt certain he was on the adjacent land and then he turned to look out over the town. He had a view of the whole valley all the way to the foothills of the Cascades to the west, and the terrain would make it easy to build a road right to the office from down near the livery. His pulse thrummed excitement in his ears. If he remembered rightly, Butch Nolan had purchased this parcel a while back. He'd just mosey out to the Nolan place and say hello.

But first, he needed to speak to the sheriff. There was no horse tied to the rail in front of the jailhouse, however, so the sheriff was probably out on his rounds.

Dixie's Boardinghouse first, then. He'd see about a room. It was only practical. Hopefully, they'd be able to rent him one until he could find other arrangements. He needed to talk to the Carvers about his place, which they'd been renting—but if they had no other options? He couldn't simply ask them to vacate. They'd been good tenants. On the other hand, it wouldn't be practical to remain at the boardinghouse long-term.

His gaze angled back to the parsonage and a twinge shot through the muscles of his back. He worked a fist into the knot of tension along his spine. Sharing a room with Tommy and Isaiah wasn't going to work if Kin was expected to get enough sleep to function during the daylight hours. So for now, the boardinghouse was his only hope.

As he picked his way through the field back past the church and toward the path that led down to town, his stomach crimped. He realized that in the rush to get Isaiah out the door to school, he hadn't taken time to eat much of Aurora's oatmeal.

That could be easily solved with a stop into the diner for one of Dixie's cinnamon buns and a hot cup of coffee. Then he could see if the little missionary still worked there. He hadn't wanted to ask PC and Aurora about her last night for fear of giving them ideas. But it sure wouldn't hurt his feelings any to lay eyes on Cora Harrison.

Just to see how she was faring.

That was all.

Chapter Nine

ora had pushed the entry desk's stool aside in favor of standing as she collected payment from two men for their meals. The last notes of the morning school bell stroked the air as she handed the second man his change.

He gave her back two pennies, then tipped his dirty slouch hat. "Fer you, Miss Cora, simply for brightenin' my mornin' with yer beauty." His grin revealed a dark gap between yellowed teeth that seemed no more than a chomp or two from falling out.

She tucked the pennies into her skirt pocket and gave him a polite reply, knowing his intentions were harmless. Regardless, she might have fled his scrutiny and gone back into the dining room, but at this time of morning, it was her duty to remain here and collect the payments from customers as they left. Thankfully, when she looked up, both men were stepping onto the front porch.

Behind her, the doors of the dining room swished open and several other patrons stepped out. She gathered their payments and wished them good day. They tipped their hats politely and headed toward the doors as she bent to mark their receipts as "paid."

Footsteps stopped before the desk. "Busy morning."

She glanced up, her trepidation rising.

Dr. Polson smiled down at her, seeming to be on a mission of some sort.

And just like that, Cora's earlier nerves reappeared in full force. Surely he wouldn't ask her anything too forward this early in their acquaintance?

She realized he was waiting for a reply and blurted, "Oh my, yes. But it's almost always this busy until the breakfast hour is past." Maybe she could sidetrack him from the question her intuition told her he'd planned. She tucked the latest receipts into the pile of bills that had already been paid this morning, attempting to look busier than she was. That done, she pretended great focus on dusting the already dust-free desk. "Did you enjoy your meal?"

He gave a mock groan and settled one hand against his belly. "I haven't tasted any breakfast that fine in, well, ever." He held his bowler to his mouth conspiratorially. "I pray those words never reach the ears of my own dear mother."

Cora stepped to the far end of the welcome desk, keeping the duster moving. "Mrs. Griffin can certainly coax mouthwatering flavors from just about any dish."

"If all her meals are as good as the one I just ate, that's certainly true." His gaze lingered on her. His voice softened. "Would now be an acceptable time to finish our conversation, Miss Cora?"

Oh, dear heavens. The man apparently couldn't read cues, and by her calculations the rest of the diners had now departed and the doctors were the last to leave. Doc would likely spend a few minutes chatting with his wife, as was their habit. There would be no interruptions to rescue her. And yet there was no honest excuse she could offer to escape him, either.

She nodded, mouth dry. Had he really been about to ask her to dinner? Surely not since they'd only met the day before.

Dr. Polson reached across the desk and took the feather duster from her.

Cora bemoaned the loss of her busywork. She opened her mouth, intent on telling him to give it back, but then thought better of it. Let the man ask his question, receive his rejection, and then be gone.

He ran the feather fronds through his fingers, seeming to ponder his next words thoughtfully.

She couldn't seem to find a place to settle her hands. They rested on the desk for one moment, then smoothed at her apron, then fiddled with the little pile of bills. Finally, she twisted her fidgeting fingers into a clench before her, feeling prickles crawling along the back of her neck.

The door from the street opened but Cora kept her focus steadfastly on the doctor, determined that they not be interrupted. She didn't want to dread facing this conversation yet again. Whoever had just entered could simply wait until the doctor finally got up his nerve and she had politely told him they didn't know each other well enough.

Perhaps spurred on by the threat of another interference, the doctor blurted, "Miss Cora, I can see your nerves are roiling just as strongly as mine." He gave the duster a little shake. "But there's no need to delay when two people such as ourselves find such a mutual attraction."

Cora sputtered, trying to decide on a reply, but he hurried on before she could belay his assumptions.

"I wondered if I could talk you into having a 'spot' of dinner with me this evening?"

Cora's stomach gave a little roll. So he *had* wanted to ask her to dinner. A wash of relief at finally having this out in the open swept through her, and also because he'd presented her with the perfect opportunity to decline him in a kind manner. "I'm afraid that's not possible."

Immediate disappointment clouded his eyes.

She hurried before she lost the opportunity to finish her refusal. "You see 'spot' is reserved specifically for tea, so it can't be used with reference to supper." She grinned to lighten her refusal. "Also, I'll be working through dinner. Perhaps another time, Doctor." She held her breath. *Take my meaning at face value and walk away, Doctor, just walk away.*

But the man did not. Instead, he cackled and shook one finger. "I see you are a woman who will keep a man on his toes, Miss Cora." His scrutiny swept over her face once more. "I like that in a woman." Dr. Polson leaned in until his elbows rested on the counter. "Shall we say six?"

Such gumption! Cora angled so far back that her shoulders came up against the wall. The man was determined to make her cut him to the quick. She dredged up every scrap of kindness she could muster. "I'm sorry, I can't. As I said, I won't be off work yet." Surely he would give up now.

He frowned, and gave a quick glance at the patch of morning sunlight playing across her desk. "You work from now all the way past six?"

Annoyance swept through Cora. He didn't believe her? "Not all day, no. You see, Dixie's offers no noon meal. On that account, I work until ten. And then I have off until four when I return and work again until eight." Thankfully, she knew he would be preoccupied with his doctoring during those lunchtime hours.

"I see." He pondered for a moment. "In that case, perhaps we could enjoy a dessert and coffee this evening at eight fifteen?"

Cora waffled, feeling her mouth opening and shutting like a banked fish. Did the man have no social graces? Could he really not see that she was sincerely trying to put him off?

The doctor leaned even closer. "I can see that my insistence has startled you. But I have to tell you that I'm not a man who lets any moss grow under my feet, dear Cora."

Her mouth gaped. How could the man address her in such an intimate manner without the least compunction?

"If you'll only say yes, you'll find my company quite agreeable, I assure you."

Cora felt at a loss. To decline him again would plunge her rudeness to a level to which she wasn't sure she could descend. And maybe having coffee and dessert would be a way to ease into knowing him better? If she didn't grow to like him more—a skeptical thought that didn't bode well for their future, she realized—she could gulp down her pie and beg off to her room. And if they did end up being as incompatible as she now feared, perhaps it would only take that short torture to get the message across to him.

The doctor's feet shuffled. "So? What say you?" The hopeful arch of his brows was the last nail in her coffin.

She released a lungful of air. "All right." She would have to scarf down something to eat as soon as she got off work or she'd be famished with only dessert, but at least this would all be over by tomorrow.

Near the door, the newcomer coughed pointedly and shifted.

It was only then that Cora remembered someone had entered. "I'll see you tonight." She offered the parting words to the doctor and turned toward the new customer. "Good morning. How may I help—" Her knees went so weak that she collapsed against the high stool beside her. Her heart was suddenly dodging about like a kite on a fickle wind.

Kin Davis stood in the entryway, hat pressed to his chest. His contemplative gaze swept over the doctor before swinging to her. One corner of his mouth tipped up, nudging to life the slash of a dimple in his cheek. His eyes sparkled. "Morning, Missionary Harrison. How have you been?"

Cora fumbled to grip the stool and settle onto it more firmly. Heavens! Had Dixie added too much wood to those kitchen stoves?

Kin Davis had started calling her "missionary" the moment she'd spoken to him about his need for Jesus. He'd left town on the very next train, but now, here he stood, bold as you please. She felt like the room had gone all hazy around the edges.

Love him.

As though hearing them afresh again, she remembered the words that had reverberated through her when she'd prayed for the Lord to show her how to help Mr. Davis. And just as she had the first time, she felt her face blaze at the thought.

How many times had she thought of this man over the past few years? Too many to count, which was just plain inexplicable.

Yet every curve and angle of his face, the exact shade of those brown eyes, the maddening quirk of his full lips, and the way his stubbled jaw had tempted her fingers to feel of the texture that last morning—even while she was witnessing to him, Lord forgive her—none of that had ever faded in her memories.

The Lord's instructions were unaccountable since Kin had made it clear he didn't need God, and as the Word instructed, she had determined to hold out for a godly man. She surely hadn't heard the Lord right. Or maybe she simply hadn't understood how the Lord meant for her to love the man. There were any number of ways to show a person the Lord's love other than loving them, well . . . in the way a woman loves a man. Drat her heated cheeks!

The stool wobbled beneath her so severely that she had to put out one foot to brace herself. For she couldn't deny that Kin Davis, with all his pulchritude and charm, stirred every last one of her worldly senses in a most heady way.

His small smile had turned into an outright grin now. "I can see that I've surprised you."

Dr. Polson made a sound of displeasure at the back of his throat. He stepped forward and held a hand toward Kin. "I'm Doctor Polson, newly arrived. And you are?"

Kin's focus lowered to the dust mop the doctor still held in his left hand. "Doctor, huh? You'll forgive me for thinking you must be one of Dixie's help." A glint of mischief filled Kin's eyes as his broad brown hand engulfed the doctor's smaller pale one. The muscles in his taut forearm flexed as he squeezed the doctor's knuckles and Cora saw Dr. Polson wince.

She pressed her lips together. Really. There was no need for Kin to flaunt his obviously stronger physique.

"Name's Kin Davis, *not* newly arrived. Miss Cora and I are old friends, aren't we, Mish? In fact, we were nearly forced into a shotgun wedding." Devilment tugged at his lips.

She flicked the perplexed doctor a look. Sure she hadn't been ready to take a meal with the man, but she didn't want to smash any bridges before they could even be crossed. "It was *not* as bad as he makes it sound!" After that, Cora couldn't seem to find any more words. She ought to toss him to the wolves by retorting that they barely knew one another, yet she couldn't seem to bring herself to do so.

He'd been handsome when he left town two years ago, but looking at him now, she realized that a boy had ridden the train out of town and a man had ridden it home. His hands were dark and thick with a strength that only came from hours of hard work. His face was more angular and his shoulders . . . Mercy! The man couldn't have looked broader or leaner if he were chiseled from stone.

Cora was saved from staring longer when Doctor Griffin stepped into the entry from the dining room.

"Well, I'll be!" He rushed past Dr. Polson to enfold Kin in a manly embrace complete with several slaps on his back. Kin's Stetson was crushed between them. "Kin Davis, I fully confess I wondered if we'd ever see you back in these parts!" He set Kin back from him. "It's so good to see you! What brings you home?"

Cora noted the irritated twist of Dr. Polson's lips as he rushed toward her and tossed the duster down onto the desk, but she was too fixated on wanting to hear Kin's reply to give the doctor's annoyance much thought.

Kin fixed the crown of his hat, then swung it toward the street outside. "I'm home to set up a law practice. Just here to see if there's a room available for a few days and then I'm heading out to talk to Butch Nolan about that property he owns behind the church."

"A law practice!" Doc chuckled. "I can't believe it." He strode to the dining room doors and pressed them open. "Dixie, get out here, darling. You'll never believe who's here!"

"Who is it?" Dixie bustled into the entry, drying her hands on her apron. The moment her gaze landed on Kin, her eyes shot wide and her fingers flew to her mouth. "Oh my lands! Kin, it is so good to see you."

This time Kin had time to move his hat to the side before it was crushed a second time. He chuckled warmly and returned Dixie's embrace. "It's right good to be home."

Dixie released him, brushing tears from beneath her eyes. "When did you get here? Are you hungry? Breakfast is over, but I still have one of those big cinnamon buns you're so fond of, and plenty of black coffee."

There was a brief flash of disappointment in Kin's eyes before he wagged his head. "You do know how to tempt a man, but really, I just ate up at the parsonage, and I've got some business to take care of, so I can't take the time, even if the thought of your cinnamon buns does have me all aquiver inside."

By his tone, Cora figured that he'd wanted breakfast but didn't want to be a bother.

Dixie and Doc laughed. But from the look on Dr. Polson's face, he likely would never find humor in anything Kin Davis said.

"Do you need a room?" Dixie asked.

Kin nodded. "I got in last night and slept at the parsonage, but . . ." He made a show of stretching out his back. "After only a few hours, it became clear that sharing a room with Tommy and my protégé, Isaiah, wasn't going to work. I know it's short notice, but do you happen to have one available?"

"Of course!" Dixie flapped a hand in Cora's direction. "You remember Cora, I'm sure. She'll get you fixed right up and—" She gave Kin a sly smile. "—I'll be right back." With that, Dixie bustled toward the kitchen, leaving the dining room doors flapping in her wake.

Doc stepped forward to clasp Kin's hand once more. "So good to have you home again, Kin. If you'll forgive us, Doctor Polson and I need to be on our way to Camp Sixty-Three." Doc Griffin clapped the younger doctor on the shoulder and nudged him forward, not giving him any leeway to linger.

Cora was left alone in the entry with Kin. She hoped he wouldn't notice the sheen of moisture suddenly drenching her brow.

His gaze drilled into hers, warm and curious. "Got to admit, Mish, that I figured at least one of the lunkheads in these parts would have swept in and married you by now. Instead, I arrive to find the new doctor fumbling all over himself in an attempt to ask you to dinner. That must mean you aren't yet spoken for." There was a hint of anticipation revealed by the crinkles at the corners of his eyes.

Cora's chin nudged upward. "He wasn't fumbling. And it wasn't an attempt." She nipped her lower lip between her teeth. Why in the world was she defending the man? He and Kin could both fall off the edge of the world as far as she was concerned, and she wasn't even sure why she was upset with Kin.

He squinted one eye and cocked his jaw to one side. "Seemed like he was fumbling to me—and it was an attempt because he only asked you to dessert." He grinned at her cheekily. "Dunderhead didn't even think about the fact that you'll likely be hungry after finishing your shift. You can do better."

Cora felt like a rod had been strapped to her spine. "I'll thank you to keep your opinions to yourself, Mr. Davis. You'll be needing a room, you said?" She lowered her eyes to the register, but drat if she could get anything to come into focus.

She heard him sidle closer, and then felt the brush of air from his Stetson as he settled it onto the high top of the desk. "With two beds, if you have one." He pressed his arms on the counter and leaned over to peer down at the book, which brought his face to within several inches of her own. But where Dr. Polson's similar action had made her retreat, now she was tempted to lean forward.

Cora's heart kicked up like a fawn in sunshine. She swallowed and scooted the book a little way down the desk, forcing more space between them.

She heard him give a low chuckle, but he was at least polite enough to remain where he stood. She could, however, feel his undivided scrutiny.

If only she could concentrate. See. *Think.*

"So how have you been, Mish?" His tone was low and layered with true interest.

She could still feel him studying her. "Fine. Good, really. This job that you got me before you left that day has been a true godsend." She lifted her gaze to his.

Heavens.

Meeting his gaze had been a mistake, because now she couldn't seem to look back at the book.

His expression was soft and serious, and somehow even the way he looked at her was more grown up than before. It filled her with an awareness that she had no business feeling for such an ungodly rogue. Why couldn't she dredge up even a fraction of this feeling for the well-intentioned doctor?

There were new lines at the corners of Kin's lips. And the stubble on his jaw was even thicker than she remembered. He must not have taken time to shave this morning. But my, it was a good look on him. Her hands trembled against the pages of the register.

Kin's gaze flickered from her face to her fingers and back again. One corner of his mouth angled upward. "I knew it would be. I'm glad it worked out."

She tucked her hands out of sight in her apron pocket. "And you?" She hadn't meant to continue their dialogue, but curiosity burned within her. "How have you been?"

He waved a hand and, thankfully, turned his focus to the desktop, where he seemed to be looking into the past. "Been good. Worked in Seattle for the past few years and studied law. And, as you heard, I recently passed the exams." He swept one hand around the back of his neck. "So I guess that means I ought to do something with that honor. Ran into a kid that needed my help, and suddenly had a longing for home and—" His gaze rebounded to hers. "—for the people here."

Her mouth was as dry as overdone toast. His soft scrutiny brought to mind the golden-brown top of one of Dixie's pecan pies—tempted her to believe he could be just as sweet.

With a quirk of his lips, Kin pointed past her to the key hanging on the rack behind her. "If I recall, room two has a couple beds. Seems like that might be your last one?" Humor sparkled in his eyes like he knew she might have been having trouble focusing earlier.

She swung her gaze to the sole remaining key on the wall. "Yes. Ah—" She spun the ledger to face him and lifted it to the higher part of the desk. "If you'll just sign here." She nudged the fountain pen closer as she added, "And indicate how many nights you will be needing it." She tapped the head of that column.

He signed his name with a flourish, but when it came to the column indicating his desired number of days, he hesitated. "Number of nights depends on a few things. Can I pay for two weeks and then let you know in a few days if I'll be needing it longer?"

"Yes. That ought to be fine."

Her heart did a little flip. Her room was only across the hall from room two. For two weeks he'd be coming and going. Maybe bumping into her in the hallway. Why did that thought give her traitorous heart a little thrill?

Dixie bustled into the entry holding something wrapped in brown butcher paper. "All settled?"

Kin tugged a leather wallet from his jacket pocket and withdrew several bills. "Just finishing up." He set the bills on the counter. "Will that cover it?"

Cora quickly penciled out the cost for two weeks and then returned the unneeded bills. She held up the remainder. "This will cover it."

"Excellent." Dixie stepped forward and held the packet out to Kin. "This is for your travels today. And I won't take a penny for it." She smiled wide and held up a hand to reject any money he might try to hand her.

Kin tucked his wallet back into his coat and sniffed the package as he accepted it. "Mmmm. You sure do know how to spoil a fella, Mrs. Griffin."

Cora caught a waft of delectably yeasty cinnamon and sugar. It must be one of Dixie's cinnamon buns.

Dixie only waved him on his way. "Just my way of saying welcome home."

Kin lifted the package in a gesture of acknowledgment. "Thank you kindly." His gaze settled on Cora as he gave a little salute and added, "See you this evening." With that, he moseyed out the door.

Cora stared at his signature in the book, her pulse tripping along like a gangly colt.

Belle's warning about not rushing into anything came to mind and she clutched at it like a lifeline.

Cora Harrison, there can be no future between a woman who wants to do things God's way and a heathen charmer like Kin Davis!

Love him.

Gracious saints! She really needed to take herself in hand.

This would not do.

It simply wouldn't do.

Chapter Ten

saiah settled into his desk in the middle row at the schoolhouse. It would have suited him better to be in the back row with the bigger boys, but he was so happy to be at school that he didn't let that bother him too much. He was always taken for much younger than he actually was.

Ms. Kastain had given him several test papers along with the instructions that he was to ignore today's lessons and concentrate only on the tests so that she would know at what level to place him. In all honesty, he had no idea what level he ought to be at since Pa had never told him.

His heart panged something fierce at the thought of Pa, and he had to blink real hard to hold back tears.

He tugged the mathematics assessment closer.

If a wedge of gold weighing fourteen pounds and three avoirdupois ounces is valued at $514 what is the value of each troy ounce?

His breath caught. How many ounces were in a pound of gold? Had Pa ever taught him that? Was a troy ounce different than a regular ounce? And what in tarnation was this "avoirdupois ounce"?

A longing for Pa's steady presence made him curl his arms over his aching stomach. He rocked a little, staring at the question. Not daring to look at the next.

It was nice having Mr. Kin and all, but he would give anything to have Pa back. To be able to feel the strength of Pa's arms swinging him in a wide circle just one more time—even though it had been a long time since Pa had actually done that, since Isaiah was too old for it. To hear the hearty guffaw of his laugh or the way he could coax such a haunting melody from the old hymns he was fond of singing at the piano in their parlor.

"Ike?" A hand settled against his shoulder. "Are you all right?"

He blinked and looked around. The room was empty save for him and Ms. Kastain. He glanced at the door. Where had everyone gone? Fear filled him and he lifted his gaze to the teacher. He hadn't even answered one of the test questions. Would she be mad? Banish him from ever coming to school again?

Ms. Kastain sank into the desk next to his and leaned close to look at the top test in his stack. "Ah. The old troy ounce question. That one gets me every time. It's a very mean question for them to have put first on that test, don't you think?" Her sincere gaze held nothing but kindness.

Isaiah wondered if he'd ever seen a pair of eyes so blue as Ms. Kastain's.

She met his scrutiny with a gentle, frank gaze. "Did you ever go to school, Isaiah?"

He shook his head, still trying not to think about Pa, but failing miserably. His vision blurred with moisture. "My pa taught me because . . . the schools wouldn't have me." He sucked his bottom lip in. He shouldn't have told her that. Maybe she would decide that she didn't want him either.

Ms. Kastain's chin trembled a little and she massaged one slender finger across it. After a moment, she asked, "And you lost your pa, did you?"

Her voice was barely audible, and Isaiah felt an immediate kinship for her obvious understanding of his pain.

He nodded.

Ms. Kastain squeezed his elbow where it rested on the desktop.

She smelled like vanilla and the English lavender in their garden back home, and Isaiah came to a sudden comprehension of Tommy's affinity for the pretty teacher.

Ms. Kastain poked at a knot on the floor with the toe of her shoe. "I lost my pa a few years ago. There's no pain quite like it. I'm very sorry for your loss."

He couldn't find his voice, so he only nodded again.

"I know this settling-in process isn't really much fun. But I want to assure you that we'll find a place for you here and we will figure out what level to place you at."

"Yes'm."

"For now, all the children are outside for morning recess. Why don't you take a break and then when you come back in, you can try the reading assessment, okay? If you don't know the answers, it's okay. There's no shame in that. There's always more for everyone to learn, even me."

She smiled and something like a ray of hope shot through Isaiah's chest.

He sat a little straighter. "Yes'm."

"All right then, go on with you." She flapped a hand toward the door. "I'll ring the bell in a few minutes. After that, we'll have a couple more hours of class and then a break for lunch."

"Thank you, ma'am." Isaiah escaped down the aisle, feeling his dread of the tests slip away like dirt in a washtub on bath day.

Lincoln Nolan leaned against the rail on the porch with a blade of grass between his teeth and two baseball gloves under one arm. He straightened when Isaiah stepped out. From his pocket, he pulled a knotted green apple with a blush of pink on it. "Brought you an apple from our tree."

Isaiah took the apple, lifting his gaze to the older boy. A wave of sheer awe filled him. He'd never had a white kid voluntarily speak to him before. Much less one who towered head and shoulders above him. "Thank you."

Lincoln shrugged one shoulder and a grin brightened his face. "You might want to wait to thank me till you've tasted it. Those apples will pucker the inside of your mouth so tight that you'll be lucky to get in a spoonful of anything else all week."

Isaiah turned the fruit in his hand. He liked apples well enough, though this one looked a bit wilder than the kind Pa had purchased at the fruit market. He took a big bite and relished the tart sweetness dancing on his tongue. The skin though—the moment he chomped down on a bit of that, he couldn't resist a grimace accompanied by a shiver.

Lincoln raised a brow. "See? Don't say I didn't warn you."

A laugh slipped free. A niggle of guilt weighed down his heart over the joy begging to be freed. He ought not allow himself too much joy on account of Pa not being here. Yet even a hint of joy was a stark contrast to the low way he'd been feeling only moments earlier. He drew in a breath of contentment and blew out anxiety. Pa had gone on after losing Ma, and Isaiah knew that he'd loved her with his whole heart. If Pa could do that, then maybe he could face the future one day at a time as well.

"Want to play ball?" Lincoln motioned with one hand to a group of boys under the large oak nearby. "The fellas are playing catch. I've got an extra glove." He held one out to Isaiah.

Isaiah bit the apple and held it with his teeth while he slipped his hand into the glove. Then he removed the apple and offered a ready smile. "Sure."

As they trotted down the steps, Lincoln bumped Isaiah's shoulder with his own glove. "You have to watch out for David

Hines's slider. And Hugh LeGrado will always say he's safe, even when he knows he's out."

When the bell rang a few minutes later for them to return to class, Isaiah climbed the stairs with a great deal more hope buoying his steps.

Kin stepped onto the boardwalk in front of the diner, still savoring the scent of Dixie's cinnamon bun. The brown paper crinkled invitingly beneath his fingers, and an ooze of frosting dripped over the edge onto his finger.

He relished the sweetness, lifting his gaze to once more study the piece of land he was considering behind the church. But his mind wasn't on the land. It was on the pretty blonde he'd just left at the desk inside. As sweet and inviting as the frosting that now danced on his tongue.

And it seemed that she remained unspoken for.

Unless one counted the fumbling doctor whose invitation he'd interrupted.

Kin smirked. Nah. He wouldn't count the doctor. She had said yes to the man's invitation, but it had seemed a reluctant yes.

Any fool could tempt a lady away from a man such as that. At least, he thought so. And it would sure be fun to try.

He grinned, suddenly even more happy that he'd brought Isaiah home to Wyldhaven than he had been before. He took a hearty bite of sweet cinnamon goodness, turning toward the jailhouse.

"Kin Davis! Well, I'll be." Sheriff Reagan Callahan strode toward him from his office, which was just two doors down. He stretched out his hand. "Doc stopped in and said you were here. Had to come see for myself." The sheriff's smile was warm and welcoming.

Kin quickly swallowed as he accepted the sheriff's handshake. The hitching rail that had stood empty in front of the jailhouse a few minutes ago, was now occupied by the sheriff's horse.

"Sheriff." He offered the man a nod and a smile. "I was just about to come and see you."

A light of caution filled the sheriff's eyes. "Oh?"

Kin figured the sheriff was likely remembering all the trouble he'd caused as a rambunctious lad. It would take time to prove to the town that he wasn't the same irresponsible kid who had left. "Got a minute?"

"Sure. But not much more. I was just heading out to Sixty-Five to see about a theft. Come on down and I'll get you some coffee to go with that cinnamon bun."

Kin suppressed an audible groan as he trailed in the sheriff's wake. It was well known about town that the sheriff made coffee strong enough to rattle a skeleton's gizzard. Not only did he make it strong, but he left it simmering on the wood stove in his office all day. Often his coffee was so thick that it practically glugged from the pot. At least it was early enough in the day that the coffee would likely not be too thick at this point. Still, he would be jittery all day if he had to drink more than a sip or two of the sheriff's brew.

On the other hand . . . He suppressed a yawn . . . After the night he'd had, maybe it was just what he needed.

Sheriff Reagan led the way into the jailhouse. "Sit. Sit." He nudged the chair in front of his desk to create more space and motioned for Kin to make himself comfortable.

As the sheriff tugged two tin mugs from the hooks by the stove and filled them with coffee, Kin turned his attention to the cells at the back of the room. His stomach churned. He would never be able to be in this building without remembering the way his pa had flown into a rage and died right there on the floor.

The sheriff stopped before him, holding out one of the cups. "Go ahead and eat. Don't let me stop you. What brings you back to town?"

Kin accepted the coffee and then balanced it on the edge of the sheriff's desk, within reach. He folded back the paper on the cinnamon bun and reluctantly broke it in half, offering one portion to the sheriff.

Settling into his chair behind the desk, the sheriff held up one hand. "No. Thank you though. I'm getting old enough that I can't handle too many of Dixie's sweets." He patted a hand against the flat of his shirt.

Kin chuckled. He squinted, trying to envision the sheriff with a paunchy belly, but he couldn't quite get the picture to form. Ever since he'd known the man, he'd been lean and hard as shoe leather.

"I find that difficult to believe." But he wasn't going to push to divvy the treat that he hadn't wanted to share in the first place. He took a big bite and chased it with a sip of caffeinated death. He resisted a grimace. "As for what brings me home, that's what I wanted to talk to you about."

He explained how he had been helping Isaiah and about the sailors who had been looking for the boy. He also mentioned Farnham's actions at the train station. He ended the story with a lift of one shoulder. "I just thought you should know. I have a feeling we haven't seen the last of them, though I don't know why they would be after the boy. Maybe something his father did. His family apparently comes from money. After I get my law practice set up, I plan to take some time to go to California and help him get all his affairs in order."

"Doc told me you are now a lawyer. Congratulations."

Kin resisted a proud smile. "Thank you. I was just headed out to the Nolan ranch to ask him if he might be willing to sell me that piece of property behind the church. But I did want to give you warning about those men who seem mighty interested in Isaiah."

"Thank you for letting me know." The sheriff stood from behind his desk and stretched out one hand. "Really good to have you home."

"It's good to be home."

After they said their goodbyes, it only took Kin a few moments to rent a mount from Bill Giddens down at the livery, and soon he was on his way out of town. The children were out for recess as he rode by, and it did his heart good to see Isaiah playing ball with Lincoln Nolan and some of the other boys.

Despite the spring colors in the leaves, indicating that the weather had turned cool, the day was warm and sunny. His shadow stretched away behind him as he rode in the direction of the Nolan ranch. Two blue jays chittered at him from the low branch of a pine tree, and a squirrel dashed across the path ahead with a pine cone twice the size of itself in its mouth.

Kin smiled.

Nostalgia washed over him as he topped out on the ridge above the Nolan ranch. How many times had he come here and felt that this place was more of a home to him than his own? How many meals had he eaten at the Nolans' table, always jealous that Wash had so many brothers? How many times had Mr. Nolan given him fatherly advice, right there on the hard-packed dirt of that barnyard? Other than the half-built cabin in the distance, which was new, the place looked exactly the same.

He shook the sentimentality away and, with the click of his tongue, urged his mount forward. When he rode into the yard, Mr. Nolan stepped out of the barn.

"Well! My stars!" A huge grin split the man's bushy red beard. "Kin Davis, get down here and let me shake your hand."

Kin dismounted and stretched out a hand, but when Mr. Nolan wrapped his own beefy one around it, he didn't seem satisfied with just a handshake, and pulled Kin into an embrace that just about smothered him. Thankfully, it was short-lived and then Mr. Nolan set him back at arm's length.

"Let me look at you. Hang, but time does fly. I remember when you barely came up to my bellybutton." He guffawed heartily. "How have you been, son? Linc tells me you're a law man or some such now?"

"Lawyer. Yes sir. In fact, that's partly why I'm here to talk to you this morning. You still own that piece of property behind the church?"

"Sure do."

"You interested in selling?"

Butch Nolan squinted one eye, pondering thoughtfully. His gaze skimmed the breadth of his land.

Kin took it all in with a critical eye. The roof on the cabin was in need of new shingles. And there were a few broken boards on the near side of the barn—maybe more on the other side that he couldn't see. One window in the cabin was covered over in butcher paper and the chimney was leaning and in need of repair.

Mr. Nolan scratched his fingers into his beard. "For the right price, sure."

Kin grinned, immediately recognizing the negotiator in Mr. Nolan, even though it was clear he needed the money. "I'm happy to pay a fair price. In cash."

Mr. Nolan nodded. "Well, all right then. I'm happy to sell."

When Mr. Nolan named his price, Kin was pleasantly surprised at the amount. He'd be able to pay cash for the land and still have plenty left over to cover the cost of building an office.

They shook on the deal and then Mr. Nolan invited him in for coffee.

Kin was much happier with this invitation than he had been with the sheriff's.

And he was much relieved about having a place to build his office.

It was good to be home.

Chapter Eleven

After catching up some on the family with Butch Nolan, Kin handed him cash for a down payment with a promise to bring the rest of the money by the next day. Then he hurried back to town so that he wouldn't be late to pick Isaiah up from the schoolhouse.

The closing bell was just ringing as he trotted into town, and by the time he stabled his horse and walked up the hill, Isaiah was waiting on the top step with his satchel beside him.

Kin ruffled his hair. "Howdy, kid. How was your day?"

To his surprise, Ike lifted eyes brimming with big tears. "You think they gonna let me come back if I failed all them tests?"

Kin sank onto the step beside him and propped his forearms across his knees. "Tests harder than you expected them to be?"

Isaiah nodded. "Ms. Kastain, she's as nice as can be, but those questions . . ." The kid shook his head in disgust. "Those questions, they was not nice. No, suh. Not nice at all."

A chuckle escaped before Kin could prevent it. "I suppose we've all felt that way a time or two when faced with a test." He scrubbed a knuckle along his jaw, searching for the right words. "Meantime, let's not expect skunks when we might get kittens."

Ike's attention flew to him. "We gettin' a kitten?"

"No. I—Never mind." He made sure he had Ike's full attention. "I've known Zoe—Miss Kastain—almost my entire life and I can guarantee she's not going to keep you from school."

Isaiah's whole countenance lifted, but then fell just as quickly when Kin raised a finger to indicate he wasn't through.

"However, that doesn't mean that you might not have some catching up to do. We'll see. Let's just take things one day at a time."

Isaiah released a sigh that sounded like a blowing horse. "Yessuh."

"Come on." Kin nodded his head for Isaiah to follow him. "I've got something I want you to see."

He led Isaiah out behind the church and strode to the center of his new property. He stretched his arms wide and indicated for Isaiah to take in the view. Below them the buildings of Main Street gave way to the townhouses separated by trees beyond. Wyldhaven ended where the ruffle of the shaggy evergreen forest began. And in the distance, the misty gray blue mountains rested against the horizon like a rumpled goose-down tick bursting at the seams.

Isaiah smiled. "My pa, he would've liked the way those mountains is all covered with snow. In California, he often bellyached 'bout the lack of snow."

Kin settled a hand against Isaiah's shoulder. "I kind of like them myself."

The kid nodded. "Me too. Yessuh, I sure do."

They returned to the parsonage after that, and Aurora had a hearty snack waiting for Isaiah. He wolfed down the cornbread and milk like a child who had been denied food for three days.

Kin grinned at him. "Slow down there, kid. Don't want you choking to death on Aurora's cornbread."

Isaiah swiped the back of his hand at the milk clinging to his upper lip, and pushed back from the table. "I have to hurry, so's I can get to the lessons Ms. Kastain gave me." Isaiah unhooked the leather satchel from where he had left it on the hook by the door and tugged several books from within. He was back at the table in moments with a furrow of concentration creasing his brow.

Kin mentioned his meeting with Zoe and asked Aurora if she would mind keeping an eye on the boy while he went down to the diner. She acted offended that he would even think he needed to ask and practically swatted him out the door with her kitchen towel, much to Isaiah's amusement.

Kin felt a wash of thanksgiving as he strode down the path toward town. How many times was he going to be overwhelmed with thankfulness to be home before it finally settled in that he really was here to stay?

The diner was busier than a frog in a swamp when Kin walked in. Zoe hadn't yet arrived. The batwing doors had been pushed open and latched to give free access to those coming and going. Kin waited there, finding no difficulty in the task. He enjoyed watching Cora bustle from table to table.

She had a water pitcher in one hand and a coffee pot in the other. A perpetual smile graced her face as she refilled cups and glasses and made small talk with the diners. Tonight, she wore a blue blouse that matched the exact shade of her eyes. It was tucked into a black skirt that drew his attention to how thin she'd become. Was she that tiny when she'd first come to town? He remembered how thin and hungry she'd been in the Cle Elum saloon the night he'd first met her. Yeah, she'd always been that small. She was beautiful, but needed some more meat on her bones.

He frowned. Hoped she wasn't working herself too hard.

A noise behind him drew his attention.

The new doctor strode across the entry and paused in the diner's doorway beside him, bowler hat in one hand. His gaze latched onto Cora.

Kin felt a roil of something ugly stir inside him. He shook it away. Whatever Cora might have going with the man was no concern of his. He only hoped the man would treat her right if he happened to win her heart.

He thrust out a hand. "Evening."

The doctor gave him a startled look as if only just then realizing he was there. "Oh. Good evening to you as well. Davis, was it?"

Kin would give him points for the fact that he had a firmer grip this evening. "Kin Davis, yes."

"Alexander Polson."

"I remember. How was your day?"

The man blew a breath. "So many needs and such a lack of necessary medical personnel and facilities, not to mention equipment."

Kin felt another coil of an ugly feeling toward the man. "I'm sure Doc is doing the best he can."

"Oh, I'm sure he is. I didn't mean to imply otherwise. But medicine is advancing so rapidly now. He should . . . Well, there are many opportunities available that we could be taking advantage of."

Kin was prevented from coming to Doc's defense yet again by Cora's greeting.

"Good evening, gentlemen."

Both men turned to look at her.

She divided a glance between them, hands twisted into a clasp before her.

"Mish." Kin snatched off his hat. "You're looking lovely as ever this evening."

It gave him great pleasure to see color rise in her cheeks.

"Evening, Cora." Dr. Polson stepped forward to insert himself. "I'll take whatever table you have available, please."

Kin could have protested that he'd arrived first and therefore ought to be seated first. Instead, biting back a devilish grin, he asked, "I thought you two were having dinner this evening after Cora's shift?" When the doctor tossed him a sheepish look, he feigned remembrance. "Oh! Yes. That's right. You changed it to dessert and coffee. Please, by all means . . ." He swept a hand for the man to allow Cora to lead him to a table.

Cora gave him a glower that could be interpreted as nothing other than *behave* before motioning for the doctor to follow her. "Right this way, Doctor Polson."

As they moved away, Kin heard the man admonishing her to call him by his given name. He clenched his teeth and searched the entry beyond the nearby desk. Still no Zoe.

When he turned back around, Cora was approaching once more. "A table for one tonight, Mr. Davis?" She searched the room. "I'm afraid the doctor has just taken the last table, but it should only be a moment for another. Several groups are just finishing."

"Not a problem. And for two, please. I'm meeting Zoe—Miss Kastain—for dinner."

"Oh."

He tilted his head. Was that disappointment he'd heard in her tone? He'd better not conjure false hope from thin prospects. "You eating enough, Mish?" His gaze drifted the length of her.

"What?" Her frown revealed that his question truly had perplexed her.

"You look like a strong wind could blow you away."

"Such flattery, Mr. Davis." Her lips pinched into a thin line.

He chuckled. "I didn't mean it as derogatory. Didn't you believe me when I told you just a moment ago how lovely you look?"

There she went blushing again and making his stomach get all tight and dodgy.

"If you'll forgive me, I need to deliver desserts to a couple. I'll return to seat you just as soon as we have a free table." She rushed away without giving him time to respond.

Kin grinned. Her fluster ignited a little hope in a man.

From across the room, Doctor Polson scowled. And, well, if that made his smile grow bigger, Kin couldn't help himself.

Zoe rushed through the main boardinghouse doors, puffing. "I'm so sorry to be late. I was grading papers and I'd wager Ma's last jar of peach preserves that sometimes time decides to play tricks on people and simply takes off at a sprint!"

Kin swept his hat to dismiss her concerns. "Don't worry about it. All the tables are full right now, but Cora said she'd come get us as soon as one comes available."

Zoe's stomach rumbled, loud and long. She laughed and covered it with one small hand. "Oh dear. I'm afraid I'm rather starving. One of my students didn't remember their lunch today, so I gave them mine."

Kin winced. "And you probably could have gone home immediately after school to get something to eat, but were waiting for our dinner?" How often was she giving away her lunch? That was probably partly why she was so boney. Where Cora was maybe a little too thin, Zoe was downright skeletal.

She took his arm and smiled up at him, unconcerned. "And it was worth it. It's so good to have you home, friend! I can't wait to hear all about how you've been the last few years."

"And I, you." He relished the warmth of her welcoming smile. On one of his first weeks of school, when he'd had no supplies, Zoe had been the one to organize all his classmates to each give him something. He'd arrived at school one day to find a small pile of pencils, papers, a slate, and even a ruler on his desk.

For many years he'd been halfway smitten with her, but as soon as it became clear that Washington Nolan had staked a claim on her heart, Kin's feelings had changed. He would never try to horn in on Wash's girl. And that had made his feelings for Zoe change to mere friendship. Or maybe they'd always extended only as far as friendship, because if he'd truly loved her, would he have backed off so easily? Not likely, even if Wash was his best pal.

For some reason, those thoughts made his gaze bounce between Cora and the annoying doctor.

"What are you looking at?" Zoe giggled.

Kin snapped his focus back to her.

"Just relishing being back home with all the people I love so much."

A group of loggers brushed past them and Cora stopped before them.

She cleared her throat. "I have a table for you now."

"Excellent. Thank you." Zoe showered a bright smile on Cora who led the way to the last table in the far corner of the room.

Kin pulled out Zoe's chair and seated her before taking the other chair that would leave his back to the wall and offer him a good view of the room. And if his choice made it to where he could delight in the sight of Cora moving about the room for the remainder of the evening, so much the better.

He and Zoe placed their order and then made conversation until their meals arrived. Kin filled her in on his time in Seattle and how he'd come to study law under Mr. Townsend. And Zoe regaled him with tale after tale of shenanigans her students had pulled over the past few years.

He tried to focus on Zoe's stories, but his attention kept wandering to the beautiful woman in blue. The new doctor's gaze followed her too. But it wasn't only the doctor. Kin didn't like the sweeping looks some of the loggers kept giving her when her back was turned.

Why had he thought this job would be good for her? He should have talked to Jacinda instead, and gotten Cora a job sewing dresses for the town's womenfolk. If she were his wife—

The thought was such a surprise that it died mid-rise.

He dropped his gaze to his plate. Zoe was still recounting something about an apple and a beetle and a kerfuffle it had caused in the schoolhouse.

Kin finished the last of his food and set his plate aside. When her story wound down, he said, "Speaking of your students, I wondered if you've had a chance to look at the tests Isaiah took today?"

Zoe swallowed the last of her mashed potatoes, then wiped her mouth with her serviette. "Yes. Those were what I was grading just before I came down."

Drawing his coffee closer, Kin twisted the cup on the saucer. "He seemed concerned over his performance."

Zoe's lips twisted to one side. "I wouldn't say he needs to be concerned. But I think there are gaps in his education. However—" She waved a hand. "He's young. If need be, I can give him some extra tutoring."

"What kind of gaps?" He felt his brow slump.

Zoe rushed to say, "I don't think it is anything to be concerned with. He got several questions right that were levels above where he should be, yet some of the other questions that he should have known, he missed. Some of that could be because he was educated elsewhere, but none of it is anything that will keep him from excelling."

"He'll be relieved to hear it. Do you mind if I ease his mind tonight by telling him? He'll likely sleep a sight better."

Zoe smiled. "Ah a true scholar, is he?"

Kin chuckled. "You've no idea. In fact, when I came down to dinner, he was hard at studying the lessons you sent home with him."

"Excellent. See? He'll be caught up in no time."

While he tried to formulate the wording of a question about how Wash was faring, Kin watched Cora clear Polson's table.

Zoe leaned forward and spoke through a sly smile. "You haven't taken your eyes off her all evening. You should ask her on a picnic. Not many more cool days before the heat of summer sets in."

Kin cleared his throat and concentrated the cup he was still fiddling with. "I won't deny that's a temptation. But she deserves someone better than an old reprobate like me. Besides, she's taking coffee and dessert with the new doctor this evening as soon as she gets off work."

Zoe blew an unladylike sound. "Once a reprobate does not mean always a reprobate. And the Kin Davis I knew and loved never backed down from a challenge."

He grinned at her. She'd obviously never known how hard it had been for him to step aside for Washington. The thought of his friend sobered him. "How is Wash, Zoe?"

Her humor fell away, and to his dismay, large tears filled her eyes.

"I don't know, Kin. I honestly don't. I haven't heard from him in weeks. He wrote regular as clockwork. Sometimes I'd get two letters with the post each week. Then they just stopped. I've written to him countless times without reply. My only hope is that Butch has had no word of his demise. Surely the cavalry would let his father know if something had happened to him?"

"I'm sure they would have." Kin reached across the table to squeeze Zoe's hand. "I'm sure he's fine." If only that were true, because he wasn't sure at all.

"I hope so." She clasped his hand in both of hers. "I have simply felt so hollow."

Cora paused by their table with coffee and water. Zoe released Kin's hand and declined both, but Kin nudged his cup and saucer closer to the edge to indicate he would accept more coffee.

With his cup filled, Cora gave them a smile and then bustled off, yet Kin couldn't help but feel her cheer seemed a bit forced. Maybe she was just tired? Hungry? Or maybe she wasn't looking forward to her dessert with the doctor. That thought buoyed him rather more than it ought.

Zoe yawned expansively and Kin realized he'd kept her too long. He gulped one more scalding swallow of coffee and then rose. "Let's get you home, Zoe. You're about dead on your feet."

He knew she truly was tired when she didn't protest. "I am rather, at that."

They moved together to the front desk. When Zoe tried to pay for her meal, Kin brushed her money aside. "This one is on me. You can catch me next time." He knew she didn't make much in her position as Wyldhaven's teacher. For the amount of work she did, she really ought to be paid more.

She gave him a disgruntled look, but again, didn't protest.

When Cora returned his change, he pushed a silver dollar back in her direction. "Get yourself something to eat before your dessert with the doctor. You look done in."

Cora's eyes widened a little. "It's too much."

"Nonsense." He'd better beat a retreat before she thought of another reason to decline it. Kin withdrew with a tip of his hat and then helped Zoe don her coat as they left the diner. He couldn't resist one glance over his shoulder as the door swung shut behind them.

Cora remained behind the desk, watching them.

Chapter Twelve

Cora stared at the silver dollar still resting on the desk before her. He'd just doubled her day's wages with one coin. She often had patrons give her an extra penny or two, but she'd never had anyone give this much before.

Her mouth watered as she thought of Dixie's venison steak meal. It came with a big side of mashed potatoes, and green beans fried with bacon and onions. The meal was the most expensive one on the menu at a whole two bits, so she'd never ordered it before. Dixie gave her a dollar a day plus meals, but Cora had never felt right asking for the venison. But with this money, she could order it and pay for it with ease.

She took up the coin and thrust it into her pocket. As she did so, her gaze snagged on the blue jar on the desk's high counter. Charlotte Callahan had placed it there with a note taped to the front. *Donations for Wyldhaven's new schoolhouse.*

Before she could think better of it, Cora dropped the dollar in with the few other coins that had been collected over the past few days.

Soup and a roll would do her just fine tonight.

She flicked a glance at the clock on the wall. Almost closing time. She'd best get to clearing tables. Thankfully, it hadn't been too busy. Some evenings she ran so hard and fast that she was practically in a lather by evening's end. Tonight, she was grateful the doctor wouldn't have to see her in that state.

As she wiped down a table, hoping the last group of diners would leave soon so she'd have time to slurp down her soup before the doctor arrived, she pondered Zoe and Kin.

A week ago, she would have laid money on the fact that Zoe would end up with Mr. Ecklund, the mill owner, if her friend Washington Nolan never came back to town. But tonight . . .

First, before Zoe's arrival, Kin's compliment on how nice she looked had filled her with such warmth. She really oughtn't be so vain, but his words had reverberated on repeat in her head all evening.

Mostly in confusion because just after his compliment to her, as she'd arrived to seat him and Zoe, she'd overheard Kin say something about loving Zoe so much.

The man was a conundrum!

And then Zoe had held his hand! Right in public! And she'd said something about feeling so hollow. Had she meant that was how she'd been feeling since Kin went away? And now she was feeling better? She'd certainly *looked* happy and bubbly with him all evening. He'd paid for her meal too. A man didn't do that for a woman he only considered a friend, did he? No. Of course not.

Yet then he'd given her a dollar tip.

Forget conundrum! The man was a scamp. A rapscallion. A rogue!

And what had he meant by saying it looked like a strong wind could blow her over?

She worked hard! And she'd bet she was a lot stronger than he gave her credit for.

Dixie poked her head through the swinging doors to the kitchen. "Cora, I'm getting ready to put out the stove. What should I make for you tonight?"

Cora smiled, suddenly feeling quite proud of herself for her choice. "Just a bowl of soup and a roll, please. Oh, and—" Cora strode closer to her, lowering her voice. "The new doctor wanted to have dinner with me this evening, but I told him I would be busy. However, he's going to come down so we can have dessert and coffee in just a few minutes. I hope that's okay? I'll be sure to clean up after."

"Of course." Dixie smiled, but then her eyes widened and her smile fell away. "But I didn't know that was the case and I just realized we've sold all but the last slice of pie this evening. Of course, Charlotte will bring more in the morning, but . . ."

Cora waved away her concern. "It's fine. Mr. Polson can have it and I'll just have coffee."

"But that's not the same. I wish I'd known. I'm so sorry."

"Really, it's okay. Please don't worry about it. I should have thought to say something earlier." Cora forced a smile, but despaired internally. She'd really been looking forward to the treat. Maybe the doctor would share with her.

The last of the diners were soon gone and Cora cleaned their table. She set up a tray in the kitchen with the one piece of pie and cups for coffee. Made sure the coffee pot was keeping warm on the back of the stove and then hurried to her meal.

Sitting across from Belle Kastain at their usual table in the corner of the dining room, she savored her soup and the warm buttery roll.

Belle looked displeased. She checked the foyer doors, apparently to make sure the doctor wasn't in sight, before she whispered, "I thought you weren't going to rush into anything?"

Cora swiped her mouth with a napkin. "I tried to decline the man. I truly did. But somehow, he worked me into a corner."

With her lips thinned, and one brow quirked, Belle hummed a derogatory note. "That notch he climbed yesterday? He just fell back to a lower level."

"I can't say I disagree with you." Cora spooned up more soup. She wanted to be finished before the doctor arrived. But it was not to be.

She'd only made it halfway through the bowl when he poked his head into the room.

"Ah, there you are. Finished for the evening then, are you?"

Belle gave Cora a sympathetic look as she rose.

"Yes, I'm just finishing." With a sigh, Cora nudged her soup bowl, indicating Belle could take it with her into the kitchen, where she would likely finish her own meal before heading home for the evening.

As Belle departed for the kitchen, Cora gave Dr. Polson her best smile, hoping it wasn't too wan around the edges. "Let me fetch our coffee and pie. You can sit anywhere." Standing, she swept a gesture to the empty dining room.

In the next room, Belle held her soup out to her. "You should finish."

Cora shook her head. "I don't want to keep him waiting. I had enough. I can finish the rest after he leaves. Just leave the bowl on the stove, would you?"

"If you're sure."

"I'll be fine."

She settled the coffee pot onto the tray, then hefted it and hurried to meet the doctor. As she set the tray on the table and handed him a cup, she offered an explanation about the pie. ". . . so, you see, there was only one slice left. It's cherry."

She'd brought two plates in case he offered to share. Her mouth watered at the thought of Charlotte's delicious cherry pie. Her cherries were always the perfect blend of sweet and tart. And, somehow, she turned out the flakiest crusts. Cora had tried her hand at pies and they always ended up dry and crumbly with centers that were passable, but not delicious.

Doctor Polson shrugged one shoulder. "Cherry is not my favorite, but it will be fine."

Cora placed the pie before him and scooted the tray to one side of the table as she sank into the opposite chair. Her tastebuds abandoned hope as he forked off a big bite and savored it.

"Mmmm. After eating this cherry pie, though, I might just change my mind about my favorite. Did you make it?"

"No. Actually the sheriff's wife makes all the pies we sell here in the diner."

"Well, she does a fine job of it." He slurped a sip of coffee and took another bite. "So tell me about yourself, Cora." His gaze rose to hers and lingered.

Cora rattled off a rote description of her childhood and what had brought her to Wyldhaven, but as she spoke, her thoughts were occupied elsewhere. And one thought was the most prevalent.

It was a surge of amusement over how steadily her interest in the good doctor kept plummeting as she got to know him. Now, all she could think about was how much she wanted this to be over so she could finish her soup and go to her room.

And if a handsome face with twinkling brown eyes and a swoop of brown curls popped into her mind's eye once in a while as the doctor blathered about a little of this and that? Well, she was the only one that knew her smiles were because of that and not the doctor's unheard words.

After walking Zoe home, Kin headed to the Clays'. PC had the chessboard set up, and since Isaiah was still finishing up some arithmetic at the table, Kin dallied over the game.

Tommy sat in a chair next to him, enjoying watching them battle it out. At one point he blurted, "K-Kin you sh-shouldn't'a moved th-there."

PC chuckled with relish and swooped in to take Kin's queen.

Kin winced and clutched his chest. "Tommy! Why didn't you warn me sooner?"

Tommy laughed heartily. "P-PC is the o-one who f-feeds m-me."

Both Kin and the parson threw their heads back at that proclamation.

The game didn't last much longer. Kin had thoroughly enjoyed the time, even though PC beat him.

"Your mind elsewhere tonight?" the parson asked. "It's not often that I beat you at chess."

Kin shrugged. "Just out of practice, I guess."

Truth was, no matter how much he tried not to think about it, he couldn't help but wonder how Miss Cora's dessert with the doctor was going. He'd like nothing more than to tromp through the entryway and interrupt them, but he made himself stay and make small talk with PC and Aurora.

Finally, after Aurora had filled him in on all the details about the upcoming social, which they hoped would raise the final costs for flooring and desks for the new schoolhouse, he fetched Isaiah's satchel and informed the boy that it was time they returned to the boardinghouse.

Ike was quiet on the way down the hill, and after all the talking Aurora had done, Kin was thankful for it.

As they moved through the boardinghouse entryway, he caught the glow of a light emanating from the dining room. He looked over the doors. The dining room was empty, but there was still a light in the kitchen, and a sound indicated someone still worked in there.

Surely both Dixie and Cora had long since finished for the day?

Kin dropped a hand against Ike's shoulder. "Stay here. Give me just a minute."

"Yessuh."

The kid was tuckered out, and with school tomorrow, he needed to get him off to sleep, but he really should check to make sure everything was all right.

He soft-footed through the dining room, not sure quite what had raised caution in him. He pressed his back to one wall and quietly eased open one of the batwing doors to the kitchen.

There was a clatter and an indistinguishable mutter of frustration. After a few swishing sounds, the light extinguished, throwing the room into complete darkness.

Kin's heart thumped. Was this an intruder?

His Colt slid easily into his palm and he was just ready to push through the doors when he felt the brush of air as someone made to hurry past him.

On instinct, he reached out and latched hold of an arm. "Don't move. I have a gun."

A loud squeak followed by a gasp instantly had him holstering his gun. "Sorry, Cora, it's just me. Kin."

"Kin Davis!" Cora walloped his shoulder, but good. "You practically stole a year off my life."

He couldn't withhold a chuckle. "Sorry. Really I am." Now that his eyes had adjusted to the darkness, he could see her staring daggers at him. His chuckles probably weren't helping him any. "I thought . . . Well, I thought you would have retired by now."

"I have not, as you can see. But I would like to, so, if you don't mind . . .?" She started away, but just then her stomach gave a loud rumble.

Kin's hand shot out again, this time of its own volition. "I thought you were going to eat before the doctor came?"

She sighed. "I tried. However, he arrived sooner than I expected and I was going to finish after. But I knocked the soup on the ground and just finished cleaning it up. I really am quite exhausted. I'd just like to return to my room."

"You'll sleep better with a full stomach. Give me but a moment. Here sit." He pulled out a chair and urged her into it. "I'll be right back."

Cora relinquished hope of ever making it to her room this evening. Weary as she was, she realized there was no sense in sitting here in the dark. She lit the lantern on her table.

Kin returned only a moment later with a young boy at his side.

"There's someone I'd like you to meet." Kin settled his hands on the boy's shoulders. "This here is Isaiah Coleman. He's staying with me for a while." He nudged the boy forward slightly. "Isaiah, this is Miss Cora Harrison."

The boy smiled and stretched out a small hand. "Pleased to meet you, ma'am." His searching gaze settled on her face and seemed to hitch a little.

Was he just a little embarrassed? Or was it something more?

Cora returned his smile. His handshake was firm. "Lovely to meet you, Isaiah. How is it that you came to company with such a scoundrel as Mr. Davis?"

The boy searched her features for a second longer, but then he grinned up at Kin over his shoulder.

Kin's soft laughter warmed her rather much more than it ought.

"Well, ma'am, Mr. Kin, he come to my rescue, I guess you could say." The boy would one day be sweeping ladies off their feet right and left. His skin was the most beautiful golden brown touched with cream, and his blue eyes were so mesmerizing she found it hard not to stare.

"Indeed, I did," Kin supplied.

Isaiah's scrutiny settled on her again. He tilted his head and squinted one eye. "Do I know you, ma'am? From somewhere else, I mean?"

"I don't think so, no. I would have remembered a handsome fellow such as yourself. Why do you ask?"

The lad's lips twisted. "Don't rightly know. You seem familiar somehow."

Cora lifted one shoulder and an awkward silence fell.

Kin angled Isaiah toward the doors. "All right, I just wanted you two to meet."

Good. Maybe now she could get some sleep.

But when she started to rise, Kin stretched out a hand. "Give me one more moment, Cora? Please?"

When she sank back into her seat, he nodded.

"Thank you. I'll be right back."

He urged the boy to the entry and she could hear him giving instructions for him to head up to room two and get some sleep.

Isaiah responded in the affirmative and then Kin's steps returned in her direction. "Are your meals provided with your pay?"

"Yes."

"Good, then Dixie won't mind if I fix you something."

"It's really not necessary."

"Nonsense. You can't sleep on only a slice of pie and a few bites of soup."

She didn't bother filling him in. She doubted Kin would have anything good to say about the doctor if he knew the man had sat before her and eaten a whole slice of pie without offering her even one morsel.

The man had also lingered much longer than was comfortable, telling story after story of his medical accomplishments. She hoped that all his stories were true, because Wyldhaven really could use someone of such expertise in the medical field. Doctor Griffin did his best, but most days he was quite literally run off his feet. She remembered Dixie telling of the time he'd arrived home so exhausted that he'd passed out on the stairs up to their apartments and nearly given her the scare of her life.

Kin nudged her to her feet. "Come sit in the kitchen so you can instruct me where things are."

Cora had to wonder over his tender treatment when he'd only just returned from taking Zoe home. Before she could think better of it, she blurted, "Don't you think Zoe would rather you leave me be?"

He stilled. Frowned. "What does Zoe have to do with my wanting you to get a good meal in you?"

Cora felt her perplexity rise. "You two seemed . . . rather . . . intimate." She rubbed her thumb into the center of her palm.

Kin barked a laugh. "We were just two old friends catching up, Mish. In fact—" Devilment danced in his eyes. "She encouraged me to ask you on a picnic."

Cora spun toward the kitchen lest he see the pleasure in her countenance at that thought. "Perhaps she was just testing you to see what you would say."

"Nah. Not Zoe." His tread kept pace behind her. "But maybe *I* was just testing *you* to see what you'd say about a picnic?"

She could hear the grin in his voice.

Cora willed away the temptation to say yes. "I'm afraid I'd have to decline, Mr. Davis. It's much too dark out and I'm far too fatigued."

"I see. Well, that's my loss then."

He didn't pursue it further and she had to admit her thankfulness for the fact, because in her current state of weariness, he probably could have convinced her to say yes, just as Dr. Polson had. Chalk one up for Mr. Davis for taking her at her word.

Once they were in the kitchen with the lantern once more lit, she started toward the pantry. But he stepped in front of her with raised hands.

"No. No. You sit there." He indicated the little table in the corner of the room.

When she sat, he moved the other chair from the two-person table around to her side. "Here, prop your feet on this seat and boss me around."

Cora laughed tiredly. "I don't need to prop my feet up."

"Suit yourself. How does bacon, eggs, and toast sound?"

Cora's stomach rumbled greedily. "That actually sounds rather grand."

"Good." He grinned broadly. "Because it's the only thing I know how to cook. Now where do I find the bacon?"

Cora instructed him and watched in awe as he built up the fire, set the cast iron on the stove, and quickly layered several slices of bacon. "I know where the eggs are kept," he said, moving to the bowl on the sideboard, "unless Dixie has moved where she keeps them. Aha! I guess she hasn't." He withdrew two and held them up like prized gold nuggets for her to see.

She smiled, feeling a wave of weariness drooping her eyes. Her four a.m. waking hour had been a long time ago, and tomorrow's was fast approaching. He was right, though, she would sleep much better on a full stomach, and what woman would turn down a meal cooked especially for her by a handsome man?

Kin worked quietly, but efficiently. He flipped the bacon, whisked the eggs, and even added two slices of bread to Dixie's long-handled oven toaster.

A hand settled on her shoulder. "Cora?"

She startled and realized with embarrassment that she'd drifted off to sleep. A plate sat before her—scrambled eggs, crispy bacon, and golden toast.

Kin nudged a crock of butter and a jar of jam nearer. "Wasn't sure if you'd want butter and jam on the bread. Hope you don't mind that I snooped a little in the larder to find them."

"Not at all." Cora lifted the fork he'd angled across the plate and bowed her head to say grace.

When she lifted her head, he was watching her carefully. "Wasn't sure if you were praying, or if you'd nodded off again." He smiled.

She felt heat in her cheeks. "Sorry. It's been rather a day."

Kin wiped his fingers on a kitchen towel. "If that man was any kind of a good doctor, he would have recognized he was overstaying his welcome."

Cora didn't come to the man's defense. She couldn't have agreed more.

The first forkful of eggs melted across her tongue. She hummed a little note of pleasure. "These eggs are impeccable. What's your secret?"

He shrugged one shoulder. "Onion, a little garlic, salt, pepper, and—" He grinned roguishly. "—some good old Davis wrist work."

Cora scooped up another bite. "You could open your own diner with cooking like this."

He shook his head. "Folks would get mighty tired of bacon and eggs, I'm afraid. Not to mention, I have no desire to cater to grumpy, hungry loggers day in and day out."

Cora chuckled. "Isn't that the truth."

Kin used the poker to separate the coals in the stove and then set to cleaning up while she finished the rest of her meal. With her plate practically licked clean, she released a contented sigh and stood. She approached the sink, intent on washing her plate and utensils.

"Ah-ah." Kin held out a hand. "Tonight, the cleanup is on me. Get some sleep."

Cora felt bad, leaving him to wash her things. "'Twill only take me a moment."

"Less than a moment." He tugged the plate and fork from her hands and dunked them in the soapy water.

"Thank you, Mr. Davis." She hoped he knew she meant her thanks for more than just him washing her plate.

He rested the heels of his hands against the lip of the sink and gave her a nod before he leveled her a look. "Thought we talked about you calling me Kin?"

She recalled the moment as if it had been yesterday. Her, hunkered against the cold in the Cle Elum alley where she'd planned to sleep, and him towering over her.

Shaking away the memory, she started toward the door. "We did talk about it and I distinctly recall telling you it wouldn't be proper."

She pushed through the doors, taking the warm sound of his chuckle with her.

Chapter Thirteen

Kin woke Ike the next morning, and hurried him down to breakfast. They were running a bit late, so he was thankful that a table was immediately available. He was also thankful to see that Cora looked well-rested when she seated them and poured his coffee.

"I'll be right back with a glass of milk from the icebox for you, Isaiah."

"Thank you, ma'am." The boy grinned at her shyly. "You can call me Ike, if you like."

Cora plunked a hand on one hip and gave Kin a pleased look. "I think I've just been paid a rather high compliment, Mr. Davis."

He nodded. "I do believe you have."

Cora ruffled Ike's hair and bustled off to fetch his milk.

A gaggle of women who were gathered around a table in the corner laughed and chattered, sounding more like a congregation of geese than one of the fairer sex. He recognized Mrs. Rodante, Mrs. Callahan, and Mrs. Holloway among them, as well as Susan, Zoe's mother. He'd heard she'd remarried but didn't know her new name.

When Cora returned and set the milk before Ike, Kin tipped a nod toward the table. "What's that all about?" He knew all too well, but he had a plan.

She smiled. "Oh, they are planning the last social to raise funds for the schoolhouse. We are set to start building in April and just need a little more money to complete the purchases of supplies—lumber and such."

"I see. Will there be dancing?" He swept her with a look intended to let her know he had her in mind as a partner, then leaned back on two legs of his chair, looking up at her with what Mrs. Griffin had once labeled his "mischievous grin." He knew what was coming and wasn't disappointed by the rise of color in Cora's cheeks.

"I suppose there will be, yes."

Kin dropped his chair to all fours and propped his arms on the edge of the table. "Well, I'll look forward to seeing you there then."

Across the table, Ike grinned, bouncing a look between them.

One of Cora's pert brows winged upward. "I'm afraid I'll be rather busy right here, manning the diner."

Disappointment reared. "Ah. Everyone's loss, then."

They gave Cora their orders, which included a sandwich, apple, and bottle of milk for Isaiah's lunch, but Kin determined that between now and the social, he would figure out a way to get her out of this diner and to the social. It seemed she spent far too much time working.

After they'd both gulped down a bowl of oats smothered in cream and brown sugar, he hurried Ike to the schoolroom. Ike was chipper, prancing along like a frisky fawn. Kin bade the kid a good day and then headed for the livery.

He rented two horses and then picked up Tommy from the parsonage. The ride out to his pa's old place filled him with memories, and surprisingly some were not as painful as expected. A few times they'd gone fishing or picked blackberries. Those times Kin had almost been able to catch a glimpse of the man his father had been before Ma passed. But the glimpses had always been fleeting. Only an ungraspable hope between the anger and the beatings. The man had been living with his own emotional pain, Kin knew. Still, a stronger person would have realized that he needed to be a comfort for a son who'd been experiencing his own grief at the loss of his mother.

Before he crested the rise above the house, he pulled his mount to a stop and simply rested his forearms on the pommel of his saddle for a moment. Working up his courage, he supposed.

"Y-you okay, K-Kin?"

"Yeah, Tom Tom. Just give me a moment."

He closed his eyes and listened. Birds chattered. Wind sighed through branches that clacked together once in a while. Off to the north Wyldhaven Creek burbled happily. Robins chirped, and nearby the sharp caw of a blue jay warned them not to come closer to her nest.

He searched her out.

The jay perched on a tumbled tree, fallen so long ago that it had already started to crumble on one end. The bright blue of her plumage seemed at odds with the browns of the fir bark beneath her little black feet. She hopped several steps, tilting her head to assess the danger they presented. He smiled and lifted his gaze to the hills.

All around him lay the greens of a typical Washington forest. Emerald pines and olive oaks. Here, the blue-green of a cypress. There, the brighter golden-green of a larch that would turn yellow come autumn. Glimpses through the branches revealed the shocking greens of spring moss climbing the trunks of the trees. Had he ever before realized how many shades of green there were?

As a boy, his only desire had been to escape this place. He hadn't seen the beauty. Only the pain.

But it had taken leaving to realize that memories were things that couldn't be escaped. He could either let them bend him or break him.

He blew out a breath. *Lord, bend me into a better man than my father was.* A better man than he was now.

Surrender, PC had said.

But Kin didn't quite know how to do that.

While he'd been studying the terrain, Tommy had been studying him. "I p-pray for y-you, K-Kin. All these y-years. I p-pray."

Kin felt heat slide down from the base of his neck as surely as if someone had drenched his back with warm oil. His gaze sharpened on Tommy, who now studied the blue jay with an intrigued smile.

For such a time as this.

The almost audible impression hit him at the same time that he felt a palpable presence. He squirmed in the saddle and rubbed at the goose flesh on his arms.

The words came in answer to the question he'd asked himself about what God needed with a man like Tommy. He knew it beyond a shadow of doubt. He simply hadn't expected God to answer. At least not like that!

God needed Tommie for prayer? Could such a small thing really be so important?

"P-prayer h-helps." Tommie declared as though able to read his thoughts. "You d-different. G-good different." He nodded. Smiled. "God l-loves y-you. And me." His smile broadened. "H-he's still g-got a l-lot of w-work to do. But I c-can s-see you. You c-coming."

Even though Tommy straightened and clucked his mount into a gentle walk, Kin knew his statement had nothing to do with their physical destination and everything to do with a spiritual one.

With a shake of his head, he urged his horse in Tommy's wake. Who was he that God would be speaking to him?

He grunted and forced his thoughts to other things. The clouds in the sky. The plummet of an eagle diving into Wyldhaven Creek just over the ridge, only to rise with a fish flailing in its claws. The way his horse's ears turned all the way from front to back as it listened to the morning's sounds.

When he topped out on the rise, the little cabin lay before him just as he remembered it—but in much better shape. The Carvers had taken good care of the place. The yard was swept. Bright red and yellow flowers bloomed in two pots on either side of the porch steps. A wisp of smoke spiraled from the chimney.

As he neared, he could see there was new clear glass in the windows and the corral had recently been rebuilt. The split cedar rails still had a new golden glow to them.

A yearling Dun peered at him from behind the rails, ears perked in curiosity. It was a gorgeous creature with a coat that glimmered more silver than gold. It had a mane and tail that were almost coffee black, and stripes of the same dark color around its legs that reminded Kin of pictures he'd seen in schoolbooks of the Dark Continent zebra. A black stripe along the ridge of its back seemed to divide the beautiful creature in half. Despite only being a yearling, its chest was already massive. Once it reached full growth, the horse would be impressively powerful.

"Aren't you a beauty," he cooed to the horse.

Footsteps drew Kin's attention.

Kane Carver stretched out a hand. "Davis, good to have you home." Though he said the words, there was a glint of defeat in the man's gaze. Carver's focus flicked around the property and Kin could almost see the man assessing how much work he'd put into the place in the past couple of years.

It was that look that solidified Kin's change of mind. He'd honestly come out here to tell them that they needed to find a different place. However, now that he was here . . . Well, it was one thing to realize one couldn't escape memories, but quite another to force oneself into an environment that dredged them up with every other blink.

There was the chopping block that Pa had dragged him to while in a drunken stupor. His father had threatened to cut off his hand because he'd spilled the last cup of milk in the larder. Kin's gut churned at the memory; he could still taste the fear on the back of his tongue. And, though the boards were different, those were the steps his father had pushed him off countless times. It was a miracle he'd never broken any bones. One winter night his father had locked him in the barn for some infraction he couldn't recall. With no fire for warmth, and a coat that was barely adequate, he'd spent a sleepless night, pacing, and swinging his arms. On another winter night, he'd been banished to the porch. That night, he'd wished for the fractional warmth of the barn.

He could go on, allowing the memories to crash over him in a crippling flood. Instead, he turned off the spigot.

Kane was watching him. "Would you like to come inside?"

"Thank you." Kin nodded.

Tommy had crawled between the slats of the corral and was petting and cooing to the horse.

"You want to come inside, Tommy?"

He shook his head. "Nope. I stay here with Z-Zoom."

"Zoom?"

Kane smiled. "He comes once a week to help me with my horses. That's what he named him. He'll be fine. Come on in."

Kin complied, following him toward the house. "I hope I'm not intruding on your day?"

A brush of Kane's hand waved away his concern. "The work will wait. Another cup of coffee is always better than another wheelbarrow full of manure."

Kin chuckled.

Inside, Maude, Kane's sister, already had the pot of coffee settled on the hottest part of the stove. She gave a little dip of her knees. "Mr. Davis. Nice to see you again." Her gaze flicked off her brother's and there was a hint of the same concern he'd read in Kane's expression outside. "Coffee will be ready in a moment."

Kin wondered at her still being here with her brother. He would have thought that she and Jackson Nolan would have gotten married by now. He supposed that Seth, their younger brother, was likely still in school.

"Thanks, Maude." Kane stretched a hand toward the table. "Please, have a seat, Mr. Davis."

"Kin, please." He gave the gentle reprimand as he sank into a seat at the table.

Kane settled a jar before him. "This is the twelve dollars and two bits that I owe you up to this point. The rest of the rent money has gone to the Kastains just like you asked to cover the boarding of your horse."

Kin scooted the jar onto a lace round that graced the middle of the table. "Seems like you've done quite a few improvements around here. I think it would only be fair that those be paid by me. Did you keep a tally?"

"Nah." Kane shook his head. "I figured doing those things was only my duty as an occupant of the home. I'd do them for my own place too."

Kin studied his folded hands. He really ought to wait to broach business until the coffee had arrived, but now that he'd decided, he really didn't want to wait any longer. He lifted his gaze to Kane's. "Would you be interested in buying the place?"

From her spot by the stove, Maude gasped. Her eyes sparkled at her brother.

Kane wasn't so quick to get excited. "You sure you want to sell? This is a nice piece of property."

Kin didn't hesitate. "I'm sure." He avoided searching the side of the stove for the mark that used to indicate where his shirt had melted to it the day his father had shoved him up against it. Only a moment after, Pa had blubbered and sobbed in repentance and hurried him into town, but of course the damage had already been done. Doc Griffin had been kind enough to pick the pieces of melted material from his burn for free. Kin wondered if the mark on his back had faded any since the last time he'd paid attention to it.

He realized a silence had stretched, and filled it with, "I just bought a piece of land in town. I'm planning to build there." He'd planned to build an office, but he could build that on the first floor and a home on the second, similar to what Dixie had done at the boardinghouse. Or maybe he'd choose another piece of land somewhere along Wyldhaven Creek and build a proper cabin. If he ever married and had children, that would be the better solution.

Again, it was Cora's pretty blue eyes framed by blond wisps that came to mind and he quickly banished the vision.

He looked at Kane. "So? What do you say?"

"I'm overjoyed. Honestly, this place suits us perfectly. I've had some ideas for improvements I'd like to make specifically for breaking horses, but didn't want to implement them because it wasn't my place." His face broke into a broad grin. "I'm more than happy to buy your spread. More than happy. I've been saving up and can give you a substantial down payment."

Kin did some quick figuring. "Land is going for around fifteen dollars an acre right now. Add on the house and barn for a hundred, and we'll call it a deal."

Kane did some calculations of his own. "At thirty acres, that comes to five hundred and fifty."

"It does. I'm willing to count the twenty-four dollars you've paid over the last two years as a down payment, and we can draw up papers for you to repay the rest over, say, the next ten years? That comes out to four dollars and thirty-nine cents a month. Can you swing that?"

Kane shook his head. "Won't be that much. I can give you almost half of that as a down payment. And maybe you're interested in that horse outside?"

Kin's brows shot up. Was he ever! "Is he available?"

"Sure is. He's on pace to be fully broken by early July."

"What are you asking?"

"Hundred dollars."

A whistle escaped. But after a moment of thought, he realized it was a fair price. His mare came from good stock and was still young enough to foal a colt or two. The pair could be the start of a good line.

Kin grinned. "Well, all right then." He thrust out a hand. "It's a deal. You keep him and feed him until July, and I'll endeavor to have a place to house him by then." He suddenly knew he didn't want to live in town. And having that hefty influx of cash would also give him more leverage when it came to buying property along the creek. He felt as if a great weight had just been lifted from his shoulders.

Maude brought coffee. He thanked her, then asked Kane to tell him what his plans were for improving the place. He spent several minutes listening to the man's excited explanations and finishing his coffee, and by the time he was ready to leave, he was even more sure that he'd made the right decision.

They set up a time for Kane to come to town to sign the contract and make the down payment, and as Kin and Tommy rode away, Kin paused at the top of the hill and looked back over the land. He didn't plan to come here any more often than he was required to and he wanted to seal the vision of the place in his mind's eye one last time.

Finally, satisfied, he loosed a breath and reined his rented horse toward the Kastains'.

It was nice seeing the legacy of the old place being changed and that was certain.

Now he just had to figure out what to do about a place for him and Isaiah to live.

Chapter Fourteen

After picking up his horse from the Kastains with many thanks, Kin led it out to the Nolan ranch and paid Butch the rest of what he owed for the town property. He asked Butch if he knew anyone who might want to sell a small property along the creek. Butch pondered for a moment and then recalled that Ewan McGinty had a small five-acre parcel just east of town, right along the creek. Butch had once heard him mention that he'd like to sell it.

Kin felt his hopes deflate. Ewan wasn't a man he really wanted to have doings with. The canny barkeep knew too many of his weaknesses.

He thanked Butch and made his way back to town. He paid Bill to stable his mare and then headed toward the boardinghouse to talk to Dixie about extending his stay.

He grimaced. This moving-back-home business was getting expensive. Thankfully, Kane's sizable down payment would help. But the expense at Dixie's couldn't be avoided. There was no way he could find a piece of land and get a home built inside two weeks. Having the mill right in town would speed up the timeline considerably, but he and Ike might have to move into a shell of a place at first. Then he'd have time to finish it out before winter.

As he moved down the street, he eyed McGinty's Alehouse with dread. Much as he didn't want to talk to the man, there was nothing for it. Properties didn't just up and appear out of thin air. If he wanted a piece of land, he'd have to approach the man.

He had just started toward the alehouse when he heard the caterwauling of a loud conversation coming from inside the diner.

With a frown, he changed course and pushed into the entry of the boardinghouse as he snatched his Stetson from his head.

Cora stood behind the entryway desk, pinching the bridge of her nose, eyes closed.

Kin strode forward and didn't let the desk stop him. He rounded it and stopped by her side, speaking low. "What's going on?"

She startled and spun to look at him. Her eyes were red and he could tell she'd been doing her best to hold back tears.

He would throttle anyone who'd hurt her. "Are you okay?" He glanced around, but the rest of the entry lay empty.

She nodded and reached to touch his arm. "Oh, Kin, I'm fine. But you should get yourself into the dining room right this minute."

He ought to have relished her use of his first name; instead he found dread mounting up inside him. "What is it?" He was already backing toward the batwing doors. And now that he was this close, he recognized Mrs. Hines's strident voice.

Cora flapped a hand for him to hurry. "Just go."

When he pushed into the dining room, he found Mrs. Hines pacing the aisle between two tables. Seated at one of the tables were Mr. and Mrs. Olann on one side, and Charlotte, Reagan, and Zoe on the other. He glanced at his pocket watch. What was Zoe doing here? It must be time for recess up at the school. It wasn't yet lunchtime.

Mrs. Callahan rose. "Kin. We're so glad you're here."

"Me?" What did this have to do with him? His gaze slid to Mrs. Hines and his stomach dropped.

So . . . Here it was. And much sooner than he'd expected it.

He clamped his teeth to keep himself from saying something he shouldn't, and tossed his hat onto one of the empty tables. He folded his arms. Leaned into his heels. Wanted to be anywhere but here.

"Where's Ike?"

Zoe motioned toward the church. "He's at recess with the other children."

That was a mercy. At least the kid wouldn't have to witness whatever this spectacle was about to be.

"What is it?" He addressed the question to Zoe.

She shook her head morosely. Swiped at her eyes. He could see now that she'd been shedding tears too.

Zoe's voice was soft when she spoke. "Kin, Mrs. Hines has called for a meeting of the school board and asked me to be present. She doesn't feel—"

"It's not only me!" Mrs. Hines interrupted. "Some of the other parents feel the same!"

With a withering glower at the woman, Zoe pressed ahead. "*Mrs. Hines* has demanded that Isaiah should not be allowed to remain in school."

Kin leveled the contemptible woman with a glare. "What sort of interaction have you even had with the kid?"

She faltered and opened her mouth. Covered her lips with her fingers and swallowed convulsively.

So much anger seethed that before he realized what he was doing, Kin took a step toward her.

She scampered to plunk herself into the empty seat next to the Olanns, folded her hands, and lowered her gaze without so much as another word.

Defeated, Kin slumped to prop his palms against the nearest table.

Compassion radiated from Zoe's soft blue eyes. "The board rules state that if even two parents ask for an emergency vote, we are required to convene and put the matter at hand to the question."

She remained silent for a long moment, but Kin was determined to wait her out.

Finally, she continued. "Mrs. Hines and Mrs. Olann asked for a vote."

She hadn't said, but he needed to confirm. "About Isaiah?"

Charlotte sank against the slats of her seat. "Yes." The word was weariness itself.

Kin's gaze slid to Zoe and on to the Olanns, then back to Charlotte and Reagan.

Mr. and Mrs. Olann refused to meet his gaze. Reagan's eyes glittered with a hard anger that Kin knew wasn't directed at him or at Ike, and Charlotte studied the table, failing to disguise the tears shimmering in her eyes.

"So you six comprise the board?"

Zoe's shoulders slumped. "I'm not on the board. Not allowed to vote."

Kin felt a muscle pulse in his jaw. So the vote would not go Ike's way. "The Olanns don't even have children of school age."

Mrs. Olann's chin shot into the air. "Our Carmen will be in school next year. Close enough. She's smart as a whip and Zoe tried to talk us into enrolling her this year. We've decided to take her up on the offer."

Distress drooped Zoe's and Charlotte's shoulders.

But Kin's back was suddenly ramrod straight. He strode to the table and pinned each of the three culprits with a steely-eyed scrutiny. "What's he done!?"

None of them seemed able to meet his gaze.

Rage made his vision blur. His fists clenched so tight that he trembled.

"Kin," Reagan said.

Mrs. Olann, the closest of the three, flicked him a glance, then scooted her chair closer to her husband's.

Kin took Reagan's warning and hauled in a calming breath. But by all that was just, he wasn't about to let them proceed with this travesty unchallenged. He spoke more calmly this time. "I demand to hear your reasons for calling this meeting."

Mrs. Olann fixated on the lace gloves she'd strangled in her lap.

Mr. Olann cleared his throat, Adam's apple bobbing.

Mrs. Hines worked a finger over her lower lip.

"Cowards." Frustration tempered his next words. "Every one of you."

Mr. Olann's nose shot into the air. "It's the— It's the—"

"It's the what?" Kin planted his palms in the middle of the table and leaned so far across it that Mr. Olann flinched back, angling his head away.

Kin was close enough to see the trembling of the man's lips when he whispered, "It's the . . . well . . . he's a . . ."

The man's gaze darted to Charlotte who, much to Kin's appreciation, was scowling at the man from across the table.

"A black . . . child."

Kin surged back, lest his fury get the best of him and he pummel the man into the next room. He paced several steps and then spun to face the table once more. "*Child*, yes. Child, is the operative word you should be fixed on. A child whose father died only a few weeks ago. A child whose mother loved his father and married him. A child who can no more help the color of his skin than you can help that you're pale and pigheaded!"

Mrs. Hines and Mrs. Olann gasped in unison. Mr. Olann sputtered.

Reagan chuckled, drawing a glare from the banker. "Hey, pigheaded is nicer than what I've been sitting here thinking you are," he groused.

"Well, I never!" Mrs. Hines slapped her hand on the table. "I demand that we take our vote."

Kin knew he had lost. There was no more point in fighting. But he had one more thing to say. "I grew up in this town. None of you three"—his gesture took in Mrs. Hines and the Olanns—"were here back then. And I have to say I'm thankful for it. Because this is the first time that I can think of where I've ever felt embarrassed to say I'm from Wyldhaven." He snatched up his hat. "All right. Get on with your travesty of a meeting then, but before you cast your vote, I want you to think on one thing." He pointed toward the schoolhouse. "That kid up there is just an orphan who wants the chance to learn like any other child. The color of his skin doesn't make him a danger. In fact, I'd wager he's much less of a danger than a couple of the forked tongues in this room right now."

Mrs. Olann hissed her outrage, but Kin pressed ahead, ignoring her.

"That boy would go out of his way to help every one of the other students in any way that he could. No matter that their skin is paler than his. As I said, his father died not more than a few weeks ago. Is this really what you want to burden him with? The poor little fella . . ." His voice broke and he had to take a breath and calm down before he could regain the use of his voice. "He's barely holding on. Missing his father every moment, but doing his best to live in a way to honor his memory." He cleared his throat. "Yeah. So you go on and have your vote."

Mrs. Hines looked at him. "If you'll just step from the room—"

"Oh no, Mrs. Hines." Her eyes widened, but Kin didn't care one whit if his manner may have offended her. "I'm not moving an inch. If you are going to have your vote, you're going to have it in front of me. Why would you need to hide anything if you are voting for what's right?" His heart was pumping so hard he felt as though it could burst out of his chest at any moment.

Zoe stood and turned by his side to face the board. "And in front of me." Her chin lifted.

Mrs. Hines gasped. "We could have your job for such impertinence."

Zoe didn't budge. "Yes. You could."

A sound rustled behind them and Kin felt Cora stop beside him. "I agree that the voting should not be private. I'm not leaving, either."

Her aunt flashed her a withering glower, but Cora gave back as good as she got, adding, "In fact, I think it would be good for every school board vote to be conducted in public."

Charlotte sniffed and brushed her fingers under her eyes. "What a grand idea, Cora. I think I'll bring it up with Mr. Heath the next time I speak with him." Her chin jutted in a determined set. "Which will be tomorrow."

"Oh, for heaven's sake," Mrs. Hines slapped her fingers against the tabletop to get everyone's attention. "All in favor of banning this boy from attending school, raise your hands." Her hand immediately thrust into the air, followed by Mrs. Olann's.

For one short moment, Kin's hopes had life as Mr. Olann kept his hands beneath the table, but a sharp jab from his wife's elbow had him slowly lifting a hand.

Kin grunted, spun on one heel, and stormed from the room. The doors slammed against the side walls as he passed through, then clattered and squeaked as they toiled to close behind him. He strode onto the boardwalk and looked up the hill toward the church where the children were all at play for recess.

His chest felt tight and hot.

How in the world was he going to find the words to tell Isaiah?

Charlotte rose from her seat, hearing Reagan do the same beside her. She clenched her fists so she wouldn't follow through on the temptation to slap the satisfied smirk from Mrs. Hines's face. After they'd had such a connecting talk the other day with regards to having children, Charlotte had felt that her prodding should have had more sway with the woman. But she hadn't been moved by anything Charlotte, Reagan, or Zoe had said in the boy's defense. She didn't want her stepson, David, taking lessons with a child she'd termed "neither here nor there."

Charlotte would have liked to show her where both here and there were!

She rushed from the room and through the boardinghouse entry. When she stepped onto the boardwalk, her heart clenched.

Kin presented such a defeated picture. His hat was pushed back on his head, his shoulders slumped. His thumbs, hooked in his back pockets, looked like they might be the only thing keeping him from sagging to the boards of the walk.

She stopped by his side, tugging her gloves as though they needed adjusting. "Kin, I would like to make you an offer."

He glanced at her.

Still fiddling with her silken fingers, she hurried on. "I was just saying to Reagan the other day that I needed something more to do and I think this fits perfectly with my qualifications. I'd like to offer to privately tutor Isaiah."

Behind them, Reagan's boots sounded on the boardwalk.

Kin blew out a breath and gripped the back of his neck. "That's very kind of you, Mrs. Callahan. But he's just a kid. How am I supposed to tell him he's been removed simply because of the color of his skin?"

Charlotte didn't have an answer for that, only shook her head in dismay.

After a moment, Reagan spoke. "You simply tell him the truth. That in this world there are some small-minded people who can't see that differences can be a strength. He's going to have to fight that thinking all his life. It will be his choice whether he rises above it, or lets it push him down."

As though holding up his own weight had grown too burdensome, Kin sank onto the boardinghouse steps. His arms, propped against his knees, bore the weight of his torso. "Why do people have to be so unbelievably unfair?"

Again, Charlotte had no words and was thankful for the quiet wisdom of her husband.

Reagan cleared his throat. "I don't know, Kin. But even in the Good Book, Jesus says, 'In this world you will have trouble, but take heart, I have overcome the world.' All we can do is take our pain and sorrow to the Creator and beg Him to help us be more like Him than those who've caused our pain."

Kin sighed and lumbered to his feet. "Thanks. I guess I'd better not put off talking to him." His gaze landed on her. "As for your offer, Mrs. Callahan, thank you. You let me know what your salary needs are and I'll make it happen."

"Oh. No." Charlotte felt her ire rise once more. "Don't you worry about the cost of my salary, Mr. Davis. I have a meeting with Mr. Heath in the morning and I'm sure the town council will be most happy to pay my wages. It is our duty as a town, after all, to ensure that all the children who live here are supplied an education. I'm sure the bank and the mercantile will be happy to have their taxes raised for such a worthy cause!"

"Well . . ." Kin started toward the church. She could tell he hadn't really registered her tirade. "Just let me know."

Charlotte stood and watched until he'd walked all the way up the street to the churchyard. She saw the moment when Isaiah heard his call and trotted over to him with a big grin. And the moment when Isaiah's smile fell away and his shoulders drooped. The boy bent and tugged up a blade of grass, methodically shredding it with his thumbnails as Kin spoke to him. And then both of them headed on up the hill and disappeared into the parsonage, with Kin's hand resting on Isaiah's shoulder the whole way.

"Come on, Charlie." Reagan touched her back. "I'll walk you home."

She followed Reagan without protest, but as she did, she realized it was a good thing her meeting with Mr. Heath wasn't until tomorrow. Her blood was boiling so tumultuously, she didn't think she'd be able to string two sentences together right now.

She needed to pray and plan.

With the right words, hopefully she could get Mr. Heath to agree to her requests, if not reinstate the boy in the regular school.

Chapter Fifteen

Kin paced the small confines of the parsonage parlor, while PC spoke quietly to Isaiah. He hoped he hadn't bumbled too badly in telling Isaiah what had transpired. There had been no good way to inform the boy that he couldn't rejoin the classroom. His only thought after the deed was done was to bring the kid to the parson.

The man had certainly encouraged him enough times throughout his life. Maybe he could do the same for Isaiah.

Despite the fact that Kin could tell the news had been shattering, Isaiah had yet to shed a tear. He currently sat on the settee, staring at the floor as he listened respectfully to the parson.

PC sat beside him, leaning forward with his elbows on his knees. He looked sideways at the kid. "Rejection is never easy, Isaiah. Especially when it's over something that is so out of our control."

Isaiah nodded.

"Jesus was also rejected."

Another nod. "Yessuh. By all them people He came to save."

"That's right."

PC draped an arm across Isaiah's shoulders and gave him a gentle squeeze before releasing him. "What do you think about Mrs. Callahan's offer to tutor you?"

Isaiah's face scrunched up. "Been thinkin' 'bout that. But I'm not sure. Maybe the Good Lord is tryin' to tell me that it's time for my schoolin' days to be over." His little lips pooched in thought. "Pa said I was good at shovelin'. Know anyone who needs to hire a shoveler?"

PC bounced a glance off of Kin.

Every muscle in Kin's back was so tight that pain shot up his neck.

PC spoke thoughtfully. "Well now, sometimes it can seem like the Lord is saying one thing to us when He's entirely saying another. For instance, maybe the Lord wanted you to be tutored by Mrs. Callahan. You know she used to be our town's teacher. She's very good at her job."

Kin released his clenched teeth long enough to say, "She was my teacher."

Ike straightened, a hopeful look in his eyes. "She was?"

Kin nodded. "Taught me everything I knew before I went to work for Mr. Townsend."

"But I'd be all alone? No more playing ball with the other fellas?" He scrubbed a hand at the back of his head, the only indication of his agitation.

Kin felt another swell of anger pulse through him. "Leastwise, not at the schoolhouse. But I know Lincoln had a lot of fun playing baseball with you and I'm sure I can take you to his place on some weekends so you can do some gallivanting together."

The first signs of tears welled in the boy's big eyes. "You think he wants to play ball with me?"

Before he could think better of it, Kin tugged the boy off the couch and pulled him into a secure embrace. "You listen to me, Ike, and listen good. None of this had anything to do with the boys not liking you. It was two biddies and a—"

PC cleared his throat loudly.

"Two . . . *ladies* who aren't much ladies at all. And a man with no spine."

PC rolled his eyes, but let the comments go. Kin figured he couldn't disagree with the truth.

"I feel kinda sorry for them." Ike's voice emerged, muffled, from the front of Kin's shirt.

Kin closed his eyes, wrapping the boy tighter. "How's that?"

"They must be kinda sad and lonely like. Mean people usually are."

The parson coughed to cover a laugh, but then lifted one shoulder and shot a grin in Kin's direction as if to say the kid was probably right.

Kin massaged circles against Ike's back. "The important thing is that you don't let mean bid—ladies turn you into something similar to them. We have to be kind and respectful to them, even if we don't like what they did."

Ike heaved a long sigh. "It's hard to love cranky people."

"Ain't that the truth."

PC cocked a brow.

Kin relented. "But we have to try. The Good Book tells us not to pay back wrong for wrong but instead to always try to be kind to each other and to everyone else."

The parson leaned back, his jaw going slightly slack.

Kin offered the man a slant of a smile. He'd read the book the parson had given him that last Christmas a time or two. He really should start doing it more, he supposed, if he wanted to become a man with qualities like the parson.

The parson thumped a fist against side of Ike's knee. "You like to play chess? Kin here has lost his touch and I need an opponent with some skill."

Isaiah eased back from Kin's embrace and glanced over at the board. "Not sure I know how, sir."

"Well!" PC rose. "There's no time to learn like the present. Even if Kin there has grown a bit inept, he once was an excellent player. You and he can be on a team. Just don't be too discouraged when I beat you, and make sure to study all my moves so that Kin's amateurity doesn't rub off on you."

Kin was thankful for the parson's burden-lifting humor. And chess was the perfect solution to get Ike thinking mostly about something else for a while.

They whittled the afternoon away with game after game and, just as PC had predicted, Ike was a quick study.

The sun was dropping low on the horizon by the time Kin squeezed Ike's shoulder. "Best we get going, Ike. We need to get to the diner and have a meal and then first thing in the morning we'll go out to the Callahans' and have a talk about your new lessons. I'll get your tests from Zoe so Mrs. Callahan can look them over."

"Can we play some catch?" Ike lifted hopeful eyes.

Kin smiled. "We can do that. Dinner first, all right?"

The boy nodded. "Yessuh."

Kin ruffled the boy's hair. They bade the Clays and Tommy good evening and headed back down the hill.

To the west, the sun had dipped low along the horizon. Peach and gold kissed the boots of frothy clouds with a gilded gleam.

Isaiah stopped to take it all in, and Kin let him look.

After a moment, the boy continued forward. "God sure do paint good, don't He, Mr. Kin?"

"Yeah, kid. He does."

Kin couldn't help but wonder how a sunset could look so pure and beautiful on a terrible day such as this.

The next morning, the train station lay quiet in the midmorning sunlight that filtered through a thin layer of clouds. Captain Sherman was the first man off the train, followed by Farnham and Carr.

His men trotted down to the luggage car to gather their few bags. While they did that, Sherman approached an attendant. He offered his most charming smile. "Good morning."

The man faced him, his little round cap making his short stance seem even shorter. "Good morning, sir. How can I help you?"

"I wondered if you might be able to help me find a friend of mine. Last I heard he'd recently returned to these parts. His name is Kin Davis?"

The man's eyes lit up. "Mr. Davis? Yes. He just arrived a few days ago. Had a cute kid with him."

Sherman smiled. "Excellent. He'll be so happy to see us." He motioned for Farnham and Carr to join him. They were indeed in the right place. "Is there by chance a wagon that could take us into Wyldhaven?"

The attendant pointed down a set of stairs. "There's usually a boy or two waiting with a wagon this time of day."

"Much obliged." Captain Sherman tipped the man his hat.

There was indeed a lad with a wagon, and it only took them a few minutes to find themselves standing in the center of Wyldhaven. As Sherman scanned the street, he grinned. This town was so small it would only take him a couple of hours to find Davis and the boy. He'd have his deed back in no time. And there was even an alehouse!

Worry still niggled at the back of his mind. He really had nothing other than gut instinct telling him the boy had the deed. But it didn't matter. If he couldn't find it with the boy, he could go back to the pauper's grave he'd paid for in Seattle and dig the man up to search for it. But no matter how hard it was to find, he didn't plan to resume sailing until he had the deed to Cassandra's home in his possession once more.

Charlotte had thought her temper would have cooled down by this morning, but as she marched along the path toward Wyldhaven, she realized that she could spend a month of weeks and still harbor just as much anger over what had been done to that poor child yesterday.

She rounded onto the road near the livery at the south end of town and stormed up the steps in front of the bank.

Her boots snapped sharply along the boardwalk, giving her only a moment's satisfaction that she'd finally talked the town into completing that long-desired amenity last autumn.

Glowering through the bank's windows as she passed, she caught a glimpse of Mr. Olann behind the counter. He looked up from whatever he was tabulating and watched her storm by. She met him gaze for gaze for several steps. But then she noticed that there seemed to be a bone-tired harangued expression on his face. Her conscience got the better of her.

Charlotte faced forward and kept going, but her steps were a little less forceful this time.

Town founder, Mr. Zebulon Heath, had retired to a little home he'd built for himself across the bridge and just west of the mill about a mile.

Charlotte spent the rest of her walk praying. She prayed first for Isaiah to know that his worth was not tied up in the meanness of a few sorry souls. She prayed for Mr. Heath to be moved to help. And she prayed for her own bitterness and anger to ease into forgiveness.

By the time she knocked on Mr. Heath's door, she felt in a better frame of mind.

Still, Isaiah deserved justice and she didn't plan to change her mind on that.

Mr. Heath answered the door, leaning heavily on his cane. "Charlotte, my dear. So good to see you. Do come in."

He left the door open and tottered across the room to his table. She remembered how frail she'd thought him all those years ago when he'd first come to see her in Boston, but that had been nothing compared to now.

The man hardly had any meat on his bones, and by the way he nearly collapsed into one of the chairs at the table, barely any strength in his legs.

Charlotte tugged off her gloves and accepted the chair kitty-corner to him.

"Anja, you can bring in the tea now," he called.

His voice was so soft, that Charlotte wondered if anyone could have heard him. But she was thankful to learn that someone was caring for him.

A woman bustled in, carrying a tray. Charlotte blinked in surprise. How had she not heard that Mr. Heath had hired such a young and pretty housekeeper?

"Hello." She smiled at the woman.

Mr. Heath gestured between them. "Charlotte, meet Anja, my great-niece, fresh here from Boston. Anja, Charlotte here also hales from Boston. I'm sure you two would have much in common."

The girl, who had her blond hair plaited into a long braid that wrapped around her head like a crown, dipped her knees. "It's pleased, I am, to meet you, Miss Charlotte."

Charlotte stretched out a hand. "I feel the same. I'm sorry I haven't come around to meet you sooner. I had no idea you were here. How long have you been in town?"

Anja slid the tray onto the table, and then settled a slender pale hand against her uncle's shoulder. "Uncle Zeb found himself in need of some house help and I came . . . what? About a month ago now, Uncle?"

Zeb nodded. "A great help she's been, too."

A month? Charlotte knew she was a bit isolated, since she no longer interacted as much with those in town, but she hadn't realized she was so secluded that she would miss news of this magnitude. She smiled at the man, relieved. "I'm glad to know you have some help."

"I'm afraid she's been working herself to the bone, and hasn't gotten into town much." Mr. Heath motioned to the tray as Anja poured their tea. "Cream? Sugar?"

"Oh," Charlotte hesitated, not wanting to offend. "I'm afraid that I can't drink black tea, Mr. Heath. Something in it gives me debilitating headaches."

"I'm very sorry to hear that. Can we offer you something else?" There was nothing but kindness in Anja's gray eyes.

Charlotte held up a palm. "I really don't need anything. I only need a few words with Mr. Heath and then I must hurry back home."

Zeb liberally scooped three heaping teaspoons of sugar into his mug and stirred. "Thank you, Anja." He gave the girl a nod that she seemed to take as dismissal, for she hurried off to the kitchen with a parting smile. Zeb's rheumy gaze settled on Charlotte. "If you are here about that school board debacle, I've already heard." He puffed a weary sigh. "I've tried to settle this town with good, decent, God-fearing folks, Mrs. Callahan. But it seems that at least in part, I have failed."

"I don't see it as a failure on your part, Mr. Heath. But I do think we need to do something about it. I know they are duly elected members to the school board, but I also know that most in town who voted for them would be horrified by their actions."

He nodded. "I agree with you. I have a plan, but it must wait until the evening of the fundraiser."

Charlotte felt her pulse trip with hope. "A plan, Mr. Heath?"

The old man smiled mysteriously. "Indeed. Can you keep a secret, ma'am?"

"From everyone except my husband, yes."

His smile grew. He sipped his tea. "That's fine. I don't think the sheriff will cause any trouble."

He took another slow sip of tea and Charlotte felt ready to jump across the corner of the table and shake the information out of him.

Finally, his cup clattered into his saucer. "There is a line in the school board bylaws that some of the more outspoken members of our board may have missed." He added another spoon of sugar to his tea.

Charlotte literally clamped her teeth against her tongue, determined not to badger the man to spit it out.

"You see . . ." He sipped his tea once more and smacked his lips, seeming satisfied this time with tea that Charlotte could only assume tasted like syrup. "I foresaw that there might come a day when the school board voted in a policy that many disagreed with. So I inserted a clause that allows anyone in town to call for an overriding vote. I plan to ask for this vote at the fundraiser."

Relief crashed through Charlotte. "Oh, that's wonderful!"

"But!" Mr. Heath held up a knobby finger. "It has to be a fair vote. With no preparation or manipulation. No trying to coax anyone to certain sides. Just a quiet vote without a lot of drama, if you please, Mrs. Callahan."

Charlotte nodded. "Thank you, Mr. Heath. That seems more than fair. And sways me to leave off my planned request that you quadruple the taxes on the mercantile and the bank."

Mr. Heath bellowed a laugh. "God love you, Mrs. Callahan. The Lord was certainly watching over Wyldhaven the day I hired you as our teacher all those years ago."

Charlotte grinned. "Why thank you, kind sir." She relayed that she planned to tutor Ike until after the vote and the man assured her he felt that was a grand idea.

"Now, let us get to the reason we set this meeting in the first place, shall we, Mrs. Callahan? I presume you asked to meet with me to discuss the details of the fundraiser?"

"I did indeed." Charlotte filled him in on all that they'd accomplished so far, but she was thankful that this meeting had been set merely to keep the man informed of the progress they were making for the fundraiser, because she didn't think she would have been able to keep her mind on anything more serious.

An hour later when she left to walk home, her heart felt about nine hundred pounds lighter.

Because if there was one thing Charlotte believed about the people of Wyldhaven, it was that most of them would never stand by and tolerate such blatant racism.

Isaiah would soon see that not everyone in town ought to be tarred and feathered!

He would, wouldn't he?

She placed a hand over her churning stomach. "Lord, please don't let me be disappointed in anyone else in this town." She paused on the Wyldhaven Creek bridge and peered into the crystal-clear water burbling below. "Forget about me. Don't let Isaiah be disappointed in anyone else in this town."

Speaking of Isaiah, he and Kin would likely be arriving soon.

She released her cares to the Creator and hurried toward home.

Chapter Sixteen

ora was wiping down the last of the tables in the dining room when she heard footsteps in the entry. She rolled her eyes. If these people were here to eat, they were too late. All the food had already been put by, and the stove extinguished until this evening. She was weary and wanted nothing more than to get to her room and read more in her copy of *Following the Equator*. And maybe take a nap. Though she did need to finish crocheting the largest piece of lace for the schoolhouse fundraiser.

She dropped her rag into the little bucket of soapy water Dixie kept by the doors, and then hurried into the entry, drying her hands on her apron.

Three men stood on the other side of the desk. But they didn't have the look of hungry loggers about them. One was taller than the other two and stood at the front. He wore a mariner's cap and a loose-fitting jacket with tight cuffs. His beard was long, but neatly trimmed, and his long brown hair was swept back and bound at his neck. The other two—who both wore tied down pistols—stood spraddle-legged, spanning him like dedicated protectors.

"Good day, gentlemen. How may I help you?" She stepped behind the desk and tugged the register closer. If they wanted a room, she needed to see what was still available. Perfect. It seemed that the group from room seven had left. That one had three beds in it. She wondered if Dixie or Belle had found time to clean it? The morning had been busy.

She'd been studying the register for a few seconds, when she realized that none of the men had spoken. Slowly, she lifted her gaze to them once more.

The dark man in front was gaping at her like he'd seen a ghost.

She actually touched her face to see if she'd smeared something on it without realizing. Nothing seemed amiss.

The leader spoke first. He snatched his cap and pressed it to his chest. His voice shook when he spoke. "Ma'am, if you'll forgive me for staring . . ." His words trailed off. He cleared his throat.

Cora felt her heart tap a rhythm against her breastbone. The man was making her more than a little uncomfortable. "What is it?"

One of the lackeys leaned toward the leader, his gaze still fixed directly on her. "Cassandra didn't have that accent." To her, he next said, "Your name's not Cassandra, is it?"

"No." So it was only that she looked like someone they knew? That relieved some of her tension.

The other man with the guns gave a low whistle. "Sure are the spitting image of a woman the captain used to know back in California. He keeps one o' them daguerreotypes of her. Her name was Cassandra McKnight."

"Coleman," his fellow protector corrected.

"According to the captain, she was McKnight before she was Coleman," the other retorted.

Cora tilted her head. Coleman? Isaiah's last name was Coleman. Something uneasy raised her awareness.

Throughout their conversation, the man at the fore remained silent. He simply kept staring. Her tension soared right back to its peak. There was something unsettling in the way the man searched her over.

Kin had never said why he'd needed to come to Isaiah's rescue. In fact, she knew next to nothing about the situation, but it seemed odd that Kin would suddenly show up in town with a boy in tow, and then only days later, three strangers would arrive spouting nonsense about some woman with the same last name.

Thankfully, Kin and Ike had left earlier to go to the Callahans. But . . . Had they said anything about when they planned to return? She had a distinct feeling that nothing good could come of these men bumping into Kin and the boy. She'd better try to find a way to warn Kin.

The two sailors were still engaging in their row.

But the leader's gaze remained fixed intently upon her. He waved his hat at both his men in frustration. "Shut up, both of you!" He took a step forward and gave a courtly bow, with his cap pressed to his chest. "If you'll forgive us, ma'am. You truly are the exact replica of a woman who was very dear to me. So much so that I could have sworn I'd seen a siren when you walked through those doors."

His smile stretched wide, but there was something possessive about his eyes that sent a shiver down her spine.

"I'm Captain Bartholomew Sherman. These are my men. Roy Farnham and Kip Carr."

"Pleased to make your acquaintance. How may I be of assistance?" She hoped to return his mind to business and wasn't in the habit of giving her name to strangers—especially not ones who made her uncomfortable.

Thankfully, though he looked a tad disappointed, he seemed to take her hint. "We've come to see about getting a room? The man down at the mercantile said this was the only place with beds in town."

"Yes." Cora spun the book toward him. She pointed. "If you'll sign there. I have a room with three beds. I'll just need to pop up and make sure it's been tidied."

He asked for three nights and as soon as he'd paid, she closed the book and handed over his key. "Please wait here. Can I get you gentlemen some coffee while you wait?"

Captain Sherman shook his head. "We'll be fine. Thank you."

His two companions looked a little disappointed by his denial, but Cora decided not to reiterate her question.

"All right." She gestured to the bench along one wall. "Feel free to sit while you wait. I'll return to let you know just as soon as the room is ready for you. It should only be a few minutes and then you can fetch your luggage up. You'll be in room seven, as you can see on the key."

To keep herself from nervously blathering further, she lifted a double handful of her skirts and took the stairs as quickly as she could, hoping Kin and Ike wouldn't return and stumble upon the men in the entry while she was upstairs. She shoved her master key into the lock and pushed open the door to room seven.

Thankfully, it appeared that either Dixie or Belle had cleaned the room after the other men had departed. All the beds were made up with clean linens and the room was ready for the men below. Only a scent of someone's tobacco lingered. She quickly crossed to hoist the window sash, then spun back toward the door.

"Oh!" She froze.

Captain Sherman's hulking frame blocked the door. Below stairs, she hadn't realized just how large the man was. But his head nearly reached the top of the doorway and his shoulders almost brushed the frame on either side. She would be helpless against such a hulk, not to mention unable to dart past him.

Her heart beat from the region of her throat, blocking off her airway.

He stepped further into the room, but didn't move aside. A predatory smile parted his lips. "I didn't catch your name downstairs."

She lifted her chin, clenching handfuls of her apron. "That's because I didn't give it. I'll kindly ask you to allow me to pass, sir."

He remained where he stood. His gaze slipped over her.

Cora's heart pounded. She glanced around for anything she might use as a weapon, if it came to it. The only thing available was a small silver candlestick on a side table between the beds. She inched toward it.

He took another step, still blocking the doorway. "Come now, there's no need for the fear I see in your eyes, miss."

Cora snatched up the candlestick and held it like a hammer.

A sound came from the landing. "Cora?"

The sound of Dixie's call eased the pounding of her heart only slightly. Cora never took her attention from the man near the doorway. "In here!"

"There you are." Dixie stepped into the room. Her eyes widened at the sight of the man who was only now stepping to one side. "Oh hello. You must be with the men downstairs. Welcome to our boardinghouse. I'll send your men right up with your luggage." Dixie stretched an arm toward Cora. "Cora, please don't dawdle, you're needed downstairs."

With a surge of relief, Cora rushed past the man without giving him another glance. Her legs trembled so badly that she barely made it down the stairs. Dixie's arm remained wrapped around her shoulders the whole time.

In the entry, she instructed the two men, Farnham and Carr, that they could proceed upstairs. "Turn right at the top of the stairs, gentlemen. You'll see the number seven on the door."

With that, she prodded Cora into the dining room and all the way through it into the kitchen. She gripped Cora's shoulders and spun her until they stood face to face. Dixie assessed her, once over. "My land almighty, Cora, are you all right? I know you always follow my rule about never letting a man be in a room with you. What happened?" She pried the candlestick from Cora's tight grip and plunked it onto the sideboard.

Cora pressed one hand to her chest, gulping big breaths. "I asked them to stay in the entry. I wasn't sure if the room had been cleaned, so I went up to check. He followed me. I didn't hear him. Just . . . Suddenly there he was, blocking the doorway." She shook out her fingers, hoping to dispel some of the trembling in her hands.

Dixie pulled her into a gentle embrace. "I'm right sorry. That must have been terrifying. Bless your heart."

Cora eased back, needing to pace. "Thank you. I'm so glad you came when you did." She wrapped her arms around herself. "That man sets my insides all to quavering. He says I look like a woman he used to know." Her eyes shot wide and she pivoted to face Dixie. "I need to speak to Kin right away!" she whispered. "Dixie, I think those men might be here looking for Isaiah. The woman I apparently look like was also named Coleman—I think. It was all rather confusing. But . . . The other day, Isaiah said I reminded him of someone! I think it was his mother! I need to warn them!"

"Oh, good gracious." Dixie flapped a hand toward the side exit. "I'll go into the entry and make sure to distract them if they come right back down. You go out that way and hurry to the Callahans to tell Kin. It might be nothing. But, better to raise an alarm for no cause than to let it go and later be sorry."

"Yes. I agree."

Dixie was already bustling toward the entry.

Cora rushed outside and hurried around to the front of the building. Thankfully, room seven was at the back of the boardinghouse, so the men wouldn't be able to see her from their window.

She poked her head around the corner and checked the street just in case Dixie may have missed delaying the men if they wanted to come outside. However, the only person she saw was Kin—with his hand reaching for the main boardinghouse door.

"Kin!" She rushed forward.

He glanced at her, stopping in surprise.

She practically ran toward him, but she didn't want to talk here. She pushed his arm and pointed him toward the alley between the boardinghouse and McGinty's Alehouse. As she passed the door, she cast a furtive glance through its arc of glass windows. Blessedly, the entry lay empty except for Dixie, who stood at the desk.

Dixie made a shooing motion, urging her to hurry, and Cora pushed Kin again. "Keep going."

"What—?" Kin tried to face her to get an explanation.

Cora grabbed his shoulders and adjusted his angle. "Just—" She pointed past him to indicate he should keep moving. "I need to talk to you a moment. Where's Isaiah?" She gasped and glanced back over her shoulder. "Is he already inside?"

"No. He's at the Callahans."

"Oh. Good." She nudged him into the alleyway.

Finally, she allowed him to stop and face her.

He plunked his hands on his hips. "Will you please tell me what this is all about?"

They weren't far enough into the alley. Cora flapped a hand at him to indicate he should move deeper.

With a huff, he took her arm and trod several steps, then swung her to one side until her back pressed against the wall of the boardinghouse. He propped one hand alongside her head and leaned in. "What in thunder is going on?" A muscle in his jaw ticked in irritation.

Or was it concern, she wondered, as he scanned the alleyway both up and down, one hand resting, ready for quick action, on his gun.

His gaze returned to hers and he waited silently.

Cora swallowed. He was so close that she could see amber flecks in the brown of his eyes. But despite the intensity in his gaze and the fact that he was just as large as Captain Sherman, being this near to him didn't give her any qualms. Well . . . At least not the fearful kind of qualms.

Butterflies in her stomach. Damp palms. Quavering knees. Yes.

But no fear.

"Cora?" The word was almost a growl.

Right. He was still waiting for an explanation. "Th-three men came into the boardinghouse."

He straightened and assessed her from head to toe.

"I'm fine," she hurried to assure him.

He seemed to relax a little.

"But . . ." She took a breath. Lowered her gaze to her clenched fingers. Was this all just silly? Was she overreacting simply because that man had terrified her?

Kin leaned in, hand once more planted on the wall by her head. He reached with his other to touch her chin and raise her gaze to his. His voice was soft when he spoke. "What is it, Mish? You can tell me anything." His thumb stroked soft caresses that threatened to derail her thoughts again.

Darting her tongue over her dry lips, she hurried on before she could get too distracted. "The men. They, well, they mentioned that I looked like a woman they used to know. A woman named Cassandra McKnight *Coleman*." She bit her lip, waiting to see if the name filled him with as much angst as it had her.

Kin darted a look toward the front of the alleyway. His free hand moved to cup around her shoulder protectively. "Three men, you say? Did one of them have red hair and a short curly beard?"

She felt her eyes widen, even as she nodded.

Kin muttered something unintelligible under his breath. "Where are they right now?"

Cora gestured. "Upstairs. In room seven. Dixie was watching for them until I could warn you!"

He squeezed her shoulder. "Thank you, Mish. Your warning is indeed warranted. I thought they might be coming. Even said something to the sheriff the other day."

So those men *were* dangerous. Cora tried not to focus on the tingle of horror that skittered through her. She pinned her thoughts instead on the pleasant feel of Kin's thumb caressing her upper arm. "Who are they? Would they hurt Ike?"

Kin released her, paced two steps away, then two steps back. He stilled and folded his arms.

She laced her fingers, missing the warmth of his touch on her shoulder.

He worried both sides of his lower lip with his teeth. "I'm honestly not sure why they want him. Ike was on the captain's ship with his father. His father died."

"Oh, I didn't know. That's terrible."

"It is. I found Ike on the streets of Seattle—I suppose it's more accurate to say he found me—and then later bumped into these goons who were asking around town about him. They never said what they wanted with him. Ike swears up and down he owes them nothing. I couldn't very well approach them to ask why they were looking for the kid without revealing that I knew his whereabouts. So I brought Ike here. Unfortunately, the red-haired man, his name is Farnham—I worked with him repairing the streets of Seattle for a time—anyhow, he saw us at the station and . . ." His brow slumped. "Made a threatening gesture at the kid. We were already on the train and it was pulling out, so there was no danger at the time, but I worried that something more would come of it. Now . . ." He sighed. "It seems it has. That poor kid has been through too much in the last few weeks. But . . ." He continued to pace. "You said the man claimed you looked like a woman with the last name of Coleman?"

Cora nodded, feeling a shiver work through her.

"Do you have any siblings? Cousins?"

"No. My mother almost died giving birth to me. I was her first and only child. And Aunt Betsy is Ma's only sibling, so her youngsters are my only cousins. I don't know much about my pa's side of the family, however Ma told me one time that he was an only child."

Kin paused. He dug his toe at a clump of dirt, brow crimped. "Likely you looking like this Coleman woman is only a fluke, then."

"I would imagine so. Will you have to leave?" Cora's heart sank at the thought.

Kin gripped the back of his neck. "I'm not sure. I need to talk to the sheriff. Mrs. Callahan said he ought to be home for lunch. I'll ride back out there. You'd best return inside."

Cora's stomach clenched. Her room would be only a few doors down and across the hall from that awful Captain Sherman. She'd never be able to relax with him in the same building, much less just down the hall.

"Can I come with you?" she blurted.

Kin gave her a surprised look. He assessed her from head to toe again. "Something happened, didn't it? Did one of them touch you?" There was a savage note in his voice that filled her with terror and comfort all at the same time.

Her laced fingers clenched so tightly that the muscles ached. At least that kept them from fidgeting. "The one who seems to be the leader . . . He surreptitiously followed me into room seven and refused to move aside when I asked him to. He didn't touch me or even make any threatening gestures, but it scared me and that's putting it mildly."

Kin glanced down the alley and rasped something too quiet for her to catch. His words were dark, threatening, and yet somehow made her feel protected.

His focus rebounded to search her face. "How did you get out of there?"

"Dixie came to my rescue. I'm honestly not sure how she knew to come looking for me, except for the intervention of the Lord . . ." She searched his face. Had his feelings about God changed any in the years he'd been gone?

Though he didn't disparage the idea, as he might have in the past, neither did he agree with her assessment, nor did he thank the Lord for rescuing her. His face remained grimly impassive.

Cora's vision blurred with moisture and she blinked hard to dispel it.

"Hey. Come here." Kin reached for her slowly.

And she didn't hesitate to step into the comfort of his arms, even though she probably should have.

He wrapped one hand around the back of her neck and settled his chin against her hair. His other hand came to rest against the curve of her spine.

She inhaled scents of juniper and leather cream. Spread her hands across the softness of his waistcoat. Her heart steadied. Her breathing settled.

Kin was like a sheltering rock. He remained still. His hands didn't move, yet his arms seemed the safest of shelters. His feet, planted wide, braced to accept her additional weight without shuffling or adjusting. His breaths whispered steadily. His heartbeat thumped calmly beneath her ear.

Why, oh why did she feel such a strong draw to a man who didn't share her love of the Lord? He was a temptation that could never be satisfied. And she had made provision for sin long enough. She forced herself to step back.

He gripped both her shoulders and searched her face for a long moment. "You okay now?"

Cora nodded and dashed at the remaining moisture beneath her eyes. "Yes. Thank you. I'm sorry. I'm not usually one to fall apart."

"You didn't fall apart. You suddenly came to terms with how much danger you'd been in. It's a natural reaction in anyone. Ready to ride?" One corner of his mouth ticked up.

She lifted a hopeful gaze. "I can come?"

"Of course." He released her.

"Then, thank you, yes."

They turned toward the front of the alley.

Cora froze, as did Kin by her side.

Doctor Polson stood on the boardwalk in the gap between the two buildings. He was staring at them, hands on his hips.

Kin's hand shot out to protectively rest against her spine, but then he must have thought better of it, for he pulled it back.

The doctor only remained where he stood for half a second before gritting his teeth and turning to storm down the boardwalk.

Cora pressed her lips together. Truth was, she couldn't summon even a hint of regret to have the man upset with her. Maybe this would save her from having to decline more invitations from him.

"Sorry about that." Kin angled her a look. "I'll be happy to explain to the man that nothing was—or is—going on between us. I'll catch up with him just as soon as I can find a moment."

She met Kin's gaze as disappointment eased out on a long breath. Apparently Mr. Davis hadn't felt the same attraction she had only a moment ago. Surely if he had, he wouldn't be offering so blithely to smooth things over with the doctor?

All she could think to say was, "It's fine. Let's not worry about him at the moment."

"Right."

With that, he strolled out with purpose, leading the way to the livery.

Chapter Seventeen

Charlotte stood at the window smiling as Ike swung on the metal rim of an old wagon wheel that Reagan had fastened with two equal-length strands of rope to the giant maple at the top of the hill. The ancient maple tree with its jutting branches was perfect for the swing because the boy could run from the ground at the base of the trunk to push out into the empty space where the land dropped away. The wheel would swing in an arc until his feet could push off again.

Balancing on his stomach, he currently had his arms spread wide as the swing swept through the air. She covered her smile with one hand, hoping he wouldn't lose his balance and find himself in a jumbled heap of arms and legs after a long tumble.

Reagan tromped toward her, a grin as big as a crescent moon splitting his face. He entered through the kitchen door and came to stand behind her at the window.

With his hands on her shoulders, he leaned close to rumble in her ear, "I haven't had that much fun in a month of Sundays, Charlie."

Charlotte reached to cover one of his hands with her own. Together, they continued to watch.

Apparently tiring of flying in a wide circle, the boy climbed inside the rim, so that he was sitting on the lowest part of the circlet. He then proceeded to look up and spin in a circle, watching the ropes above him twist together into a tight skein.

With a firm grip on the wheel, the boy lifted his feet off the ground and let the swing unwind.

They could hear his squeal of laughter all the way in the house.

Reagan chuckled. "Who knew so much joy could come from an old broken wheel?"

Charlotte squeezed his hand and glanced over her shoulder at him. "Thank you for taking time to make that for him. It will give him some relief from his studies in the middle of the day."

"My pleasure." Reagan leaned close to sweep his lips over hers.

No matter that they'd been married for several years now, Charlotte still felt her stomach warble each time her husband kissed her. Easing back, he teased her nose with the stubble of his chin.

She giggled. "Stop that."

"You're no fun," he groused, returning his focus to Isaiah. Suddenly, he bent to take a closer look at the road that passed near the tree.

Two riders had crested the hill and were trotting toward the house.

Isaiah left the swing and ran to greet the pair.

"That's Kin and Cora," Reagan said.

Kin reached down to haul Isaiah onto the saddle behind him and they continued down the hill.

Reagan stepped out to meet them, while Charlotte quickly pushed both a coffee pot and a tea kettle to the hottest part of the stove and set to gathering cookies, sugar, and cream onto a tray.

It was only a few moments before Reagan was leading the trio through the front door. The easy pleasure that had been on his features only moments ago had been replaced with tension.

A business call then. Her heart sped, as it always did when Reagan would soon be heading into danger. It wouldn't slow until he was safely home and tugging her firmly against his chest.

Charlotte hurried forward. "Please come in. I'll have coffee and tea ready in just a moment." A tightness pulsed through her as she noted the protective way that Kin kept a grip on Isaiah's shoulder.

Charlotte stretched a hand to the boy. "Ike, why don't you come get a snack while you read a little more of *Huckleberry Finn*."

"Yes'm." The boy flicked Kin and Cora a worried glance, but didn't hesitate to do as she'd asked. She led him into the kitchen and settled him at the little table in the corner with a plate of oatmeal cookies and a tall glass of milk.

The water boiled. She poured it over the raspberry leaves in the pot, and added several cups to the tray. She could hear the low murmur of Kin's tense voice as she worked. Something wasn't right. She sent up a prayer for the Lord to please keep everyone in town safe. She wasn't sure what might have brought Kin and Cora to the house, but knew it couldn't be anything good.

It was only a moment before the coffee was ready and she carried the whole tray into the dining room.

Reagan looked up at her. Keeping his voice low, he said, "Apparently some men have arrived in town and are staying at the boardinghouse. They seem to be searching for Isaiah—all the way from Seattle. I think it's best we get some answers straight from him. Can you please ask him to join us?"

Charlotte nodded. She started to return to the kitchen, but then stilled. "Reagan? Go easy on him, would you? You can sometimes be quite intimidating when you are interrogating."

Reagan's serious expression softened, even if he didn't smile. "I'll be as gentle as I can, I promise."

Charlotte fetched Ike and seated him at the head of the table next to Reagan. Kin and Cora sat on the other side of Reagan. She took the empty chair on the opposite side of the table.

The poor child folded his arms on the tabletop and rested his chin on them, looking between the adults with a great deal of anxiety in his gray-blue eyes.

"Son . . ."

Charlotte was gratified to see Reagan give the boy a smile before he leaned forward to touch Ike's elbow.

"First thing I want to say is you're not in any trouble. But some men have come to town looking for you, and Mr. Davis says they were also looking for you back in Seattle."

The boy's eyes widened a little. His gaze flicked to Kin. "That gang of reavers?"

Charlotte frowned as she poured coffee for the men, feeling her heart expand toward the boy. A child shouldn't know anything about such terms. Besides, what was a *gang* of reavers?

Kin shook his head. "No." Kin took a moment to explain to them about the group of men who traveled the streets of Seattle, killing people for money.

The coffee pot clanked onto the tray louder than she'd intended. Her eyes were likely as wide as the saucers beneath the cups. What indeed was this world coming to? Killing people for money?

Kin, however, didn't seem fazed. He looked back at Ike. "These were different men, by my calculations. That first day when you were in my apartment and I got home? They were asking my landlady if she'd seen you."

"I see." Ike frowned. "What'd they look like?"

Charlotte realized she hadn't yet poured for Cora. At her lifted brow and short gesture between the choices, Cora indicated that she would also take coffee. Charlotte handed her a cup and then poured the herbal tea for herself, sinking against the back of her seat.

Kin pondered. "One had red hair and a curly beard. The other . . ."

"Clean-shaven and blond," Cora supplied. Tugging at her earlobe she added, "With a gold loop in his ear."

Kin kept a careful eye on the boy. "There's also a man named Captain Sherman. He has long dark hair and a full beard."

Isaiah straightened. "The men from the ship? The captain of our ship coming up from California looked like that, and his name was Sherman."

Reagan nodded. "Yeah. Kin said he already talked to you about them and you didn't know why they might be following you. You sure you can't think of any reason?"

Isaiah pondered for a long moment and Charlotte could hear the *swish, swish* of his shoes scuffing against the floor under the table. Finally, with the lift of one shoulder, he answered simply. "No."

"Did you ever talk to any of them?" Kin asked.

"Not much. Only a little after Pa passed. The captain, he paid for Pa to get buried. Then, like I told you, he kept all the money Pa'd had in his poke and I scrammed. That first night, the reavers almost got me, but I didn't recognize any of them. I don't think they was from the ship."

Charlotte closed her eyes, feeling a bit ill at the thought of sweet little Isaiah having to run for his life from monsters who held no value for life whatsoever.

Cora leaned forward. "Did your pa give you anything before he passed?"

"Good question," Kin encouraged.

Ike shrugged one shoulder. "Only his old coat." He pointed.

They all turned to look at the plain black coat hanging from the peg by the front door. It was worn through in one spot near an elbow, and frayed in a couple places around the hem.

Charlotte pressed her lips into a pinch. Highly unlikely that anyone was looking for the boy because of that ratty coat.

As if everyone were thinking the same, all the adults exchanged looks.

Kin leaned forward, setting his coffee to one side. "Miss Cora mentioned that Captain Sherman said she looked like a woman named Cassandra McKnight Coleman. Does that name mean anything to you?"

Isaiah nodded. His eyes widened a little as his gaze snapped to Cora. "That's why I thought you looked familiar! You look like my ma. Pa kept a picture of her in his poke. But he only let me look at it if he was near. I used to look at it more when I was younger."

"So Cassandra Coleman was your mother's name?" Reagan prodded.

Charlotte realized he wanted to be certain.

Isaiah nodded. "She passed, giving birth to me."

Kin continued the questioning. "And you had a house near the beach in California?"

"Yessuh. It were my ma's house before she married my pa."

Charlotte bit her tongue to keep from correcting his speech. This wasn't the time.

"Right near the water, it was. I miss waking up to the sound of the waves."

"Do you know what your pa did with the house before you left on your trip?" Reagan asked.

Isaiah pondered with a frown. "Some people was moving in the day we left. Pa told me later that he'd let it out to them."

"You're sure your father didn't sell it to them?" Cora blew on the surface of her coffee before taking a sip.

"No. He didn't sell it. Pa told me we'd go back someday." Tears flooded his eyes at that proclamation, but he showed a strength of character by remaining where he was.

Kin and Reagan looked at each other.

Reagan ventured, "Maybe they think he has something that he doesn't?"

Charlotte's attention was captured by Cora, who kept darting looks at Isaiah's coat. After a moment, she rose and went over to the coat hooks.

Kin and Reagan didn't pay her any mind.

Kin said, "Should we just confront these men and ask them what they want with him?"

Reagan rubbed his jaw. "Couldn't hurt, I suppose. But it would reveal to them that he's for sure here. Might cause trouble down the line."

"True." Kin scooped his fingers through his curls. "I don't like this. Not at all. Presumably the kid owns a house in California, but without a deed or even a will, we can't prove that it's his. Did his pa just tell him they would go back to soothe him? Or——"

"No!" Isaiah shook his head. "My pa wasn't like that. He told things like they was. If he said we would go back and live in that house, he meant it." The boy's voice had risen with each word. "Besides, like I said, he told me it was rented."

Kin held up a hand. "Okay, I believe you." He focused on Reagan again. "In that case, he owns a house that's likely bringing in a goodly amount. Maybe that's what these men want? But . . . Where is that money going? And how would we prove that this boy is Isaiah Coleman's son?"

Cora returned to the table with the boy's coat in one hand. She scooted her coffee cup to one side and flopped the coat onto the table.

Kin startled a little, leaning back to look up at her.

Cora shrugged. "This was the last thing his father gave him. I find it odd that his father would insist on him having a coat that is three times too big for him. And all torn in places to boot."

Ike hung his head. "Those rips is from me runnin' from those killers that first night."

"I see." She started feeling the material all over. First at the shoulders. Inside the lapels. All along the sleeves. In the pockets.

All revealed nothing.

But as she felt of the material at the back of the hem, there came the sound of crinkling paper.

Everyone froze and looked at one another.

Cora smiled. She carefully lifted that side of the coat and examined the stitching. "Charlotte? Do you happen to have a small pair of scissors?"

Charlotte leapt to fetch them and they all watched as Cora carefully snipped the stitching along the bottom seam of the coat.

Soon she was able to pull a thin onionskin paper from between the layers. There was also a thicker piece of paper, folded in thirds.

"Well, I'll be!" Kin tugged the pages closer. "Cora you're a genius." He bent to examine the onionskin first.

"Read it out loud," Charlotte asked, unable to curb her curiosity. She pushed her teacup to one side.

Kin began to read. "'I, Isaiah Solomon Coleman Senior, being of sound mind, do hereby bequeath all my worldly goods to my son, Isaiah Solomon Coleman Junior.' Then there's his signature."

Reagan tapped the table repeatedly with one finger—a sure sign of his tension. He jutted his chin toward the letter and looked at Kin. "Will it hold up in court?"

Kin rubbed one finger at a spot on his cheek beneath his eye as he continued studying the letter. "There's no witness signature, but possession is nine tenths of the law. Since the kid is in possession of a coat that used to be his father's, and since this letter was in that coat and witnessed by all of us,

I think any fair judge—if it comes to court—would make the connection between the two."

"What's the other paper?" Cora asked.

Kin set the letter aside and took up the folded page. He smoothed it open on the table. It wasn't but a moment before a smile crooked up one corner of his mouth. "This here . . ." He tossed the page onto the table in front of Reagan. "Is the deed to one California beach house, complete with address, and history of ownership. See here?" He leaned forward and pointed. "Isaiah Solomon Coleman Junior has been added under the original two names. And a Cassandra McKnight Coleman has been listed as deceased. There's even the name of their solicitor."

"Can I see my pa's letter?" Ike asked softly.

Kin's exuberance over their find faded. "Of course." He slid the onionskin page toward the boy.

Charlotte felt a lump in her throat as Isaiah traced a finger soberly over the strokes of the pen on the page.

Reagan reached out a hand and simply rested it on the boy's small forearm.

Kin cleared his throat and scrubbed at a knot on the table.

"I wondered why my pa insisted I take his coat. I woke up one night when we were on the ship and saw Pa hunched in the corner doin' somethin' with his coat. But when I asked him about it, he told me to go back to sleep. I figured maybe he was just usin' it as an extra blanket of sorts. The next day he pressed it into my hands. He tried to say somethin', but he was already quite sick by that point and I couldn't understand what he was sayin'. Maybe he was tryin' to tell me the deed was in the linin'. I almost had the men put it back on him for his buryin'." Isaiah swallowed hard and worked to maintain his composure. "Even at the last, he was tryin' to take care of me, weren't he?" Isaiah searched each of their faces.

Reagan gave his arm a gentle squeeze. "Yeah, son. It sounds like he certainly was."

The boy's face crumpled. "I miss him."

"I know, kid. I know." Reagan scooted his chair back, and without hesitation, held his arms out to the boy. When Isaiah lurched forward to take advantage of his invitation, he gathered the boy onto his lap.

Isaiah curled into a tight ball and rested his head on Reagan's shirt pocket. Though his tears fell, he hardly made a sound or movement.

Reagan pushed the chair up onto its back legs and rocked, and Charlotte didn't even reprimand him for it. He rubbed a hand over the boy's back. There was a distinct gleam of moisture in his eyes.

A glance at Kin and Cora revealed the same.

Charlotte pressed weary hands into the table and rose. Her gaze landed on the deed resting in the middle of the table.

She had a terrible feeling that piece of paper was about to upend the peaceful little town of Wyldhaven.

And her dear husband would be right in the thick of it.

Chapter Eighteen

Cora helped Charlotte clear the dishes from the table, and by the time they returned to the dining room, Isaiah was sound asleep in Reagan's arms.

"How old is he?" Reagan adjusted the boy to a more comfortable position, directing the question at Kin.

Kin shrugged. "You got me. He's never said and I didn't press him about it. Wasn't sure if remembering birthdays would add to his grief."

Charlotte, who had moved to stand behind her husband, reached over to squeeze Kin's shoulder. "You are a good, kind, and thoughtful man, Kin Davis."

The truth of those words struck Cora at her very center. He *was* a good, kind, and thoughtful man.

No. There she went again, giving in to temptation. She gritted her teeth, determined to follow the instructions in the Word not to be unequally yoked with an unbeliever. For if she gave in to her burgeoning feelings for the man, his strong personality would inevitably draw her away from the Lord she loved.

She put a hand to her throat and looked at the table. *Father, forgive me for even being tempted with the consideration of what life might be like with Kin. Help me to ever be mindful of the truth of Your Word. Please change my feelings for him.*

When they went back to town in a bit, she could go to her room and escape his nearness. She would spend the evening looking up every verse she could find about not being unequally yoked, and maybe even commit a few to memory. Then she could repeat them to herself anytime the man came close.

But the thought of being just down the hall from that terrible captain, no matter that Kin would be nearby, too, to protect her, sent a roil of nausea through her. She covered her stomach with one hand. Took a breath.

"Cora?" The very man occupying her prayers looked at her with concern filling his expression. "Everything all right?"

She realized she'd closed her eyes at some point during her entreaty and following thoughts. "Yes. Fine." She sank into the seat across the table that Charlotte had occupied for most of the evening.

Cora wished he'd quit searching her face with such soft scrutiny.

Kin folded his hands on the table. "You must be exhausted. And with that man causing you distress earlier, I wonder if it might not be better for you to stay away from the boardinghouse and from work for a few days? Until they leave town?"

Reagan's attention snapped to her. "A man caused you distress?"

Cora nodded, but couldn't seem to get her mouth to form an explanation.

Kin came to her rescue and filled them in on what she'd told him earlier.

Charlotte rushed to Cora's side and wrapped her in a side-hug. "That's terrible. I'm so sorry. We've plenty of room here."

Cora felt a wave of relief at the thought. "Thank you." Tears choked off more words of gratefulness. That would also put a greater distance between her and this tempting man.

The sheriff looked at Kin. "Might be good for you and the boy to stay out of sight as well, until we can do a little more looking into this." He swept a gesture at the papers still on the table.

"We've a bedroom for you too, if you don't mind sharing with Isaiah," Charlotte offered, her hands still resting on Cora's shoulders.

Cora despaired. It seemed she couldn't escape the man. Kin staying here in this small house with her? Likely right across the hall? It had been bad enough to think of him in a nearby room at the boardinghouse, but this . . .

"On second thought, I think I'd better go back to town," she blurted. "I'd hate to leave Dixie in the lurch."

There was a glint of humor in the look Kin gave her, as if he might know the reason for her rapid reversal. "If you're worried about the diner, I think I could ride out and ask Maude Carver to fill in for you for a couple of days. I'm certain she wouldn't mind."

"That's an excellent idea." Charlotte squeezed Cora's shoulders again. "Dixie will totally understand. And I'm sure Maude could use a little extra cash for an upcoming . . . event." When Cora glanced up, Charlotte's eyes twinkled like stars, as if she might know something she wasn't sharing.

Cora's interest rose. She twisted to get a better look at Charlotte's face. "Has Jackson finally proposed?"

Charlotte pressed her lips together, the bunch of wrinkles on her brow indicating she was trying to decide how to respond. Finally, she offered, "I'd better not say. Only, something I witnessed Jackson buying in the mercantile the other day has me suspecting that Maude will soon have a big day to celebrate."

Regan huffed a breath of humor. "You've just said what you said you ought not say, dear wife."

Charlotte covered her mouth with a giggle. "Oh dear. I guess I did at that."

Kin's gaze was still fixed on Cora. She could feel it. She transferred her attention to him. The impact of his concern filled her with a blaze of yearning. Her ribcage didn't seem big enough for the expanding of her heart. Or for her lungs, which suddenly couldn't seem to find enough oxygen.

Gracious. It was as though her recent prayers had not changed her one whit. Maybe she would need to fast to relieve herself of these sinful desires. She snapped her attention to her clasped hands.

"Let Maude cover for you." His voice was soft and cajoling. "Just for a few days. I wager you could use the rest, anyhow."

Cora remembered turning around in room seven to find that horrible man blocking the doorway. A shudder quaked through her. She suddenly had no hesitation. "Yes. Thank you." She bounced a glance between Charlotte and Reagan. "I really don't want to be an imposition."

"Nonsense." Charlotte released her with a flap of a gesture. Inching up her skirts, she gave Reagan a nod of her head. "Bring him on down the hall, sweetie, and let's get him tucked in. Poor child has been through too much recently." To Kin and Cora, she said, "If you'll just give me but a moment, I'll have both your beds ready."

With a soft word of acknowledgment, Reagan gathered the boy into his arms and followed his wife from the room.

Cora missed the comfort of Charlotte's hands and wrapped her arms across her shoulders to ward off a chill.

Kin was immediately on his feet. "Cold?" He was already shucking out of his duster.

Her mind traveled to another night in a cold alley in Cle Elum when he'd come to her rescue with a similar gesture. Her pulse tripped.

She held out a palm. "No. Truly. Please keep your jacket. It's just been a bit of a crazy day." She noticed Ike's jacket still on the table and, rising from her chair, took it up. "I really ought to repair this seam."

"Tomorrow will be soon enough." Kin tugged it gently from her fingers and dropped it back onto the table. He didn't step back, but remained where he was, only a handspan away. The brown of his eyes softened like melting caramel, and he tucked one side of his lower lip between his teeth.

Cora felt the invasion of her space as surely as she had with the man back at the boardinghouse. And yet there was such a contrast in the way her heart responded this time. Her breaths came in short, rapid puffs, but not of fear. Heaven help her; this was anticipation. She really ought to retreat but her feet seemed unresponsive. Her pulse thrummed like the wings of a hummingbird. Where were those Bible verses when she needed them?

His hand inched forward and his broad first finger hooked around her pinky. The warmth of his tentative grip was better than the wrap of a coat, any day.

His thumb caressed her knuckle, and then his fingers tantalized the skin of her palm as he skimmed his hand beneath her own to get a better grip. "Cora . . ." His voice was rough. Barely audible.

"All right, you two, I've got— Oh!"

Kin yanked back his hand and put it to use, smoothing the hair at his neck. He turned to face Charlotte by the door, as Cora retreated to the other side of the table once more. She willed the flames in her face to extinguish.

Fasting. Yes, indeed. Many long days of it.

"I'm sorry to interrupt." Charlotte smiled knowingly between them.

Kin gestured to the coat. "Cora was just saying she ought to repair the hem and I was telling her it could wait until morning."

"Yes. I think it can." Charlotte hurried forward and gathered up the jacket. She carried it to the hook by the door. "I intended to see if he'd let me resize and repair it, anyhow. Jacinda will be happy to help me do that. But I didn't want him to feel we were taking away the last thing his father gave him."

Kin flicked Cora an assessing glance, as though making sure she wasn't too horribly embarrassed. "Yes," he replied to Charlotte. "It might be better to put it away for him without changing it, and make him a new one. He won't be the size he is now for long, and then he'll be grown out of it."

"Yes. True. That's an excellent idea, Kin." Charlotte pressed her palms together. "Are you two ready for some sleep?" Her focus bounced between them. "Reagan said he would ride into town to fill Dixie in, and then on to the Carvers to talk to Maude."

"I don't mind making the ride," Kin offered.

Charlotte shook her head and brushed away his concern. "He doesn't want to risk you being seen by any of those men." She squeezed Kin's arm. "It will only take him a short time and he's used to riding out at all hours. Don't concern yourself. Now—" She started toward the hall. "If you'll just follow me, I'll show you to your rooms."

Charlotte showed Kin to the first room down the hall on the left. Isaiah was already sound asleep on one of the room's beds. The other bed was turned back. Kin offered his thanks and closed the door quietly.

"Yours is just here." Charlotte pushed open the door to the room across the hall. "Since you've come to us unprepared, I laid out a sleeping gown for you. It might be a little big on you."

"Thank you, kindly." Cora rushed to assure her. "I'm sure t'will be fine."

She was thankful that Charlotte left her then without any questioning looks or smirks of womanly knowing. She only offered that she would see her in the morning and pulled the door closed behind her.

The room was cozy, despite the rough log walls. White lace curtains hung at the window. And someone had spent a great deal of time crocheting the huge lace panel that covered the white down tick. A white milk-glass lamp spread a soft golden light from where it sat on the knotty pine bedside table. And the dressing screen that angled across the far corner had center panels padded with white silk. Each was embroidered with single nosegays of lavender.

Weary to the bone, Cora lifted the long white gown Charlotte had provided, and moved behind the partition to shimmy out of her dress.

Once she'd extinguished the lamp and was securely snuggled under the tick, she was frustrated to discover that her mind seemed preoccupied with scenarios of what might have happened in the dining room just now if Charlotte hadn't popped back in when she did.

Father, forgive me for I am a sinner. Weak of flesh, and prone to temptation.

Her fingers stroked her palm as she remembered the glide of Kin's caress in the same spot.

With a huff, she flopped onto her back, gripping the tick in tight fists as she stared at the ceiling. "Cheese and crumpets, Cora Harrison! Go to sleep!"

No matter her command, her mind remained in a rebellious state that refused to relinquish thoughts of the man across the hall.

The next morning, after a fitful night, Cora arrived at the dining room table. Reagan and Kin were already having a conversation.

"You'll leave today, then?" Reagan asked.

"I think it best." Kin spun a cup of black coffee in a circle on its saucer. "I'll go straight to talk to this solicitor. I don't want the kid to lose out on his inheritance because we delayed."

"You're right, of course. I'll do my best to keep word of your departure from reaching this Sherman and his cronies. Once you've established Ike as the legal heir, there won't be much they can do."

"Do you think I should take him with me?"

Reagan scrubbed his fingers across his jaw. "Much as I hate to keep his schedule in upheaval, it might be best. The solicitor might know him by sight and that would strengthen your case."

Kin nodded. "My thoughts exactly. I'll need to fetch Ike's and my things from town. Ike doesn't have much."

Reagan shook his head. "I'll fetch them for you. I'll be back inside an hour." With that, he stood, gave Cora a nod of acknowledgment, and then headed out the door.

Cora found herself once more alone in the dining room with Mr. Kin Davis.

"Morning, Mish. How'd you sleep?" His eyes sparkled as though he may have been able to hear her tossing and turning the whole night through.

She notched her chin a few degrees into the air. "I slept just fine, thank you. And you?"

"Had some trouble." He wagged his head in distress. "Couldn't stop thinking about a beautiful blonde woman with the comeliest blue eyes a man ever did see." He grinned at her wickedly.

Cora felt a traitorous thrill. Heat blazed into her cheeks and she pressed her fingers to them before she thought better of it, and then quickly snatched her hands down, hoping he hadn't noticed.

"But she turned me down not long ago when I asked her on a picnic, so I don't suppose there's much hope for me anyhow."

Cora bit down on a coy retort and only offered, "Well, I hope this fictitious woman of yours was worth the sleepless night, Mr. Davis."

His grin broadened. "Oh, she is, Mish. She truly is."

Cora fled to the kitchen, throwing over her shoulder, "I think I'll find myself some coffee."

Kin's soft chuckle chased her.

Charlotte was already bent over the stove frying sausages and eggs. "Morning," she greeted. "Help yourself to some coffee. Then—" She nodded at a bowl of dough. "If you don't mind, you could scoop those biscuits onto the cooking sheet there."

"Happy to help." Cora took her coffee to the sideboard, but as she measured out the biscuit dough, she couldn't help but fret over the fact that Kin had only just arrived and was again set to depart. At least she would be separated from the temptation of him for a time. Maybe that would help her get herself in check. How long would it take them to travel to California, settle Ike's affairs, and then return to town? Her gaze blurred against the green hills out the window.

"You look like you're sifting through cobwebs," Charlotte interrupted, reaching for the now filled tray.

Cora started, and stepped out of her way. "Yes. Sorry." She offered an embarrassed smile.

Charlotte eyed her. "He's very handsome."

Cora spun to look out the window once more. "Isaiah?" she prevaricated. "Yes, he really is a handsome little fellow."

Charlotte giggled as she slid the biscuits into the oven. "That's not who I meant, and you know it very well."

Cora blew out a frazzled breath and faced her friend. "Even though you're right, naught can ever come of it. I'm determined to only marry a man who loves the Lord as I do."

Charlotte tilted her a look. "So last night? What I saw near the table? What was that?"

Cora slashed her hand through the air several times, trying to come up with words. "That was . . . Well . . . Confound it, but I can't seem to think, move, or breathe when the man is near me, talking all soft and looking at me with those mesmerizing eyes of his. All my determination to do things God's way seems to flee right out of my mind."

With a laugh, Charlotte stepped near and bumped her arm. "Oh dear. You've got it rather bad, haven't you?"

Struck by how true Charlotte's words were, Cora whimpered dramatically and let her shoulders slump. "I'm afraid I do. And not one of my prayers has seemed to help."

"I think he's changed quite a bit over the last two years. I haven't heard even one story of him being at McGinty's since he arrived back home."

Cora gave her a withering look. "He's been home for less than a week."

Charlotte laughed. "Well, that's true enough. But when I came out this morning, he was already up. He was in the parlor reading Reagan's Bible." One of her brows winged upward.

Hope burst to life in Cora's chest like an exploded feather pillow. "He was?"

"I might not have believed it, if I hadn't seen it with my own eyes." Charlotte patted her shoulder and then hurried to turn the sausages. "You just keep praying for him, dear Cora. I've known ever since he was a boy that God had big plans for Kin Davis. He has a heart bigger than all the mountain ranges in Washington."

As Cora helped Charlotte scoop the sausages and eggs from the pan onto a serving platter, and gathered butter and jam onto a tray, she already found herself praying.

Dear God. Dear God. Dear God. Please let it be true.
She'd been praying for her feelings to change for him. Why not

pray that his feelings would change toward God? She recalled a verse from 2 Corinthians. *The weapons we fight with are not the weapons of the world. On the contrary, they have divine power to demolish strongholds. Lord, in the mighty name of Jesus, I pray against any stronghold that might be keeping Kin from completely surrendering to You. Demolish those strongholds. I have no power, Lord, but You have all the power. And I ask once again that until that time, You would give me the will to resist these tempting feelings for him.*

She felt helpless to do more as she followed Charlotte to the table, carrying the coffee and tea pots.

Kin had disappeared, leaving his empty cup on the table.

His absence made her thoughts flash to that moment in the alley the day before when Dr. Polson had seen them together. She remembered Kin's words. "I'll be happy to explain to the man that nothing was—or is—going on between us."

Her heart fell. Questions rose. Perhaps she was the only one feeling attraction?

But if so, what had he meant by clasping her hand the evening before?

She blew out a frazzled breath.

Mercy. She was going to twist her thoughts into a tighter tangle than Isaiah's swing.

More to pray about, she supposed.

Chapter Nineteen

ackson Nolan rode toward the Carver place, thanking the Lord that Mr. Ecklund had agreed to give him the day off. His boss had tortured him a bit before agreeing, however.

"A day off, you say, young Nolan? Och . . . This is a thing that here in the Americas is done?"

"Well, sir—" Jackson twisted his cap in his hands. "—you don't have to give me the time off. I'm just hoping . . . Well . . . There's something I was hoping to do, you see. And I wanted to do it during the day and not later in the evening after I get off of work."

The ring he'd purchased felt like a leaden weight—albeit a joyous one—in his jacket pocket. He was terrified of losing it before he could get it on Maude's finger. She was a very early riser and he knew she regularly was asleep by eight. He hadn't wanted his proposal to feel rushed, or to catch her when she was already exhausted from a long day.

"I see . . ." Mr. Ecklund drew out the words. "So, 'no' I am allowed to say, ja?"

Jackson couldn't withhold a sigh. "Yes, sir."

Mr. Ecklund burst out laughing and slapped his thigh. "I am just kicking your leg, young Nolan! The day off, you may have."

Jackson grinned, relieved. "Pulling, sir."

"What is this 'pulling'? This is what you will do on your day off?"

"No, sir. The phrase is, 'pulling your—' Never mind. Thank you, sir." He had rushed out before the man could change his mind, leaving the still chuckling Mr. Ecklund to his bookwork.

Now Jackson stood on the crest of the hill, looking down at the Carvers' cabin. Seth and Kane were going to be some put out by having him take their cook and housekeeper, he supposed. But he couldn't worry about that.

Maude meant everything to him, and he felt certain that she felt the same way about him. If he could just ask her, she would say yes, and they'd live happily to a ripe old age, if the good Lord tarried.

Hauling in a fortifying breath, he trudged down the hill and knocked purposefully on the door. While he waited for it to open, he quietly practiced his proposal. "Maude, ever since I first laid my eyes upon you—" He shook his head at himself. "No. That sounds disgusting."

He paced a few steps and tried again. "Maude, I used to stare at you from the back of the church— Watch you from the back of the church? No."

He headed for the other side of the porch, stomach churning. That sounded more than slightly creepy. Why hadn't he taken time to practice what he was going to say? And what was taking her so long to answer?

"Maybe I should just blurt a short, 'Maude, will you marry me?'"

"You should probably say something about loving her." A chuckle accompanied Kane Carver's words, spoken from behind him.

Jackson whirled toward the voice.

Kane stood laughing up at him, wiping dark axle grease from his hands onto a dirty towel. After only a second, however, Kane's features hardened. "I guess you weren't planning on asking me for her hand?"

Jackson felt like his collar might cut off his air. "Well, I, ah . . . You see, with you being her brother, I wasn't quite sure what the etiquette might be. I planned to ask her and then have her tell me how to approach you."

Kane kept glowering.

Jackson slipped a finger beneath the top button of his shirt. "I meant—mean—no disrespect."

Kane's expression didn't change.

Jackson gulped. "Does this mean that you are denying me permission to ask for your sister's hand? Because I have to tell you, I love her so much that I don't plan to let you stand in my way."

He realized that at some point he'd thrown back his shoulders. He pushed out a breath and tried to relax a little.

Kane's hard expression softened and then split into a smile. "Ease up, Jackson. I was just seeing what you were made of. But I have bad news . . ."

A frown slumped Jackson's brow. "You do? She's not sick, is she?"

One of Kane's hands patted the air. "Sheriff Callahan came by last night and asked her to fill in at the diner for Cora today. That's where she is."

"Oh." The tense anticipation he'd been feeling all morning drained out of him so quickly that it sapped the strength right out of his legs. He sank onto the top step. "So, she'll be there all day?"

Kane eyed him, still working some grease off his fingers. "Had to be to work at six. Works until ten. Then she has a six-hour break until four when she'll finish out the remainder of her shift until eight."

"I see." Jackson scrubbed at the tension paining the back of his head. She would definitely be too tired after finally arriving home at the conclusion of such a day. He sighed.

Kane seemed mighty interested in making sure his fingernails were clean. "Told me that she plans to walk up to the church to read her book during that looong break in the middle of the day."

"I see." Despair still weighted Jackson's head toward the ground. "Wait!" His focus snapped to Kane and his back straightened. "She did?"

Kane chuckled. He angled a look at the sun hanging just above the treetops in the distance. "I'd wager you have just about enough time to run home and pack a picnic lunch for two. She's rather fond of that wildflower field up toward the Kastain place."

Jackson lurched to his feet. "That's a great idea!"

He'd taken several strides toward home when he realized his ill manners. He pivoted and returned to stand before Kane, hand outthrust. "Thank you, Kane. And thank you for your permission to marry your sister. I'll do good by her, I swear I will." With that, he offered a huge grin then turned at a run for home, calling, "Good day to you!"

At the top of the ridge, he glanced back. Kane Carver remained in the yard, shaking his head and laughing.

Breakfast was finished. It had been a quiet affair with Kin mostly filling the time by informing Isaiah of the reasons for their trip to California. The boy was a quick study and asked intelligent questions. Now Cora and Charlotte were in the kitchen and Reagan had harnessed the team. He'd earlier ridden into town to fetch Kin's and Isaiah's bags from the boardinghouse, and they were in the process of loading the wagon.

Cora watched from the window as Kin helped Isaiah onto the seat. They would take the train to California and return only when Isaiah's affairs were in order.

Cora clenched her hands, wondering again how long they would be.

At the sideboard, Charlotte rolled out dough for several pies. "You could go out and offer a farewell, you know. Men do like to know that the women who hold their hearts return the sentiment."

Cora glanced back at her. "You think I hold his heart?"

"Sweetie, I've never once seen Kin Davis look at a woman the way I saw him looking at you last night." Charlotte raised her eyebrows to make her point.

Cora blushed and returned her focus to the wagon. "I'm not so certain you are correct."

"Do tell." Charlotte's tone was dismissive of the idea.

Resilient hope raised its head. She quashed it. "Doctor Polson saw Kin . . . consoling me after Captain Sherman accosted me at the boardinghouse."

"Ah. *Consoling* you." Charlotte chuckled. "I always like it when Reagan consoles me."

Cora batted a hand at her. "Oh, do stop. It was only a hug. But afterward, Kin said he would be sure to inform the doctor that there was naught between us."

Charlotte blew a scornful sound. "That's because he is a gentleman who doesn't want to stand in the way of your happiness, and he's not yet sure what would make you happiest. You have to show him."

"There's still the question of where he stands with the Lord."

Charlotte tilted her head. "Have you asked him?"

She shook her head. "No."

"Seems to me that since it's such an important matter, a conversation ought to be had before you go jumping to conclusions that are incorrect."

The problem was that Cora wasn't so sure she was incorrect. Despite her certainty that she was right, maybe she ought to give him a chance to come out and tell her. Because until she did, there would remain a lot of questions in her mind where that man was concerned.

Cora very much wanted to dash out to the yard and, at the very least, tell him to return safely. But she forced herself to remain where she stood. A real lady didn't throw herself at a man. Especially not at one who might not want her.

"You really saw him reading Reagan's Bible this morning?"

"I did." Charlotte nodded.

Cora returned her gaze to the group by the wagon, willing down the hope taking flight in her chest.

Kin propped his hands on his hips and glanced toward the house. He said something to Reagan and started toward the door, but Reagan pulled his watch from his vest, consulted it, and then said a few words with a shake of his head. Kin reversed course and climbed up onto the wagon seat by Isaiah. As they drove away, there seemed to be a little bit of defeat in the slump of his spine.

As Reagan drove the cart away from the house, Kin forced himself not to look back. She hadn't come out to say goodbye and that was that. He'd thought there was time to offer his farewells, but Reagan had said there wasn't. He realized suddenly that he'd be leaving town without having the chance to give an explanation to the new doctor. He could only dredge up a marginal amount of sorrow over that realization.

He smirked. Let the good doctor stew and wonder for a bit. He would eventually learn that Cora was free and clear and be the happier for it.

Reagan took the backroads to avoid town, and Kin was surprised when they took the turn off toward the Rodante farm. "Where are we going?"

Reagan only smiled. "You'll see. Something important."

When he pulled the wagon to a stop near the barn, Joe was there to greet them. "Right this way," he said. He led them to the farthest stall and pushed open the gate. There in a clean pile of hay, lay a calico cat with five tiny kittens all jumbled in a ball.

Ike's eyes grew wide. "Kittens."

Reagan nudged his shoulder. "Go on and pick one out. They're too young to leave their ma yet. But a couple weeks after you get back home, you can have it."

As Isaiah fell to his knees beside the feline, Kin frowned at Reagan.

He waved a hand. "Oh, you'll be fine. Cats don't take up much room." His gaze was soft as he watched Ike lift and examine each kitten. "Every boy needs a little joy in his life, Kin. Every. One."

Yeah. Kin figured if anyone knew that truth, it was him. Still, he couldn't help feeling a little irritated that he hadn't gotten to say goodbye to Cora on account of a kitten-choosing.

Kin was beginning to fear they would miss the train, but finally Ike held up a gray kitten with black markings and green eyes.

Joe promised that he'd keep her for Ike, and they all climbed back onto the wagon.

Once they reached the station, they had plenty of time to buy their tickets and stow their cases in their berth and still had a few minutes left over.

Back out on the platform, Kin stretched a hand to the sheriff. "Keep an eye on Cora, would you? She was really rattled by that captain." His stomach roiled at the thought of anything happening to her while he was away.

Reagan gave him a serious nod. "I've already planned a meeting with Joe and Zane. One of us will keep an eye on those men at all times until they leave town. And Cora is more than welcome to stay at our place for the duration. She'll be fine. On my word."

The words eased Kin's tension a little and he thanked the sheriff and then prodded Isaiah to say his goodbyes.

Surprisingly, Ike rubbed a toe at the boards beneath their feet and shook his head.

Kin frowned. It wasn't like the boy to be impertinent. He gave Reagan an apologetic look.

Reagan swiped away his concern with his hat. He ruffled a hand over Ike's hair. "I'll be waiting right here to say hello when you get back, all right, kiddo? And maybe we can go pick up that kitten together in a couple weeks?"

Ike peered up at him, but only pinched his lips together with a little frown.

Sudden understanding struck Kin. Ike was worried that something might happen to Reagan while they were away. It was with a little jealousy that he realized that in the few short hours the boy had spent in Reagan's presence, he'd already come to see him as a father figure. But the jealousy lasted only momentarily as an idea sparked.

He wasn't sure why Reagan and Charlotte hadn't yet conceived, and of course it wasn't a question he could ask. But they would be the perfect parents for Isaiah.

It would solve a lot of his concerns over whether he'd be a good father figure, too. He could be a brother figure easily. He'd been doing that for years with Tommy.

He wouldn't broach the subject now, but he'd talk to Reagan and Charlotte when they returned.

"All aboard!" the conductor called.

"That's us, kid." Kin bade Reagan farewell, then nudged Ike along the platform. "Don't worry. We'll be back in just a few days."

Before they entered the train, Ike paused and looked up at him. "You won't leave me in California?"

Kin lowered to his haunches so he could look the boy right in the eyes. "You got any family in California?"

Gray eyes wide, Isaiah shook his head. "None that I know of."

"All right then. You and me. We're family. Got it? And when we get back, Mr. Reagan and Mrs. Charlotte, they're going to be like family too. Lots of people in this town will. The parson and Mrs. Aurora . . ."

Isaiah turned and hefted himself into the car. He ambled along the aisle and pushed into their berth. He flopped onto one of the benches, stretching his legs along the length of it. He leaned his head against one wall morosely. "Lotsa people here don't like me."

Kin took the opposite bench with a shake of his head. "That's just not true. You can't let a couple bad apples spoil your view of the whole tree. You gotta pick those bad apples and toss them out and then you'll see that the rest of the tree is filled with nice juicy crisp fruit."

Ike giggled. "I don't think Miss Cora would like to hear you callin' her a crisp fruit."

Kin smiled. "I think you're right. Now, tell you what. We've got a long trip ahead of us. Why don't you catch some shuteye. It will make the trip go faster for you."

"Yessuh."

The boy was fast asleep before the train even began its chuffing exit from the station.

Chapter Twenty

Maude Carver sat on the back bench in the sanctuary, simply enjoying the silence and the freedom to sit and do nothing. She'd worked hard this morning in the diner, seating customers, making change, refilling drinks, running food to tables . . . But that wasn't anything on rising with the sun to milk three cows, slop seven pigs, feed chickens, fork hay to the horses, and feed two brothers who some days didn't seem much different than the pigs.

She welcomed this break in her routine. Would dare say she relished it.

With a happy sigh, she reached for the biography Missionary David Livingstone had written about his adventures on the Dark Continent. The man wrote with a wit and turn of phrase that had her giggling more often than not. However, he'd also undergone some serious, even treacherous situations that at times had her holding her breath and flipping the pages to see how he'd extracted himself from the danger. She was almost finished with this one and was already looking forward to spending the extra money she was earning today on more books at the mercantile.

She had just started reading when she heard the stairs up to the church porch creak. She frowned. Someone was coming?

She lowered her book to her lap and studied the doorway to her left, unsure if she ought to be concerned or not. She heard the outer door of the church open and held her breath.

When Jackson stuck his head around the back partition, she relaxed against the pew. "Oh hi. It's just you." She frowned. "Are you off of work?"

He stepped further into the room, fiddling nervously with his hat.

"Everything all right?" She rose, concern mounting. "Did something happen to Kane or Seth?"

Jackson held out a hand. "No. No. Everything is fine. I just . . . wondered if you'd like to take a picnic with me? I hear that you have a few hours until you have to be back to work?"

Something inside her melted. Jackson came regularly to their house on Fridays, but he spent more time talking with Kane than he ever did with her. It was nice to think that he actually wanted to spend some time with her. Maybe his intentions were firming toward her. "Aw, Jax. That's right thoughtful of you. But . . . aren't you supposed to be at work?"

He grinned at her. "Don't worry about that. I got the day off because I . . . well . . . I wanted to spend it with you. Come on." His hand extended, inviting her to slip her fingers into his.

She didn't hesitate. His grip was warm and firm around hers. She sidled close enough to boldly rest her chin on his shoulder and blink up at him. Maybe Jax just needed to know that she wanted to get to know him better. "This is much nicer than sitting in the dim light of the church trying to read. Thank you for thinking of me."

"Sure." Jackson looked pleased and yet at the same time he seemed kind of green around the gills.

She pulled back. "Are you feeling okay? You don't look so good."

"I don't?" He gave her a surprised look as they descended the church steps. His wagon waited for them and a large basket, covered with a patchwork tablecloth, sat in the back. "I'm fine." He helped her up to the seat. "Why do you say I don't look so good?"

"I don't know. You look a little . . . peaked."

"Huh."

He made no reply after that, and Maude let it go. Still, she couldn't help feeling that something was odd. This was very out of character for him.

As Jax climbed onto the seat beside her and clucked to the horses, Maude pulled in a lungful of wonderful spring air. It was probably her favorite time of year. Birds chirped. The creek burbled. And flowers of every color had burst into bloom—some of them so tiny that one could almost miss them if they were moving too fast, and others, like Mrs. King's large pink hydrangea at the back of the post office, simply made her want to sing with joy. Of course, she never did. She would be terribly embarrassed to have someone come upon her while she was singing. But the urge to do so brought a smile.

She was surprised—a bit alarmed even—when Jackson turned the wagon, not toward town as she'd expected, but toward the area north of town. "Where are we going?"

He gave her a tight smile. "You'll see."

She glanced back at the receding town. "Jackson, we can't go off on our own. It's not seemly. We should take the picnic on the lawn near the mill."

"It'll be fine."

"It won't be fine if Mrs. Hines gets wind of it. We should go back."

Jackson kept the wagon on its course.

She smacked his shoulder with the back of her hand. "Jackson Nolan, take me back to town, at once."

"Maude, will you hush. Kane is the one who told me just this morning that you like that little wildflower field north of town. That's where I'm taking you."

He'd spoken to Kane? Maude's mouth rounded into a small oh.

Jackson's shoulders were stiff, and he seemed intent on avoiding her scrutiny. He maneuvered the team around a washed away part of the road.

He'd spoken to Kane!

Her eyes rounded. Her heart hammered. She clutched for the iron arm of the wagon bench. Jackson Nolan was about to ask her to become his wife!

Her thoughts flashed to Kin Davis. She was ashamed to admit that she'd been rather more excited than she ought to have that handsome man back in town. Two years ago, she'd been naught more than a girl and he hadn't seemed to notice her. But he'd been right gentlemanly the other day when he'd stopped by the house and Kane had invited him in. She'd even caught him looking toward the kitchen a time or two. And he'd spoken to her like a friend.

Jackson was . . . well . . . Jackson. He was hardworking. Plain spoken. A man who could be depended upon to stick to his routine—other than his showing up to take her on a picnic today! And sure, she'd just been sending him signals that she'd like to get to know him better. But . . . marriage? Was she really ready for that?

Surely if she loved him like that, she wouldn't even be giving a man like Kin Davis second thoughts, would she?

Surreptitiously, she eyed Jackson. He was handsome, sure. And dependable. But . . . Did she want to spend the rest of her life with him?

Why, in the past two years she hadn't known him to vary his routine even in the slightest. He'd gone to work for Mr. Ecklund only a few weeks after the mill had opened, and since that time, Maude had been able to set her clock by his routine.

He always stopped by the house right after his shift on Fridays. Only Fridays. They even waited dinner for him on that day of the week now. After the meal, he and Kane would have a game of checkers. Then Kane would make some excuse about needing to see to whatever horse he was training. Seth would settle on the settee with a book. That left Jax at the dining table with her for ten minutes—their conversation never lasted longer. Jackson was always a gentleman. He asked after her week. Listened quietly as she told him—again—about her mundane chores.

One time she had asked about his work at the mill to which he responded, "Oh you know, same as usual."

She had waited an interminably long amount of time for him to give more detail, but he never had. She had wanted to rail that she had no idea what the "usual" was because he'd never told her! Instead, she'd cut him another slice of pie. She sometimes wondered if he only came around because it gave him a chance to escape his bachelor father's cooking one day of the week. Silently, he'd eaten the pie and finished his second cup of coffee, and then he'd stood a moment later to bid her goodnight, as he always did.

The next time in the week that she would see him would be at the church services, when he would give her a nod from his place with his family on the back row as she passed to sit with Kane and Seth across the aisle. After church, he would approach to offer a polite greeting and benign conversation about the weather. He and Kane might get into a discussion about a horse, or a gun, or a new type of wagon-bench spring that someone had added. After a few minutes, he would tip his hat and bid them farewell.

And then she wouldn't see him again until his regular Friday visit.

Despite the fact that he'd been coming around for nigh on two years now, she didn't feel like she really knew anything more about Jackson than she had the first time he'd stopped by.

And now he planned to ask for her hand?

A wave of irritation rose inside her. Her teeth locked together. Her jaw ached. "Stop the wagon!" Her command was so loud, she gave herself a start.

Jax yanked the reins on pure instinct, she felt sure. The horse, unused to such a quick change of pace, bobbed its head and peered at her over its shoulder.

Jackson blinked at her. "What in tarnation, Maude?"

She soothed her hands along her skirt, willing herself to composure. But after only a moment, she realized that she didn't care that her actions seemed out of sorts. She *felt* out of sorts. "What's my favorite hymn, Jackson Nolan?"

He frowned at her.

"My favorite flower? My favorite color?" She threw a gesture to the air. "My favorite *food* even?"

Perplexity had him fiddling with the wagon's brake handle. "How should I know?"

Maude huffed her irritation. "You're supposed to care enough about me to *ask*. Are you really planning to request my hand with as little as we know about each other?"

He blinked at her. "You know? How?"

"I'll tell you how!" She rubbed her palm at the heat building beneath her temple, taking a breath to ease the pounding of her pulse. Her next words were spoken with quiet defeat. "I know, Jax, because you haven't broken routine once since you've started coming to call. If I didn't know better, I'd say you were more excited about seeing Kane and playing checkers each Friday evening than you were about seeing me. And now— Now, you show up in the middle of the day, claiming you've spoken to Kane and you want to take me on a picnic in my favorite spot. But you didn't know that was my favorite spot until he told you, did you?"

She felt her guilt rise when he hung his head like a whipped puppy. "I guess I didn't."

She ought to relent, but couldn't find the charity to do so. She folded her arms and glowered at him. "Do you even know when my birthday is?"

He angled her a look filled with bafflement. "I need to know that?"

Her fists clenched into the material of her blouse. "Take me back to town this instant, Jackson Nolan." Unmoving, he focused on the branches of a large pine tree overhead.

Maude maintained her stiff pose.

Birdsong filled the air, the creek chattered happily, a soft breeze teased the branches. Their argument had meant nothing to nature at large. It would go on.

And she simply would not cry over a man who cared for her so little!

Jackson remained still for the longest of moments, and she thought he might not do her bidding. But finally, he clucked to the horse and managed to turn the wagon in the middle of the roadbed.

It was only a short way back to the church, but the silence stretched as long as the Cascade Mountain Range in the distance.

When he helped her down from the seat, quietly returned to the driver's bench, and drove away, she dashed up the church steps and flopped onto the back pew.

Despite her resolve, she gave in to the flood of tears that begged for release.

The San Francisco train station made Kin long for Wyldhaven. Even the Seattle station hadn't been this crowded or cacophonous. He set Ike directly in front of him and told him to walk. Kin thrust his satchel forward to one side of the boy. He was so close on the kid's heels, that he had to walk like a duck to keep from treading on him, but in this crowd, Ike needed the protection of the case to give him space to move. It might have been easier with Ike behind him, because his strength could have pushed through the crowd, but he hadn't wanted to risk losing the kid in this melee.

"Excuse us, please." He bent and pointed past Ike's ear. "That door over there. Head that way."

When they finally burst from the hot station onto the even hotter street, Kin drew in a big lungful of air. At least out here, there was room to maneuver a little. He instructed Isaiah to pause, then set their cases on the walk and shrugged out of his coat. "You can take yours off too." Isaiah did.

Kin folded both jackets over his arm and hefted their cases again. He consulted the address he'd jotted on a scrap of paper. "Right. We're looking for Ashbury Street."

Ike pointed. "There's a cab."

Kin hailed the driver and handed over the address. The man gave a nod and helped them inside.

When they arrived at the law office, Kin gave the cabby a coin and asked him to wait for them. They were going to need a nearby hotel.

"Oh, yes sir," the man assured. "I'll git you fixed up right good, I will. Know just the place."

Even so, Kin didn't feel comfortable leaving all their luggage in the cab. He handed Isaiah his small bag, once more folding their coats over his arm and hefting his satchel.

"We might be a while."

The man waved away his concern. "I'll just park in the shade of this here tree and read the paper. Take your time."

Isaiah stood on the walk. His eyes were a bit wide as he looked up at the tall brick building with white marble columns lining the front steps. Crowds of people milled past them, coming and going. "I been here before."

Kin was relieved to hear it. That meant they were in the right place. "Excellent. Come on, kid. I wired ahead from the last stop requesting a meeting with the solicitor. We've got . . ." He consulted his watch. "Fifteen minutes."

Ahead of them, a broad man with a limp used a cane. He wore a black Stetson and his amble was slow and methodical. With people crowding the walk on either side, Kin wasn't able to pass him. A little impatient with the delay, Kin wondered what had happened to the man. He seemed muscular and strong, other than his right leg, which didn't seem to be working correctly below his knee.

A group of people left the walk to cross the street, giving Kin the opening he wanted. He nudged Isaiah into the space. "Excuse us, please, sir." As they passed, he turned to doff his hat at the man and nearly dropped everything he was carrying.

Chapter Twenty-one

Washington Nolan could hardly believe his eyes. How in the world had he fled all the way to San Francisco only to bump into his closest childhood friend on a busy sidewalk?

He huffed amused, bitter annoyance. God just seemed to have it in for him lately, didn't He? His gaze drifted to the smokey blue of the brazen sky.

"Sea air will be good for you," the cavalry doctor had said.

For the past several weeks, Wash had been wondering if any of that sea air was making it past the smoke and steam of the factories.

"Wash? That you?"

Wash held his silence. Behind his long scruffy beard, he imagined that it likely was difficult for Kin to recognize him. There was also the jagged scar through his eyebrow from his fall.

The last thing he wanted was for word of his injury to get back home. Better for all his friends and family to remember him as the man he'd been back before traitorous honor and prideful glory had lured him into the cavalry.

But this was Kin; he couldn't just ignore him.

Or could he?

He could see Kin assessing him from the scar on this face down to the boot that hung at the base of his crippled leg.

He lowered his gaze to the walk, not wanting to see the sympathy in his friend's eyes. He stabbed the tip of his cane against a leaf. "'Fraid you've got the wrong man." And he did have the wrong man. Wash would never be the same man Kin had known. "Good day to you."

He made to brush past them, but blast if Kin didn't step in his way. "Wash, wait."

He almost toppled on account of having to stop so fast. He had to hop on his good leg a few times to catch his balance.

"I'm so sorry." Kin reached to steady him.

He yanked his arm free and glowered. He didn't need anyone feeling sorry for him. That was exactly why he hadn't written or gone home.

Kin retreated a step and raised his free hand. "Sorry." His other hand clutched a satchel that Wash recognized as the one someone in the town had given to him that last Christmas before he left for Seattle. Had it been the Rodantes? No. The Griffins, he thought.

The pocket watch Kin checked indicated he was in a hurry to get somewhere. Wash dropped his gaze to the quiet boy by Kin's side. He had both brown hands wrapped around the handle of a small case. A handsome kid with gray eyes and almost black curls that tousled in the wind.

He felt his curiosity rise. Was the boy Kin's? No. He was too old. Wash would have known about him before he left town, if he was.

Kin's feet shuffled. His gaze flicked to the cane and then back to Wash's eyes. He settled a hand on the boy's shoulder. "This here is Isaiah. Isaiah, meet my best friend, Washington Nolan."

"Pleased to meet you, suh." Isaiah held out a hand.

Wash eyed it but didn't reach for it. What had come over him? He'd never in his life refused to shake someone's hand when they offered it. He just couldn't seem to summon the energy to transfer his cane to his other hand and reach out. If his nurse hadn't hounded him out of the apartment, he wouldn't even be walking along this blasted street. He'd still be at home with his blankets pulled over his head like he'd wanted.

He huffed a breath and glanced down the hill toward the Pacific. He was tired all the time, these days. Plain tired.

With a glance at Kin, the boy slowly withdrew. The kid looked down at the back of his hand, rubbed it against his trousers, and then returned it to grip his suitcase handle. His gaze remained lowered.

Wash's guilt mounted. The kid thought he hadn't wanted to shake his hand because of the color of his skin. He grabbed the handle of his cane with his left hand, made sure he had good balance, and thrust out his right. "Sorry, Isaiah. I'm just a little slow these days."

The lad shook his hand. Met his gaze once more. He smiled, but a question still lingered in his gray eyes.

Wash gave his hand a squeeze. "What are you doing in San Francisco with this miscreant?" He tipped his head to indicate Kin.

Isaiah's smile was like a beam of sunshine. Good to see that the lad had a sense of humor. But instead of answering, he only lifted his eyes to Kin.

Some of the tension seemed to have eased from Kin's shoulders. "We have an appointment, but . . . I'm really happy to have bumped into you like this. I mean—what are the chances? The good Lord must have wanted us both in this spot at this exact moment, wouldn't you say?"

Wash turned his focus on Kin. He seemed serious. The irony nudged up one side of Wash's mustache with wry humor. He returned his gaze to the horizon. Kin spouting religious platitudes? Wasn't that a role reversal. He'd always been the one trying to encourage Kin to have faith. And now . . .

Well . . . He wasn't sure what to believe. He certainly still believed there was a God. Still believed that he needed Jesus as his Savior. But somehow, he felt betrayed by the Almighty. He'd always done his best to live by the rules in the Good Book. To be kind to people. Love God. Serve heartily. And look where that had gotten him.

There simply was a heaviness about all of life right now. Like a cloak had been thrown over the sun and large sacks of rocks tied about his neck.

"If it's not too much trouble, could you wait in our carriage until I'm done with this appointment? I really would love to catch up."

Of course, Kin hoped to spend some time with him. They'd been fast friends. But Wash's capacity to be friendly had long passed.

He didn't even like his own company. He certainly didn't think that Kin would like it. However, there would be no escape if he outright denied Kin's request, so he forced a smile. "Sure. That carriage right there?" He jabbed his cane toward the cabby beneath the shade of the large oak just a few paces behind them.

Kin dipped his chin. "That's the one. We won't be but thirty minutes or so." He gently patted a hand against Wash's back. He could tell that his friend wanted to hug him, but was afraid of knocking him over. What kind of an encumbrance had he become when people were even afraid to hug him for fear of breaking him?

He gimped toward the carriage, and paused by the door. He waited until Kin and the boy disappeared into the nearby building, and then he hurried out of sight. In a town this size, Kin would have to search long and hard to find him. Hopefully, his commitments wouldn't allow him to do that.

After his injury, he'd begged his commander not to send word to his father about his accident on the pretense that he wanted to be able to tell Pa in person.

Now, his only regret was that news of his disability would reach those back home.

Thirty minutes later, Kin breathed a sigh of relief as he and Isaiah left the solicitor's office and returned down the hall toward the stairs. Getting the deed updated to Ike's name had been quite simple because the lawyer had been sympathetic toward Ike's plight and because he'd remembered him being in his offices with his father only a few months ago. He'd accepted Ike's story about his father's death at face value. And agreed that the handwritten will signed by Mr. Coleman was evidence enough that he'd intended for his son to have the house upon his death.

Now, all that remained was to take the documentation to the tenants and instruct them to send their rent money via Western Union to Isaiah in Wyldhaven. From them, he could find out just where they'd been sending the money up to this point.

He was relieved to have the technicalities of helping Isaiah coming together so easily. And was still shaking his head about bumping into Washington outside.

He remembered some verses he'd read in Reagan's Bible from the Proverbs just the other day. *A man's heart deviseth his way, but the Lord directeth his steps.*

He'd resisted the idea of the Lord directing his steps for so long, but he couldn't deny the Lord's orchestration that had started all the way back when Wash had been so kind to him as a boy. Then in Seattle after one bad day at work, he'd made a poor choice to get drunk and Isaiah had found him on the docks. Would God have used someone else to help the kid if he hadn't gotten drunk that evening? Kin had to figure God had used his own stupidity to bring about the encounter, otherwise he wouldn't have ended up here to bump into Wash. Kin couldn't quite wrap his head around that one. But there was no denying that his meeting with the boy in Seattle had led him to this place and time, and there had been Wash on the sidewalk.

He felt another wave of wonder as he pushed open the outer door for Isaiah. What course had brought Wash to this place? He obviously had been injured. In the cavalry? Kin couldn't help but speculate on his friend's attitude.

Wash had always been the most giving, helpful person he knew. He'd been warm. Thoughtful.

The man they'd met on the street had seemed . . . different. In fact, he'd seemed downright put out to have bumped into an old friend. So it was with a great deal of sadness, if not a whole lot of surprise, that Kin opened the cab's door, to find the interior empty. He scanned the street. His friend wasn't in sight.

"Did a man with a cane come by?" he asked the cabby.

The man folded his paper and tucked it beneath his leg. "He came by, paused for a moment, then hurried off like the devil had lit a fire under his tail. Turned that corner just there, and that was the last I saw of him."

Kin sighed.

"Why did he go?" Isaiah asked.

A helplessness washed over him. "I don't know."

Ike frowned. "You think he didn't like me on account of . . . you know." He held out one arm for Kin to look at his skin color. "Like them other folk back in Wyldhaven?"

Kin rested a hand on the boy's shoulder, wishing he could take that unchangeable burden from the kid. "Nah. He's not like that. I think he's just going through a hard time. Last time I saw him, he didn't have that cane."

"Oh." A soft light of understanding softened the boy's eyes. He scanned the street. "Didn't seem like he could have walked too far. We should look for him."

Kin's heart warmed three times over toward the boy. "I think we should give him the night to get used to the idea that we're here. Let's get a room. In the morning we'll go talk to your tenants. Then we can come back here in the afternoon, maybe."

Isaiah lifted one shoulder. "Okay."

Helping the boy into the cab, Kin scanned the street again. Wash was still nowhere to be seen.

With a burden weighing down his heart, he climbed up and sank onto the bench. He realized with growing concern how much it had shaken him to see Wash in the state he was in.

Broken. Bitter. Angry. All that was so much unlike him.

One thing was certain.

Kin wasn't leaving town without taking his childhood friend home with him.

No matter what it took.

Lord, change his heart.

The prayer surprised him. And it was in that moment, Kin realized that despite all his resistance, the chasing love of Jesus which PC had preached about for so many years must have finally caught up with him.

In the place where he used to doubt God's existence, he found only faith. In the place where he used to carry cynicism, he found only compassion.

He tipped his head against the back of the cab and closed his eyes. *Lord, I'm a worthless sinner, so undeserving of Your love, but I've tried it my way for too many years. I'm tired of devising my own way. Please direct my steps from here on out.*

A flood of peace filled his soul, bringing tears to his eyes. He dashed at them with his thumb. So this was what it felt like to turn his life over to God in unmitigated surrender? He'd been a fool to resist for so long.

From across the cab, Isaiah reached over to pat his knee. "Don't worry, Mr. Kin. I prayed for God to take care of me, and He sent you. And I'm gonna pray for God to take care of your friend too. Maybe God sent you here to help him, just like you helped me."

Kin smiled at the boy through his blurry vision. "I think you're right. Thanks, Isaiah."

"He's the one Miss Zoe is waiting for?" The boy's tone indicated disbelief.

Kin blew out a breath, feeling the weight of having to tell Zoe what he'd seen if they couldn't find Wash again. "Yeah."

"You okay?" The boy tilted his head with the question.

Despite losing track of Wash, joy flooded to the surface. "Yeah, kid. I'm going to be just fine."

More than fine, actually. Better. Better than he'd ever been.

He leaned to glance up at the sky. Was it bluer than it had been a few moments ago? Or was it only the lightness he felt in his heart making it seem that way?

Isaiah stood on the sidewalk, facing his old house. He'd thought that he might hate being here because it would only remind him of all he'd lost. Instead, he found himself smiling.

"See that orange tree?" He nudged Mr. Kin and pointed. "Pa said my ma was so excited when she got that to grow from the seed of an orange she'd bought at the market." He smiled at the memory of the way Pa's eyes had lit up with humor as he told how Ma had planted the seed in a chipped teacup without much hope for it to thrive. And now the tree was huge and blooming with the promise of a full harvest.

He took in the walk that he'd helped Pa lay, brick by brick. And the white porch swing with the bright red pillows where Pa used to rock with him after dinner while he told him stories.

He appreciated how Mr. Kin seemed content to let him take his sweet time.

Finally, he tugged down the hem of his coat and gave his friend a nod. "Okay, I'm ready."

Mr. Kin rested a hand on his shoulder, and together they moved up the walk. The door chimes were loud inside the house, bringing with them a nostalgic memory of playing tricks on Pa by ringing them and then hiding around the corner.

A maid in a black dress with a white apron answered the door. She glanced between them, then focused on Mr. Kin. "How may I help you?" Her lips were pinched into a tight line. Maybe she was frustrated to have her day interrupted.

Isaiah expected Mr. Kin to do the talking, but instead he nudged Isaiah to the fore and directed the maid's attention to him. "I'm just the lawyer. He's the one you want to speak to."

Isaiah swallowed. What was he supposed to say? Mr. Kin's hands on his shoulders were warm and supportive. He gulped a breath and blurted, "We here to see my tenants, if you please." He wished his voice hadn't warbled so much. But there was nothing he could do about it now.

The maid's brow quirked, and humor lit her dark eyes. "Your tenants?"

"Yes'm. I own this house now you see, on account of that my pa, well, he . . ." His voice broke. He coughed. Mr. Kin's thumbs massaged his shoulders gently. "He passed a few weeks back."

The woman's features immediately softened. She exchanged another look with Mr. Kin and then stepped aside to let them in.

Ike braced himself for more waves of sorrow, but when he followed her through the door, he was actually relieved to see that the tenants had changed things quite a bit. They'd repainted the entry. Instead of the bright blue that Pa had liked so much, it was now a boring white. Even the colorful carpets were all replaced with ones that were a muted gray.

Somehow it didn't bother him. He knew that he would forever have the memories that mattered tucked away in his heart.

The maid saw them to the parlor, a great big room with massive windows that overlooked the beach and the Pacific beyond. Isaiah strode to the nearest window and took in the view, hands clasped behind his back. The ocean had always made him feel small and wondrous. One time, Pa had mentioned how immense God must be if He'd brought the oceans into being with one command.

The view still stirred him.

But, marveling, he also remembered the feeling of joy he'd experienced back in Wyldhaven as he'd watched the leaves of the big oak spinning above him while he'd let the swing unwind. The light playing off the spring-green leaves. The feel of air swirling all around him.

He smiled.

The same God who'd made the vast ocean, had also made the expansive forests. There were other awe-inspiring views. This one, he would cherish. But if he allowed himself, there would be other memories to cherish in other places too. And one day, if he moved on from Wyldhaven, he could go back there and find fond memories of that place as well.

He closed his eyes. *Lord, thank You for taking care of Your Ike. Please tell my ma and my pa that I'm gonna be all right 'cause You done brought some good folks along to help me.*

With that, he turned his back to the windows.

The matron of the house bustled into the parlor.

He had to look way up to see her face. She had wispy gray curls and eyes that looked like they used to be blue, but at some point, someone had scrubbed most of the color out of them.

Beneath her missing chin, several flaps of skin jiggled. She was so big around that her head and hands looked too small.

She took one glance at Ike and then hurried forward to smother him with a hug. "Oh, you poor child. I'm so sorry to hear about your daddy."

Ike fought for air beneath her plump arms. He pushed back from her, straightening his rumpled clothes. "Thank you, ma'am."

Mr. Kin was grinning in a way that made Ike want to stomp his toes.

"Please, sit." The lady—he couldn't remember her name—motioned him and Mr. Kin toward the settee. "Are you here to tell me that you plan to sell the house?"

Ike shook his head. "No, ma'am. Only to ask that you send the rent money to me in Washington."

Mr. Kin thrust a paper toward her. "This is the Western Union information."

She took the page, but let it dangle limply from her fingers. "Land almighty, child. How old are you? You aren't living on your own in the wilds of Washington, are you? Why! I hear there are still *natives* running around those mountains!"

Ike bit back a grin. "I'm ten and a half, ma'am."

From the corner of his eye, he saw Mr. Kin dart him a look of surprise. He knew that everyone must have thought him younger. Pa had always told him he was small for his age, but that one day his growth would catch up with him.

Ike pressed forward. "And the good Lord give—gave me—good people to take care of me, thank you kindly. I ain't seen one wild native yet, besides Mr. Kin here."

The woman gave Mr. Kin a wide-eyed scrutinization. Her voice was low with awe when she asked, "You're a native?"

Mr. Kin tried to turn a bark of laughter into a cough. "No, ma'am. Leastwise, not in the way that you mean. Before we go,

I wonder if you might tell me where you've been sending the rent money until now?"

"Why to San Francisco First Bank over on Pacific Avenue."

Mr. Kin shook the lady's hand. "Thank you. That's very helpful. You'll have no trouble sending the money to the new place?"

She shook his hand as she skimmed the instructions on the paper Mr. Kin had given her. "It all seems pretty straightforward, young man. Yes. I think it will be fine."

"Very good. Then all the best to you, ma'am. We'll see ourselves out."

Ike rose. There was no more they needed to do here and he suddenly felt a great push to get going. They still had to go to the bank and then they needed to find Mr. Kin's friend. Somehow, he felt an urgency to find him quickly.

He held a hand out to the woman. "Thank you, ma'am."

Ike would have liked to see upstairs. His old room. Maybe Pa's. But they were also likely changed and he decided that keeping the memory of them unmarred was probably better anyhow.

As he and Mr. Kin headed back down the walk toward the carriage, Ike gave a sigh of relief to have this part of their task complete.

He tapped Mr. Kin with the back of his hand. "We need to hurry at the bank so we can find your friend."

Mr. Kin frowned at him. "What is it?"

Ike shook his head. "Just a feeling in my insides that something's not right."

Chapter Twenty-two

Over since Ike's comment earlier, Kin had felt a little jittery inside. He knew PC would have told him to pray. The problem was, he wasn't sure what it was he should be praying about. So while they waited at the bank, he sent up a general prayer for God to watch over Wash and help him not to be stubborn about coming home.

Whatever was going on with him, this was a time in his life that he needed to be near family, not cordoned off on his own in an entirely different state.

A few moments later, the banker returned to say that everything was in order and Isaiah's money was on the way to the bank in Wyldhaven. Kin was thankful that the process had gone smoothly. The banker assured him that he had wired Isaiah's funds directly to Mr. Olann with instructions to put it in Isaiah's name. Kin was in a little awe over the amount. The kid likely had no understanding of just how much money he had. Kin couldn't wait to see the look on Mr. and Mrs. Olann's faces when they found out that detail. After filling out the required paperwork to close out the California account, he and Ike were free to go.

Now they stood in the same spot in front of the solicitor's office where they had encountered Wash the day before.

Ike looked up and down the street. "He was walking that way yesterday. You think he was heading home? Or just stepping out?"

Kin remembered the cabby saying Wash had stopped by the carriage and then hurried off. As he'd said that, he'd pointed up the hill—the opposite direction that Wash had been moving when they'd encountered him. "I think he'd likely just left his place. The cabby pointed this way when he said he left."

"That's right!" Ike exclaimed. "Said he turned that corner."

"As good a place to start as any."

They knocked on doors for the remainder of the morning, giving a description of Wash and asking if he lived there.

Tenement after tenement proved a disappointment.

"Sorry, no one of that description lives here."

"No idea who you're talkin' 'bout." *Slam!*

The same scenario was repeated down the length of the street and up the other side.

Isaiah looked to him for guidance, but a crimp of worry pinched his brow.

"Guess we start on the next block," Kin said, trying to curb his own concern.

This time, he had Ike work one side of the street while he worked the other. He was starting to feel deeply discouraged when they'd made it through ninety percent of that block and still didn't have any idea where Wash might be.

"Mr. Kin!" Isaiah called.

When Kin glanced over, the boy was waving his arm.

Kin dashed between two carriages and leapt up the stairs to the porch of the tenement Isaiah stood at.

An older woman with a scarf tied around her head looked him up and down. "Was your friend in the cavalry?"

Kin's heart skipped an anticipatory beat. "Yes, ma'am. Sure was!"

She nodded and pointed around the corner. "Halfway up Crescent is a house used for convalescing cavalrymen. Number seven. Maybe he's there."

Kin thanked her and he and Ike practically ran up Crescent Street to number seven.

Each window in the tall, red-brick building was framed in black, and a huge black door towered above the brick stairs leading up to it.

The woman who answered this door wore a white cap with a red cross on it. A clean, crisp apron covered her light blue dress.

At Kin's description of Wash, her eyes lit with recognition. "I'm so glad someone has finally come to visit him. I couldn't even get him out of the house today. He's in quite a state. Please, follow me."

Kin swept his hat off, relief whooshing out on a huge puff of air.

She led them up two flights of stairs and along a dim hallway to a door about three-quarters of the way down. She gave a brisk knock. "Sergeant Nolan? I'm entering in ten seconds whether you like it or not, so please make yourself presentable."

No sound came from inside the room.

After a brief pause, the nurse levered the handle and thrust open the door. She swept a gesture for them to feel free to enter. "The doctor has been concerned about his state of mind, so you'll find the room rather sparse. I apologize, but it's for his own safety."

They were afraid he might harm himself? Kin's teeth clenched. This malaise was so unlike him!

He worked the crown of his hat as he stepped through the entrance. The room was a small box, painted a flat gray, with a dormer window at one end. The window had metal bars across it. The only items in the room was a thin mattress directly on the floor, and one drab gray blanket.

Wash lay with his back to them and the blanket up to his shoulders, despite the suffocating heat.

Kin strode over and cranked the handle on the casement. A waft of fresh air drifted in, and even though it was warm, it felt like an arctic blast compared to the temperature in the room.

Wash didn't even turn to see who had entered the room. Was he asleep?

The nurse remained in the doorway, lips pursed grimly.

Kin motioned with his hat. "How long has he been lying there like that?"

"Ever since he came home yesterday, except for one trip to use the necessary down the hall."

Taking in the dreary room again, Kin couldn't help but feel there was good reason for Wash's doldrums.

"Does he have to stay here? Or can we take him home?"

"Nothing is keeping him here. He's paid up through the end of the month. The money comes from a benefactor of some sort."

Wash grunted from his place on the mattress, the first indication that he was awake and listening.

Kin's resolve to take his friend home only intensified.

"So if you remove him to another location," the nurse continued, "the benefactor needs to be informed." She retreated then, her heels clicking smartly against the floor.

Kin exchanged a look with Isaiah.

The boy made a talking motion with his hand and then pointed to Wash.

Kin cleared his throat. "Wash, Ike, and I have concluded our business in town. Come on home with us. We'll take you to our hotel tonight and be on the train first thing."

"Not going home," Wash grumbled. Other than that, he didn't move.

"You seeing some fascinating piece of art on that gray wall in front of your face?" Kin tried for levity.

No response.

"Your pa, Jax, Linc, and Grant—they've all been missing you. And worried something fierce since your letters stopped."

Silence.

"You just going to ignore me all day?"

"Working on it," came the reply.

That got Kin's hackles up. He marched over and yanked the blanket off his friend, chucking it to the end of the mattress.

Wash was dressed in nothing more than gray long johns, which were soaked through with sweat. Kin saw then, too, that Wash's hair was limp with moisture.

The man was so morose that he'd been lying there boiling to death!

He bent and touched his friend's shoulder. "Come on, Wash, just come home—"

Wash flipped over so fast that Kin didn't have time to react. In one blink, he had a revolver in his face.

Kin put his hands up, eyeing the gun. He could see brass in every visible chamber. Fully loaded.

Something told Kin that Wash was not supposed to have a weapon in his current state of mind. A cold wash of horror swept through him. Had his best friend—the one who'd always been so strong and caring and capable—had he been lying there trying to get up the nerve to shoot himself?

Wash scrambled to stand on his one good leg. His eyes glittered above the barrel. Sweat dotted his forehead and his hand trembled against the grip.

Kin swallowed. "Ike? Step into the hall please."

"Yessuh."

Relieved that the kid immediately did as he'd been told, Kin moved to keep himself between Wash and the boy.

A pained look crossed Wash's face. "I'd never hurt a kid, Kin."

"You might have thought of that before you pulled a gun on one."

"I didn't—never mind."

Wash's gun didn't waiver.

Kin could hear Ike's footsteps running down the hall. Help would soon be on the way.

Wash's jaw was clenched so tight that his next words were barely understandable. "Why'd you have to come here?"

"Here to the city? Or here to this room?" Kin knew which he'd meant, he was simply trying to get him talking.

Wash only glared.

"Maybe you meant both. So, as I told you yesterday, I had business on the boy's behalf. His pa died. It was an estate issue, but it's all cleared up now." As he spoke, Kin kept his hands in the air. "As for here, to your room, well that took some doing. Gotta tell you, we asked at a lot of places before we finally found you."

He hoped Wash would see the care that had gone into searching for him. Hurting people could rarely comprehend how they were splashing their hurt onto others. Though Kin had been more than a little saddened to have Wash abandon him yesterday, he didn't figure his friend was in any frame of mind to hear how distressing his actions had been.

What frame of mind he *was* in remained to be seen. "You really going to shoot me with that thing, Wash?"

Defeated, Wash lowered the weapon.

Footsteps clattered along the hallway.

Kin quickly reached to take the revolver.

As a man in a long white coat rushed in, followed closely by the nurse and Ike, Kin held the gun up between two fingers. "It's all right. It's all right. Everyone just take a breath. We're all fine and no one is in danger."

The doctor pressed his lips into a grim line and strode to Wash's side, extracting a brown bottle from the pocket of his coat. "Here, drink this."

Wash grimaced and turned his head away.

"What is that?" Kin stepped closer, tucking the gun into the back of his belt.

The doctor scowled at him. "It's a concoction of poppy, laudanum, and whiskey. Very effective at calming a distressed mind." The doctor once more reached toward Wash's mouth with the bottle.

Kin snatched it from the doctor's hand. "He doesn't need that."

"Well! I never!" The doctor stepped back, jaw gaping in surprise.

"Trust me." Kin thrust the medicine back at the startled man. "What he needs is to come home to his family where he belongs. Now I'll ask that you give us a minute." He pointed for them to leave the way they'd just entered.

Still sputtering, the doctor stormed from the room. The nurse looked uncertain and hesitated near the door, but finally followed in his wake. Isaiah lingered outside in the hallway.

Wash looked defeated. "I'm not coming home, Kin. Just leave me be."

Kin plunked his hands on his hips. "Can't do that. Not after all the times you've helped me in the past."

"I don't need your help."

Kin gestured to the room. "Oh yeah, it looks like you're doing real well for yourself here, Wash."

That earned him another glare.

"Come home," Kin pressed. "Come heal at home."

A flash of anger stiffened Wash's shoulders. He leaned forward. "Heal? There is no more healing, Kin." He swept a gesture to his leg. "This sorry excuse for a leg is what I'm stuck with for the rest of my life!"

"So we'll figure it out. But this is the time to be around family, not running from them!"

Wash huffed a breath and sank onto his mattress, curling his hands around his head. "I can't run anywhere. Just go, and leave me be."

Kin was at a loss for what to do. He exchanged a look with Ike, who peered past the doorjamb. The boy shrugged one shoulder.

Kin sank onto the mattress beside his friend. "Does it hurt?"

Wash looked over at him, one brow lifted.

"Your leg."

"No! I thought you meant my arm!"

Kin hung his head, realizing Wash's look had not been meant as a question but instead had been meant to silence him. "Sorry I asked. You don't have to talk about it, if you don't want to."

To his surprise, that seemed to loosen Wash's tongue. "When I stand on it for too long, move too fast, twist at the wrong angle, breathe. Other than that, I'm just fine."

Kin studied the floor between his feet. Bitterness didn't look so good on anybody, but it seemed magnified on Wash because he'd always been so easygoing. How did he go about helping him when he clearly didn't want to be helped? Maybe just keeping him talking would help.

"How'd it happen?"

A snort revealed Wash's continued irritation. Kin wasn't sure if it was with his questioning, or with the incident that had injured him. After a silence that stretched so long Kin thought he might not answer, Wash finally flopped back on the mattress and scooped both hands into his hair.

"This here was what they call a fratricide incident. Only, lucky me, I'm not dead!" The sarcasm in his tone clearly portrayed his wish to the contrary.

A chill swept down Kin's spine as he once again considered the gun. What might have happened if they'd been a few minutes later?

Wash continued his story. "Son of a forestry tycoon was forced into the cavalry by his pa. Only thing he'd ever been taught to operate was his silver spoon. He'd never shot a gun before. I was walking into the mess tent when he accidentally discharged his weapon. Bullet took me through my calf."

"That must have been terrible."

Wash opened his mouth as if to retort, but then snapped it shut. He turned his head toward the wall.

"Wash." Kin infused every level of coaxing that he could muster into his tone. "Please. Come home with me. Your pa and your brothers, they're sore worried about you."

Wash didn't move, didn't respond, didn't even have the decency to look concerned.

"Jackson, he's working himself to the bone at the mill. And Lincoln is even taking on extra odd jobs outside of school hours, like driving customers from the train station into town."

Wash snorted. "And I suppose Grant is still whining up a storm about having to attend school."

Kin grinned, pleased with the first hint that his old friend was still somewhere inside the shell of a man that looked like him. "I can't say that I had a chance to see Grant before I left town, but I'm sure, knowing him, that you're probably right."

Washed stretched across his mattress and reached between it and the wall. He tugged out a brown leather poke and tossed it in Kin's lap. It landed heavily with a metallic clatter.

Kin hefted it. Tested the heavy weight in his hand. He looked over at Wash.

Washed shrugged. "That kid that shot me? I mentioned his daddy was a lumber tycoon. Well, he's been paying for me to stay here and then some. I've been saving whatever I haven't used." He rolled onto his side and curled his arm around the small pillow, punching it into a more comfortable position. "Just take that to my pa, Kin. And I'll thank you kindly to tell them that I'm doing just fine. And leave out the part about me being a cripple."

"He'll know that's a lie. You haven't written in weeks."

"I'll get around to it this week, honest."

Kin despaired of convincing his friend to come home with him. His gaze once again landed on Isaiah, who remained by the door. The kid shrugged a shoulder and mouthed, "Miss Zoe?" His brows arched and he spread his palms as if to say he had no other ideas.

Of course. Why hadn't he thought of it. Kin scrubbed a hand over his face. He only hoped this last tool in their arsenal would do the job.

Zoe.

He hated to use their childhood friend as a weapon, but Wash wasn't giving him much choice here.

He pushed to his feet. "All right. I'll leave you be, I guess. I sure hate the thought of Zoe thinking she's not as important to you as she thought she was." He settled his hat on his head and stomped toward the door. "She's been worried sick since you quit writing, and isn't eating right. Sure hope she'll perk up when she hears how *fine* you are." Kin grimaced at the sarcasm in his angry tone. He ought to curb his irritation, but Wash was being downright exasperating!

Isaiah perked up, catching on. "Yeah! She sure is skinny, isn't she, that Miss Zoe. I wondered why her dress was all saggy on her. You think it's on account of *him*?"

Since his back was still to Wash, Kin didn't resist a grin. The kid ought to join the theater.

He glanced over his shoulder. Wash still lay on his mattress with his back to the door. "Bye, Wash."

The man lifted one lackadaisical hand, but didn't look.

Teeth grinding, Kin settled a hand on the boy's shoulder and nudged him down the hall. He raised his voice so Wash would be sure to hear his next words. "There's no accounting for love, Ike. But hopefully Zoe will allow herself to move on."

"That miller? He comes around the school right regular, I hear."

Kin grinned again. The kid had raised his voice too. He motioned Ike into the corner of the hallway and put a finger to his lips. He glanced back down the hallway to watch Wash's door.

Now they would wait.

Chapter Twenty-three

Wash's jaw was clenched so tight that it ached as Kin's voice receded down the hallway.

Why hadn't he considered how Zoe would respond if he went silent? All he'd been thinking about was the fact that he didn't want anyone to feel sorry for him. Nor did he want to be a burden to anyone. He hadn't stopped to think what worry might wreak in the lives of those who cared about him.

He lolled onto his back and stared at the ceiling.

Blazes, it was hot in there, and Kin had not only taken his gun, but he'd also prevented the doctor from giving him that blessed mind-numbing medicine.

The details about his family tormented him.

Jackson working all hours. Lincoln taking on odd jobs. Pa never would have allowed that if it weren't absolutely necessary. Had something happened to the livestock? Pa had always worked as a sawyer for Zebulon Heath's logging outfit just to make ends meet as he raised four boys on his own. But he'd never made his sons do more than he felt was good for their maturity. In fact, many a time he'd downright forbidden them to work because he wanted them to concentrate on their schooling. They didn't have a lot of cattle. Just enough to sell to get them through the hard winter months. Something must have changed.

Wash pressed fingers and thumb to his eyes.

He needed to stop thinking about it. There wasn't any more he could do. He'd sent money with Kin, and he would make it a point to send money more often.

But would he? Despite not getting the most recent dose of the doctor's special concoction, his thoughts were still a little fuzzy from this morning's administration. He worried that once the doctor gave him more, all thoughts of helping out back home would flee. When he was on the medicine, every concern seemed a little farther away. No thought could ever quite fully be captured.

He stared at the ceiling. Was this truly to be the remainder of his existence?

What if he leapt up right now and hollered for Kin to wait for him? He could go back home to the people who loved him. Sure, he'd have to contend with the pitying looks in their eyes, but . . .

Zoe's face came to mind, her blue eyes soft and full of humor. Somehow, he knew that she would be the strong one. She might look at him with compassion, but never with the condescension of pity.

The image in his mind transformed. Instead of looking up at him, Zoe stood looking at some other man whose face refused to come into focus. That familiar soft sturdiness filled her eyes. Behind the couple lay the Wyldhaven church aisle, all decked out with wedding bouquets. Parson Clay smiled from the front of the sanctuary, Bible in hand. Aurora played a lively tune on the piano. Townsfolk filled the place, all laughing and congratulatory. Zoe and the interloper started down the aisle, hand in hand.

Wash surged to a sitting position with a violent shake. He cupped his head in the curve of his hands. His heart beat in his throat and his breaths came fast and unsteady.

A stench reached his nostrils.

Tarnation, but he needed a bath! When was the last time he'd even cleaned up? He couldn't remember.

He raised his head.

Was this the life he wanted? Lying on his thin mattress in this blistering room, trying to work up the gumption to end it all?

The empty corners of the room drew his scrutiny.

He didn't even have his rucksack, because the doctor didn't trust him with it. How in the world was he supposed to hurt himself with a rucksack? Strangle himself with the straps?

He snorted at the thought.

If he really wanted to hurt himself, he could do it on one of those blasted walks they made him take. Maybe down at the docks. There were plenty of ways a man could end his life down there.

That wouldn't look so good for the cavalry in the papers.

Cavalryman Injured in Friendly Incident Kills Himself on Pier 82.

Yeah, Uncle Sam wouldn't like that story one bit. A good way to get a little recompense. Yet . . . He'd bought a pistol and brought it back here, instead.

Wash sighed and studied his palms. Truth was, he didn't really want to end his life. He just wanted to end this part of it. The part where he had to face the fact that none of his dreams would ever come true. The part where he needed to come to terms with being a cripple.

The part where he had to go on without Zoe Kastain.

Realization straightened his spine. That was it. The main pain that had kept him from going home—and kept him from writing.

It was the fact that Zoe could no longer be tied to him. She had to be released to live her life with someone else. Because he wouldn't tie her down to a cripple. That wouldn't be fair.

Somewhere in the back of his mind, he'd hoped that staying away would ensure she moved on. He'd always planned to go back home at some point, but figured that by then she would have happily started a life with someone else.

Wash hadn't considered that she'd pine away with concern for him.

His gut clenched.

What should he do?

Stay here? Take more of the doctor's concoctions and selfishly slide through the rest of life in the gentle blur of a half-comatose euphoria?

Or go back home and face the people who had always loved him? See what kind of help Pa needed with the boys.

He swallowed.

Watch Zoe move on to live her life with some other whole man.

He forked his fingers into his too long hair, feeling the itchiness of the tangled mass. His face felt sweaty beneath the cover of his long beard.

Bumping into Kin on the streets of San Francisco . . . what were the odds of that? He'd lay money on "just about zero."

He glowered at the invisible God on the other side of the ceiling. *You sure are asking a hard thing of me, Lord.*

Silence.

Yeah, that was just about what he should have expected.

Still . . . He had to go back home. To help Pa, yes. But something much more important than that. Before he'd left town, he'd asked Zoe to wait for him. What a young fool he'd been.

The most important reason to go back home was to release Zoe from her commitment to him.

And if that meant that he had to watch her walk down the aisle with another?

He would do it with a smile plastered on his face, even if it killed him. Because she deserved to be happy.

He surged to his one good leg and hopped as fast as he could toward the door. "Kin! Kin wait!"

The days of Kin's absence passed slowly for Cora.

Reagan had informed her that the men from Seattle were sill staying at the boardinghouse. He and his deputies were keeping an eye on them, but so far, they had created no further problems so he had no cause to question them. They ate at Dixie's, played a few rounds of poker at McGinty's, and walked the streets. Other than that, they'd been keeping to themselves.

Reagan assured her that the townsfolk were safeguarding her whereabouts.

"Even Mrs. Hines." His eyes twinkled.

The lady had apparently come to see him in his office to report that the strangers had come into the mercantile asking after Cora. Mrs. Hines had told the men that Cora had been called out of town for a few days.

"She even told them she had no idea where Kin and Isaiah were."

Which was likely true enough, unless one of the workers from the train station had passed information along to her.

Thankful for Mrs. Hines's discretion, surprising though it may be, Cora had to admit that the extended quiet days at the Callahans' had been a blessing. She'd slept long hours and felt more rested than she had for months. She relished the luxury of getting to sleep all the way to six thirty and chuckled with Charlotte about how grumpy she would be when she had to return to her normal schedule with a five o'clock rising time.

She helped Charlotte with the chores where she could, though there weren't many things she could do since Reagan had instructed her that it was best she remain inside so as not to accidentally be seen if the strangers from Seattle decided to take a ride out this way.

The rest of her time she whiled away with reading and crocheting her lace doilies and—she would have to admit, if only to herself—pondering way too many irritating thoughts about one Kin Davis.

What was he doing? Was he safe? How long would it be before he came back home? Why was she even thinking about him when she knew he didn't share her faith?

She'd thought so much about Kin that she felt rather guilty when Reagan came home on his lunch break one day to report that the new doctor had come to see him, worried about her whereabouts.

It seemed that Dr. Polson had first raised his concern with Dixie, who obviously had been informed of Cora's situation and had blithely brushed away the doctor's distress.

Reagan chuckled rather forcefully over the doctor's report that the last person he'd seen Cora with was that "scoundrel" Kin Davis. "He was adamantly insistent that Kin must have absconded with you."

Cora blushed, which only caused Reagan to chuckle all the more.

Now, as he rose from the lunch table, Reagan wanted to know, "So, is it all right to have the doctor over for dinner?"

Cora felt a curl of dread at the prospect. She looked to Charlotte, waiting for her to respond to her husband, but then realized both of them were looking at her. "Oh! You're asking me?"

Reagan and Charlotte both had amusement dancing in their eyes. Reagan tilted his head.

"Why, I— I guess, yes, that would be fine, I think, yes." She lowered her gaze to the sturdy calico tablecloth and traced a finger over the intricate checkered pattern.

"All right then." Reagan lifted his hat from the post on his chair and bent to drop a kiss on his wife's cheek. "We'll see you at dinner." He exited the room, leaving Charlotte grinning at Cora across the table.

Cora wrinkled her nose and quickly set about gathering their plates.

With a chuckle, Charlotte followed her into the kitchen, carrying the cutting board with the remainder of the bread and the breadknife on it. "That poor doctor doesn't realize that he's already lost out to Kin Davis."

Cora plunked dishes into the sink and worked the pump handle with gusto. "We've been over this, if I recall." She gave Charlotte a mock glower over her shoulder.

Charlotte stepped to her side and dusted breadcrumbs into the sink. "Yes. Quite right. I apologize. What do you know about this new doctor?" she asked, as she strode to the stove and lifted the kettle of boiling water.

Cora blew out a frazzled breath. "I know that cherry pie isn't his favorite, but he still likes it enough to eat the whole piece when there is a company of two and only one piece left."

An appropriately outraged gasp escaped Charlotte's throat. "He didn't!"

Cora laughed. "Yes, ma'am. I'm afraid he did." She motioned for Charlotte to pour the kettle of boiling water into that which she'd already pumped into the sink. "I'm afraid the choices of eligible bachelors in Wyldhaven are quite thin, indeed."

"Well!" Charlotte plunked the now empty kettle onto the shelf near the stove. "I can guarantee you that Kin Davis would never act in such a selfish manner!"

No, indeed. Taking up the dishrag and going to work on their plates, Cora let the silence settle while Charlotte cleared the rest of the table.

Rogue heathen that he might be, she could never see Kin Davis treating her with such inconsideration.

It was the morning of the fifth day before Kin felt Wash was dried out enough to travel.

After Wash had come hopping from his room, screaming Kin's name, they'd helped him collect all his things from the cavalry facility—to much protest from the outraged doctor, who claimed Wash would die inside a week if they took him. Kin figured the man must be skimming some of the money Wash was getting from the rich patron who was paying for his care. But when the doctor had been called away to deal with a screaming man down the hall, he had managed to get the nurse to fetch him the patron's address.

After he'd sent a street boy to the address with a request that further money be sent to Wash in Wyldhaven, he'd taken his friend back to their hotel room. Wash hadn't done much but tremble, sweat, and fitfully sleep for the past several days as he dried out from whatever medicine that quack had been forcing down him.

Kin made sure to get a good meal into him at least twice a day. But each time it had been a battle.

His concern mounted over how scarecrow-thin his friend had become. He really needed to get him back home, where Dr. Griffin could examine him, but Wash had been in no condition to travel. Until this morning.

For the first time since they'd arrived, Wash woke with clear eyes. Weariness still weighted his shoulders, but Kin's heart sparked with hope when Wash swept a hand over his face and gritted, "Kin, I need a bath."

Kin surged to his feet and sent word to the front desk for hot water to be brought up. He worked to set up the screen, and laid the clean clothes he'd bought for Wash on a small stand by the tub. He also set scissors and a razor nearby. A small mirror already hung on the wall in that corner of the room.

While Wash bathed, Kin and Isaiah went down to the dining room to get food. Kin ordered a thick beefy stew and slices of cornbread, with apple pie, whipped cream, and plenty of black coffee to go with it. It was a great deal more than the broth he'd been coaxing down Wash's throat for the past several days. He asked for it all to be brought up as soon as it was ready.

As they stepped back into their room, Wash was just emerging from behind the screen, leaning heavily on his cane.

Despite the weary droop to his shoulders, Kin felt a wave of relief. "There's my old friend."

Wash looked a thousand times better than he had just a few minutes ago. His trimmed hair lay in damp strands against his head. And shaving that scraggly beard had taken years off his countenance.

"How are you feeling?"

Wash scooped a hand through his hair as he sank onto the room's settee, with his bad leg stretched out before him. "Weak as a newborn kitten."

"You've no idea how good it is to see you up and about. I've been rightly worried about you all week."

Wash glanced around the room. "How long have we been here?"

"Today's the fifth day. That cavalry doctor had you on a pretty strong . . . concoction." He hesitated to call it medicine. "I figured you could use a few days to clear your head before taking the trip home."

Wash tipped him a nod. "Thank you."

"Sure." He knew his friend wouldn't have wanted his family to see him in the state he'd been in. "Ordered some food. It should be here in just a few minutes."

Wash's stomach loosed a loud grumble. He chuckled. "I guess my stomach is offering its appreciation as well."

Isaiah giggled.

Kin grinned, but when Wash quickly grew serious, he did as well.

"Let's go home, Kin. It's time for me to see my pa and . . . well . . . it's time for me to go home."

There was some unspoken dread in his tone, but Kin let it slide. Of course, he would have some sadness in returning home in his condition, but he'd be fine. It was the best thing for him. He'd see that the town would rally around to support him, and be the happier for it.

Kin was just happy to have his friend headed in the direction of his normal personality.

Chapter Twenty-four

Reagan brought the news with him when he returned for dinner with Dr. Polson. He spoke even before the door was fully closed. Kin had returned home, miraculously bringing his friend Washington Nolan with him.

Cora's pulse surged with a joy that she did her best to tamp down.

Too late, she realized that Dr. Polson had taken the excitement on her face as pleasure to see him. She quickly transferred her attention to Charlotte, who bustled in from the kitchen.

"Oh, Reagan that's wonderful!" Charlotte's eyes glittered with happiness as she set the bowl of salad in the middle of the table. "Please, Doctor Polson, do come in and make yourself at home."

Reagan hooked his hat on a peg in the entry. "It is, but . . ." His brow knitted with concern. He motioned that Dr. Polson could have the peg next to his.

Dr. Polson shrugged out of his overcoat, but didn't move to hang it or his hat.

"Reagan? What is it?" Charlotte asked.

Before Reagan could respond, the doctor blurted, "I spoke to Doctor Griffin, who was immediately called to see this Nolan fellow. It seems that he was injured slightly. I'm hoping to visit him tomorrow and take a look at his leg. There are surgeries now that can sometimes repair things like this."

Cora searched the sheriff's face. "Do you know anything more?"

He shook his head. "First I heard of it was when Doctor Polson here told me."

Dr. Polson wagged his head. "Poor lad. But I'm sure we can have him returned to top shape in no time."

Cora felt surprised. After her last dessert appointment with the doctor, she wouldn't have pegged him as magnanimous.

His next words, however, immediately dispersed any charity of spirit she may have felt toward him.

"It would be wonderful to have a patient to practice such a surgery on, at the least. Could be of great benefit to me in the future."

Cora stared at the man, feeling Charlotte and Reagan doing the same.

His gaze darted between the three of them. "I mean, you know . . . a benefit to my patients." He bumbled to a stop and fiddled with the bowler hat he still held.

Disappointment with the man churned through her. What kind of a person reveled in someone else's misery because it would benefit them? No matter that he'd tried to correct his faux pas with that last remark about a benefit to his patients; it was clear that he was only thinking of himself.

Her heart went out to Washington Nolan. She wondered how he'd come to be injured. Cora had only met the man very briefly the Christmas she'd arrived in town. Then both he and Kin had left— Kin to Seattle, and Wash to join the cavalry a few months later.

She focused on the sheriff. "Surely it can't be too bad if he was able to travel with Mr. Davis?"

"I hope you're right," was all he offered. "I didn't get to see him."

Charlotte motioned toward the pegs in the entry. Her words were clipped when she spoke. "Doctor Polson, if you'll please hang up your things, Reagan can show you where to wash. Dinner is served." With that, she spun on one heel and practically glided back to the kitchen. Evidence of her annoyance was revealed only in the way her heels snapped smartly against the plank floor.

Reagan led the doctor to the washroom, and Cora remained to pace in the dining room as she tried to tame her curiosity over when she might get to see Kin again.

Charlotte and the men returned only moments later, and they all took their seats. The meal commenced with Reagan's prayer for Wash and his family as they adjusted to their new reality.

An awkward silence followed.

The roast venison, new potatoes, and fresh garden salad that Cora and Charlotte had worked so diligently over for several hours, tasted flat and lifeless amidst the doctor's oblivious prattle. He spoke about the patients he'd seen earlier in the day, giving specific details that Cora felt certain Dr. Griffin wouldn't be comfortable with. And then he moved on to speaking of some of the cases he'd worked before coming to Wyldhaven—all of which he had singlehandedly solved to the satisfaction of the patients.

Cora pressed her lips together. *The man is certainly newsworthy in his own broadsheet.*

Charlotte fetched the fresh strawberry pie that was still warm from the oven.

The doctor kept talking, patently unaware that he had dominated the whole meal and was grating on everyone's nerves.

Cora sensed that they were all relieved when Charlotte finally stood and removed the last empty dessert plate.

"Reagan, if you'll take the doctor to the parlor, Cora and I will do the cleaning up."

Cora felt a bit sorry for the sheriff.

He tossed down his serviette and rose with a glum look that decried his being saddled with the task of entertaining the doctor.

Cora couldn't think of any way to come to his rescue. She hefted the bowl of leftover potatoes in one hand and the empty salad bowl in the other. She had almost made it to the kitchen door, when the doctor raised his voice.

"Miss Cora? If you don't mind, would you allow me a moment with you in the parlor? I'm sure the sheriff wouldn't mind helping his wife with the cleanup."

Cora hesitated and glanced back, eyes wide.

Though there was a surprised look on Reagan's face, he hesitated for only the briefest of moments before he rushed toward her and snatched the bowls.

Cora glowered at him, but the sheriff looked unrepentant as he hurried into the kitchen to join his wife.

Dr. Polson grinned and swept a grandiose gesture for her to precede him into the parlor.

Hands clenched tight, Cora took the lead. How had she ever thought the man suitor-potential in the slightest? She determined to end whatever this was before it even got started.

Because there was something she suddenly realized.

Even if Dr. Polson was the last man on earth, she wouldn't want to spend another moment in his presence.

Kin thanked Lincoln Nolan for the ride as they arrived at the Callahans' kitchen door. After dropping Washington off at his pa's place, Kin had felt it best that they avoid the boardinghouse until they were able to talk to the sheriff and determine if the sailors from Seattle were still in town. Lincoln had offered to drive them to the sheriff's place.

Kin hoped the Callahans wouldn't be put out by having him ask if he and Isaiah could stay again, but knowing them, he figured it would be fine.

He settled a hand on Ike's shoulder and together they headed across the hard-packed yard.

At his knock, Mrs. Callahan opened the kitchen door with a towel in her hands. "Kin! Isaiah! I wondered who might be arriving in a wagon at this hour. So happy to have you back. Please come in."

To Kin's surprise, the sheriff stood at the sink with his hands immersed in sudsy water as he washed dishes. The sheriff narrowed his eyes as if to say that news of his current chore had better never reach the folks in town.

Kin couldn't resist a grin as he followed Ike into the kitchen.

"Have you eaten?" Charlotte closed the door behind them, giving Ike a quick hug. "I was just putting the food away."

Ike's stomach loosed a loud growl. He hung his head sheepishly.

Mrs. Callahan chuckled. "I'll take that as a no. Both of you sit yourselves at the kitchen table there and I'll fix you some plates."

Kin rotated his hat through his fingers. "We don't want to be any trouble." He should have thought about getting Ike some food. He could remember what it was like to always be hungry as a growing lad.

"No trouble. None at all." She flapped a hand to dismiss his concern and then ruffled her fingers through Isaiah's curls in a motherly fashion. "Let's get you a plate, young man."

The sheriff placed a plate on the drainboard and then lifted a towel to dry his hands. "Quite something, you bumping into Wash the way you did."

Still in awe himself, Kin bobbed his head. "Had to be the Lord's doing."

The sheriff and Mrs. Callahan paused and exchanged a look.

Kin realized that it wasn't like him to talk that way. It must have taken them by surprise.

He pulled out a chair at the little table in the corner of the kitchen and sank into it, hooking his hat on the post. Ike sat in the only other seat, across from him.

Interesting that it felt so natural to see the Lord's hand in things, when only weeks ago he had resisted that. What had changed his thinking?

Mrs. Callahan placed plates before them. "It's wonderful to hear that Wash is home. But terrible to hear that he was injured. When does he have to head back?"

Kin's focus snapped to her. Confusion swirled. If she knew about his injury, what did her question mean? "Back?"

"You know, to the cavalry." She scooped potatoes onto one side of his plate.

So, she hadn't heard?

Kin searched the sheriff's face to see what he might know.

The man returned his look blankly. "Doctor Polson told us he was *slightly* injured."

The weight of Kin's knowledge felt like a lead blanket. He focused on the salad Mrs. Callahan was adding to his plate. "He won't be going back."

He heard the sheriff straighten. Mrs. Callahan froze with a scoopful of salad hovering above Ike's plate.

"He's been honorably discharged." Kin offered, gently.

"What?" Mrs. Callahan's question was but a breath. She straightened and thunked the salad bowl onto the table. "But Doctor Polson said . . ."

Kin hurried to fill in the details, rubbing a finger at the pain pulsing behind his temple. "He was injured more than slightly. Apparently, they barely saved his lower leg. It's not much use to him." He couldn't bring himself to meet their gazes, not wanting to see the horror in their expressions. "He needs our prayers, if I'm honest, because he's not in a good frame of mind.

Not the same man he was when he left us, if you catch my meaning." He did focus on them then, needing to make sure they'd understood.

The sheriff nodded and moved to squeeze his wife's shoulder. She lifted a hand to cover her husband's.

No one spoke, and Kin gave them time to absorb the news. He and Isaiah ate in silence. When their plates were empty, Kin took them to the sink and started to wash them.

"Here, I can do that." Charlotte rushed toward him.

"Nonsense. If the sheriff can wash dishes, so can I." He smiled at the man. "Hope you two don't mind that we dropped in unannounced? I wasn't sure if we should go to the boardinghouse or not." He lifted a brow, knowing the sheriff would catch his drift.

"Of course we don't mind," the sheriff said. "And it was good that you came. The men from Seattle have been staying mostly to themselves, but they are still at the boardinghouse."

Kin added the last of their dishes to the drainboard and turned to Ike. The kid looked like he could fall asleep on his feet. "I'd like to talk to you about that, but it's been a long day. If you don't mind, I think we'll just mosey to our room. Can we talk in the morning?"

The sheriff opened his mouth to reply, but his wife beat him to it.

She stepped forward. "If you could just wait a few moments? It's Cora, you see. She's in the parlor with Doctor Polson and I wouldn't want to disturb them." She handed him a towel.

Kin's fists clenched involuntarily in the material. "Doctor Polson, huh?"

The sheriff chuckled. "Don't worry. I don't think he impressed her overmuch at dinner."

Charlotte batted at his shoulder. "Oh Reagan. Do be kind."

"Be kind? That man was positively— Hey now!" Reagan ducked away from a more violent swing of his wife's arm, laughing all the while.

Ike grinned at the couple from where he remained at the table. It struck Kin again how much the kid admired these two.

Still laughing, Reagan seized his wife's hands and turned her so that she was gently trapped in the circle of his arms. She didn't look like she was at all opposed to her capture as she settled her head against her husband's chin.

Reagan turned serious. "Since it appears my wife has imprisoned you in this tiny kitchen for at least a few minutes, how did your business go in California?" His gaze darted to Isaiah and then back to settle on Kin.

Kin suddenly didn't want to talk about California. All he wanted to do was march into the parlor and tell Dr. Polson to head on down the trail. Instead, he forced himself to remain steady and tell about their trip.

But all the while, he couldn't help but wonder what might be happening in the parlor.

Still, a thought had occurred to him on the long train ride home. "You know, I've been thinking about why these men are chasing Ike. We know Sherman told Cora that she looked like Ike's ma. And then he followed her into room seven and continued to stare. We already decided that this would indicate that he knew Mrs. Coleman at some point. Seemingly before she married Ike's father. We also know that Ike's pa sewed the deed to the house into the lining of his coat—perhaps on the night when Ike saw him acting strangely on the ship. Which means he was trying to keep it hidden—likely from someone aboard the ship. Do you suppose this Captain Sherman feels that the deed to the house ought to be his? Maybe he even planned to—" He cut off his words in the nick of time as he bounced a glance off Ike.

But the kid was too sharp. "You think he planned to kill me? For the deed to our house?"

Kin did. But he didn't want to burden the boy further.

Reagan released his wife and planted his palms against the sideboard behind him. His fingers tapped as he pondered. "Could be, I suppose. They figured Ike had it. And that it would be easy to take it from a kid."

Ike squirmed uncomfortably in his seat. Seemed he didn't much like being referred to as a kid, but the boy was polite enough not to kick up a fuss.

Kin nodded. "Yeah. He would have had no one to vouch for him and no one in Seattle or our area would be any the wiser about his house in California. Or his disappearance, for that matter. If no one had investigated, it would have been Ike's word against a ship's captain."

"And we all know how that would have gone." Reagan's fingers were still drumming the sideboard. "Ike, son, you're young, so I hope you'll listen to me. Do you trust Mr. Davis?"

Ike didn't hesitate. "Yessuh."

Kin felt his heart swell with love for the kid. But wondered where Reagan was heading.

"All right then," Reagan continued, "I think it might be good if you put everything in Kin's name until you come of age. I don't think these cowardly crooks will want to take on a full-grown man who can fight back. Then we let the word slip that you've signed over your inheritance. With that knowledge generally known, the balance of power should shift to our side and maybe we can get rid of these men peaceably. What do you think?"

"I'm fine with that if you think it will help," Isaiah said. "I know Mr. Kin will do right by me."

Kin pondered. He didn't mind the risk to himself. "Think it will work? I know a man in Seattle that can draw up the papers for us."

The sheriff lifted one shoulder. "It's one thing to commit such a crime when it can be easily hidden by snuffing out an innocent with no family or connections. But the way these crooks have been acting . . . I'm inclined to think that once the general public will recognize their crime for what it is, they'll give up and find some other poor soul to hound."

Kin pondered. It was a valid idea, but . . . "Ike? We don't want you to feel any pressure."

Ike scooped a hand over his hair. "I'm not sure what to think, if I'm honest. I don't rightly like the idea of puttin' anyone in danger, but I like it even less that those men're still lingerin'—especially that they makin' Miss Cora uncomfortable. You think puttin' my house into the sheriff's name would be safer than yours? I don't want you gettin' hurt on my account. And they wouldn't hurt a lawman, would they?"

Kin looked at Reagan. "That might be better. Then I can draw up the paperwork without there being a conflict of interest. Won't have to go back to Seattle."

Reagan rubbed a hand over his cheek, his gaze on Charlotte.

She had busied herself with drying the dishes on the drainboard and though she couldn't have helped but overhear their conversation, she seemed intent only on her task.

Kin thought again about Ike's reaction to leaving Reagan at the train station. He'd rolled the situation through his mind so many times but couldn't seem to settle on a good way to bring it up. He didn't want Ike to think he didn't want him.

Reagan scratched the back of his head wearily, and met Kin's scrutiny. "Let's sleep on it and talk again in the morning. Bottom line is we want both Isaiah and Cora to be safe and able to resume their lives without risk. And unless those men try something, my hands are tied. This seems like the best way to protect both Ike and Cora."

"If they go near her again, they'll have me to deal with," Kin ground out.

Reagan lowered his chin. "I think you mean they'll have the *law* to deal with."

Kin snorted. "I'll come get you after I've had a chance to say my piece." He smiled slowly.

Reagan chuckled. "Just see that your say doesn't cross any lines. Anyhow, tomorrow will come soon enough and that doctor has overstayed his welcome. Let's all head to our rooms."

Kin was happy for the release from the kitchen, but he had no plan to head to his room just yet. His destination was the parlor.

Chapter Twenty-five

Cora sat stiffly on the settee across from where Dr. Polson lounged in a wingback chair. He'd removed his evening jacket and loosened his tie as though he planned to stay for a long while. She despaired because she was already weary of his small talk.

So far, she had been subjected to several of his musings about how Dr. Griffin might be beyond his prime, a gruesome story about a sawyer who had nearly lost his hand when his crosscut saw stuck fast on a knot and his hand slipped off the grip, and now yet another tale of his medical heroism—he'd apparently saved a foreman's wife and baby from "sure death" at a birthing out at the camps today.

Cora smoothed her skirts and waited for him to take a breath. The moment he did, she blurted, "Doctor Polson, if you will forgive me—oh, dear . . ." She hid a yawn behind her hand. "I'm afraid I'm rather exhausted and must cut our evening short."

Outside the parlor window, a cricket and a bullfrog increased the volume of their duet, as if the Almighty Himself were aiding her in emphasizing the lateness of the evening to the doctor.

He leapt to his feet, eyeing her with concern. "Is your health in compromise?"

She would have to give him credit for the fact that he appeared to be truly concerned, but rose calmly, hoping to assure him on his way. "I'm fine, really. I've simply grown quite weary."

That was true enough. If she had to listen to even one more of the man's tales, she might doze off right there in the parlor! She stepped toward the door, hoping he would follow, but he remained by his chair. With an inhale meant to calm, she stopped and faced him.

He tilted his head. "You aren't working yourself too hard, are you, my dear?"

She folded her arms and clenched them tight at the unlicensed endearment.

He tossed a squint toward the door behind her before lowering his voice. "The Callahans don't have you toiling excessively for them, do they?"

"No. Of course not! Nothing of the sort." She struggled to find something truthful to say that would relieve her of his presence while at the same time easing his mind. "We've the schoolhouse fundraiser to prepare for is all. And I've still a little work to do on the lace I plan to donate."

"Oh. I see. Well . . . don't fret yourself overmuch about that. I doubt a little bit of lace will bring in too much money."

Cora's jaw went slack, but she managed to bite off a retort.

He bent and retrieved his jacket from where he'd draped it over the arm of his chair, but instead of moving to leave as she'd hoped, the doctor only drew a step closer.

Cora felt her nostril's flare.

"Before I take my leave, Miss Cora. I wondered if you would do me the honor of meeting me at the boardinghouse for dinner tomorrow evening? Since you are not working there any longer, I thought it might be a good opportunity for us to enjoy one another's company over a meal, since we've yet to accomplish that feat." He smiled.

The thought of bumping once more into that odious Captain Sherman staying at the boardinghouse made her palms damp. Much as she longed to be free of her present company, it was pleasant by comparison. "I'm afraid I cannot do that, Doctor Polson."

He straightened and his hand turned white where it adjusted his cuffs. "Oh?"

Was he really oblivious to the reason she'd removed herself from town?

"There is a man at the boardinghouse, you see. A man that I'm trying to avoid."

His eyes widened as they swept her from head to toe and back. "Was it that Davis fellow?" Outrage filled his tone.

"It certainly was not!"

As she whirled to face the voice that had come from the doorway behind her, Cora gasped, placing a hand over the joy leaping to life in her chest.

Kin Davis lounged there, with one shoulder planted into the frame and arms crossed over his chest. He offered her a bold wink. "Howdy, Mish."

She oughtn't be so happy to see the rogue, but she couldn't resist a smile of welcome. She offered a spare curtsy. "Mr. Davis."

Dr. Polson stepped forward and swung his hat toward Kin. "Is this the man?"

Cora would have laughed if the situation weren't so troubling. "No. A different man. He arrived only a few days ago from Seattle. He said I reminded him of a woman he once knew."

Polson glowered at Kin as though he might not believe her. "Did this man from Seattle assault you?"

"Yes. No." She focused on the poker handle by the fireplace. "Not exactly. Perhaps I overreacted. Maybe he was simply stunned to see me. I apparently look very much like someone he loved. He followed me into one of the rooms, but he didn't touch me."

"You didn't overreact," Kin assured her in a gentle voice that filled her with warmth.

She hoped he recognized her gratitude in the nod she offered him.

For a moment, she and Kin simply looked at one another. His gaze was soft and full of a mellow ease that filled her with the unaccountable desire to dash across the room and throw her arms around his neck in welcome. Flames licked her cheeks and she jerked her focus to the floor.

"Well." The doctor stepped closer and reached out to press her arm gently. "Whatever the case, I'm glad to hear you weren't physically hurt. For what he did to make you uncomfortable, I'm very sorry, Miss Cora. I'm happy you have friends like the Callahans to stay with." He gave "Callahans" emphasis, as though sending Kin a subtle message.

The compassion in the doctor's tone reminded her for the first time this evening of the qualities that had elicited her interest those first few days he'd been in town. The man could be kind when he put his mind to it.

"Thank you, Doctor Polson."

"I'm also glad to learn that it isn't my presence you've been trying to avoid." He smiled at her wryly. "See me out?" He offered her his elbow.

The gesture was a purposeful challenge to Kin, but she couldn't very well snub the doctor without being very rude.

She nodded and self-consciously slipped her hand into the crook of his arm.

When she lifted her gaze, however, Kin was still blocking the doorway. His focus drilled so steadily into her hand on the doctor's arm, that she could almost feel the burn of it.

She withdrew and buried her fingers into the folds of her skirt. "If you'll excuse us, Mr. Davis?"

He lingered for another moment, but finally straightened and stepped to one side with a languid stretch.

Dr. Polson scurried past him as though worried that Kin might issue a challenge he knew he couldn't win.

Following the doctor to the entry, Cora marched toward Kin with a glower.

The maddening man only grinned at her. As she drew abreast, he leaned close and spoke low. "You're looking lovely this evening, Mish. There's a fire in your eyes that makes a man want to sidle up to its warmth." He pumped his brows.

Cora jabbed a finger toward the hall and whispered fiercely, "I'll thank you to leave, at once."

He made a clicking sound in his cheek before he retorted, "Is that any way to say 'welcome home'? I can think of several much nicer ways for you to say it." His gaze dipped to her lips for one brief second before rebounding to her eyes.

She lifted her chin, refusing to even give the man another look. She breezed past him and met the doctor in the entry, doing her best to ignore Kin's low chuckle behind her.

At the door, Dr. Polson hurried into his overcoat and hat, then faced her. "Rest assured that your whereabouts will be safe with me, Miss Cora. Since you can't join me in town, will you permit me to come calling again?"

No matter his kindness just now, Cora didn't want to encourage him in a pursuit. "Doctor Polson, if you'll forgive me. Now is not . . . I'm simply not in a position to . . . start anything with . . . anyone." So why was it that her ears were straining to hear whether Kin had followed her instructions, or whether he had lingered to banter with her a little longer.

"I see." The doctor's feet shuffled. "More's the pity. If you'll allow, I don't plan on going anywhere. So when you are ready, I'll be waiting—even if I have to wait for *hours*."

She darted him a despairing look, and then realized by the sparkle in his eyes that he was having one over on her.

She smiled. "Good evening to you."

He settled his bowler and tugged on the brim. "And to you." With that, he stepped into the darkness.

When Cora turned around, Kin was gone.

Chastising herself for her disappointment, she hurried to her room.

Cora rose the next morning and dressed quickly. She paused before the mirror in her room and assessed her reflection with a critical eye.

Church service would be in just a few minutes, but she didn't think she would go. There was still a mire of alarm in her stomach each time she thought of the way Captain Sherman had looked at her. She didn't want to chance bumping into him at the church. But what was she going to do if the man remained in town for months? She couldn't just hide out here at the Callahans' forever.

If she asked him, Kin would sit with her, she felt sure. That would give her a measure of assurance and certainly protection if the captain approached her again. But it would also set tongues to wagging. Not to mention she'd just told the doctor the evening before that she wasn't in a position to start a courtship.

She hesitated.

If she was so certain Kin wasn't serving the Lord, why did she feel sure that he would be at services today? Of course there was the fact that the parson was like a father to him. But there was something more. Something in his demeanor lately that had her second guessing her concerns. Perhaps it was only that he'd been all rogue when she'd first met him and now he seemed to be at least partially tamed?

She blew a frazzled breath.

For all that she had been restless while Kin was away, she had just passed a sleepless night because of the thought of him across the hall. Her heart still pounded much faster than it ought at just the thought of seeing him at breakfast.

For protection at church, she could just as easily stick close to the sheriff's side, so why had her first thought been to ask Kin for protection?

She narrowed her eyes at herself in the mirror, knowing the answer even as her mind formed the question.

Heavens! This simply wouldn't do. She spun away from the mirror and paced to the window.

Sunrise had splashed a crimson and peach blush across the dome of the sky this morning and a thick bank of clouds lingered on the horizon east of Wyldhaven. Whether the clouds were coming or going, she wasn't sure. What she did know was that she couldn't keep hiding from Kin here in her room.

She smoothed her hands against the front of her bodice. "Just go to breakfast, you ninny. And keep in mind that the Lord is much more important to you than your emotions that go all hullabaloo every time that man so much as glances your way."

With that, she took a fortifying breath, and eased open the door of her room. The hallway was empty—thank the Lord for small blessings. At least she would have the buffer of others' company to insulate her from Kin's charm.

The man was indeed seated at the breakfast table, as were the sheriff and Ike. Charlotte was just bustling in from the kitchen with a big pot of oatmeal.

Immediately feeling guilty, Cora rushed forward. "I'm so sorry I overslept. What can I do to help?"

"Please don't fret. I don't need you to do a thing except sit yourself down." Charlotte set the steaming pot that exuded a homey, nutty fragrance onto the trivet in the middle of the table.

Kin rose and pulled out a chair for her. A soft welcome crinkled the corners of his eyes.

When her knees went all to mush, she was thankful for the seat and plunked into it.

His warm chuckle accompanied the scraping of her chair as he scooted her in. "Morning, Mish." His greeting was spoken softly, and so close to her ear that she felt the warmth of his breath.

She straightened the spoon by her bowl, giving a little nod. "Mr. Davis."

Reagan, who up to that point had been twirling his coffee cup on his saucer, spoke. "Charlotte and I have talked at length throughout the night and we've come to a decision that we'd like to present to all of you. Especially Isaiah."

Cora focused on the sheriff, curiosity piqued.

She heard Kin sink into his chair across the table, but her attention had been captured by the fatherly look that the sheriff leveled on Ike.

The boy studied the porridge Charlotte was scooping into his bowl. "Me, sir? I know I been a sight of trouble since my arrival in town and I'm right sorry 'bout that."

"Nonsense!" Charlotte scooted the pot of oatmeal toward Cora and ruffled a hand over the boy's head. "Reagan and I don't view you as trouble at all. In fact, quite the opposite. We've been blessed to get to know you these past few days."

It made Cora feel all doughy inside when the boy hung his head in pleased embarrassment.

"It was the talk of him signing over his inheritance until he comes of age that first got us to thinking on this." Reagan's focus remained fastened to the boy. "We think we have a better solution. One that will be even a stronger deterrent to anyone who might want to harm you. But we'd need your permission, and Mr. Davis's, to go through with it."

Ike's brow furrowed as he apparently tried to figure out where the sheriff was headed.

But Cora suddenly knew, and excitement surged through her. "That's a great idea!"

Kin turned his spoon end over end, waiting for the sheriff to continue. There was a tension about his shoulders that told Cora he had a lot riding on this conversation.

The sheriff set aside his coffee cup and bowl, and folded his hands on the table before him. "Son, we'd like to adopt you."

Ike's eyes widened. "Ya would?!" Excitement shone through his eyes, until they swung to Kin, then some of the light dimmed. He returned his attention to the sheriff.

"I want to assure you that this has nothing to do with your money. All of that would remain in your name and we wouldn't touch it. We only want to offer you protection and, well . . ." His gaze pinged off his wife's. "A family." He and Charlotte exchanged a soft smile.

Charlotte had tears shimmering in her eyes. She clasped her hands beneath her chin. "Isaiah, in just the few short days we've known you, we've come to love you. And we want to be sure to say that we mean no disrespect to you, Kin."

"Right," Reagan nodded. "I meant to say that."

"It's just that if you are going to name us guardians over your property, we feel adoption would be even stronger and offer you more protection. But——" She held out a hand and rushed to add, "——we don't want you to feel like we are only offering to adopt you for that reason. We truly do want to be your ma and pa. And of course we realize we can't be replacements for your pa, who you lost so recently. We understand this might be a difficult decision for you and want to assure you that we only have your best interests at heart. You won't hurt our feelings if you say no."

Cora could tell by the expression on Charlotte's face that she would indeed be hurt if the boy chose a different route, but she could also tell that the Callahans truly did only want the best for the boy. In fact, they might already love him like a son.

Ike's loyalty to Kin, however, might hold him back. Would Kin want to adopt the boy?

Even now he was watching Isaiah who, in turn, had resumed a study of his oatmeal.

Kin took a sip of his coffee and Cora could tell by the way his focus blurred against the liquid that he was trying to decide what to say to the boy. Finally, he plunked his cup back into its saucer. "At the risk of sounding like you've been a burden, which you haven't, I think you should take the Callahans up on their offer, Ike."

The boy glanced over at him, brows shooting upward. "Ya do?"

Cora hid a smile behind her own coffee cup. It was plain from his expression that the boy wanted to accept the Callahans' offer, but had been afraid of hurting Kin.

Kin nodded. "I do. Much as I—" He cleared his throat, took up his spoon, and set to intently stirring his black coffee. "Much as I love you, I'm going to be busy, you know, building a practice, and so at this point in my life I'm much better brother material."

"So . . ." The boy searched his face carefully. "It won't hurt ya if I say yes?"

"Of course not. In fact, I'm glad the Callahans brought it up, because the thought had already crossed my mind before we went to California. But *I* was worried about hurting *your* feelings." He grinned at the boy.

Ike chuckled, filling Cora's heart with glee. "We a pair, ain't we?"

Kin set his spoon into his still empty bowl. "I'll forever be grateful to the Lord for bringing you into my life, Ike."

Cora stilled. Had she truly just heard what she thought she'd heard?

Ike pondered thoughtfully, then dipped his chin. "He did bring us together, didn't He? I done prayed for God to he'p me, like I told ya."

Kin nodded slowly, and for some reason his gaze lifted to her. "God uses me like that sometimes."

Cora felt a warm wash of understanding. He was talking about her. God *had* used Kin to come to her rescue in Cle Elum all those years ago. Ike may have prayed for help, but *she* had prayed for an angel of rescue. And God had sent Kin. He hadn't been willing to admit, back then, that the Lord had sent him, yet here he was, admitting it now. And looking her right in the eyes as he did so.

Her mouth went dry. And her pulse pounded like a carpenter in her ears. Had the last barrier to a relationship with the man just been removed?

She ought to look away, but she seemed to have been captured by some current that refused her release.

In the distance, she heard Isaiah say something indistinctly and then several joyous exclamations broke the spell she seemed to be under. She gave herself a little shake and tore her gaze from Kin's to find Reagan, Charlotte, and Ike sharing a hug. Charlotte had her arms around Ike, and Reagan had his arms around both of them. His eyes were closed and his face was tilted toward the ceiling. A huge smile split his face.

Cora pressed one hand to her chest. It did her good to see the happy new family.

After a long moment, Reagan released them and stepped back. He rubbed his hands together. "Right. I think we should make this announcement today at church. I believe Captain Sherman and his men will be in attendance. And we can pray that will make them realize Isaiah is protected and there's nothing more they can gain here. Hopefully, they'll move on."

"And if they don't?" Kin asked.

Reagan plunked his hands on his hips. "I guess we'll have to cross that bridge when we come to it." He transferred his attention to Isaiah. "What do you say, son? Ready to make an announcement at church that will hopefully send these blaggards packing?"

Ike nodded. "Think it will work?"

Reagan waggled his head from side to side. "Only one way to find out."

Cora wished she could be optimistic. But with a shudder, she recollected the look in Captain Sherman's eyes as he'd blocked the doorway. She reached for the oatmeal and added a dollop to her bowl. "I think I'll stay home from services today, if that's all right with you?" She directed her question to the Callahans. After all, it was their home she'd be in.

"Of course," Charlotte said. She stretched a hand toward Isaiah's place. "Here Isaiah, let's get you fed before church." To Cora she offered, "We have no problem with you staying here. But . . . will you feel safe on your own?"

"I'll stay with her."

Cora's gaze darted to the man across the table. She could feel heat blazing in her cheeks. Did he even realize what he'd just said?

Reagan and Charlotte exchanged a look.

"Outside!" Kin blurted, palms out. "I don't mean to be in the house."

Cora raised a finger to draw attention away from his embarrassment. "You mentioned that you think Sherman and his men will be at church?"

Reagan lifted a shoulder. "I think that's a reasonable assumption, yes. They were there last week."

Relief wafted through her. "Good. I've been yearning for a little fresh air. Do you think it would be all right to take a walk? I mean . . ." She picked at one fingernail intently. "If Mr. Davis wouldn't mind?"

A quick peek revealed that he'd relaxed into his chair. "I don't mind at all." He tilted his head, bemused relief relaxing his features. "I think it's a grand idea."

Technically, it wasn't quite proper for them to be alone outside together either, but she trusted Kin and knew the Callahans did too and wouldn't say anything about it in town where it might cause problems.

Charlotte clapped her hands. "Excellent. I'll put some tea and cake into a basket for you. For now . . ." She swirled her hands at the now cooled oatmeal on the table. "We'd better eat."

Cora sprinkled some brown sugar over the contents of her bowl, feeling a little bit giddy inside. Not only would she be able to avoid the odious Captain Sherman, but she would also get to spend some time alone with one very handsome Kin Davis. Maybe they could have a conversation about his faith so that she could once and for all determine if she could let her guard down around him.

Chapter Twenty-six

"Breathe, Zoe."

Zoe did her best to follow Belle's command, but she was so jittery that she was only able to inhale in fits and starts. Exhaling wasn't much better. She was going to get to see Washington Nolan again this morning—after years of being apart, and weeks of wondering if he was even alive.

Zoe's sister gripped her shoulders and demonstrated her command. "In. Out." They stood behind the church building, where Zoe had fled the minute their stepfather, Elijah, had pulled the family wagon to a stop in front of the church.

After only a moment, Zoe spun away. She flapped her tingling hands and paced. "When Grant came by, he said Wash was injured. Do you think it's bad?"

Belle quirked a brow and adjusted her reticule at her wrist. "You've already asked me and I'm telling you Grant didn't say any more to me than he said to you. All he told me was that Butch sent him over to let us know Kin brought Wash home."

"God bless Kin Davis!"

Belle released an impatient sigh. "We better go in, Zoe, or we'll miss the service altogether."

"Yes. You're right. I know. How do I look?" She pinched her cheeks to add color as she'd already done about a dozen times this morning.

"Stop that," Belle chuckled, "or the only color you'll have in your cheeks will be black and blue. He asked you to wait for him, didn't he? Everything is going to be fine. Now come on."

Taking her firmly by one arm, Belle dragged her around the side of the building toward the front. But as they came in view of the front, the Nolan wagon sat right at the bottom of the steps. Butch and Lincoln Nolan were just disappearing through the church doors at the top of the stairs.

"They're here!" Zoe froze and covered her heart with one hand. "I didn't see him. Did you see him?"

Jackson, the only Nolan who remained on the wagon, clucked to the team to set them in motion. He would take the wagon to the hitching post beneath the old oak and tie the team in the shade.

"Come on, Zoe!" Belle vehemently lugged her a few paces, then just as quickly jerked her to a stop and dropped a little curtsy to the Hines and Olann families, who were just starting up the church steps. "Morning."

Zoe copied her sister's action. "Morning."

"Ladies." Mrs. Hines eyed them suspiciously as she slowly ascended the steps.

"Now look what you've done," Belle whispered fiercely.

"What I've done? You were the one dragging me like a plow behind a mule. Besides, I can't help my jitters! If you only understood how close I am to casting up my accounts." She massaged her stomach.

Belle grinned. "Wouldn't *that* give the ladies something to talk about at this week's fundraiser meeting?" She led the way up the stairs but paused on the porch.

"Indeed. Oh, Belle, do haul me inside." Zoe felt like the church doors were the gaping maw of doom itself. "I don't think I have the strength to take the trip on my own, but I'll not relax one smidgen until I've laid eyes on him."

Belle wrapped her tightly in one arm. "Together then."

Zoe had never loved her sister more than in that moment. Normally, she was the steady head that prevailed while Belle felt her emotions more strongly. But today . . . Well, Zoe had never felt this heady mixture of terror and anticipation all at once. Anticipation of course because she was about to lay eyes on the love of her life for the first time in two years. But terror because . . . what if she was aghast at his injury? What if he'd lost an eye? Or was missing part of his face? Or even missing a limb? She mustn't let him see revulsion. She mustn't *feel* revulsion. She knew she would get past whatever the first shock would be and she would love him eternally, no matter what. But she didn't want him to forever remember her looking dismayed or horrified.

Lord, I'm counting on You to give me the strength I need to be the woman he needs. He asked me to wait for him and I've done just that. I know our future is tied together, so help me be the strength he requires during this time. Please, God, please *keep my face impassive, friendly, welcoming, loving. Anything that will encourage him and not disappoint him.*

With that, she took a breath and allowed Belle to lead her through the double doors at the back of the church and around the partition to the aisle.

The Nolans' pew was just to the right. She turned with a smile—that immediately died.

Butch Nolan met her gaze for the briefest of moments, but then gave a tiny shake of his head and looked down. Lincoln and Grant sat beside him, both morosely studying their clasped hands.

Wash was nowhere in sight.

Her gait faltered.

Belle caught her arm in both of her own. She leaned close and hissed, "Do not fall down, Zoe Kastain, or I swear I'll leave you in the aisle where you land."

Zoe blinked at her. How could Belle be smiling so sweetly while throwing around such commands like a barbed whip? She hadn't known Belle had that in her.

"Come on." Belle's words were like syrup now. "We can find out more later. For now, you just have to make it through the service. One foot in front of the other. That's right. Good. Now sit."

Somehow, Zoe realized she was on their pew seated next to Shiloh, but she didn't remember traversing to their pew.

He hadn't come?

After two years of not seeing her, he hadn't even cared enough to come to church to say hello? Of course that wasn't the proper reason for attending services, she chastised herself. But today she would have to admit that her excitement about services had not been because of her love for the Lord.

Her thoughts raced like a wild stampede. What did it mean? Had he stopped writing because he'd found someone else? Her eyes widened. Maybe he'd lost his hand! Or . . . something worse?

Belle pressed a fan into her palm and Zoe put it to use, thankful for the cool air against her hot cheeks.

Lord, I'm going to need more of that strength than I first realized, I think.

The parson was speaking, but Zoe couldn't seem to make out anything he said. All she could think about was how quickly she could get to Jackson or Butch once the service was over. Because she needed some answers or she was going to go plumb crazy.

Reagan and Charlotte had already left for services in town and Cora was just reaching for a shawl on the hook in the entry when a knock sounded on the door.

Hand frozen in the air, she frowned. Kin had told her he would wait for her outside and it had only been a few minutes, so she couldn't imagine that it was him knocking.

This wasn't her house, so she hesitated to answer the door. On the other hand, she'd just been ready to meet Kin outside so they could leave for their walk. To not answer would essentially be to trap herself inside.

Cautiously, she nudged the door open. Relief flooded her when it was only Dr. Polson standing on the porch. Her solace at having it be someone she knew was short-lived, and her tension quickly climbed again. What was he doing here?

"Good morning. If you are looking for the Callahans, I'm afraid they've already left for church."

"Oh. No." He smiled. Gave her a once-over. Slid a finger beneath his collar and swallowed. "You look right nice this morning. More than nice. Beautiful. Very beautiful. I'm here to escort you to church."

Cora's mouth opened and her lips seemed to be testing the air for words that would not come. Hadn't she made her refusal of his suit clear the evening before? She'd also mentioned the men from Seattle to him!

"Morning, Doc." Kin sauntered onto the porch and propped one boot onto the bench to the side of the door. He rested his weight on arms folded over his knee. A long strand of grass dangled from one corner of his mouth. "Hope you had a restful evening?"

The doctor spun to face Kin, lurching a step back. "I-I-I did. Yes. Thank you."

Cora bit back a grin. He obviously hadn't heard Kin's approach. The poor man looked as if he'd just been slapped.

Cora couldn't help but compare the two. The doctor was small, pale, and soft. His inset chin almost disappeared into his neck.

Kin's dark hair and skin made the doctor look ghostly by comparison. And his broad shoulders that stretched the leather of his long brown duster, only emphasized the doctor's narrow frame.

The two men seemed to be having a stare down.

Cora cleared her throat.

"Good. Glad to hear it, Doc." Kin dismissed him by turning his attention to her. His brows nudged upward and his eyes lit with appreciation as he scanned her from head to toe and back again. He loosed a low whistle. "Wow, Mish."

He didn't offer anything more than that, but Cora felt a curl of pleasure twist through her. Why did his short exclamation of appreciation warm her through so much more than the doctor's more verbose compliment?

She slid her palms over the smooth coral watered silk of her best dress. When Reagan had fetched her things from the boardinghouse, this was the only Sunday ensemble that Dixie had packed. It was a bit fancy for a stroll along country roads, but she hadn't felt right wearing her plain everyday skirt and blouse.

Okay, that was a lie, she conceded, if only to herself. She'd wanted to look nice for Kin. And it did her good to realize that she'd succeeded. Now she just had to get rid of the doctor.

"If you'll forgive me, Doctor Polson. As I previously told you, there is a man at the boardinghouse that I'm trying to avoid, so I'm not attending services this morning, even though I hate to miss them. Mr. Davis and I were just about to take a walk."

Kin straightened and offered her his arm. With a glance in the doctor's direction, he tilted his head. "Would you like to chaperone, Doc?"

Cora jabbed him with her elbow to indicate he should behave, for the way he'd said "chaperone" clearly told the doctor that he was on the outside looking in.

"N-no. I'll just . . ." Dr. Polson swung his bowler in the direction of the town, then hesitated. "But *shouldn't* you two have a chaperone?"

Kin led Cora down the porch steps, causing the doctor to have to move out of their way. "We promise to be on our best behavior, Doc."

The doctor made no reply and as Kin led her out of the yard, Cora tossed a glance over her shoulder. Dr. Polson remained on the porch, head hanging as he massaged the back of his neck.

Cora let go of Kin's arm. "You shouldn't be so hard on him."

Kin only grinned mischievously. "What are you talking about? I was downright gentlemanly! Besides, he'll survive. I give it two weeks before he's got— Well, never mind talking about the stuffy doctor. Let's go this way."

Cora released her concern for Dr. Polson and drew in a deep breath of refreshing morning air. It felt so good to be outdoors!

Sunday morning, Maude followed her brothers into the church, and when Kane stopped and gestured for her to take the lead, as was his norm, she preceded them down the length of the aisle and turned into their pew. She plopped onto the bench in her usual spot near the outer wall of the sanctuary, feeling anything but reverent and joyous to be in the Lord's house this morning.

She oughtn't still be so angry with Jax, considering the news about Wash. But she couldn't seem to help herself.

This anger boiling inside was unlike her. But, after her quarrel with Jackson the other day, she'd thought he would at least stop by to apologize. Maybe come by the church again to have a conversation. But he hadn't shown up. Not at home, not at the diner, and certainly not at the church, where she'd spent the majority of each break for the past week.

She worked to remove the fingers of her gloves, yanking at each one as though she were plucking Jackson Nolan's head bald. With her fingers finally freed, she clenched her gloves in one fist and crossed her hands in her lap. Her teeth ground together and her shoulders slouched. He would walk in at any moment and give her that annoying nod of acknowledgment.

Seth settled onto the bench beside her, gave her a quick once-over, and then scooted a little closer to Kane on his other side.

She felt her jaw jut to one side. She didn't even care that she was letting her ill temper show.

Jackson Nolan was a cad of the highest proportions!

Fine. If he wanted to be that way she could—

Movement down the bench caught her eye.

"Excuse me. Pardon me."

Kane gave her a quick wink as he and Seth scooted away from her.

Jackson Nolan sank onto the seat between her and Seth, and tucked his Stetson beneath the pew. "Maude." He gave her a nod as he scooped his hands through his hat-indented mop. "Morning."

Her traitorous heart did a little happy dance and she had to remind herself that she was still angry with him. She jerked her face to the fore.

But, land sakes . . . He was sitting by her! In church. In front of God and everyone.

He leaned toward her until his shoulder brushed hers as he whispered, "You look very pretty today, even with your nose hitched as high in the air as it is."

She stiffened and shot him a narrow-eyed scowl, which only grew when he grinned at her maddeningly.

"I know you're upset with me. I was going to come by that next day, but Mr. Ecklund sent me out to Camp Sixty-Three to oversee a load of cedar he purchased. And the next day, it was to Camp Sixty-Five to supervise a load of pine. I wanted to come, honest."

She wasn't ready to forgive him yet. "That doesn't account for the rest of the week."

"I know it doesn't, but we had a wire from Kin while he was in California telling us that he'd found Wash you see, and Pa wanted me home as soon as I could get there each day to help him prepare a cabin on our property. Pa had started it a while back so that when Wash came home, he could have his own place. But we had to take off the stairs and put in a ramp on account of his injury."

Maude's anger was immediately softened by shame. At the pew where Jackson normally sat with his family, his pa and two younger brothers were just taking their seats, but there was no sign of Wash. "How is he?"

Jackson's face pulled into a pucker of worry. "Not so good, Maude. I'm worried about him. Pa and Doc Griffin figured that the cabin Pa had already started would be good for Wash's independence, since it's just down the road from us. Doc said it would be beneficial for Wash to have to get out and walk a little each day—you know, coming down for meals and such. So Pa, he about worked himself to death the past few days finishing that cabin and clearing the road between it and us so it would be smooth and offer nothing to trip Wash up. But Wash, he flat refused to even get out of bed this morning, much less come to church."

The slump of his shoulders was her undoing. She reached over and settled her hand on his arm. "I'm right sorry, Jax. I've no desire to be angry with you when you have so many burdens right now."

Jackson covered her hand with his and his eyes were soft when they met hers. "No, it's me who ought to be sorry. And you're right. I'm not so good with—" He flapped a gesture of frustration. "Talking. But it's not because I don't care about you. So . . ." His millwork-roughened fingers caressed the back of her hand and one side of his mouth tilted into a crooked smile. "Want to tell me when your birthday is?"

Maude laughed. She couldn't help herself. She opened her mouth to reply, but was interrupted by the parson's voice.

"Happy Sunday, everyone." Parson Clay stood behind the pulpit at the front of the sanctuary with a big smile to greet them. "If I can have your attention, I'll open our service in prayer."

Jackson pulled a face. "Great," he whispered. "Now I'll be in suspense all service."

Maude swallowed a laugh and shushed him, and if she had a hard time concentrating on the parson's opening prayer, well that had a lot to do with the fact that Jackson's hand was still covering hers where it rested on his arm, his thumb rubbing short caresses against her wrist.

After the prayer, she realized that the sanctuary had filled chock-full with people while she was distracted by her conversation with Jackson. The parson always drew a crowd, but today it seemed that the jam-packed room was abuzz with an expectant energy.

As she scanned the congregants, she noted that the three men who had been staying at the boardinghouse all week sat on the back pew across the aisle. Two of them seemed to be searching for someone, but the third man had his gaze fixed on the boy sitting with the sheriff and Mrs. Callahan.

After a few songs, the parson launched into his sermon, and if she were a confessing woman, Maude would also have to lay bare the truth that, as with the prayer, she didn't catch much of the sermon, due to the pleasure of having Jackson by her side.

Maybe others were having trouble concentrating today too, because throughout the message, there seemed to be a low hum across the room. Papers crackled. People wriggled. Children whispered to each other behind their hands.

However, at the end of the sermon when the parson announced that the sheriff had something to say, silence fell so thickly that Maude could hear the swish of Mrs. Hines's Sunday fan from where she sat all the way on the front pew.

The parson took a seat in a chair on the platform as the sheriff stepped to the front of the sanctuary, and Maude was surprised when Charlotte and the boy joined him.

The sheriff grinned and tugged Isaiah in front of himself, turning him so that he faced the congregation with the sheriff's hands on his shoulders. "It is with great pleasure that my wife and I announce that we are adopting Isaiah Coleman as our son."

Congregants gasped and a murmur of surprised pleasure rippled through the room—at lease most of those gathered were pleased. However, Maude noticed that Mrs. Hines's fan snapped back and forth like the tail of an irritated cat and the Olanns shifted uncomfortably on their bench across the way.

From her place at her husband's side, Charlotte practically radiated happiness as she excitedly thumped the boy on one shoulder. The kid returned her smile with a huge one of his own, but there was something hesitant about it. Maybe even fearful as his gaze darted to the back of the room.

Maude frowned. Surely he wasn't afraid of the Callahans. That couldn't be it. What was it? Maybe someone sitting in the area where he'd just looked? But the only people over there were the strangers from Seattle. She frowned. Did the boy know those men?

"Many of you know that Kin Davis and Isaiah just returned yesterday from California. Isaiah's father was recently killed, you see, but he owned a house down there. Beautiful place, right on the beach, so Ike tells me. For a while, there was some question as to the whereabouts of the legal papers, but we're pleased to have found them and Kin was able to help Ike here get all the property switched into his name. Now that we're adopting him, we'll be keeping it in trust until he comes of age. What's ours, is now his," the sheriff continued. "And what was his, is now ours." When he said those last words, his gaze landed threateningly on the three men across the aisle.

It did have something to do with them!

Several in the congregation turned to glower at the men in the back, including Marshal Zane Holloway and Deputy Joseph Rodante.

"Olann," the sheriff continued, "you can expect to be hearing from us with regards to his financial matters."

The banker squirmed more pronouncedly. "I-I'll look forward to that, Sheriff."

The sheriff's eyes narrowed. "I'm sure you will."

Maude pressed her free hand to her lips. She'd thought it a bit odd that the sheriff was making so many details public, but she now understood that he was making a point to several in the room that the boy was under his protection. And if the kid had a lot of money, wouldn't that serve the banker right for his participation in booting the child out of school!

Maude couldn't resist a grin. Oh, how she hoped he did have a lot of money!

Charlotte took her husband's arm. "We've asked Parson Clay to say a prayer of blessing over us as we begin this journey as a family."

She looked up at her husband with such adoration that Maude's stomach swirled. Would she ever feel that way about Jax?

Her heart threatened to stop and then rushed to catch up with itself. Because with sudden clarity, she realized that she already did feel that way about him. It was why she'd gotten so irritated with him the other day. And he'd made a huge effort today to show her that he'd heard her concerns, so maybe he felt the same way about her? Maude blew a long slow breath of relief. There was hope for them after all. She relaxed against the pew for the first time that morning.

The parson had leapt from his chair and now stood on the same level as the Callahans. "It is my great pleasure to pray such a blessing!" He beamed, stepping behind the little family to put a hand on both the sheriff's and his wife's shoulders.

As he began to pray, everyone bowed their heads, but a fumbling rustle drew Maude's attention. Across the aisle, the man with long dark hair and bleary eyes slid gracelessly from the pew. He gave one final scowl toward the family at the front, and then tromped unsteadily from the room.

Had he come to church drunk? It was rather early for that, but it certainly appeared so!

His two cronies exchanged a glance and then followed him out.

Maude gave a little shake of her head. What was the world coming to when people showed up to church in their cups? And why had he seemed so upset about such happy news?

Chapter Twenty-seven

Captain Sherman crashed through the church doors and stormed to the shade of the oak in the yard. Several horses hitched to parked wagons blew and bobbed their heads. Hands on his hips, he paced first one way and then the other. His men stood by watching him like the buffoons they were.

"What are you looking at?!" He kept his growl low, mindful of the full congregation of townsfolk still in the church.

"What do we do now?" Farnham asked.

What did they do now, indeed. He tugged the flask from his jacket and downed a healthy swig of whiskey. Then another.

It was one thing to steal the deed when no one but an orphan kid knew about it. Quite another now that legal authorities had stepped in and were in the loop. And the lawman had definitely known something. And his two deputies too. How? He and his men had been keeping to themselves ever since they'd come to town. Laying low. Biding their time.

Kin Davis!

The lawman had mentioned him. And since Farnham had played the fool back in Seattle, Kin likely knew they were after the boy. But now the deed would be out of reach. He couldn't take out a lawman and his family without raising suspicions. He might want that house. But he didn't want it bad enough to risk a hemp necktie!

Blazes and rattlers!

He kicked a pinecone, sending it scuttling across the grass. After catching his balance, he gulped more whiskey.

And still no sign of his dear Cassandra.

Cassandra?

He scrubbed a hand down his face.

No. He shook his head. That wasn't right. Not Cassandra. But close enough.

Where had she taken herself off to?

It was sheer torture that he'd glimpsed her only once and then she'd seemed to disappear. Had he imagined her? None of the townspeople seemed willing to share any information about her. When he'd asked the other woman at the boardinghouse, she had brushed away his questions as though they were of no concern. She'd said the woman—what was the name she'd called her? It didn't matter, he supposed. To him, she would always be Cassandra. The boardinghouse owner had said Cassandra had needed a vacation and was out of town for several days.

So because he hadn't known where the boy was, and because he'd also wanted to wait for Cassandra's return, he'd bided his time. And maybe he'd consumed just a little too much whiskey. But that alehouse owner had been more than happy with his business, even if he'd also been a bit tight-lipped with information.

But now what? The whole town had just learned about the California house. If he tried anything, there would be too many questions. Questions that would only lead straight back to him. He tugged at the itchy skin of his throat. He'd stayed alive this long by being very careful what illicit activities he participated in.

He growled. Maddening as it was, the deed was out of his reach. He'd lost dear Cassandra's house.

But . . . if he couldn't have the house, he would at least have Cassandra.

He just had to find her.

But where? He needed to think, and walking aways helped him think. He waved his men off. "I'm going for a stroll. Wait for me in town."

With that, he left them there and headed down the hill. It wouldn't hurt to stop in at the alehouse and refill his flask on the way.

Hang it, was the ground moving? Sure seemed like it was.

Cora took deep breaths of the crisp spring air, relishing the feel of the sunshine warming her through and trying not to dwell too much on thoughts of her handsome companion.

At least an hour had passed since they had left the Callahans' cabin.

Kin had led her along a narrow wagon track that angled west toward the mountains. He walked in one rut and she in the other. They had ambled slowly, pausing to watch a doe and her splotchy fawn at one point, and then a gorgeous blue butterfly sipping nectar from wildflowers at another. A mama duck and her six waddling ducklings had stopped them just a ways back. She and Kin had laughed when the first golden duckling in the line had stopped to study them and all of his hatchlings had crashed one after the other into each other. The poor babies had ended up a chirping, wriggling mass of yellow feathers until the hen had sorted them out with her bill.

Cora and Kin had watched the little family until they'd faded into the cover of the meadow, and then had ambled onward.

The grass in the strip between them rustled softly in a gentle breeze and when they crested a low hill, Cora stilled, drawing in a breath of awe. Below them, the road curved off to the left, but beyond that, a field of wild poppies stretched to meet a copse of trees nestled against the foot of the mountains. Clear blue sky domed the valley, filling her with an overwhelming realization of her smallness.

"Oh, Kin. It's beautiful!"

"It is, indeed."

Something about the tone of his voice drew her attention away from the view and she discovered he was not looking at the scenery at all, but instead was studying her.

The intensity of his scrutiny made her feel suddenly shy. She tucked one side of her lower lip between her teeth.

The gesture drew his focus to her mouth and Cora's heart tripped over itself.

He tore his gaze to the valley below and this time he studied the landscape while she studied him. Broad shoulders encased in the brown leather of his duster tapered down to a lean waist. Skin bronzed by long hours toiling in the sun. And even beneath the shadow cast by his Stetson, the brown of his eyes brought to mind delectable caramel swirled with molten chocolate ganache. Once again, it seemed he hadn't used his razor that morning, and his stubbled jaw tempted her fingers to explore the rough planes.

She clasped her hands tightly, instead.

A low grumble drifted from his throat and his gaze snapped over to capture hers. "You're making it very hard to be a gentleman this morning, watching me like that."

Caught.

Embarrassment flared through her and she forced her attention beyond him. The mountains, yes, she would study the mountains. "Looking at you like what, Mr. Davis?"

He laughed, low and soft.

And heaven help her, the sound of it sent a tremor straight through her.

"Like I was a piece of pie you wanted to devour." Before she realized what he was about, he'd stepped onto her side of the road and right into her space. He nudged his hat back with the touch of one finger and then his hands skimmed across her forearms and curled warmly around her own. His fingers slid between hers and he moved even closer, looking down at her languidly. "I dare you to deny it."

"I-I-I most c-certainly d-do deny it," she stammered, not able to lift her focus any higher than the glimpse of mountaintop she could see just above his shoulder. She couldn't move. In fact, could hardly breathe for the nearness of him.

Love him.

The memory of the words she'd heard all those months ago as if from the mouth of God Himself, did nothing to soothe her anxiety.

From the corner of her eye, she caught sight of his maddening grin.

He leaned close until his words brushed warmth against her ear. "I like it when you get all flustered, Mish."

She extracted one of her hands and gave his chest a gentle thump. "I am not flustered."

With a quiet chortle, he trapped her fingers against the beat of his heart. He nudged the laced fingers of their other hands to the small of her back, and swayed her a little, as though he were hearing a tune she couldn't.

Cora closed her eyes and dredged up every scrap of willpower she possessed, for this had gone far enough without her knowing for certain where he stood with the Lord. "I have a serious question." The scent of leather and sage enveloped her in a heady cloud.

"What is it?" His voice rumbled soft and low against her ear.

"I need to know— That is— I want to know— You see, this morning, you mentioned something about the Lord using you and the way you said it made it seem that you, well—"

Kin eased back just enough to look down at her. "You're wondering if this stubborn old coot has finally surrendered his will to the Lord's."

She nodded, relieved to have him put it so succinctly. "Yes, you see, because—"

"Because you don't want to be unequally yoked."

"Yes." Again, relief swept through her.

He quirked a brow at her.

"Oh heavens! It's not that I expect you to propose! It's only that I've determined, you see, that if a man doesn't share my faith, I'll never even court—" Her face blazed hotter than Dixie's kitchen stovetop. Could she put her foot any further into her mouth? "Not that we're courting, I understand, but—"

He touched her chin, holding her gaze with his own.

There was a solemness about his eyes that captured all her focus and made her forget her bumbling.

"It was meeting Wash in the middle of that busy street in San Francisco. Of all the places in all the world, we happened to both end up within feet of each other in a strange place that neither of us had ever planned to be." He tucked her head beneath his chin and turned so they could both take in the gorgeous valley below. "It was as if the Lord reached down and thumped me upside the back of my head. I thought if God could care enough about Wash to put me there at the exact right moment—me of all people—well . . . I might as well admit that He was trying to get my attention as much as Wash's. I'm telling you, Cora, if we had been one minute off on either side, we would have missed each other. I just felt this overwhelming love that God has for us and I don't think I even realized that's what it was at the time. But I just surrendered. There's no fighting that kind of love. No point in trying to run from it."

It was Cora's turn to lean back, and this time she gave in to the temptation to curve her hands around his cheeks. She let her thumbs sweep over the smooth skin near his lips and then onto the rougher territory of his cheeks. "I have prayed for you, Kin Davis. For two long years. Just like I told you I would. I fully confess that I felt you were an immovable rock, yet the Lord has shown me how small my faith is."

One corner of his mouth quirked upward. "Even rocks can sometimes have honey in them. The Lord is the sweetest of blessings. Thank you for praying for me, dear Cora."

She closed her eyes, tears of joy and thankfulness overflowing. *Oh Lord, You are so good and merciful. Your lovingkindness is from everlasting to everlasting. Forgive me for my lack of faith and thank You for bringing this man that I love into Your fold.*

Man that I love? Her eyes flew open.

"What is it?" Kin's brow furrowed.

Gracious, she couldn't answer that, because no matter that he'd drawn her near and pulled her into his arms, she couldn't be the first to admit her feelings! "Just a thought that surprised me, is all." Were her cheeks as rosy as they felt?

"Cora I—"

"Well, I'll be keelhauled!"

Cora gasped and spun toward the terrifyingly familiar voice.

But she only caught a glimpse of Captain Sherman before Kin swept her behind himself, using his left arm. "Easy there, fella. No one has to get hurt."

With a quake of fear, Cora realized that Kin had pushed his long duster back with his right hand and had settled it on his Colt.

The strength of her legs threatened to fail her. "Kin, do have a care." She peeked from behind his shoulder.

Captain Sherman stood in the middle of the track just up the hill, gun already drawn and leveled on them. He took a swig from a small metal flask and staggered a couple of steps. "Well now, here she is! Goes missing for days on end and where do I find her but consorting with the one man who has just cost me everything!"

"I think you have me mixed up with someone else," Kin said, his voice level and calm. "I don't even know you."

"Oh you know me!" Captain Sherman exclaimed, squinting one eye to sight unsteadily along the barrel of his pistol. "Leastwise, you will."

Kin bumped into Cora, and she realized he wanted her to back up. She glanced behind them and saw a large wild rose bush not too far down the track. If they could put that between themselves and the drunken captain, maybe they would have a chance to escape into the trees beyond. She retreated a step, relieved when Kin moved with her.

"You disappeared from town too, Kin Davis. You take that little whelp to California to sort out his inheritance?"

"I took a boy to California. But there wasn't a whelp in sight." Kin ground the words with such venom that Cora laid a hand against his back, hoping to remind him to remain conciliatory. She retreated several more steps, tugging him with her.

"Stop moving!"

The sound of a hammer ratcheting froze Cora in her place. *Dear Lord, dear Lord, dear Lord . . .* It was the only prayer she could muster. Was she going to lose Kin so soon after finally allowing him close?

"We're not moving," Kin offered soothingly.

"Batten your hatch and get your hand off that gun!" The captain snapped.

Slowly, Kin raised his palms. "Listen, friend, I'm not trying anything. See? My hands are right here in plain sight."

It was the tremor in his voice that sapped the last of Cora's hope. Why, oh why had she insisted that she needed some fresh air?!

"Cassandra there is mine! Already lost her to one man and don't intend to lose her to another." His words were slightly slurred and the next few steps he took were so faltering that Cora felt certain he might trip himself at any moment.

Kin adjusted his stance, his heel nudging her toe.

Cora took another step back.

It was the wrong move.

"I said don't move!" The captain's voice carried the threatening quietness of a man used to having his orders followed.

It was as though Cora watched the next moments from a place very far away.

As he spoke, the captain thrust his pistol to arm's length, the barrel pointed right at them.

Kin hunkered into his shoulders, pushing Cora further out of sight. His hand dropped toward his gun.

Cora leapt back. The grass in the center of the road hampered her skirts, which encumbered her ankles. With a cry, she realized she was falling.

Kin's feet tangled with hers.

He grunted. Tried to catch his balance.

A loud shot ripped through the morning.

Then Cora collided with the embankment and all the air left her lungs.

Chapter Twenty-eight

Alex Polson never made it back to town. He ought to be at Sunday services, but he no longer had the gumption. Instead, he'd trekked off into the forest until he'd found a little hill overlooking a pretty valley. He sank down at the base of a large cedar to sulk and lick his wounds.

He'd known asking to escort her to church had been a long shot, but it galled him to know she was at the Callahans' with that rapscallion, Davis.

Of all the bad luck, why had a charming interloper like Kin Davis arrived in town just when Alex had worked up the courage to ask that pretty woman to dinner?

Truth was, from the way she'd reacted the first moment Davis had walked into the boardinghouse, Alex had known that he'd already lost. Today had simply been the final nail in the coffin. Cora Harrison was not the woman for him. Maybe he wasn't destined to be a married man. That wouldn't be so bad. It would give him more hours to dedicate to his work.

But maybe he ought to do that work in a different place?

This town was not what he had thought it would be. Perhaps he ought to start sending out feelers to other larger areas? The pay would certainly be better, and likely with much less of a time commitment.

He picked up a dried cedar cone and chucked it down the hill. It cascaded through the brush, sending a flock of quail launching into the air.

Startled, he lurched back so violently that he whacked his head on the trunk of the cedar.

"Ow!" He rubbed at the spot morosely.

Proof right there that he wasn't a country lad. He would do much better in the city.

He would leave to head back to California today if it weren't for his concerns about Dr. Griffin's health. He really did hate to leave the man in a lurch. They needed more doctors in this area, not less. And they needed a clinic.

Dr. Griffin had confided that he would love to build one, but he simply hadn't had a spare moment to set it into motion. Twice on their rounds this past week, the doctor had handed the reins of his bright red wagon to Alex and caught a few moments of sleep between logging camps. The poor man was simply exhausted. With an expecting wife and a young daughter, it probably wasn't only medical calls keeping him up nights.

No, Alex's conscience wouldn't let him leave. But maybe he could find his own replacement and then he'd feel free to move on.

A gunshot ripped through the morning.

He was on his feet, looking around, heart racing, before he even realized he'd moved. Where had that come from?

Another shot had him ducking behind the cedar.

From the valley!

Was it just someone hunting?

Wait!

That was the direction Cora and Kin had been heading when they left the yard!

He was running down the hill before he could think better of it.

Cora rolled to her hands and knees, fighting for oxygen. Her mouth gaped, but no air would enter. Several poppies lay crushed and lifeless in the place where she had fallen. An odd thing to notice when her lungs were refusing to give up their stranglehold on her airway. She tried for another inhale, arching her back to aid the effort. The loamy soil broke easily where her fingers gouged into it, but cut painfully into the tender areas beneath her nails. Darkness invaded the edges of her consciousness.

And then, finally, blessed air streamed past her lips.

She collapsed into a coughing fit that shook her long and deep and painfully. After several moments, she lay spent, staring at her hand where it rested on the broken, dirt-marred grass in front of her face. Dark half-moons of soil were packed beneath her fingernails.

Beside her, someone moaned.

"Kin!" She forced herself upright.

He lay beside her in one track of the roadbed. Blood already pooled beneath his head, turning the dirt a murky black.

Cora scrambled forward on all fours. "Kin?!"

Other than his profusely bleeding head, he didn't seem to have any other injuries. But he wasn't moving!

She shook his shoulder gently. "Kin?"

Captain Sherman grabbed her arm.

"No!" She tried to fight him off, but the man's fingers were as strong as a bear trap.

"Got you now, dear Cassandra. Got you now. Don't worry. He didn't feel any pain." Captain Sherman hauled her to her feet.

The stench of sour whiskey made her want to retch.

Anger flared and she planted her hands against his chest and shoved him. "You monster!"

The captain only took a bracing step as though riding out a storm aboard his ship.

"He didn't do anything to you!" She tried to push him again, but this time his reaction was swift.

His palm cracked against her face with the force of a mule kick.

Pain exploded as Cora shot backward, arms flailing. She crashed once more against the embankment. She blinked at the sky. Her ears rang. Black spots danced in her vision, circling against the blue overhead.

And then Captain Sherman leaned into her line of sight. "Now, you ready to behave yourself? Or do you need another dose of that discipline?" He spat just to the side of her.

Cora worked her jaw from side to side.

He reached down a hand, and on instinct she accepted it, immediately wishing she hadn't.

He yanked her to her feet. "Good. Now, you're coming with me." He prodded her with the point of his gun toward the trees in the distance across the poppy field. "Walk."

With no recourse, she inched up her skirts to keep from tripping on them and did as she was told. One glance over her shoulder revealed that Kin still hadn't moved and the pool of blood beneath his head had expanded.

Facing the trees once more, Cora bit off a whimper of despair and another of terror.

Her dearest Kin had just been killed and she was all alone with his murderer.

A man who thought she was someone else!

The whole world felt as if it had just gone dark.

Alex burst from the brush that covered the hill he'd been on, and since there was no cover, he crouched low to assess the situation. Far off, on the other side of the road and moving quickly into the distance, he could see two figures.

"Cora!" She was immediately detectible by the color of her dress.

Just as he had feared.

The other was a man, but not Kin, based on the bow-legged way he was walking. What had happened to Davis?

Those shots . . .

He shook the thought away. That didn't matter at the moment. He must save Cora.

Keeping low, he ran forward.

He had no idea what he would do once he reached her, for he had no weapon, but he would take that field when he came to it.

The embankment fell away down to the roadbed, and he jumped down. He dashed across and crouched to peer just above the grass, assessing the couple in the distance to see if the outlaw might have heard the sound of him landing in the road. It didn't seem so, for the man didn't look back. He would have to be more careful from here on out. Keep low and out of sight.

He started into the field but the moaning of a man behind him made him freeze.

He glanced back.

Just around the bend in the roadway, a cowboy boot lay in sight. At first it was still, then it moved.

Another moan.

Davis. It had to be. Unless someone else had been part of this altercation.

Alex ground his teeth, looking to where Cora was still being prodded across the field. To help Kin, might cost Cora her life. However, Cora was still in good health and Kin, it seemed, was not. Besides, Kin had a gun!

He retreated and scrambled to Kin's side.

Kin lay in one of the tracks of the roadbed, a deep gash splitting the skin at the side of his forehead near his temple. His hat had tumbled into the grass, and his left shoulder was oddly misshapen. Alex could tell that even through the leather of the duster Kin wore.

Kin rolled his head from side to side, drawing attention to the amount of blood he'd lost. His feet moved erratically, a sign of the agony he must be in.

Alex eyed Kin's pistol, still in the belt around his waist. It looked huge and heavy. He could take it, but even if he did, he'd have no idea how to use it. However, if he could patch Kin up. Maybe together they could save Cora.

He leaned forward and pushed Kin's duster away from his shoulder. Grabbing his shirt near the buttons, he gave one quick jerk. Buttons flew. He pushed the material back from the shoulder so he could see what he was doing.

His fingers palpated the protrusion. "Kin, it's me. Doctor Polson. Hold still, I'm seeing what I'll need to do to put your shoulder back into place."

With another groan, Kin cracked one eye open. "You? Where's Cora?" He tried to sit up, bracing himself with his bad arm, then cried out and fell back.

"Lie still."

Kin at least listened to that command this time, but he insisted, "Where's Cora?"

Alex took a good grip of his arm and prepared himself. "That other fellow took her," he said.

Just as he'd suspected, Kin surged to a sitting position again. Alex used the momentum to give his arm a good twist. A loud *pop* made Kin gasp.

"Blazes, Doc!" He rubbed gently at his shoulder.

Alex waited, crouched away from the man. Had it worked? If it had, Kin should be feeling much less pain now, but if not, he'd need to try again.

Kin's lips thinned into reluctant humor. "Feels better. Thanks."

Alex blew out a breath. "Good. Now I need to look at your head."

Kin frowned. "What's wrong with my head?"

Alex motioned to the bloody dirt and grass. "I think you were shot."

Kin muttered a few comments about the lineage of the man who had shot him.

As Alex leaned close to examine the wound, he asked Kin if he knew who had shot him.

"I only know him as Captain Sherman. He has a couple companions. You seen anyone else around?"

"No. No. Just the one man leading Cora away. Do you have a knife?"

"He has Cora!" Kin tried to stand.

"Easy. I can't let you go anywhere like this." It only took a little pressure from Alex's hand on Kin's recently reset shoulder to make him grunt and fall back to the ground. "Sorry about that, Davis."

"I'll bet you are," Kin groused.

"Just needed you to know what kind of shape you are in. I need to stop this bleeding or you won't make it half a mile. Knife?"

Kin reached into the top of his left boot and extracted a bowie. He handed it over, hilt first. "Be quick."

Alex was thankful the blade was honed to a razor-sharp edge, as he quickly cut a strip from the bottom of Kin's shirt. Once he had two full-length strips, he padded them together and wrapped them good and tight around Kin's head. "This will need stitches later, but it looks like you were lucky. If that bullet had been half an inch closer, we wouldn't be having this conversation. Now give me your belt."

"Wasn't my day to meet my maker, I guess." Kin shucked off his belt and handed it over without question.

Alex measured it against Kin's torso, then buckled it at about the right size and looped it behind his neck. "That will give you something to rest your arm on."

Kin scrambled to his feet. "Can I go now? Whoa." He broadened his stance to catch his balance.

Alex pressed his lips together grimly. They would be lucky to catch up to Cora at all with the state he was in. "This way, come on, I'll lead the way."

"Oh, no you don't, Doc."

"What?"

Kin pointed toward town. "You have to get back to town and tell the sheriff I need his help. I'll go after Cora."

"But—" Even as he protested, he couldn't deny a little relief.

"No buts. Get moving."

With that, Kin stumbled into the field and lumbered in the direction indicated by the crushed grass.

Alex grimaced. Cora and her captor were nowhere in sight. And in his current condition, Kin would be no match for a man crazy enough to capture a woman in broad daylight.

He'd better hurry.

Chapter Twenty-nine

They'd walked for miles. How many, Cora didn't know. The going had been easier before, but here the brush was thick and her skirts hampered their progress. Cora was actually thankful for the hindrance, because it slowed them.

The moment they'd moved into the trees, the captain had changed their direction. Instead of continuing west, he had turned them to the south. And even in his drunken state, he'd started being more careful about their trail. He used rocky ledges and creek beds to disguise their trail for the first couple of miles, and her fledgling hopes that Kin might still somehow be okay and would be able to find her had died. But now with the slowdown, she thought there might at least be a chance for her to escape. Maybe someone from town would have found Kin by now—a sob caught in her throat. If they found Kin, then they might think to look for her.

Her feet throbbed. Since their trek through the creek, she'd been walking in wet boots. And much of her forced march had been blurred by tears, so she'd stubbed her toes a couple times and twisted her ankle once.

Why had God taken Kin away, just when she'd come to realize she loved him? Just when he'd finally surrendered his will to God's?

She prayed like she hadn't prayed before for Kin to be found and helped. And because she had no other choice with the captain's pistol prodding her back, she put one foot in front of the other.

But now, blessed relief, the captain took her arm and pulled her to a stop. They had come free of the thick underbrush and were in a little clearing between three massive evergreens. The ground beneath them was liberally padded with pine needles.

"Sit."

The captain shoved her against the base of one of the trees and took off the bandolier he wore across his body. He unbuckled it, draped it around her, and used it to cinch her firmly to the tree. He pulled the leather strap so tight that she could only pull in shallow breaths, and it cut painfully into her middle.

"Don't go anywhere. I'll be right back."

She heard him crash into the brush.

She tried to wriggle free, but it was no use. Her ribs prevented her from squeezing out one way and her hips and crinolines, the other.

Hopelessly, she gave up fighting the restraints.

He returned and cleaned a spot in the center of the trees free of needles. After placing several rocks in a circle, he built a fire. To her, he spoke not a word.

She watched him carefully. Even though it couldn't yet be more than mid-afternoon, his eyes kept drooping. The liquor he'd consumed was finally catching up to him.

She must act now. "Excuse me?"

He blinked slowly, giving himself a little shake. His dark gaze settled on her.

Cora worked the dryness out of her mouth. "I need to use the necessary."

He huffed, but to her surprise, he didn't deny her request. He rose and loosened the bandolier, then tugged her to her feet. He motioned for her to move behind one of the trees. "Try to run and I'll shoot you before you go more than three steps."

Cora's brows rose. So had he come out of his stupor enough to realize she wasn't his Cassandra, now? Seemed like it. She didn't think he would have threatened "Cassandra" in such a way. Except, he *had* slapped her when he'd thought she was Cassandra.

She moved to the other side of the tree, but she didn't need the privacy. She knew she couldn't escape him by running. But if he fell asleep . . .

She waited what she hoped was an appropriate amount of time and then returned to the circle near the firelight. "Thank you."

"Sit," was all he said.

She did. And this time, when he went to cinch her down with the bandolier, she took the biggest breath she could muster and pushed every muscle in her torso out just as far as they would go.

He took his time, tugging on the leather and assessing the tightness of the bonds. He seemed to realize something was amiss, but his inebriated weariness must also be clouding his mind, because he finally gave a grunt and moved once more to the other side of the fire pit.

It was all Cora could do not to blow out the breath she'd been holding in one great whoosh. Instead, she managed to release it in a slow quiet stream. Excitement shot through her at how loose the band was. She mustn't let him see that. She leaned forward and let her head droop as if she intended to go to sleep herself.

A few minutes later, when she lolled her head back on the pretense of finding a more comfortable position, she noted that the captain had slumped into the pine needles by the fire. He was sound asleep.

However, the moment she stirred, he sat up with a start. Glancing around and seeing her still tied to the tree, he slumped over again and went back to sleep.

Cora twisted her lips in despair. She was going to have to wait for him to fall more deeply asleep before she tried to escape again.

She didn't relish the idea of taking a bullet in the back.

He wouldn't hesitate to dispatch her now that he was sober enough to realize she wasn't his beloved. Kidnapping a woman was still a hanging offense in these parts. If he thought killing her would help him escape, he wouldn't hesitate. She felt certain of that.

Kin collapsed against a tree, giving his head a shake. His vision was blurry and things around him warbled like a mirage. But Cora was in these woods somewhere and he wasn't going to let a little dizziness stop him.

A few steps farther in, he came to a small creek. It cackled over stones and sand, cascading downhill.

He fell to his knees and drank thirstily from one of the little pools, then splashed a double handful of water against his face. His head still throbbed, but the cool water helped. He swiped most of it away and looked both directions.

Which way had they gone? The ground didn't seem to hold any clues. He hunted for several feet in both directions and found nothing.

Discouraged, he came back to the creek for another drink. As he bent to scoop a handful, his focus honed in on one of the rocks in the bottom of the bed.

Moss had been scraped off of it!

There another! And still another a little farther on.

The captain was smart. He'd made Cora wade the length of the creek bed!

Kin sent up a prayer of thankfulness and headed downstream.

After what Cora figured must be fifteen minutes, the captain started snoring.

She set to work on the buttons of her jacket. If she took that off, the silk of her blouse beneath would help her be able to slide out from under the leather restraint. It would also give her an extra half inch of space.

She had one arm out and was working the jacket off the other arm when the captain grunted and stirred.

She froze. Held her breath.

He rolled over and started snoring again.

But there wasn't a moment to lose. Who knew how long the man would sleep? He could wake fully at any second!

With her other arm free of the jacket, Cora set it quietly onto the ground beside her and then went to working the bandolier up over one shoulder. It was a task, especially with the rough bark of the tree continually catching at the leather of the bandolier or gouging into the tender skin of her back, but she finally had the leather above one shoulder. The other was easier to free, after that. But now the leather was around her neck!

She turned her head to the side and tried to push the restraint up over her head, but it was so tight! Her hair caught in the bark and came loose. Several strands caught and pulled. She clenched her teeth against the pain. Her right cheek scraped against the sharp bark, but finally, the bandolier slid off! She was free.

She froze and glanced across the fire.

He was still asleep.

Taking her jacket, she stood as quietly as she could. Her first step crunched loudly against the dry pine needles. She winced. But he slept on. She backed slowly around the tree she'd been tied to. And only when it was between her and the slumbering man, did she move more hurriedly.

After pushing as quietly as she could past several bushes, she gave up being quiet and chose speed over stealth.

It was only when she'd run to exhaustion that she realized she'd made two mistakes.

She hadn't even tried to disguise her trail.

And because she'd only been concerned with putting distance between herself and the man, she had no idea which way town was. Was she moving away from town? Or toward it? What if some wild animal came upon her? She had nothing with which to protect herself!

Cora paused, braced her hands on her knees, and looked around.

Nothing gave her any idea which way to head.

Kin smelled the smoke first. He slowed, and tested the air.

Not coming from behind him, obviously, or he would have noticed the scent sooner. The wind was coming toward him. But the brush was so thick here, it was hard to determine whether to the right or to the left.

He chose the right, and pressed ahead quickly. A wave of dizziness caught him unexpectedly and caused him to lose his balance. His boot came down on a branch that snapped loudly.

He froze. Cringed. He may as well have called out to announce his presence. But no sound indicated that anyone had heard the noise. He proceeded, more cautiously this time.

The scent of the smoke grew stronger and his anticipation mounted. He was close. But he willed himself to draw a long slow inhale. He needed to approach with caution so that he didn't get Cora hurt.

There! Through the brush he could see the light of the fire that must be the source of the smoke.

Why would the man have stopped after only several miles and built a fire to boot? Didn't he know that Kin would have hunted him to the ends of the earth? The man's drunkenness must not have him thinking too clearly. It didn't matter. All that mattered was that he had found them. If that man had hurt Cora in any way . . .

His teeth slammed together, and he shucked his Colt. Inched forward. Paid careful attention to where his feet fell. There were three large evergreens, with the fire built in the center. He leaned against one of the trees, took a quick breath, and swung around to the other side, gun at the fore.

Disappointment slammed into him.

The area lay empty.

He dropped to a low squat.

Had stepping on the branch earlier alerted Sherman? He could even now be hiding in any of the surrounding brush, taking aim.

Kin slunk back into the bushes just far enough to give himself some cover.

He searched the surrounding area methodically. Every shadow. Every bush. Every tree.

There! It wasn't Sherman, but it was a broken path through the brush!

Something had moved through here quickly.

His heartbeat quickened. Had Cora escaped?

He scooted over and bent to study the ground. "Yes!" The imprint of a small boot lay clearly visible in the soft dirt beneath a juniper. The toe of the print was slightly deeper, indicating she'd been moving fast.

She *had* escaped! Good for her!

But overlaid partially atop Cora's print, was the larger heavier print of Captain Sherman.

Sherman was on her trail.

Kin moved out at a lope, giving his head a shake to dispel the blur that had crept into his vision. "God, I need a little help here."

Chapter Thirty

ora figured moving, even if it was away from town, was better than standing still. She wanted to put as much distance between herself and the captain as possible. So she pressed forward.

But she made herself move more cautiously now. The ground was soft, and she couldn't prevent her boots from leaving prints in the dirt. But wherever she could, she jumped from tree root to tree root, or tree root to rock. And if she did have to land on soft soil, she took a moment to sprinkle some leaves over the area.

Maybe that would at least slow him down if he made a pursuit.

Then she came to a place where a huge patch of wild blackberries grew so thickly tangled, that she couldn't push through. If she had a hatchet, she could have hacked her way through. But of course, she didn't have one. And anyhow, it would void all her efforts at keeping her trail hidden. But she could hear a creek on the other side!

If she could follow the creek downstream, she would likely come upon a settlement of some sort where she could get some help!

She must find a way through!

A branch snapped behind her. With a gasp, she spun around.

Captain Sherman glowered at her above the round black hole at the end of his pistol. "Thought you were pretty smart, did you?"

Cora licked her dry lips. Despair sapped the strength from her legs. She sank to the ground and hung her head.

But just as quickly as the fight had drained out of her, it rose back up again. She fisted her hands by her sides. "Whatever you intend to do with me, I wish you would get on with it." She cast him a defiant squint, and immediately wished that she hadn't.

Because a glint of anticipation filled his eyes and his lecherous gaze slithered over her. "It would be my pleasure." He moved toward her.

Cora's heart hammered so loud and fast that she felt a bit faint. She scrambled away from him, but the tangle of thorny vines behind her blocked her progress. "Get away from me!"

Sherman only laughed.

He snatched for her ankle, but Cora kicked out with both feet. One of her boots caught his gun hand across the knuckles and sent his pistol flying into the brush.

He cursed loudly as she clambered away on all fours.

Lord, please. There was no time for more of a prayer than that.

Her breath hissed through her teeth. Panic threatened to choke her.

No longer worried about the thorns, she grabbed several brambles and tried to squirm and break her way through the thick shrubs. But the green branches didn't break easily or give way to create a path. Sharp protrusions caught in her hair, blouse, and skirt. One scraped a cut along her arm. A spear-shaped one, broken off at some point in years past, jabbed her so sharply that she instinctively jerked back with a gasp.

Sherman was on her again. He grabbed her leg and yanked.

She clawed for a grip, but thorns stabbed her palm and she cried out. It was no use.

Dragging her on her belly, he hauled her out of the patch, then dropped her on the ground at his feet. He fell onto her, pinning her legs. "Come on now, darling. You can't have it both ways. You just told me I could have my way with you." He flipped her over.

"I did no such thing!" Cora scrabbled one hand along the ground, searching for any weapon to use against him but only came up with a handful of sandy soil and pine needles. She flung it into his face.

He yelped and lurched back, clawing at his eyes.

Frenetically, she leapt up to run, but before she even got one step, he shot out a hand and clasped a handful of her hair.

With a cry, she toppled backward. She grappled and kicked and clawed. Yet, try as she might, she could not get free.

He took his time clearing his vision. Holding her captive without a word, he blinked his watering eyes. Rubbed them. Blinked some more.

"I'm going to kill you," he ground out. "Gah!" He growled in pain. Muddy tears streamed into his beard. He stretched his face, open-mouthed, eyelashes fluttering.

"People will be looking for me by now." Cora didn't really believe her own words, but it was the only thing she could think to say.

"Naw. Even if they have figured out you've gone missing. It'll be hours before anyone even knows where to start the hunt."

Cora tried to extract her hair from his grip once more and cried out when he gave her a vicious shake.

Using her hair as an effective tool, he flopped her onto her back and reached to undo his belt. A lecherous grin split his lips, bunching the skin near his red-rimmed eyes.

Cora's horror mounted as for the first time it registered what he truly planned to do to her. "Dear God, please." The prayer emerged as a whimper. Then she said more boldly, "Kin will have told them where to look!"

Sherman grunted a laugh. He leaned over her and grabbed her face in one meaty hand. His fingers sank painfully into her cheeks. Spittle clung to one corner of his lips. His hungry gaze roamed her face. "He won't be talking. In case you've forgotten, we left him lying dead back there."

Cora couldn't stop her tears. She had not forgotten.

All was lost, for she was powerless against his brute strength.

Something crackled in the brush. "I wouldn't be so sure of that."

"Kin!" Her hopes surged.

Shock washed over Sherman's face. Eyes wide, mouth gaping, he involuntarily loosened his grip when he looked up.

Cora reared back her head and then brought it forward like a battering ram. Her forehead cracked against the bridge of his nose.

"Ah!" Blood spurted everywhere as he clapped both hands to his face.

"Get off her," Kin roared. A broad, brown hand appeared on the captain's shoulder.

And then Captain Sherman was airborne.

He crashed into the blackberry bushes a pace away. Sherman's hand dropped to his hip, but Cora saw the moment it registered that his gun was still off wherever she'd kicked it.

His eyes bulged and he lunged in that direction. But the blackberries had firm hold of him now. He cried out, thrashed once, then froze. He gingerly lifted his hands above his head. "Don't shoot!"

Kin thrust his revolver toward the man. "Why shouldn't I?"

Cora scrambled forward. "Kin. Don't."

Attention and gun still focused on Captain Sherman, Kin reached his free hand to help her up. "You okay?" he asked, without looking at her.

"Yes." She rested a hand on his arm that still stretched toward Sherman. "Kin, you got here in time. Please. Let's let the law take care of him."

"Yeah, good idea." Sheriff Callahan stepped into the clearing, followed by his two deputies. He mercilessly hauled a howling Sherman from the brush. "On your belly!"

Sherman complied without hesitation, and with the deputies standing guard, the sheriff cuffed his hands.

Cora could see that he was bleeding profusely from several long scratches.

Kin blew out a breath, holstered his gun, and sank to a crouch. He touched his fingertips to the ground to help maintain his balance, hung his head, and gulped great breaths several more times.

Then, very shakily, he stood and gathered her into his trembling arms. "Thank God. Thank God. Thank God." He pressed a kiss against her temple.

"Good job, Kin. I didn't think we were going to catch up to you in time. I forgot how good you are at moving through the woods like a ghost." Sheriff Callahan approached and clapped Kin on one shoulder.

Kin winced. "Go easy on the shoulder."

"Sorry."

Reluctantly, Cora stepped out of the shelter of Kin's arms.

Reagan arched a brow. "Were you going to shoot him?"

Kin glared at the man, who was being led away by Deputy Joe. Then he met the sheriff's gaze evenly. "There was no need, once Cora was safe."

"Uh-huh." The tone of the sheriff's voice said he wasn't sure whether to believe Kin or not. He gave them both a once-over. "You two better go see Doc, right away. I'll send Joe with word for him to meet you at our place."

"Thank you," Cora said.

The sheriff nodded.

"How did you know where to find me?" Her gaze bounced between both men.

Kin shrugged. "After I came to, Doctor Polson was there. He patched me up as best he could in a quick manner. Then I sent him back to town to fetch help, and came after you."

The sheriff brushed dirt off his hands, face grim. "We were halfway home from services when Doctor Polson found us. Thankfully, both the Holloways and Rodantes were coming to the house with us for a celebration meal. Glad you are both okay. Come and see me after you talk to Doc, all right? I'll have a few more questions." With that, he walked away.

It was just Kin before her now and he looked a lot the worse for wear. His skin seemed pale and dried blood matted his hair and beard. The large bandage around his head was also stained with blood.

"Look at you." Very gently, he touched her cheek.

She could only imagine what kind of bruising she had from that slap, but she was in prime condition compared to him.

"Cora, I'm so sorry."

"I'm fine. I thought I'd lost you." Cora reached to touch the bandage around his head. "Are you okay?"

He took her hand and curled it close. The brown of his eyes softened as he looked down at her. "I am now. You sure you're okay?"

She pressed her other hand against his chest. "Yes. Thanks to you." She frowned at the belt looped behind his neck. "What's this?"

His lips thinned into wry humor and he adjusted his wrist to rest in the loop. "My shoulder got popped out of joint somehow when I fell." He gave the belt a flick. "This is supposed to be a sling. Guess I forgot about using it there for a second."

"We need to get you to Doc." She started in the wake of Sheriff Callahan and Marshal Zane, but Kin's warm fingers wrapping around hers stopped her.

With his free arm, he tugged her close again. "Before Sherman came upon us, I was about to say something that I need you to hear."

"Can it wait? I'm worried about you."

"It can't wait." His scrutiny swept across her brow, past her eyes, across her cheeks. It paused on her lips. Lingered. Hesitated.

Cora's heartbeat quieted in her ears. In the tree above them, a bird twittered. The gentle hum of a honeybee buzzed in the near distance.

After a long moment, Kin's head dipped. His lips grazed hers, tantalizing and gentle.

Her knees lost their strength and she clutched his shirt, moving as close as she could without crushing his arm.

He started to draw back, but she chased him up onto her tiptoes, capturing his lips again with her own. This was bliss. This was love. This was home.

Too soon, he pulled back. She let him go this time, relishing his nearness as he pressed his forehead to hers. "I love you, Cora Harrison. I think I fell in love with you the moment you turned around in that Cle Elum saloon and looked at me."

She grinned. "Did you now?"

He nodded. "I did. But I knew your faith wouldn't allow you to let me close."

"You were right."

"I'm going to do my best to grow in my faith. But I might need some time before, well . . ." He cleared his throat. "Before we decide if we take this further." He dipped in for another quick kiss.

"I'm okay with that. I think it's better that a courtship is slow."

"Courtship, huh?" One side of his mouth ticked up. "I like the sound of that."

"I do too, Mr. Davis. I truly do."

And as his mouth slanted over hers once more, Cora couldn't help but shoot up a little prayer of thanks to the Lord for turning her nightmare into such joy.

Chapter Thirty-one

ora was so happy on Saturday morning when she woke to see that it had dawned bright and fair. It was the perfect day for the final schoolhouse fundraiser. The whole town would be abuzz with activity.

Even though Dixie had closed down the diner for the day, Cora had left her room at her usual hour to come help with the huge amount of baking.

Dixie was donating twelve batches of her cinnamon buns, and all but the last two trays had already been pulled, brown and piping hot, from the oven. Cora was just finishing with her job of slathering on the icing and about to fetch the last two trays. They only needed a couple more minutes. After she iced them, she slid them down to Belle, whose job it was to cut the buns apart and wrap each one individually in brown paper and tie them with a bit of twine.

With twenty buns in each batch, Dixie's contribution to the fund would be no small amount. She'd planned to sell each one for two bits, but both Cora and Belle had told her not to offer them for less than fifty cents. It was for the best of causes, and hungry loggers would be more than happy to part with their hard-earned cash to get their hands on such a delectable treat, even at such an outrageous sum.

"You torturous fiends! It smells like the halls of heaven in here!"

At the sound of Kin's voice, Cora spun around with a happy smile. "Top of the morning, you."

He grinned and sidled closer, slipping his hands around her waist. "The height of the morning will all depend on if you give me one of Dixie's cinnamon buns, or not."

"Hmm. I see how much I mean to you all of a sudden."

"Let me hasten to add that it will also depend on how many sweet kisses I can steal while Belle isn't looking."

Cora chuckled, and appreciated that, with a smile of parting, Belle suddenly seemed to remember something she needed to take care of in the dining room. Cora and Kin were left alone in the kitchen.

"I like her," Kin said just before he dallied a kiss across Cora's lips. Leaning back, he smacked his own. "Mmmm. Sweet kisses indeed. I think you've been sampling the goods, Miss Cora."

She giggled and licked a dab of frosting from the tip of one of her fingers. "Perks of the job."

He released her and reached toward the pan of newly frosted buns.

"Ah-ah!" Cora smacked the back of his hand. "That will be fifty cents, if you don't mind." She pointed to the blue mason jar with the fifty-cent sign on the front.

"Fifty cents is highway robbery to a man with hunger pangs cramping his belly."

Cora only grinned. "We know."

Kin laughed. "I'll take two." He dug a silver dollar from his pocket and dropped it into the jar.

Cora beamed. "Coming right up. Would you like the hot ones just coming out of the oven? I might even be coerced into adding an extra dollop of frosting."

"You do know how to sweet talk a fella."

Lifting the hot pads, Cora pointed him toward the coffee percolator on the back of the stove. "Coffee's there. Then have a seat at the table. We're almost done and then I have the rest of the day off."

She pulled the last two trays of buns from the oven while Kin poured two mugs of coffee. She dropped her own fifty cents into the jar, then scooped two rolls onto a plate for Kin and one on another for herself. It wouldn't hurt her to sit for five minutes to join him for breakfast. She was already ahead of Belle, anyhow.

As she slid his plate in front of him and sank down across the table, she eyed him with concern. He likely didn't realize it, but he was rubbing his temples. The white bandage around his head filled her with angst every time she focused on it.

While her bruises had faded and her scratches had healed, Kin was still fighting dizzy spells and headaches.

With the judge passing through town on account of the fundraiser this week, Captain Sherman's trial had been a quick affair. Because he had shot Kin and left him for dead, the judge had sentenced him to twenty years. He'd tacked on another five for Cora's kidnapping and attempted assault. And another five simply because his intent had been to harm a child. Deputy Joe and Marshal Zane had escorted the man on the train to McNeil Island Prison. The captain's crew members had been rounded up and returned to Seattle on the same train. Word around town was that Sheriff Callahan had informed them that if they ever set foot in his town again, they would find themselves on the wrong side of a jail cell, though Cora wasn't certain how much of that particular rumor was true. She was only thankful and so relieved to have their dark threat removed from her life.

"How's your headache today?"

Kin straightened and tugged his plate close. "A lot better, actually. But Doc said I could be fighting them for months yet. I guess it's a good reminder to be thankful and keep working. God must not be done with me yet."

She reached across the table to squeeze his arm. "And I'm so glad He's not."

They said a quick prayer of thanks and then oohed and ahhed their way through Dixie's sweet rolls. Kin stuck around to help her and Belle finish the packaging, and if it was partly so that he could scoop out the last of the frosting and down it by the spoonful, well Cora could only laugh because she enjoyed his company so much.

After they'd all washed their sticky hands, they loaded up their arms with baskets and hurried, laughing and chattering, up the hill to the church.

All the pews had been moved and stacked at the sides, and there was table after table laden with goodies and paraphernalia for sale.

Cora laid out her lace rounds on her reserved space and smoothed them flat. She had managed to finish ten of them. One was significantly larger than the rest and would actually make a lovely white table cloth if anyone needed a fancy one. She wasn't sure if two dollars was too much, but considering the hours she'd spent on each piece, she hadn't been able to justify anything less.

Kin lifted one of the little paper tags she'd tied to one. "Two dollars, huh?"

She wrinkled her nose. "Do you think it's too much?"

"No. Not at all." He shook his head.

She blew a breath of relief. "Oh good. I didn't want to overprice them. Oh, there are Charlotte and Reagan with Charlotte's pies. I should go help her. Would you mind manning my booth and collecting the money if anyone decides to buy? My donation jar is there on the back corner of the table."

"Of course."

"Thank you." Cora hurried away.

The morning passed in a flurry of activity. After she'd helped Charlotte slice and plate ten pies, Belle had asked her to sit for a portrait, and Cora had obliged her with a little trepidation. But in addition to her donation of lace, she'd planned to spend a whole two dollars at the fundraiser, and since Belle was only asking two bits for her sketches, it was a bargain. Belle brought such life to her portraits with just a few strokes of her pencils, and it was only fifteen minutes later that she presented Cora with the picture.

To Cora's surprise, it was not only a portrait of her, but Belle had added Kin too. In the sketch, Cora wore an apron and held a cinnamon bun behind her back, and Kin was attempting to see over her shoulder with that adorable lopsided grin of his.

"Belle, it's beautiful!"

Belle gave her a squeeze. "You two are beautiful." She tipped a nod. "Don't you think you better go rescue him?"

Across the room, Mrs. Hines had stopped before Cora's booth and was fingering the largest piece of her lace. Kin had his hands clasped behind his back and was attentively replying to each apparent question she asked.

Cora grinned. "Maybe I should at that. Thanks again." She gave Belle a quick hug and then hustled through the crowd.

As she approached, she heard Kin saying, "The price is well worth it, Mrs. Hines, I can assure you. You won't find any finer lace here today and I can promise you that."

Cora's hackles rose. That woman was haggling over the price of two dollars she'd put on that? Why, it had taken her three months to get that piece just right!

"All right. I do believe you are correct, Mr. Davis." Mrs. Hines smiled. She patted the lace. "I'll take it."

Kin nodded. "Excellent choice, Mrs. Hines. As you can see, there's only one small one left. You'll be glad you were one of the lucky buyers of these exclusive pieces!"

Cora's brows launched into her hairline. He'd sold all but one of her pieces? Why, that would be a lovely donation of eighteen dollars already! How wonderful!

Kin carefully wrapped Mrs. Hines's lace in brown paper and handed the packet to her, accepting the money she offered. "Thank you, Mrs. Hines. Good day to you." He tapped the package. "No one will have a finer Sunday table than you will."

The woman beamed. "Indeed, I believe you are correct!" With that, she scooted to the next table over.

Kin turned and tucked the money into Cora's jar.

Cora joined him behind the table. "I'm so pleased to see that the lace has sold so quickly. If I'm honest, I wondered if it would even sell at all. But I'm very honored to be able to donate my few dollars to the cause."

Kin grinned. Nodded. "What do you have there?"

"Oh, you must see it. She's only charging two bits! Look what Belle sketched." She held the page out for him to see.

He took the paper and studied it with a laugh. "She does know us rather well, doesn't she? She's so good. I wish she would follow her dream to go to that art conservatory in Seattle."

Cora's gaze drifted to where Kane Carver stood chatting with Belle while she sketched him. Her smile turned wistful. "I think she's been waiting on a certain someone to see if he will get with the program and propose."

"Oh. I see. Did you say she's only charging two bits? She should be charging much more than that. Hang on a second. I'll be right back." Kin handed Cora the sketch and strode across the room. She giggled as she watched him steal one of Belle's pens, cross out the amount on her sign and scrawl something else. Cora couldn't read the amount from here, but she could tell that he'd increased the price by quite a bit, due to Belle's and Kin's giggles at the aghast protest Kane made with much good-natured laughter.

"My, this is lovely."

A woman Cora didn't recognize stopped before her table. Perhaps one of the wives from the logging camps? Plenty of those women rarely made it in to town.

"Thank you." Cora smiled.

The woman turned over the tag and hesitated. "Is this your only piece?"

"It's the last one, I'm afraid. All the others have sold already."

"At this price?" The woman lifted a surprised look.

People obviously had no idea how many hours went into one piece of lace. Cora only smiled. She was too happy today to haggle over prices. "Yes."

The woman dropped the tag and held out one hand. "My name is Rose Shipman. I own Shipman's General Store over in Cle Elum. I wonder if you'd be willing to sell your lace through my store?"

"Oh my, that's flattering. I'm just not certain that enough money can be made to make it worth our time."

The woman's brows arched. "I would only want twenty percent."

Cora did some quick figuring. With the cost of the thread, that would leave her a dollar and a half from each piece. It would be nice pocket money, though she'd have to spend a great deal of time to get it. Still, on her breaks and in the evenings, she could crochet a little.

"Okay, that sounds lovely."

The woman nodded. "Excellent. I'll take as many pieces as you can make by the end of the month."

"Thank you. I'll see what I can do."

Kin strode up just as the woman was leaving. "Who was that?"

Cora explained. Then added, "I'll be making very little for the hours involved, but it's flattering to have her want the pieces."

Kin grinned at her. "Check the price tag."

"What?"

"Go on. Check it." He pointed.

Feeling a surge of curiosity, Cora did as she was told. "Twelve dollars?!" She dropped the tag as if it had burned her.

Kin's gaze sparkled. He tipped a nod toward her donation money.

Cora opened the lid on the blue mason jar and gasped. Instead of the coins she'd expected, inside lay a jumbled mass of paper currency! She could see several ten-dollar bills. "What did you do?"

He grinned with the lift of one shoulder. "It was easy to add a one in front of all your twos. And a five after the two on that bigger piece."

Cora gasped. "Mrs. Hines paid twenty-five dollars for a lace tablecloth?"

"She sure did." He winked. "It's all in how you sell it."

Cora plunked into her chair, a hand pressed to her chest. "Oh my. Wait. How much is in there?" She pointed to the jar.

He chuckled. "Over a hundred and twenty dollars."

"Oh, that's wonderful. I can't believe it. Zoe is going to be so thrilled!"

"I'm sure she will be. Speaking of Zoe . . ." He searched the room. "Have you seen her?"

"No. I haven't seen her yet. I'm certain she's simply run off her feet today."

"Probably true."

"When is the ground-breaking ceremony?"

"Supposed to start at three, I think. But word is that Mr. Heath has a big announcement. He's supposed to give it at any time."

"Interesting."

"Quite."

Jacinda Callahan approached then and exclaimed over Cora's lace. She declared that she simply had to have it and purchased the last piece. Cora felt a bit like a highwayman as she stuffed the bills into her jar. But my, it gave her such a feeling of accomplishment to think about how much she would be able to add toward the building of the school.

Kin sidled close and lowered his voice. "Does this mean you are done with your commitments for the day?"

Cora searched the room over. "I suppose it does. However, I could help over at Dixie's table. And we should wait to hear the announcement."

"Meh. That wouldn't be nearly as much fun as riding out with me to see a piece of property I recently purchased."

Cora's gaze flew to his sparkling one. "You bought property? Other than the piece here behind the church?"

"I did. Want to see it?"

"Yes!" Excitement mixed with a heady curiosity swelled through her. The twinkle in his eyes told her he was up to something.

"Well, all right, then. Let me fetch the wagon. We can go right after Mr. Heath has his say."

"Okay." As she watched him leave, she couldn't help but wonder what he was up to.

Chapter Thirty-two

Zoe Kastain stood on the path looking down onto the Nolan ranch and feeling like she might lose her breakfast at any moment. Smoke spiraled in a steady whirl from both the chimney on the Nolans' main house and on the new cabin further down the road.

When she'd arrived at the social this morning only to have Jackson tell her that Wash had once more refused to come, she'd known that she must go see him, consequences be hanged.

She was missing part of the festivities on a day that she'd looked forward to for months, but there were some things that simply were too important to be put off.

Taking a deep breath, she rubbed her palms over her hips and strode down the hill. She moved past the main house, with her goal firmly set. Her knuckles rapped sharply against his cabin door. "Wash? It's me, Zoe." She pressed a hand to her stomach and whispered to herself, "Do not get sick, Zoe Kastain. Do not get sick!"

After a moment, she heard a sound like scraping furniture inside, but received no reply.

"I can hear you in there. Please, Wash. I only want to say hello." She curled her hands together in a tight clench. What would she do if he refused to answer the door?

She'd begun to despair that would be the case, when, finally, the door swung slowly open.

Wash stood in the opening, leg's wide, arms folded.

She scanned him from head to toe. Then again. Other than the frown on his countenance, nothing seemed changed. His face was unmarred. He had both arms. Both legs.

So his injury really had been as minor as that new doctor had been proclaiming about town?

Anger surged through her, hot and powerful. Her chin notched up several degrees. "Washington Nolan, I ought to pummel you! Here I have been worried sick for days that something was really wrong and you look just the same as when you left!"

A muscle pulsed in his stubbled jaw. "Good to see you too, Zo."

His words set her back. She pinched the bridge of her nose, willing away the ache in her heart. "It *is* good to see you, Wash. I just don't understand why you've been avoiding everyone? Avoiding . . . me?" Her voice turned small on that last word. Irritated by the sting of tears, she blinked rapidly a couple of times and then forced herself to search his face. Surely he had a good reason?

Arms still folded, he lifted one shoulder. "Just haven't felt much like engaging in empty prattle, I guess."

"Haven't felt much like . . ." Was that what he thought of all the dreams they'd shared? Empty prattle?

She turned her face toward the spring green of the fields surrounding the cabin. From here, due to a little rise in the road and a small copse of trees, she couldn't see anything of the main house except for the spiral of smoke against the blue of the sky. Butch's green pastures lay empty with only the barbed wire fences giving any indication that they were normally filled with cattle. She frowned, wondering where all his animals were.

Maybe he'd gathered them all into one of the farther fields.

Realizing that shock had caused her mind to wander, Zoe snapped her gaze back to Wash. She needed to understand where she stood. "Before you left, you asked me to wait for you. I thought you would at least come and see me."

He propped one hand against the door, shifting his weight a little.

Heavens! He'd been muscular when he'd left due to hard work on the farm, but this cavalry had broadened him. The bunched muscle of his arm seemed to be chiseled from hardwood, and his chest was at least twice the width of her shoulders.

He cleared his throat and looked past her toward the fields.

She realized she'd been staring and snapped her attention to the doorframe.

The knuckles of his hand that gripped the doorposts turned white. After a long pause, he grated, "I hope you didn't take that too seriously. We were nothing more than kids, Zoe."

She had to fight for a moment to get her thoughts back on track. "Nothing more than kids . . ." She felt like an echo, constantly repeating the shocking statements that were so unlike him. "I see." She retreated a step, no longer certain of anything in her life. "Uh . . . Okay. I just wanted to say . . . uh . . . welcome home, Wash. You have a good day."

She turned and hurried away then, lest she fall into a blubbering heap of confusion at his feet. Tears streamed and she swiped at them angrily. Apparently, he'd been willing to engage in *empty prattle* all the way to the conclusion of his last letter in which he'd told her how he planned to finish out his time in the cavalry and then build them a home on the farthest pasture of his father's land. He'd planned to work the land, raise cattle, maybe allow his father, who was getting up in years, to retire from his labors and rest for his final years.

And now . . .

Zoe huffed, hefted handfuls of her skirts, and took the incline back toward town with as much speed as her legs could muster.

"Nothing more than kids, indeed! Someone certainly is acting like a child!"

Wash closed the door and immediately fell into the chair that he'd scooted out of sight behind it. He bent until his forehead pressed against his knee and massaged the aching muscles of his lower leg.

For the rest of the day, he'd be paying for his pride of not wanting her to see him leaning on a crutch.

A sob caught him unaware. He scrunched his eyes tight and gulped another breath.

That had been much harder than he'd expected it would be. He almost hadn't been able to force himself to say those words. But that would have been the ultimate selfishness. It was better this way. Even if his heart felt as though it lay in lacerated pieces around his feet. She would have a better life without the burden of caring for him.

A cramp seized his calf and he cried out at the severity of it. He dug his thumbs into the pain, gasping in relief when the sharp cramp gave way to the pressure.

Yes. Zoe would be much better off without being stuck with a cripple like him for the rest of her life.

He just had to stay away from her so that his heart could come around to accepting what his mind told him was true.

Kin pulled up in front of the church with the wagon. He was just about to dash up the steps when he saw Isaiah sitting in the shade of the building, with his arms curled against his chest. He was looking out over the bustle of the town, methodically stroking something Kin couldn't see. A furrow pinched his brow.

Kin reversed course and sank onto the ground beside him. As he did, he saw that Ike held a fluffy bundle of gray fur—the cute kitten he'd chosen. He plucked a stem of grass then bumped Ike with his elbow.

"Morning, kid." He reached over to scratch the kitten behind one ear. "She old enough to leave her mama now?"

Ike shook his head. "Gots another week. The Rodantes only brought her in for the day."

"I see. Something on your mind?" Kin studied the frown still on Ike's brow.

Isaiah transferred his gaze to the sleeping kitten in his lap. "Nah. It's nothing. She sure is a cute little thing, ain't she?"

"Sure is." Kin wasn't ready to let him off so easily. "Burdens always feel lighter when shared with a friend."

Ike's face twisted toward him. "We friends?"

Kin lifted one shoulder. "I'd like to think we are."

Ike's brow slumped again. "You think the Callahans only adopted me on account of wantin' to protect me? The judge, he signed the papers and everythin' just yesterday, but I don't want to be a burden to no one."

Kin felt his heart go out to the kid. How well he remembered having that same feeling with the parson as a kid. He reached over to settle one hand on the boy's shoulder. "I've known Sheriff Callahan most of my life. And if there's one thing I know, it's that he doesn't ever do anything he doesn't want to do."

Ike shrugged. "Yeah, but maybe he only wanted to protect me?"

"I'm sure he did, but you pause and think about all the other things he's done for you. If he only wanted to protect you, would he have built you that swing? Or taken you to pick out this kitten—which I'm more than a little jealous about, by the way."

Ike chuckled. "She is a beaut."

Kin stroked her head again. "For certain." Kin jostled the boy's shoulder.

"It's just that Mr. Reagan, well, he was a bit short with me this mornin' and I just wondered . . . You know."

"I have something to say and I hope you'll be able to hear me." Ike looked over at him.

"When I was a kid, Parson Clay adopted me. I think you knew that. What you don't know is that I shared a lot of your concerns. I didn't want to be a burden, but I wasn't as . . . well-behaved as you are." He winked, pleased to see Isaiah relaxing a little as humor filled his features. "The parson, he was hard on me, and I thought maybe it was because he didn't want me. But I can see now as an adult that if that had been true there would have been any number of ways PC could have ousted me from his life. He kept me because he loved me."

He swallowed hard, realizing he needed to find the man and have a conversation with him. A word of appreciation would go a long way, he felt sure. And he knew PC and Aurora would be so thrilled with his surrender to the Lord.

He tossed aside his grass and stood. He needed to get Cora. "Today, there is a lot going on. The sheriff, he carries a big burden of keeping this town safe. Sometimes that might mean he's less than patient. But it has nothing to do with how he feels about you. I look back now on the times PC disciplined me and I realize he was doing it on account of how much he cared about me. There will be times you get disciplined too. Just let it drive home the point about how blessed you are to be loved by a good man like that."

"Yessuh." Ike's troubled furrows seemed a little smoother.

"All right then, I better—"

"Isaiah! There you are, son." Reagan barreled around the corner of the building, holding a wooden crate in his hands. He lifted the crate a little higher. "Didn't I ask you to fetch these last few pies from the wagon?"

"Oh, sorry! Linc Nolan asked me to play catch. And then Mr. Rodante gave me Blue." He held up the kitten. "Then, I was talking to Mr. Kin."

Kin tucked his thumbs into his back pockets, giving Reagan a grin.

Reagan frowned at his smile before returning his gaze to his son. "Well, when I ask you to do something, I'll ask that next time you not forget it." He thrust the crate out. "Take these in to your mother, please. I need to make another sweep of the town."

"Yessuh." Ike scrambled to tuck the kitten into his shirt and then took the crate.

He grinned at Kin over his shoulder as he carried the crate into the church. There was so much relief shining in the kid's eyes that they could have almost been the day's sunlight.

Kin couldn't help but laugh. Could there have been any more perfect timing?

He moved to follow Ike inside, but just when he reached the top of the steps, PC was coming out the doors.

"Kin." His brow was furrowed and, perhaps because of his conversation with Ike, Kin realized for the first time that the look on PC's face didn't mean he was angry—merely concerned. "You still doing all right?" PC's gaze bounced off the bandage on his head.

"I'm fine, but I'm glad I bumped into you. Have a few minutes?"

"Sure."

Kin led him to one side of the porch. He leaned his arms on the rail. PC joined him, and together they looked down over the town.

Kin swallowed, not quite sure where to start. "Got something to tell you that I think you'll be happy about."

"Oh, yeah?" PC angled to look at him.

"Know you'll be happy about." Kin grinned over at him.

A hopeful lift filled the parson's expression. "I'm all ears."

"That surrender you spoke about?"

The parson straightened and searched Kin's face.

"Well, I finally figured out what that was."

PC had him wrapped in a bear hug before he even realized the man was moving. The parson clapped him several times on the back, making him wince when a pang shot through his still recovering shoulder. But it was a good kind of pain. The kind that was worth it for the underlying joy that accompanied it.

PC set him back at arm's length and then yanked him in for another hug. "Kin, you've no idea how delighted it makes me to hear this news."

"There's more." Kin stepped back, adjusting his rumpled clothes. "I just wanted to say thanks. Thanks for taking on the task of raising me. I know it—I—couldn't have been easy. But you stuck by me and I need you to know how much it means to me."

Genuine tears sparkled in the parson's eyes. "I know I was far from a perfect guardian."

Kin shook his head. "You were just what I needed." This time, it was Kin who pulled PC in for one more embrace.

After a moment, they both stepped back, laughing deprecatorily as they both swiped tears from their eyes.

"I better let you go," Kin said. "Just needed you to know."

PC nodded. "Thank you. You've made my day."

"Where were you going? Do you need help with anything?"

"No." PC shook his head. "I'm just heading down to Zeb's place to pick him up. He has a big announcement to make, it seems."

"What's it about?"

"No idea. He wouldn't tell me. Only said to please pick him up when the crowd was full."

Kin eyed the churchyard packed with wagons. "I think this qualifies."

PC smiled. "Indeed. We'll be right back."

"Okay. See you inside."

He stood for a moment, simply relishing the joy of thankfulness as he watched PC drive his wagon past the mill toward Zeb's house.

Chapter Thirty-three

Zoe lost the steam of her anger when she was only halfway back to town. She slowed, moved to the side of the road, and sank down on a log. She must hold it together. She had a whole town gathered to celebrate her and her students!

She pulled in a breath. Then another. But it was no good.

The tears came despite her valiant efforts.

Alone. Rejected.

Heartsick.

It all welled up and seeped from her eyes. Shook her with racking sobs. Her chest ached with the pain of it, and she couldn't hold back groans and outcries.

Her breaths hitched and hiccuped.

Her hands trembled where they covered her face.

"Zoe? What has you so distressed?"

She gasped and looked up, then gave a little shriek, shocked to see Parson Clay sitting on the log beside her.

He held up his palms. "I'm sorry. So sorry."

Zoe pressed a hand to her chest, hardly able to believe the parson's wagon sat on the road only a few paces away. Mr. Heath was sitting on the bench looking down at her sympathetically.

How had she not heard their arrival?

She brushed her hands over her eyes, hauling in a big breath. "I'm sorry. I'm fine. Really." She swiped more tears and stood. "I'm expected back in town. I really should be on my way."

She had only taken two steps when the parson said, "Running from our pain rarely solves anything."

She stopped, shoulders slumping. "And what do you do when you've tried to face your pain, Parson, and it has kicked you in the teeth?"

He thought for only a moment before he replied, "Our Lord tells us to turn the other cheek, walk two miles, give away our cloak."

Zoe felt her despair mount. How did one turn the other cheek when she hadn't been exactly slapped? Sometimes the pat answers from the Word made her want to throw her hands up in frustration. But she couldn't do such a thing with the parson and Mr. Heath looking on, now could she?

"I will endeavor to determine what that means in this situation, Parson. If you'll forgive me, for now, I really must get back to the festivities."

The parson stood. "We are just heading that way ourselves. And if you'll allow me to give you a ride, I think you'll witness something that will truly lift your spirits." He and Mr. Heath exchanged sly smiles.

"Oh?" Zoe couldn't fathom what he might mean.

But all he offered was a hand to help her into the back of the wagon. "You'll see."

She accepted his help and, a few minutes later, when the parson had parked the wagon near the church, followed the men inside.

Music was playing and several couples swept by on the dance floor. Doc, with little Ellery on one arm and his other holding Dixie. Deputy Joe, smiling down at Liora as they twirled by. Kin, with his bandaged head and Cora with her fading bruises looked lovingly into each other's eyes, seemingly in a world of their own as their feet moved in unison.

Zoe sighed. Looked away. In her current state, such sights were too painful.

Mr. Heath didn't waste any time but strode to the front of the room, not pausing to chat with anyone.

Once he was on the platform, Parson Clay blew a sharp whistle to gather attention.

The music died down and everyone came to a standstill, curiously intent on the front.

The parson smiled. "Thank you. Please listen. Mr. Heath has something he'd like to say."

Mr. Heath tottered to the podium, donned his spectacles, and then peered out at those gathered. News had spread quickly, and more people were crowding in from outside.

"If I could have the school board join me up here, please?"

Mrs. Hines offered the room a simpering smile as she quickly joined Mr. Heath. Mr. and Mrs. Olann were not far behind her. Mrs. Olann took her husband's arm and beamed out at the gathering.

Zoe felt a little sick to her stomach, seeing them up there.

The Callahans, who had been at the back of the room, were slower to join the man. They looked more somber than the others.

Zoe searched the room for Isaiah and found him standing next to Cora and Kin. His lowered gaze was fastened on a cute gray kitten in his arms. Kin had one hand resting on the boy's shoulder.

Zoe gritted her teeth. If the board was about to receive a commendation for their part in these events, she just might have to retire.

While the members had been gathering on the platform, Mr. Heath had pulled several papers from the inside pocket of his coat. He glanced over at the board members. "Thank you for joining me up here."

Zoe was distracted by Parson Clay, who was placing two buckets on the floor near the podium—one on either side. And Aurora was handing out small pieces of paper and pencils.

There weren't enough pencils to go around, but as she handed Zoe a paper, Aurora instructed, "The pencils will have to be shared, but there are enough that the wait shouldn't be too long."

The wait for what?

"I'm glad to see that so many have turned out for this fine fundraiser!" Mr. Heath shot one hand above his head, drawing a cheer from the room. "As you know, these are your duly elected board members, and you have them to thank for all the wonderful entertainments this evening!"

Another cheer.

Zoe studied her fingers that were crimping one corner of the blank paper in her hands.

When she looked back up, Mrs. Hines was clapping mincingly just beneath her chin, a huge smile on her face. When the cheering continued, she dropped a little curtsy.

Mr. and Mrs. Olann gave small waves, looking appropriately embarrassed.

The sheriff and Mrs. Callahan seemed very solemn and focused on the floor at their feet.

Mr. Heath waited to speak again until the room had quieted. "What you may not know is of a recent vote the school board took."

Mrs. Hines's simpering smile froze. Her eyes angled toward Mr. Heath.

Mrs. Olann shuffled slightly. Mr. Olann stretched his neck and straightened his tie.

But it was the tiny smile Charlotte did her best to hide that sent Zoe's hopes soaring. He wasn't!

Mr. Heath swept a hand down his long white beard and searched the gathering. "Isaiah Coleman? You here, lad?"

The crowd parted around the boy.

"Ah! There you are. Come join me, if you would?"

Isaiah's eyes were a bit trepidatious as he handed his kitten off to Kin and moved slowly toward the platform.

"There's a good lad. Right here beside me if you please. Now . . ." Mr. Heath lifted his gaze to the crowd once more. "Isaiah, here, came to town with Mr. Davis from Seattle a few weeks back."

"Coleman!" Lincoln Nolan shouted encouragingly from the back before being hushed by Butch.

Isaiah smiled shyly.

A ripple of laughter filled the room.

The Olanns and Mrs. Hines looked even more uncomfortable now.

Zoe felt anticipation begin to lighten her mood. *Please God, let this be a comeuppance, even if I will have to pray for forgiveness due to my joy over their demise later on.*

"Like any responsible pupil, Mr. Coleman joined our school right away."

The room lay completely silent now.

"I'm sure many of you have heard from your students that he's been absent, but you may not know why."

Mrs. Hines looked near a full-blown panic now. "Mr. Heath, might the board and I have a word with you in private?"

Mr. Heath thrust out a palm to silence her. "No, Mrs. Hines. The time for doing things in secret has passed."

She visibly paled and pressed a hand to the base of her throat.

Mr. Heath continued addressing the gathering. "You see, due to no infraction on this boy's part other than his coloring . . ."

Isaiah's head hung and Zoe was thankful to see Reagan scoot over and rest one hand on Ike's shoulder. The boy looked up at him, gratefully.

"An emergency board meeting was called by Mrs. Hines and Mrs. Olann and a vote was passed by a margin of three to two in favor of removing the lad from school."

"That's outrageous!" Someone gasped.

"He's just a boy!" Someone else chimed in.

Mr. Heath held up a hand, once more calling for silence. "Now, I know that generally when the board decides something, it is set. But I've called you all here at this moment because of a clause in our bylaws." He nudged his spectacles up onto the bridge of his nose and scanned the papers in his hands. "Our bylaws state that if the board rules on a matter that anyone in town disagrees with, we can call for a vote by the township and if at least a two-thirds majority votes against the board's decision, it can be overturned."

Zoe's eyes fell closed. Sheer relief and joy welled up within her.

"Let's vote!" Someone called.

Mr. Heath patted the air. "Each of you should have a paper in your hands. And someone nearby will have a pencil. We are voting here on whether to maintain the decision the board made to remove this lad from school. A vote of 'yes' keeps the decision as-is. A vote of 'no' will allow the boy to go back to school. Please make your marks and drop your ballots into the buckets up here. Parson would you—" He swept a gesture to the buckets.

The parson moved forward and turned the buckets around.

Zoe could now see that one had a sign that read "yes" and the other "no."

"Just drop your vote in the appropriate bucket. If it's close, we will count them. But I think I know what the good fair-minded citizens of Wyldhaven will choose."

When the person next to her handed over their pencil, Zoe took great relish in writing in large bold letters NO!

One by one, people filed past the buckets dropping their papers in. Since Zoe was near the back, she waited patiently, inching forward as she could. When she was finally able to reach the front of the room, it gave her great pleasure to see that the "yes" bucket lay completely empty, while the "no" bucket was filled almost halfway with little pieces of paper.

Mr. Heath beamed at Isaiah. "Welcome back to the Wyldhaven schoolhouse, son!"

Zoe rushed over and drew the boy into an enthusiastic embrace. Oh, how she had needed this bit of good news after today!

Mr. Olann took his wife by one arm. "I told you this was a bad idea!" He snapped as he marched off the platform.

Zoe couldn't hear his wife's reply.

Mr. Hines stormed to a stop in front of the buckets. He gave his wife a purposeful squint as he dropped his paper into the "no" bucket and then turned to stomp away.

"Now, Jerry—" Mrs. Hines hefted her skirts and scurried after her husband. He, however, did not seem inclined to wait for her.

When Zoe glanced down at Ike, it was to see tears of gratitude shimmering in his eyes.

He peeked into the empty "yes" bucket. "Mr. Kin done tried to tell me that the Wyldhaven tree was filled with good fruit. I just wasn't sure I believed him . . . Until now."

Zoe gave him another hug. "Kin is right. Wyldhaven is filled with good people."

Her thoughts drifted to Wash. Maybe all he needed was a reminder about what it meant to be from Wyldhaven.

She had to figure out how to help him.

Cora stood chatting with Charlotte and Liora Rodante about how well the fundraiser was going. All of them were thrilled with how the surprise vote had gone.

She'd already turned her donations over to the parson, who was the one in charge of collecting and tallying all the money. Later, there would be an announcement about how much had been raised.

"Ready?" Kins voice spoke from just behind her.

She spun to face him. "Yes!"

"Well, all right then." He led her outside and helped her up onto the wagon seat.

"Are we going to see that land?" Cora called back to him as he made his way around to the other side.

"You'll see." He grinned as he sank onto the bench beside her and clucked to the horses.

"Mysterious!" Cora teased.

"A little mystery is good for the constitution," Kin retorted.

Cora smiled and let her mild curiosity fade into the background.

They drove past Dr. Polson and Dr. Griffin's medical tent, where any ailment could be treated today for a donation to the cause of the school. Dr. Griffin appeared to be in the process of extracting a tooth from a bellowing patient who flailed on his table, but Dr. Polson acknowledged them with a mild salute.

Cora gave him a wave, thankful that he'd taken her at her word when she'd told him her heart had been captured by Kin.

It was a gorgeous day. A butterfly fluttered along beside the wagon, keeping pace for several seconds before careening off on a breeze to cavort with the wind. Far overhead an eagle cried.

Cora put her hand to her eyes and searched until she saw it circling with a keen focus on a field below.

A ways out of town, the road slipped beneath the shade of tall evergreen trees. The cool of the forest interior felt lovely, especially with golden rays of sun slanting through the branches overhead.

Not much further ahead, Kin pulled the wagon to a stop and came around to help her dismount.

Wyldhaven Creek tumbled merrily beside the path he led her along. He escorted her to a low knoll that overlooked the creek and, through the trunks of a couple tall trees, a little green valley beyond.

He stretched his arms wide. "What do you think?"

"It's beautiful. But surely you don't plan to build your office all the way out here?" Cora inhaled the sweet scent of the wild lilac bushes growing nearby, then bent to admire a dark-centered daisy.

"No. I think having my office in town will be best." His voice was suddenly coming from much closer to the ground. She turned to see what he might be doing, and froze.

Kin was down on one knee, holding a ring between his finger and thumb.

Her hand flew to cover her mouth.

He swallowed. Cleared his throat. "Cora Harrison, will you marry me?"

She stepped nearer and took his hand to encourage him to his feet. "I thought we were going to wait a while?"

His brows peaked with a little worry as he sidled nearer. "I was going to, but then, I thought, 'scrap that.' I don't want to wait a moment longer to make you my wife." He grinned languidly. "What do you say. Will you have a reformed reprobate like me?"

Her gaze dropped to the ring he held aloft between them. It was a simple silver band with a small sparkling white stone inset at the top. "It's beautiful," she breathed.

"It was my mother's."

Cora spun in a circle to take in the property. "Who did you buy this from?"

"Ewan McGinty." His voice sounded like sandpaper on nails. "How long are you going to keep me in suspense?"

Grinning, she looked up at him. "I thought mysteries were good for the constitution?"

He laughed a bit nervously, wiggled the ring for her attention, and quirked a brow.

Cora raised her arms and wrapped them around his neck. She leaned back, giving him a coy look. She wanted to retort with something witty, but her mind was blank. It seemed she could only focus on one thing. She lowered her left hand to waggle her ring finger. "The answer is yes, Mr. Davis. An emphatic yes!"

He blew a breath of relief. "I wasn't certain you would have me!"

"Oh, you most certainly were!"

He shook his head as he slipped the ring onto her finger. "I most certainly wasn't."

Cora raised up on her tiptoes and dallied a kiss across his lips! "Well, concern yourself no longer, my angel."

"Thanks for being my missionary," he whispered against her lips.

Such a surge of longing swept through her that she gave him one final peck and then stepped back, holding out a hand to keep him at bay. "I'm not feeling anything like a missionary at the moment, so you better keep your distance."

He growled happily and tugged her close for another quick kiss. His cheek pressed against her ear. "We could have PC marry us today." There was a hint of humor in his words.

She leapt back and smacked his chest. "Most certainly not. I want time to plan the perfect day." She put several steps between them. "Now tell me what your plans are for this property."

He mumbled good-naturedly but when he took another step toward her, she retreated with a laugh. "Kin Davis, you behave yourself!"

He capitulated with feigned grumpiness. "Fine. I thought we could put the cabin right here. And then . . ."

Cora forgot to pay attention to what he was saying as she happily stared down at the ring on her finger.

Please Review!

If you enjoyed this story, would you take a few minutes to leave your thoughts in a review on your favorite retailer's website? It would mean so much to me, and helps spread the word about the series.

You can quickly link through from my website here: http://www.lynnettebonner.com/books/historical-fiction/the-wyldhaven-series/

Want a FREE Story?

If you enjoyed this book...

...sign up for Lynnette's Gazette below! Subscribers get exclusive deals, sneak peeks, and lots of other fun content.

(The gazette is only sent out about once a month or when there's a new release to announce, so you won't be getting a lot of spam messages, and your email is never shared with anyone else.)

Sign up link: https://www.lynnettebonner.com/newsletter/

ABOUT THE AUTHOR

Born and raised in Malawi, Africa. Lynnette Bonner spent the first years of her life reveling in warm equatorial sunshine and the late evening duets of cicadas and hyenas. The year she turned eight she was off to Rift Valley Academy, a boarding school in Kenya where she spent many joy-filled years, and graduated in 1990.

That fall, she traded to a new duet—one of traffic and rain— when she moved to Kirkland, Washington to attend Northwest University. It was there that she met her husband and a few years later they moved to the small town of Pierce, Idaho.

During the time they lived in Idaho, while studying the history of their little town, Lynnette was inspired to begin the Shepherd's Heart Series with Rocky Mountain Oasis.

Marty and Lynnette have four children, and currently live in Washington where Marty pastors a church.

Made in the USA
Monee, IL
30 July 2024

62979181R00215